LOVE AT FIRST BITE

Without their space suits, the creatures were an unnerving sight—hard, shiny integument bristling with stiff hairs, spiny legs, globular green eyes. The four-fingered claspers at their projecting rears were pincers of horn, and the forward manipulating limbs were all tweezers and hooks. They prowled the floor and balconies of the chamber, taking no more notice of the gawking humans than humans would have taken of moss on a rock.

Suddenly, before Bram could stop him, Jorv stepped up to one of the creatures for a close look at its face.

There was a blurred movement as the creature seized Jorv with its facial limbs and bit his head off.

By Donald Moffitt
Published by Ballantine Books:

THE JUPITER THEFT

THE GENESIS QUEST

SECOND GENESIS

SECOND GENESIS

DONALD MOFFITT

A Del Rey Book

BALLANTINE BOOKS • NEW YORK

A Del Rey Book
Published by Ballantine Books

Copyright © 1986 by Donald Moffitt

Library of Congress Catalog Card Number: 86-90955

ISBN 0-345-33804-9

Printed in Canada

First Edition: December 1986

Cover Art by Ralph McQuarrie

Part I

EXODUS

CHAPTER 1

The tree named Yggdrasil plunged toward the heart of the galaxy at very nearly the speed of light, safe within a cone of shadow from a sleet of radiation that otherwise would have charred it to ash in microseconds.

It still clutched the remains of a comet in its roots, so water was not yet a problem. But light and gravity were strangely wrong, interfering with its tropisms.

Yggdrasil was a very confused tree.

Ahead, always, was a funnel of dancing sparks. Behind was a terribly bright light. Yggdrasil's senses told it that it was in the terrifying grip of a one-g gravitational field that was tugging it toward that unnatural sun. It had been trying for twenty years to escape. But when it tried to turn the reflective surfaces of its leaves toward the perpendicular, something always frustrated it.

Yet, wonder of wonders, Yggdrasil never fell. An equal and opposite force applied to a small region of its central trunk prevented that. Yggdrasil knew in its vegetable fashion that a girdle of foreign substance encircled its waist, but its senses were not adequate to tell it about the tether and the gargantuan turnbuckle that anchored the girdle.

A strange thing had happened to the stars as well. They swarmed around the tree in rainbow hoops of color— violet, then blues, greens, and yellows ahead; orange and progressively darker reds behind. Both ahead and behind, blind disks had blossomed as the stars marched in both directions through the spectrum and disappeared. The rearward blind spot was larger. Over the years it had kept

expanding, compressing the rainbow hoops and pushing
them forward until now they circled the coruscating funnel of sparks like concentric halos.

Scores of times Yggdrasil had tried to pick a yellow
target star, only to have it change colors and vanish from
the universe.

Only the odd pursuing sun had not dopplered through
the spectrum. It remained fixed in color and distance,
seeming to grow ever brighter against the expanding dark
region behind it.

Fretting, Yggdrasil tried to concentrate on growing one
of its branches. Its crown—since it had been prevented
from spinning—was no longer perfectly symmetrical, and
this was a branch that needed to catch up. Fortunately,
the direction of the tug of gravity was always a guide.
Growth, Yggdrasil knew in its simple wisdom, was supposed to be perpendicular.

There was commensal life within the cavities of the
errant branch, but it was too insignificant to be noticed.
Yggdrasil ignored it. The only verities were light, gravitation, and water.

"I think Yggdrasil needs a tranquilizer again," the tree
systems officer said. "It's starting to show signs of trauma."

Bram set down the carton of housewares he had been
packing and turned to face her. "Are you sure?" he said.

"I'm afraid so, Captain," she said. "The monitors indicate enzymatic reactions in the heartwood, and gallic
acid's showing in the contents of the parenchymal cells."

Mim, coming through into the observation veranda with
another armload of empty cartons, heard the exchange,
"Oh, no!" she exclaimed. "Right in the middle of moving
week!"

Bram shot her an affectionate glance. Mim was well
past middle age now—the mirror showed fewer gray hairs
every day—but her handsome face still preserved some
of the lines it had acquired during their four decades together. To Bram's way of thinking, the lines gave her a
strength of character and a beauty that he had come to
love; it was hard to imagine Mim without them, but youth-

ing was inevitable, and he supposed he would have to get used to it.

"Have you tried readjusting the auxin balance?" Bram said.

The tree systems officer looked worried. "We're close to the limit on that, Captain," she said. "Any more might be dangerous. Yggdrasil *knows* it's edge-on to something that looks like a sun to it and that half of its crown's in shadow. We can only deceive it so far, then the separate deceptions start to contradict each other. Too many auxins on the lit side, and we could have a very sick tree."

She waited diffidently for his response. The tree systems officer was a grandchild of Jao and Ang, and like many of her contemporaries she tended to treat Bram like a monument. She had not even been born yet when he had begun the immortality project. But Bram knew that she was a first-rate botanist, and he trusted her judgment.

Bram sighed. "All right. I suppose we'd better keep Yggdrasil tranquilized at least through moving week. We can't afford a delay. The branch we're living in is getting a bit bosky. And we're already ten degrees out of plumb." His eyes crinkled humorously. "Besides, we'd have a mutiny on our hands if we held up Bobbing Day."

"Very good, Captain," she said without cracking a smile. She turned smartly on her heel and left.

Bram watched her go. She had made him feel old and hoary. There was no reason for it, he told himself. His apparent age was down to somewhere in the midforties by now. But his body still carried the memory of being much older, and it showed sometimes in the way he moved and in the habit of protective postures. That, too, would pass with time, Bram supposed.

"The new ones are so *earnest*," Mim said, reading his thoughts.

"I just wish they wouldn't call me 'Captain' all the time."

She laughed. "But you *are* captain this year. And you've been elected seven times. That's more than anybody."

"It's only ancestor worship," he said. "Exaggerated respect for all the old father figures. And mother figures," he added hastily.

"Then why was Jao elected only once?" she teased him.

"And never again—I know, it was a disaster! Jao's the first one to tell you that himself."

"Jao never wanted to be captain in the first place. I sometimes suspect he sabotaged his first term on purpose so they'd never ask him again. But pity poor Smeth. He keeps campaigning, and he hasn't been elected once yet."

"Save your pity. Give him time. He has the next five hundred years to round up the votes. I'll bet that by the time we get to the Milky Way, he'll hold the record for being elected the most often. Because by then he'll be the only one who *wants* the job."

She giggled appreciatively, though she never would have hurt Smeth's feelings by doing it in his presence.

"And when you remember how he kept telling everybody that he had no intention of coming with us—that *he* wouldn't trust *his* life to an overgrown plant and a jerry-built ramscoop drive!"

Smeth had been a surprise to both of them. Bram had been sure that Smeth would stay behind. By the time the probe project had reached fruition, Smeth had accreted a huge department, with more than a hundred humans beneath him. He had attached himself like glue to the Nar organizational superstructure, and the Nar, thinking they were stepping softly on human sensibilities, funneled everything through him, snowballing his authority. He had nothing to gain by deserting the new egalitarian society that human immortality had brought about. With eternity ahead of him, he had nowhere to go but up.

But when the day had come to board Yggdrasil or be left behind, Smeth had showed up at the shuttleport with a small bag of personal belongings and a string of six biosynthetic walkers, led by a Nar porter bearing his library, instruments, and accumulated records.

"I guess he decided that it was better to be a big floater in a small pool," Bram said.

"Or maybe he simply couldn't *bear* the idea of all of us leaving without him."

Bram nodded. "After he saw the stampede that developed."

Smeth had not been the only surprise. More than five thousand people had elected to go along on the genesis quest—almost a third of the human race. The project had tapped a deep longing. The Nar had not underestimated the strength of the buried feelings unearthed in their pets. About ten years into the project, they had begun a program to gather all candidates from the farther worlds, and it had taken another twenty years to bring them all in. Those who had waited too long or who had changed their minds at the last minute had been out of luck.

"Well, I'm glad he decided to come along. It wouldn't be the same without him."

"Yes. I have to admit he's improving."

Mim fell silent. Bram knew she was thinking about Olan Byr. Immortality had come too late for Olan. The project had been a long, hard one, even with the blueprints of Original Man to work from and the full cooperation of the Nar. There had been times when Bram had thought that he himself would grow too old to benefit from it.

Mim had had fifty years to get over her grief for Olan. Forty of them had been spent with Bram. By the time they had drifted together, she had been too old for children. But her fertility had returned during the last few years, and lately she had been thinking about having a baby after she grew another ten or fifteen years younger. But only if tree demographics permitted, she was always quick to add whenever the subject came up. Yggdrasil could easily support another twenty thousand humans—in fact, about five hundred babies had been born already. But everyone was aware that a long trip lay ahead of them.

Bram reached for her hand, and they exchanged smiles. "Go ahead," she said. "I'll finish the packing. You'd better see to Yggdrasil's tranquilizer. If the drinks get sloshed over the rims of all the glasses on All-Level Eve, Marg will have a fit."

"Life would certainly be simpler," he said, "if we didn't have to rotate our environment thirty degrees every year to keep Yggdrasil from getting lopsided."

She squeezed his hand. "But it wouldn't be half as much fun," she said.

*   *   *

It was an hour's ride to the trunk even by slingshot, but Bram always enjoyed the view. There was no real reason to make the trip—the tree systems staff was fully competent and, in fact, knew more about the operation of the tree than he did—but the approaching tree-turning maneuver made a good excuse for the excursion.

He reeled in an empty travelpod, eased it through the lips of the gasket, and clambered inside. The absurdly simple arrangement made the expense of air locks for the external travel system unnecessary; otherwise, twelve air locks would have had been installed. The main rack of cables, like an abacus one hundred fifty miles long, was anchored at a new terminus every year, thirty degrees farther along the rim of the tree's crown, leaving a couple of permanent cables behind for standby access to the abandoned branch.

So far, the only major internal fast-transit system was limited to one branch—the one the human population would be living in during the half millennium when they were coasting between galaxies, and Yggdrasil could be allowed to have its normal one-g spin again. But that was one hundred and twenty degrees away at the moment, its halls and compartments standing on their heads, its pools drained, and everything important either moved or lashed down.

Bram took a moment to check out the pod's systems. Nothing could go wrong, of course; there was an FM rescue beeper in every pod that would quickly summon help in an emergency. But for someone serving as year-captain, it would be embarrassing to be stranded halfway along the guide rope and have someone come to fetch him.

He made sure the air bladder carried enough reserve for the hour's trip and that the emergency bottle under the seat was full. He squinted through the hyaloid membrane of the docking chamber's blister and sighted upward along the elastic cable. The several hundred feet of it that he could see before it came invisible against the distant trunk were reassuringly opaque, indicating that the molecular structure was in a mostly crystalline state.

He grinned as he prepared to change that. He got the

little bottle of boron trifluoride out of the dashboard and applied a few drops with an eyedropper to the elastomer line, just forward of the bowline knot that hitched it to an interior stanchion.

The pod gave a shudder as the line began to contract. Bram could see the triggered section turning transparent as its molecular structure became amorphous. The transparent portion shot outward, erasing the cable from sight. A few minutes later, when enough miles of cable had been triggered to overcome the one-g force stretching the line, the pod picked up speed, burst through the gasket, and flew up the guideline toward Yggdrasil's distant trunk.

Bram held on. He was glad the process wasn't instantaneous. He wouldn't have fancied a snapped neck. There was a lot of energy stored in a hundred and fifty miles of superelastic line. As it was, the pod would accelerate at a comfortable rate, never passing two g's at its zenith, then slow to a bounce as the trailing cable began to tighten.

The organic elastomer, with a stretch ratio of over a thousand to one, was a by-product of the exodus research program and, by departure time, had already found wide industrial application on the Father World. The raw materials came from Yggdrasil itself—derived from the adaptive mechanism by which a tree with a three-hundred-mile diameter synchronized the turgor movements of its leaves.

Bram gazed unabashedly through the transparent skin of his rubbery container and admired the outside view.

Straight up, of course, was a silhouette of Yggdrasil's trunk seen against the swirling blizzard of sparks created by the ramscoop field some hundreds of miles in front of the tree.

The silhouette was a short, thick bar, lacking detail. The shower of light was pretty—even jolly—but Bram knew that its beauty was a lie. It was the emblem of instant death—the visible by-product of the inferno of radiation pouring into the probe's magnetic funnel. At more than ninety-nine percent of the speed of light, here in the thick of the galaxy where the H-II clouds were dense, some two hundred trillion hydrogen atoms slammed into every square inch of the electromagnetic shield every second.

Even allowing for a gamma factor of twenty thousand—the last figure Jao had given him—that worked out to twenty billion high-energy collisions per second within the ship's relativistic time frame.

If that shield were to fail for even a fraction of a second at this velocity, five thousand humans would die before their nervous systems were able to register the fact. And Yggdrasil would turn to stardust.

Bram shuddered. As frightening as that umbrella of sparks was, at least it hid the nothingness beyond—the blind spot where the crowded wavelengths of light pushed past the visible spectrum and wiped the stars from the universe. The blind spot behind, eerily framing the artificial sun of the fusion stage of the drive, was bad enough.

He let his eyes follow the long, mirror-bright shaft downward to where the fusion flames burned. The waste light had enough red in it for Yggdrasil to carry on photosynthesis, enough ultraviolet for human sunbathers to tan themselves by behind the lenticels of the recreation areas.

The long shaft threaded a dangerous course between Yggdrasil's twin domes. At its closest point it passed within forty miles of the trunk, and Yggdrasil itself had provided extra protection there—growing a shield of adventitious leaves with their silvery reflective sides facing out. The star tree could handle anything up through x-rays.

The material part of the shaft was its least important aspect. In fact, its tremendous length could not have held up under even moderate lateral stress. It was there to provide support for the winding coils that deflected the roaring streams of ionized hydrogen in their constricted path from the collection area forward to the ignition cage aft.

For a moment Bram tried to imagine what the whole crazy travel arrangement would look like to a hypothetical observer outside the craft—provided that the observer could see by undopplered light. Or, more to the point, provided that the observer was in the same relativistic frame, matching the spacecraft's course in velocity and direction. Otherwise, the collection of shapes on their long skewer would be foreshortened by a factor of twenty thousand, turning them into a stack of paper-thin disks pierced by a thumbtack.

He decided it would look like a post horn straddled by a leafy dumbbell.

Bram had seen a post horn once, at one of Olan Byr's memorial concerts. The ancient instruments, from lyres to sousaphones, had been part of Olan's legacy. He had been tireless in commissioning reproductions from hints in man's digitally transmitted art masterpieces, dictionary sketches, and clues in the musical notation itself. The post horn was based on one played by an angel in an Annunciation. It was a long, straight tube of brass, tall as the man who played it, with a flaring bell at one end and the smaller flare of a mouthpiece at the other.

Bram closed his eyes for a moment and savored the eccentric image.

The post horn that dragged Yggdrasil by the collar was twelve hundred miles long, with its slender tube aligned along g forces to keep it straight. The bell was an insubstantial net of superfilament, several hundred miles in diameter, that kept its shape by virtue of an independent spin at its rim. Around the bell was a multicolored cascade of sparks, like trumpet notes made visible. A miniature sun burned blindingly in a magnetic cage at the mouthpiece, like a divine breath. And from the flared mouthpiece issued a thin pencil of inspired light as the hadronic photons, their work done, decayed and wreaked havoc with whatever interstellar debris was still left behind in the wake of the probe's sweep.

Pleased with the image, he conjured up the other component of the queer hybrid vehicle.

Yggdrasil would make a compressed sort of dumbbell, he decided, with a short, thick handle and rather flattened hemispheres. More like a pair of fat wheels lying athwart the long axis of the probe. One hemisphere was silver with a green rim facing the fusion fire. The other was brown, laced through with the crystal sparkle of cometary ice and showing an arc of green where Yggdrasil's root system had decided to help out with the photosynthesis.

The looming reality of a wall of foliage rushing past

him only a few miles away dissipated the image, and Bram turned his eyes to the view he loved best.

Between the rushing walls of Yggdrasil's twin hemispheres, a spectacular slice of sky was visible. A rainbow of stars made a dazzling arch across the void. Optical effects had crowded the bands of color so close together that the effect was like strands of matched jewels, jumbled together in overlapping profusion.

It was so beautiful that it hurt.

Bram studied the ribbon of stars. Was it narrower than the last time he had looked? It was hard to tell. But the yellow band seemed to have moved a degree forward, and the dull, ominous blanket of reds that faded into the blind spot seemed to have been dragged along by the rainbow hem.

A star whizzed by, changing from purple to blue to green, then to yellow, orange, and red before it was swallowed by the blind spot.

The star must have been very close—only a few lightdays away. At the present gamma, Yggdrasil swept across a light-year in about thirty minutes. That was fast enough to make the nearer stars move at a crawl, changing their colors as they lined up against the background rainbow.

A second violet star popped out of nothingness, riffled through the spectrum, and vanished to the rear.

The first star's companion! Yggdrasil was skirting a double star system.

Bram tried not to worry. Even here in the depths of the galaxy the stars were light-months apart. A collision would be most improbable, Jao had assured him. Even if Smeth's instruments were to show Yggdrasil heading straight toward a star emerging from a dust cloud, there would be minutes—perhaps hours—to change course. A lateral nudge of less than half a degree, projected over a minute or two of travel, would always give them margin to spare.

He drank in the glittering spectacle again, wondering how much longer he would be able to enjoy it. As Yggdrasil's speed increased, eventually the stellar rainbow would shrink into a thin gold rim framing the forward blind spot, and the vortex of hydrogen influx would make it invisible from any part of the tree. He had tried to get a time estimate from Jao, but Jao had been vague. They were slicing the remainder of the speed of light so thin at this point, Jao said, that measurements were meaningless.

He looked up through the top of the pod and saw the trunk rushing toward him. A cluster of external housings was directly above: upside-down bubbles with suspended catwalks. Ten or twenty miles to his left, he saw a portion of the tremendous crystalline girdle that circled Yggdrasil's waist and the secondary tether that would keep Yggdrasil from sliding forward along the shaft during deceleration mode. The tether was of woven viral monofilament a half mile thick, and the double bowline knot that fastened it had been tied, with much tricky maneuvering, by a pair of space tugs. Tension would only make it stronger; with the enormous forces involved, nobody wanted to take chances with extraneous fittings.

Bram noticed that at the moment Yggdrasil was floating free within its circlet; its momentum was temporarily matched with that of the probe.

The trunk filled his view, and then the taffy pull of the counterline slowed the travelpod to a bobbing stop about a half mile below the entry blister.

Bram uttered a mild expletive as he found that the fist-size electric trolley that was supposed to wind him in the rest of the way was out of order.

For a moment he was tempted to exercise a year-captain's prerogatives and signal the hub to reel him in. But he was only a couple of hundred feet from his destination, and the pod's weight was negligible added to his own, even under one-g acceleration. A half hour's worth of muscle power would do it.

With a sigh, he bent to the two-handed windlass and began cranking.

"That ought to do it," Bram agreed.

He tore his gaze away from the massive helical housing of the high-capacity pump. There was a final gurgle that shook the floor as the last of a half million gallons of chemical solution was forced deep into Yggdrasil's sapwood.

The tree systems officer and her hovering assistant gave him bland stares. "I thought the best way to calm Yggdrasil down would be to smooth out the peaks and valleys in phytochrome balance," the TSO said with professional briskness. "There was too extreme a swing between the two pigment forms, and it was driving Yggdrasil crazy."

She gauged his expression for signs of comprehension, apparently decided in his favor, and went on. "You see, the problem is the growing Doppler shift. Unfortunately, all the far-red light comes from the same direction as the fusion light, so that side of the tree's overstimulated. The phytochrome keeps changing back and forth between the far-red-absorbing form and the sunlight-absorbing form, then back again."

Her assistant, even younger than she was, nodded agreement. They were both being patient with the old dodderer.

"Yes, yes," Bram said quickly. "I'm sure you took the right approach."

The assistant cleared his throat and glanced at his boss before speaking. "And at the same time, there's the problem of blue light tropisms at the *opposite* side of the tree. Where the band of up-shifted light is. Yggie's hormones are working overtime to cope. And you can imagine what *that* does to his biorhythms."

"I can understand why your department was so concerned," Bram told them in his best sober manner.

They both beamed at him.

"So we added a healthy dose of vitamin A to the tranquilizer to damp down beta-carotene activity," the assistant finished triumphantly.

"Fine," Bram said with a judicious nod. He looked around for a way to make his escape. "Well, that seems to take care of it, so I'll—"

"Of course, you'll want to review our total hormone strategy while you're here, Captain," Jao's granddaughter said. "Shall we start with the tree-turning maneuver?"

Bram gave in to the inevitable and let her lead him over to the far end of the hollow, where a battery of young technicians, wearing the leaf tabards that seemed to be

the working costume of the new generation, busily tended
the array of giant fermentation tanks where hormone syn-
thesis started.

A half hour later, his eyes slightly glazed, Bram found
himself blessedly alone in the brilliant corridor that ran
through the trunk's heartwood. Alcoves branched off on
either side, each with its neatly painted street sign. Here,
forty miles beneath Yggdrasil's bark, a lot of specialized
work went on—plastics manufacturing using leaf sugars
as feedstock, the Message broadcasting facility whose
vital work could not be interrupted by yearly bough mi-
grations, the central observatory.

There was also a recreation complex with guest suites,
increasingly popular with the younger set and the advanced retroyouth crowd, with facilities for sports, swimming, and small-craft sailing. After Yggdrasil left the galaxy
and acceleration ceased, it would be a center for such
weightless pursuits as flying, flat-trajectory handball, three-
dimensional ballet, and, Bram didn't doubt, free-fall sex.

Bram paused to look at the bulletin board. Some members of the trunk staff were choosing up sides for a game
of teamball in what would eventually be the flydome.
Bram was tempted to join them. But he knew that he'd
be invited only through courtesy and deference to his
position. At his present chronological age, he'd only be
a liability to whatever team was willing to suffer him;
better stick to playing with his peers on the occasional
Tenday.

Feeling pleasurably sorry for himself—refraining from
reminding himself that he was not as old as he had been
twenty years ago—he gave the bulletin board a regretful
last glance and set off down the long arcade toward the
observatory.

At least that was one treat he could give himself.

Jun Davd looked up from his work and smiled at Bram
with a third set of teeth that were as white and flawless
as they had been when he had grown them a quarter
century ago.

"Nice of you to play truant just so's you can come visit
an old man," he said.

"The captain *never* plays truant," Bram said, smiling back. "Everything I do is *always* in the line of duty."

He raised both hands, and they touched palms in the old gesture.

Jun Davd chuckled. "So your duty brought you up to Yggdrasil's attic to rummage through the stars."

He was bent, frail, attenuated, but in remarkably good shape. Bram guessed that his biological age was down to about eighty. There were even traces of gray in the cap of white curls. Flesh was returning to the dark, mummified face, filling in the wrinkles. They had gotten to Jun Davd just in time.

"Is that what they look like now?" Bram asked, gesturing at the extrapolated display Jun Davd had been studying when he came in. The screen showed a splendid panorama of multicolored stars, glowing clouds, and luminous streamers swimming past in relative motion. Quite a few of the stars had disks.

"More or less," Jun Davd said. "The computer's having a hard time keeping up. That nice orange star you see coming toward you has been reconstructed from gamma rays in the ten-to-the-minus-six-nanometer range. The light that kills. The rear view's even more of a challenge. We're seeing *those* stars by ultralong radio waves—past the hundred-kilometer range. We've got almost a thousand miles of wire with a weight on the end trailing behind us for a dipole antenna, and I really could use a couple of thousand miles more except that I haven't been able to figure a way to keep the drive from melting it, and I've got I don't know how many thousands of stiff wires making pincushions out of Yggdrasil's crown and root ball, but you can appreciate that definition's still a problem. I'm afraid the computer's taking a lot of artistic liberties."

"Stop complaining. You're living in an astronomer's paradise."

He grinned, young teeth white in the ancient face. "Don't I know it. On my way to the galactic core to make direct observations of whatever the dust clouds are hiding. The old director, Pfaf-tlk-pfaf, would've given one of his fingertips for the chance!"

"I wonder what he's doing now," Bram started to say before he remembered.

It was strange to think that the old Nar, Pfaf-tlf-pfaf, had been dead for almost fifty thousand years. And that the immortal humans whom Yggdrasil had left behind were, presumably, still alive—unless the Father World had been hit by a wandering planetoid.

A wave of nostalgia washed over Bram as he remembered how kind the old director had been to a little boy who wanted to learn about the stars and how patient a human astronomy apprentice named Jun Davd had been in explaining all the wonders of the stellar universe.

"Sometimes I wish I'd followed my instincts back then and chosen astronomy as my career," Bram said.

"I'm awfully glad you *didn't,*" Jun Davd said tartly. "Where would I be now?"

It was a sobering thought. The two of them contemplated it in respectful silence for a moment, then Jun Davd went on more equably.

"It's not too late, you know. You can have an infinity of careers if you wish. Why don't we take up our lessons where we left off? In five hundred years you might make a pretty fair astronomer."

"Are you offering me a job, Jun Davd?"

The dark face creased in mirth. "I'm going to need a good assistant. We'd better learn all we can about the Milky Way before we arrive there—including how to use its H-II regions and the hypermass at its core to match our impetus and bring us to a nice safe stop." His voice was rich with enthusiasm. "Imagine being able to study a galaxy from the *outside* before making it your home! What an incomparable opportunity!"

Jun Davd had retired, still a junior apprentice, before the immortality project had borne fruit. He had hung on longer than most, and the Nar compassionately had looked the other way, but the day finally had come when he'd had to admit to himself how feeble he had become. He had been miserable in retirement. When Bram, with immortality finally in his pocket, had sought him out, he had jumped at the chance to join the expedition as chief astronomer, with the chance to run things to suit himself.

In one swoop he had gone farther than he had in an entire lifetime on the Father World, and he had unlimited vistas before him. Bram sometimes thought that it was this, as much as the immortality treatment itself, that had rejuvenated Jun Davd.

It would be different now for humans on the Father World. Now it was the Nar who were the mayflies.

Their society had had fifty thousand years to adjust to the new truth. How had it transformed itself? Bram wondered. He would never know. And every hour another few years passed on the world he had left.

He shook off the thought and returned to the conversation.

"Are you sure we'll *find a* hypermass to brake by when we get there?" he said.

Jun Davd looked at him reproachfully. "You're forgeting all I taught you. Scratch a galaxy like ours and you'll find a hypermass at the center. Relic of the quasar epoch. It's a necessary consequence of the way galaxies are formed."

"I know. A giant black hole."

Jun Davd nodded. "A black hole with a mass of anywhere up to several hundred million swallowed suns. The centers of galaxies are violent places, and they're very crowded. They stir up brews of colliding suns and relativistic electrons. They throw off x-ray jets. Sometimes they explode. The different events depend on the size and spin of the black hole and what it has to feed on and the way it chooses to express itself. And maybe the normal galaxies we see are simply the violent ones in a quiet phase of their history."

"You paint a vivid picture. What kind of core are we diving into now?"

Jun Davd did not smile. "One that worries me," he said.

Bram was instantly alert. "What do you mean?"

"For one thing, there are more young stars than theory predicts. And the infrared radiation getting through the dust clouds keeps increasing the farther in we travel, especially at the wavelengths associated with star formation. There are too many stars being born in there."

Bram searched his rusty memory. "You told me yourself, years ago, that emissions at around the hundred-micron wavelength increase at a fairly uniform rate as you go in."

"You don't take my meaning. At this point we're seeing by light that won't reach the Father World for another fifty thousand years. We've jumped fifty thousand years into their future—and the future of those former selves of ours that made those infrared observations. The process, whatever it is, is speeding up. Something odd is happening behind those dust clouds. Something recent."

"What do you think it is?"

Jun Davd switched off the display showing the outside stars and punched in a new code. A galaxy appeared within the screen, shining by the glossy light of computer simulation. It was a very pretty spiral with a regular shape. A second galaxy appeared to its left—another spiral, slightly smaller.

"You're looking at our galaxy the way it appeared some hundreds of millions of years ago, before we collided with the Bonfire. The smaller spiral is the Bonfire as it must have looked before the encounter tore it all out of shape. You're about to see a computer reenactment."

"I'm impressed."

"It wasn't as big a job as you think. The basic computer model is an old one. I brought it aboard with my data files. I first ran into it as a young astronomy student. All I did was feed in a lot of updated data, including the fifty thousand years' worth we've collected on our trip so far."

"Go ahead. I'm ready."

Jun Davd set the display going with a final poke of his finger. The point of view rotated slightly to give more of a side view, and the smaller galaxy that was the Bonfire began moving toward the larger one. Their directions of rotation were opposite, like two wheels rolling toward each other.

"They're going to grind together with a lot of extra kinetic energy," Bram commented.

"Watch it here. We've got some tidal forces coming into play."

The larger galaxy began to draw long streamers out of

the Bonfire. At the same time its own spiral structure
began to stretch and deform.

"I'm going to punch in a couple of overlays at this
point," Jun Davd said. "The red lines are infrared, the
white ones radio."

His long gnarled fingers played over the touch pad,
and a pair of overlapping contour maps appeared, more
or less conforming to the optical shapes, surrounding them
with concentric squiggles and squeezing close together at
the centers of the galaxies and in the areas of encounter.

The two galaxies continued to tear at each other as
their arms brushed and mingled. It was not a head-on
collision, but it was damaging enough. Gauzy ribbons that
must have contained millions of stars were stripped away
and left to evaporate into space. The computer could not
infer the collisions of individual stars—such collisions
would have been rare even if the two galaxies had fully
interpenetrated—but it could visualize the effects of the
gas clouds slamming together.

"Tremendous rise in temperature," Jun Davd said. "And
intense radio emissions."

The superimposed contour maps writhed, grew brighter,
pulsed faster and faster.

"Now, watch closely," Jun Davd said.

The spiral arm closest to the encounter flared and turned
blue as millions of new stars were born out of the clouds
of disrupted gas. The Bonfire sailed past; now a blazing
blob of light that had lost its spiral shape. The larger
galaxy squeezed, then stretched, responding to the gravitational tug. The coils on the opposite side, now released,
loosened and changed their pitch. The blue arm tried to
follow the Bonfire, reaching after it and losing more stars
in the process.

"Now you know why Skybridge is blue," Jun Davd
said.

"I can see that the passing of the Bonfire rejuvenated
the nearer spiral arm as a steller nursery," Bram said.
"But what has that got to do with the interior of the
galaxy?"

"Keep looking at the radio and infrared maps," Jun
Davd said.

Over an interval that must have represented a period of hundreds of millions of years after the encounter, the heat and the radio activity pulsed inward, like ripples from a stone seen in reverse. As the computer simulation neared the present, Bram could see the pattern of infrared intensity settle into the profile he was familiar with, growing stronger as it approached the central regions.

But there was more to it than that—a winking of blue light in a shell that followed the wake of the wave and shrank toward the galactic hub.

"It's the infall of that peeled-off gas, touching off another era of star formation," Jun Davd said. "By now, it's in the core, feeding the black hole. Or maybe I should say overfeeding it."

"We can handle it even if it *does* turn out to be bigger than we expect. After all, even a black hole with a few *billions* of solar masses can't have a diameter of more than a fraction of an astronomical unit, and when we swing around it, we'll make sure to stay a safe distance from the accretion disk."

"You're considering the black hole solely as a gravitational entity. I'm more concerned with what it might be *doing* in there."

"Such as?"

Jun Davd added a couple of worried furrows to the fan of deep creases in his forehead. "You saw what our encounter with the Bonfire did to the outer geometry of the galaxy. I'm wondering if it stirred up things in the inner regions as well."

"That happened hundreds of millions of years ago."

"Exactly," Jun Davd said, showing his perfect teeth in a mirthless grin. "Time enough for it to ripen."

"Jun Davd says it's thick in there," Bram said.

"Don't I know it." Jao sighed. "We're picking up gamma too fast. The ramscoop uses whatever falls into it, and I don't dare monkey with the fields this close to the bend in our hyperbola."

"But we still haven't reached the limits of our projected gamma for leaving the galaxy?"

"No, but I'd hoped to make up most of the difference

on the way out. We don't want to be going too fast for the hypermass to grab us. And I don't want to get too close to a thing like that." He scratched his ribs reflectively. "Now I'm going to have to shave it finer than I like in there."

"Jun Davd says the black hole's going to be a lot bigger than we expected."

Jao brightened. "That'll be a help. Stronger gravity to swing us around. Stronger magnetic field to transfer rotational energy. Bigger radius to keep us from getting pulled apart by tidal effects."

"Now you're doing what I did, according to Jun Davd— thinking of the black hole only as a gravitational resource and not paying enough attention to whatever mischief it might be causing among all those close-packed stars and dust clouds."

"Astronomers worry too much."

"The centers of galaxies are active places. And this one's more active than most. I'm not just thinking about radiation, I'm thinking about material particles. Are we going to be in danger?"

Jao sucked thoughtfully at his upper lip. The bushy gray mustache there was beginning to turn a faded orange. "Barring the chance of hitting a star or planet, our magnetic fields and our relativistic state of grace ought to do a pretty good job of protecting us. Do you have any idea of how much *energy* we're carrying at this point? The universe is in more danger from *us* than we are from it!"

Bram refrained from smiling. "What about a dust particle?"

"Tear it apart. Whip it on through. Use it."

"Can we handle that stew of radiation coming from the central parsec?"

"Handle it?" Jao snorted. "We'll *use* it."

Bram said nothing and waited. After a moment Jao flushed.

"All right," he said. He squatted and scratched a diagram on the smooth wood of the floor with a stylus from his wrist pouch. Bram bent over to see.

There was an obtuse angle with a dot gouged at its

vertex. Intersecting the dot was a shallow arc whose horns curved well forward of the dot to embrace the angle.

"This is us, here," Jao said, tapping the dot. He traced the two lines forming the angle with his stylus. "Our umbrella is opened out to about this angle now, and it'll keep opening out farther as we pick up speed. Theoretically, if we reached gamma infinity, the cone of the field would open all the way out to a flat disk, but the point is that the field thrives on anything that's thrown at it. It all goes to feed the engine and make more gamma and a wider intake area. So we have nothing to worry about from up front. And from the rear, of course, all the dangerous wavelengths are dopplered down past the radio end of the spectrum by now."

"And from the sides?" Bram prompted, though the answer was plain to see in the diagram.

Jao grinned hugely. "You've just taken a ride outside," he said. "You saw for yourself how far forward the starbow is displaced by now." He tapped the two horns of the arc with his stylus. "By the time we hit the core, we'll be snug within what amounts to a dopplered lens with a curvature that looks like this. Any hard radiation forward of the red-shifted meniscus intersects the nappe of the cone made by the field."

"How long before we swing around the galactic center?"

"At the rate we're picking up speed in this hydrogen soup, probably in the next few days."

"Should I cancel Bobbing Day?"

"Don't even whisper such a thing!" Jao exclaimed in mock horror. "I'll try to slow us down as much as possible by avoiding the thickest parts of the H-II clouds. With any luck, we'll squeak through Bobbing Day and All-Level Eve before Yggdrasil starts to squeak and groan."

"And then?"

"*Then* we batten down."

"How much longer can we broadcast the Message?"

"Let's go see Trist and ask him."

The Message Center was in the thickest part of the trunk, near the spreading root system, for maximum protection. It was, after all, the most important part of the treeship and the ultimate reason for the mission.

Bram looked down the length of the enormous cylindrical cavity, which was brilliantly lit by the abundant electrical power that was a by-product of the fusion drive. The circular tracks that had been worn all the way around the walls marched dizzyingly into the distance till they blended together. They had been scraped into the wooden surface over a period of time by the necessity of pushing thousands of pieces of heavy equipment another thirty degrees farther along every year.

The equipment itself—data banks, towering stacks of naked capacitors, oscillators, control elements for the thousands of phased array antennae planted in Yggdrasil's crown and roots—made several broad avenues down the center of the chamber's temporary floor, leaning crazily inward.

A work gang of young huskies had already started the next move, sweating and hauling at the heavy housings with levers, ropes, and their own backs and shoulders. It was a tremendous job once a year, but it was a lot easier than carting everything across space from bough to bough.

They found Trist in a control booth, eating a tomato sandwich with one hand and tracing geometric diagrams on a touch screen with the other. His face lit up with pleasure when he saw them.

"What brings you two to the upper depths?" he asked.

"We're going around the bend a little earlier than we thought," Jao said. "The skipper wanted a status report on the Message."

Trist took a bite of his sandwich, then put it down. "We'll be completing one last abbreviated cycle sometime later today, and I think that about finishes it." He shrugged. "Of course, I'll keep it going till we're out of the galaxy. Beamed backward in the microwave frequencies. But it'll be a very long shot, no pun intended."

"Your signals have dopplered too far to be receivable, is that it?" Bram said.

"No, that's not the real problem. Even with a gamma factor of twenty thousand, we're still intelligible, pulse by pulse. The microwaves focused sternward lengthen into radio waves, and the long waves we send ahead of us compress into microwaves for anyone who happens to be listening on the radar frequencies. With the frequency continually adjusted for Doppler shift, of course. No, the trouble is the pulses are too far apart now because of time dilation. We've got a problem of information density."

"How long is your abbreviated cycle?"

"Twenty days." Trist grimaced. "We're down to the genetic code for the Nar themselves, plus a minimum number of simple organisms from which a biologically sophisticated civilization might cobble together a supporting mini-ecology. Plus a Great Language module, of course. And a Small Language dictionary with human loan words. And a capsule history. And a highly abridged cultural package." He peered at Bram. "We've got a touch symphony by your touch brother Tha-tha in the cultural package, by the way."

Bram found himself looking past Trist, through the window of the control booth, at what he could see of the library. Miles of shelves, containing everything the Nar knew about themselves and their world. The old touch sagas were there, unintelligible to any race but the Nar. The message of Original Man was there in its entirety.

Not all of it could be broadcast, of course. But the Nar had wanted the departing humans to have it all. In the fullness of time, it might come in handy.

Out of it all, a Nar committee had prepared their Message. Or rather a series of Messages, progressively edited. The first took a year to broadcast. Now the Message was down to twenty days.

But if a touch symphony by Tha-tha was still included, then there must also be plans for a touch reader. A future generation of reincarnated Nar, here in the inner galaxy, might yet have access to a smattering of their heritage.

Jao was already figuring in his head. "Twenty days," he said. "That works out to almost a thousand years for receiving it—with no repeats. The Message of Original Man had only a fifty-year cycle, and it was received by a very patient folk." He shook his shaggy head. "I can see why you think the program's finished, Trist."

"And on our way out of the galaxy," Trist said, "if our gamma's up to what you say it's going to be, we'll have a Message cycle of close to four thousand years. With the tail out of range of the head."

"It's probably moot at this point, anyway," Jao said. "If there's other life in the galaxy, we wouldn't find it this close to the center. Too much radiation in these skies. If we *have* managed to seed the galaxy with secondhand Nar, we must have done it farther out, with the unabridged Message."

He cocked his head as a happy thought occurred to him. "That might have been forty or fifty thousand years ago, as the galaxy ticks. They might already have spread like crazy from thousand of foci. They wouldn't have been too far behind the Father World—hell, they *started* with a technological civilization! And they'd *know* their progenitors were only a galactic blink away, waiting to embrace them with all five arms—not like *us* poor spawn of a vanished species! What an incentive! By now they'd have met, merged. And when we burrow out of this nest of stars, we'll be traveling through a solid pavement of Nar."

"Don't get carried away," Trist said dryly. "Our lateral transmissions cut a swath that's only a few thousand light-years wide. The message has probably swept about two percent of the stars in this galaxy. That's a lot of stars, but it's hardly at the saturation point."

Jao waved his arms impatiently. "What are you talking about? With the effective diameter of the phased array in the crown and all the power we've got to play with, we can beam to the opposite edge of the galaxy."

"If we could cut through the dust clouds," Trist said patiently. "But that's not the point. For each cycle of the Message, I try to aim the lateral beams at some thick cluster of stars a couple of thousand light-years away and hold them there while I compensate for the changing Doppler. By the time the beam spreads much beyond that, any civilization that's searching for intelligent signals starts getting smaller and smaller cross sections of the Message. You reach the point where you get a thin slice that doesn't look like an intelligent signal. And even if you suspect that it is, you scan and you get other thin slices that you can't put together."

Jao gave Bram a disgruntled look. "Any advanced civilization doing a sky search would run a continuous survey if they're worth their salt. They'd sweep up and down the spectrum and run a computer program to put it all together."

"Maybe," Trist said.

Jao brightened. "Look at it this way. Two percent of the stars in this galaxy comes to—what?—four billion stars. Say two percent of *those* have planets with conditions that support life—"

"Don't get reckless," Trist said.

"Two percent," Jao said firmly. "All right, that's eighty *million* target stars. And say that one-*tenth* of one percent of them have advanced societies with a little genetic engineering capability and a normal amount of curiosity."

"How about one one-thousandth of one percent?" Trist suggested mildly.

"Sure. Why not? I won't quibble. I'm a very unimaginative guy. That makes eight hundred little Nar factories. Hell, make it one *ten*-thousandth of one percent! We're *still* in business!"

"It only has to happen once," Bram said. "Once out of those four billion stars we've touched. Those are the odds the Nar were willing to settle for. They knew it could happen. It happened once with Original Man."

"More than once, maybe," Trist suggested.

"That's a thought!" Bram laughed.

"On the way out of the galaxy," Trist said, "how about using the phased array in eavesdropping mode for a few thousand years between Message cycles? See what may have developed."

"It's all right with me," Bram said. "But you'd better take it up with the next year-captain."

"That might be Smeth. He's campaigning already. He's concentrating on the new crop of voters this time. He's got them hornswoggled. The young ones flock around him to listen to his tales of the good old days, when a small band of dedicated humans under his guidance as chairman of the physics department ran the Father World and decided to initiate a grand project to return humankind to its home in the Milky Way."

"He asked for my vote," Bram said.

"What did you tell him?"

"I said he could have it."

Jao, impatient at the digression, had perked up his ears at the mention of eavesdropping mode.

"Yah," he said. "Good idea. See what intelligent transmissions we pick up. Plug in a program to look for the patterns of touch-reader transmissions. That way we know they're Nar. You know, even if there's no other intelligent life in the galaxy and this whole errand was a flop, the Nar must've spread over a sphere of a couple of thousand light-years by now, anyway. Hey, in the last fifty thousand years, maybe they sent more message probes after us. Maybe one with a second human crew. If they've developed a better drive and were willing to boost at slightly over one gravity, maybe they're *ahead* of us. Maybe we'll find them waiting for us in the Milky Way with a million years of civilization behind them. Or maybe the Nar have been spreading *themselves* at the edge of lightspeed! Why not? A few thousand years of developing the hadronic photon drive and it might be cheap enough for colony ships. Who needs probes? Who needs errandpersons? At one and a tenth g's, they could already have settled an arc of space with its leading edge ahead of us." He looked around wildly. "They could be all around us *right now!*"

"Don't get carried away," Trist said. "Next you'll have them traveling faster than light."

"Faster than light? Why not? Einstein is as Einstein does. The Nar arrived at *their* relativity by a different route. Maybe we humans missed something. You know, for the Nar, mathematics is a sensory experience. They count with the surface of their bodies. Whole digital operations, faster than you can whistle. They can plug as many Nar into a problem as they want—subunits, everything—and *feel* their way to a solution. Who's to say they haven't tackled the faster-than-light problem?"

"Here's where he drags out the tachyons," Trist said with a tolerant smile at Bram.

"Go ahead, laugh, but they could've reached the other side of the galaxy by now," Jao insisted.

"If you're still beating the dead carcass of your Klein universe with its inside-out tachyons, I thought we settled that thirty years ago when we ran it through the computer and kept running up against the problems of nonorientability and self-intersection no matter *how* many dimensions you cared to postulate."

"We only ran it up to thirteen dimensions," Jao protested. "We never solved it for a general case."

Bram intervened to squelch the familiar squabble before it could get started.

"Whatever's happening out there in the galaxy— whether the Nar really needed us or not, or whether other intelligent life forms exist and the Message got through to one of them, or eighty million of them by now—it doesn't matter anymore. We've done our part of the job. We can go home now."

CHAPTER 2

Home.

Bram leaned back in his chairpuff and savored the idea of it, as he had done for most of his life. When he had been a small child, it had been bright, real, and immediate. Later it had become an abstraction, an impossibility. The adult Bram had known too much to believe in it. Now it was tangible again.

From the wooden corridor outside his apartment came the sounds of revelry: Bobbing Day celebrants on their way to the All-Level Eve festivities in the Forum—some of them already tipsy, by the sound of it. Mim was in the next room, getting dressed. Shortly she would join him, and they would go down together to be a part of the merrymaking. A year-captain could not afford to be absent.

But for these few moments of solitude he could think about home. For that, after all, was what the annual tree-turning celebration was all about—though it had grown lately into a tradition of its own.

Home.

Thirty-seven million years ago there had been an intelligent species that called itself the human race—Original Man. They had dwelt, by all the evidence, on a planet of a yellow sun in a rather isolated galaxy that they called the "Milky Way," part of a sparse cluster consisting basically of two big spirals and their attendant swarms of small satellite galaxies.

Whether or not human beings still existed there was

impossible to know, of course, when the very light that arrived from the Milky Way was thirty-seven million years old. But it was unlikely in the extreme. It was to be presumed that those humans were long extinct—gone the way of other species before them. Or that in the immensity of time they had evolved out of all recognition, into some new species that could no longer be considered human.

But before they had vanished or changed, they had left their mark on the universe.

The heights they must have reached had been dazzling, for they had learned how to tame whole stars and squander their energy. The energy, in unimaginable quantities, had been spent on the ultimate purpose of every species—to perpetuate itself.

Only this species had defeated the final enemy—the witless yawn of time.

Transformed into radio waves, the energy had been sprayed in the direction of the local universe that contained the richest clusters of galaxies—galaxies by the thousands, each containing hundreds of billions of suns.

It had taken all of that thirty-seven million years for the radio waves, expanding at the speed of light, to reach the galaxy where the Father World resided—a sprung spiral that those far-away, long-ago humans had known as the Whirlpool. There, a race of intelligent decapods who called themselves the Nar had intercepted the radio waves and deciphered them.

And a treasure trove had spilled out.

The lessons in genetic engineering alone had transformed the Nar civilization and given it abundance. Terrestrial starches and sugars had provided cheap energy and construction materials in the form of cellulose and exotic plastics. The bioengineering techniques, adapted to the Father World's life forms, had boosted the food supply and led to a host of biological devices that had taken the place of inefficient machinery. The genetic blueprint for a fast-growing tree called a poplar, included in the kit, had paved the way for the great living spaceships like Yggdrasil which plied the spaceway at up to one-seventh the speed of light and, with their world-size environments, made interstellar exploration at last practical and inexpensive.

But the centerpiece of the great Message was the genetic blueprint for humankind itself.

A mere millennium later—a drop in the bucket of cosmic time—the Nar bioengineers had created the second human race and nurtured several generations of it. A modest cultural package included in the Message had even given the new humans the sketch of a human society to enclose them.

Bram closed his eyes and remembered what it had been like to grow up as a small human child in a world of frondlike giants who towered so far above a little boy that even their girdle of waistline eyes—the closest thing to a face that a Nar possessed—loomed higher than his own eye level.

To be something between a house pet and the echo of demigods. To be loved and pitied as someone whose physical limitations would forever bar him from full closeness in the Nar touch group that had adopted him, and would forever bar him from full membership in the wider Nar society beyond.

For humans were handicapped. By their nature they were unable to speak the Great Language in all its tactile richness. Humans had to make do with the crude unenhanced sounds of the Small Language, or their own Inglex or Chin-pin-yin. And they were painfully short-lived. They died after only a century or two, long before they could earn the honorifics that would gain them an adult's place in an adult's world.

Still, he had been cherished. The new people born aboard Yggdrasil would never know what it was like to have Nar touch brothers.

Bram let the noise of the revelers in the outside corridor fade from his consciousness, and let the old memories wash over him.

"Bram-bram, guess what?" Tha-tha had said to him that day, in the blend of Inglex and the Small Language they used when speaking to one another.

Tha-tha was Bram's favorite touch brother, even though you weren't *really* supposed to have favorites.

"What?" he said absently, staring longingly through an oval casement at the sunny world outside.

It was a splendid morning, early in the season when the lesser sun left the night sky and spent most of its time in the day. The bay was bright and cloudless, the sky a vivid lavender blue, and Bram could see the sparkling water, full of Nar bathers and colorful little V-winged pleasure boats.

He turned to contemplate with disfavor the beehive chamber where he and his touch brothers had their lessons and naps. Ranged along the far curve of the wall were the miniature tilt-top body readers against which Tha-tha and the others pressed their outspread upper tentacles—the star-shaped upper surfaces scaled down to child's size—and his own little desk with its reading screen and big-buttoned board that took the place of the others' touch pads. There was the toy box, filled with baby things that most of them professed to have outgrown—the spongy alphabet-letters for Bram, and the pyramids and cones and involute spheroids of various textures, and the small furry, mock-alive things that went through their limited tactile sequence when you squeezed them in the right place.

Two of the young decapods were wrestling, rolling boisterously around on the floor, their stubby little tentacles entwined as they tested one another's strength. Roughhousing like this was apt to go on when there was no big Nar around to supervise them. For the moment, the old foster-tutor, Voth, had left them to their own devices; they were supposed to be quietly using the touch readers or otherwise usefully occupying their time, but it was hard to concentrate when the weather was so fine and the smell of the salt ocean was in the air, and the whole world seemed to have gone swimming.

Bram gave a tragic sigh. Lessons were all right, he supposed, but some days it was better to be outside.

Tha-tha sidled closer to him, piping happily, "Voth says I can have my own grownup-size reader! And library access to grownup touch scores—the easy ones, anyway. And a real composition matrix!"

"You're too little," Bram said scornfully.

Actually Tha-tha, during the past year, had shot up a full foot above Bram's mop of rust-colored hair. But the slender decapod form did not yet outmass him, and besides, in Bram's perceptions, what really counted was eye level, and Tha-tha's five mirror-eyes, equally spaced around the narrow waistline from which upper tentacles and lower limbs sprouted, still only came to somewhere around Bram's ribcage.

"No, really. Voth says I'm getting very proficient. He submitted one of my toccatas, and they said that even though it wasn't full span, it used areas just like an adult!"

In his eagerness to communicate, Tha-tha had wrapped one of his tentacles around Bram's forearm, and Bram could feel the velvety nap of the limb's underside writhing with effort.

"*I* didn't see what was so special about it," Bram said stubbornly.

Bram knew that Tha-tha was very talented—the most talented of all the younglings in his group. Bram had tried to understand the little toccata that Tha-tha had composed, and had stretched himself across the five-pointed star of one of the readers to let his human skin sample its rippling patterns of cilia movement. But as always, the meaning had eluded him; it had only been something that tickled in structured rhythms.

"Anyway," Bram said, casting about for the perfect squelch, "it was nothing but a lot of squares inside squares that kept marching off the edge. *I* can make a touch reader do that!"

In fact, Bram had an unusual facility with the Great Language for a human of any age. He was able to manipulate a cilia board well enough to reproduce a few basic commands, and when Voth absentmindedly pressed a limb against his skin, he was often able to recognize some of the simpler morphemes, like numbers.

Tha-tha said, with a baffled earnestness that showed in the slow beat of his tentacle lining, "But it's not the *shapes* that count, Bram-bram. You can have outlines with nothing inside. It's the meaning they *enclose* that's important."

Bram felt all the blood drain from his face. He was

numb all over, as he had been the time he had slipped on a sheet of winter ice and come down flat on his belly and had all the wind knocked out of him.

"It is *so* the shapes that count," he insisted feebly. "You can tell lots of things from the shapes."

Tha-tha belatedly remembered that he had been admonished by Voth to make allowances for his four-limbed brother. He damped down the cilia movement in the tentacle that held Bram's arm and concentrated on the fluting sounds of the Small Language coming from deep within his central gullet.

"Never mind, Bram-bram, Su-su didn't understand it either." He gestured with a couple of spare limbs toward one of the wrestling brothers. Su-su was squealing in simpleminded triumph. He had his opponent pinned, with all five of the upper tentacles wrapped up in a tight bundle by Su-su's encircling grip and the lower limbs off the floor, flailing wildly for purchase.

Bram's features screwed up, and he found himself ready to cry. Tha-tha, trying to be kind, had just made it worse. Everybody liked Su-su, but he wasn't much in the brains department. He had trouble doing the simplest arithmetic and, Bram gathered, even the Great Language had been slow to develop in him. He communicated in the Small Language and in tactile baby talk, and it was obvious that Voth was becoming concerned about him.

"Leave me alone!" He jerked his arm out of Tha-tha's grasp and stomped over to his desk reader. It was the only one with a vision screen. The others' touch readers didn't need them, Tha-tha said, because the Great Language, even in its juvenile form, provided a sort of perception that was like pictures, only better—just as it was faster to count in the Great Language with its racing ranks of cilia than on a human-style keyboard. The visual crossconnection had something to do with the way the Nar brain worked. Bram's touch brothers were capable of appreciating the pictures of his vision screen, but most of the time they watched them without much interest, just to be polite.

Savagely, Bram punched buttons almost at random, but his small fingers were cleverer than his rage, and he found himself looking at some of his favorite sequences from the history lessons about Original Man.

Here were the human race's achievements in all their splendor and glory, as imagined by human artists with the help of computer reconstructions drawn from clues in the great Message, and interspersed with everyday scenes of the Father World and its family of planets.

Bram caught his breath at the sight of the shining cities as they must have been, with their pyramids and cathedrals and the cloud-reaching spires that were very much like the tall calcified spirals of the cities that the Nar had grown with the aid of humankind's bioengineering legacy.

The pictures shuffled, and he saw the forests of giant trees grown on comets in the deep beyond the Lesser Sun. And the living spaceships derived from them—great twinned hemispheres of foliage and roots, hundreds of miles in diameter, voyaging to the nearer stars.

And here was a simulation of a star itself being enclosed in a sort of sphere—the supposition was hazy—and its energy being transformed into the radio waves of the human Message and traveling across the void between galaxies. The Nar themselves couldn't do anything like that, and would not be able to match such power for tens of thousand of years, if ever.

And now there was another uniquely human glory—music. The scene shifted to the concert hall that the Nar had grown for their wards in the human Compound. The camera panned across the rapt faces of the audience as they listened to a scrap of their heritage—a grand songfest called "The Messiah," which had been lovingly reconstructed from the computer readouts of the Message. A mighty chorus of human voices rang out, singing *"Wonderful! Marvelous!"* in recognizable Inglex, while tears rolled down the faces of the listeners.

Bram was fighting his own tears. He put his palms flat against the screen, trying to absorb the experience directly.

Nothing! There never was! Only the hard smooth surface of the screen with the miniature people in it, and the massed voices coming from the speaker. It could not compare with the touch symphonies that so entranced Tha-

tha and kept him stretched out on the star-shaped body reader for hours—and that he had tried without success to explain to Bram.

Bram gave a choked sob and felt the hot tears come.

What *good* was it? What good was it to be a human and talk with your voice, when the Nar could talk with their whole bodies? It was only sounds...or symbols which, when you came down to it, could always be transcribed into sounds.

He began beating on the machine with his small fists, screaming and kicking at it while his touch brothers stopped what they were doing and stared at him in horrified silence.

Tha-tha warbled tentatively, "Bram-bram."

"Go away!" Bram screamed. "Go away, all of you! I hate you!"

He was still having his tantrum when Voth came in. The old teacher stood in the tall doorway regarding the scene, his cluster of upper limbs writhing thoughtfully. Tha-tha ran in a five-legged scramble over to him and whispered something with one outstretched tentacle, Voth dipping an upper limb to listen.

"All right, Tha-tha, you can take your brothers to the beach now," Voth said aloud in his deep tones. "I'm putting you in charge. Tell the door proctor I said it was all right."

As the little decapods swarmed confusedly around Tha-tha and flowed in an intertangled mass out the door, Voth went over to Bram and swept him up in his tentacles.

Bram made a great gulping sound. "Oh, Voth!" he sobbed.

"Hush, little one. It's all right."

He let the little boy cry himself out in his warm clasp, then set him down and lowered himself to eye level. "How would you like to go to the observatory with me and see our friend Jun Davd?" he said. "We can take a ride in the bubble car and buy some polysugar candy, and Jun Davd will let you look through his telescope."

Bram rubbed his eyes with both fists. A small coil of

rebellion still burned within him. "I want to go by myself," he said.

Voth acted not at all surprised. "You've never traveled alone before," he said. "It's a very long way to go. You'd have to ask directions in the Small Language, make yourself understood. And—" He paused delicately. "Since you can't imprint your Word directly, you'd have to use a credit transfer device, and use it correctly."

Bram said stubbornly, "Jun Davd is my human friend, and I want to go see him by myself."

Voth thought it over. "All right. I guess you're old enough. But promise me to be careful."

Bram hugged Voth around the middle where the skirt of walking members flared outward; the waxy integument was smooth and unyielding, not at all like the warm fluffy lining of the petallike arms. "I promise," he said.

"There are no human conveniences after the departure terminal," Voth said, becoming brisk. "Jun Davd will see that you're fed. Remember not to eat *anything* till you get there—not even polysugar. Not even if some well-meaning person offers you something. Many of the Folk do not realize that human and Nar chemistry are different."

"I know, Voth."

"Here's a touch token for when you get on the bubble car. Do you know how to make it say what you want?"

Voth handed him a small flat wedge with one ciliated surface, the kind Nar used in special circumstances when credit delegation was more convenient.

"Yes," Bram said. He demonstrated with a deft flutter of fingertips. Numbers were easy.

"Good. Even a lot of grownup humans never learn how to do that."

He escorted Bram down the spiral ramps to the street; this was an old defunct orthocone whose lower septa had long since been scooped of life and its nutrient pool filled in, allowing a ground-level entrance to be added beneath the original overbridge. He hailed a pentapedal carrying-beast and gave it detailed directions to the terminal before lifting Bram to the passenger howdah. Bram looked about eagerly. The white sun-bleached spires and filigree bridges of the city spread endlessly and magically before him; he had every intention of countermanding Voth's instructions as soon as the beast was out of sight, and doing a little roundabout sightseeing on his way to the terminal. He knew he could do it. The transport creatures responded to voice as well as touch.

A string of bubble cars passed overhead on their invisible cable. Bram gawked at them, hardly able to believe that soon he would be traveling in one without supervision, just like an adult Nar. Even Tha-tha had never been allowed to do that.

"I'll call ahead and have them tell Jun Davd you're coming," Voth said. He tapped one of the upright limbs that formed the framework of the howdah and Bram felt himself rising high into the air as his vehicle straightened its five stiltlike legs. A moment later the beast was trotting down the causeway that led toward the terminal. Bram turned back once to wave to Voth. The old decapod waved back in imitation of the human gesture. Bram thought that somehow Voth seemed sad, but he couldn't imagine why.

"Do you think we could look at Original Man's galaxy now, Jun Davd?" Bram asked.

"In a little while," the tall man said—tall for a human, though Jun Davd would hardly have topped Voth's brachiating midsection, even on tiptoes. "But first I'm going to give you some lunch."

"I'm not hungry, Jun Davd, honest." He looked around impatiently at the enormous chalky chasm that housed the observatory's big eye. Massive machinery loomed overhead in steel cradles. The interior extruded convoluted catwalks of polycarbonate that reached every nook and cranny. Across the immense floor was the eye itself, a great bowl of living jelly that seemed to Bram to be the size of a swimming pond. Aproned Nar attendants, some of them wearing optical girdles, glided silently about, seeing to its needs.

"I promised Voth-shr-voth I'd feed you," Jun Davd said, smiling down at him. "Don't worry—your galaxy won't go away."

Bram smiled back. Jun Davd was very nice, with a

kindly, creased face that was several shades darker than
Bram's, almost the color of stained wood. His hair was
a bush of pure white. He was old for a human, and had
risen as high as a human being could go—to a shadowy
status somewhere between an apprentice and an intern.

"All right, Jun Davd," Bram said. He took the slender
gnarled hand and let himself be led from the fascinating
chamber to the cubbyhole where Jun Davd worked and
lived amidst a clutter of instruments and a spartan few
personal possessions.

They were stopped several times along the way by Nar
personnel who wanted to greet the little boy and inquire
after the absent Voth-shr-voth. During the past year they
had become accustomed to the sight of the human child
who was brought by his Nar guardian from time to time
to be shown some of the distant wonders trapped by the
big eye's living system of mirror optics, and to be given
some rudimentary tutoring in astronomy by Jun Davd.
Voth-shr-voth was held in high esteem, and every courtesy was extended to him—though why he was encour-
aging a fruitless interest in astronomy in his human ward
was unclear, since Voth himself was renowned for his
bioengineering achievements, and presumably if he wanted
to make a place for the boy, he would do it in his own
touch group.

Bram presented the palms of his hands to meet the
proffered tentacle tips and answered their inquiries gravely
and politely. A nudge from Jun Davd reminded him to
add the honorific; it was hard to remember that the em-
inent Voth-shr-voth was the plain old Voth whom Bram
had known since his nursery days, when his own principal
gene mother, mama-mu Dlors, had given over the largest
part of his care.

Even the observatory's director, the venerable Pfaf-
tlk-pfaf, showed Voth a special deference. Voth was several centuries older than the director, and near to the time
of his Change. Bram didn't know exactly what the Change
was, but it had something to do with why you hardly ever
saw a lady Nar, except for the rare infirm and draped
individual being carried in a biolitter, and why there was
no such thing as a little girl Nar, only touch brothers.

Bram had asked about it, but Nar grownups were always evasive, the way mama-mu Dlors always changed the subject when he asked how human babies were assembled.

"Pfaf-tlk-pfaf is very busy now," Jun Davd told Bram, "but perhaps he'll be able to see you for a few minutes later on."

"And then will he show me the galaxy of Original Man with the big eye?" Bram asked.

"We'll see. The big eye is doing some very important work at the moment—a survey of the heart of *this* galaxy, the one we live in."

"But you promised."

"All in due course. First, lunch."

A short while later, Bram pushed away his half-finished bowl of chimerical soycorn porridge and wiped his lips on the damp cloth Jun Davd gave him. "All through," he said.

"Would you like a sweetcrisp?"

"No, thank you. Can we see it now?"

Jun Davd went over to a keyboard that had been haywired to a Nar touch pad. An oval screen lit up with fuzzy visual patterns generated by an interface program that Jun Davd had written himself. No one but Jun Davd could make sense of it, but Bram had resolved that some day he would learn to read it, too.

"The big eye's still busy," Jun Davd said, "but I can give you the last stored view. We swung that way about a Tenday ago."

Bram was disappointed. "I wanted to have a really now look, not a picture."

Jun Davd laughed. "You couldn't tell the difference. Anyway, there's no such thing as a really now look. The light from Original Man's galaxy left there thirty-seven million years ago, and the images are all processed one way or another."

"I can *so* tell the difference. It isn't the same thing."

Jun Davd's expression sobered. He squatted on his haunches to look into Bram's eyes. "I understand, Bram. You want to feel that you're seeing the actual light of home. But even the big eye only collects photons one at a time and assembles them into an image. Do you understand what I'm saying?"

"I guess so," Bram said reluctantly. He brightened. "Could we see it with *your* telescope—the little one?"

The telescope that Jun Davd tended in an adjacent structure was small only by comparison with the big eye; it was a huge drumlike object mounted on rocker beams. With it you could see the planets of the lesser sun, and even the gas giant that revolved around Juxt, the closest extrasystem star, almost a light-year away.

"No, it's too small," Jun Davd said. "You know that, Bram. I've explained it all before. Compared to the Milky Way, even our neighbor galaxy, the Bonfire, is practically next door. The Milky Way is so far away that when the light we detect first left it, there weren't even any Nar here on the Father World—just the little seashore creatures that were their ancestors. So we can never see Original Man's galaxy as it is *now*."

"We could if we waited another thirty-seven million years," Bram said reasonably.

"I guess we could at that," Jun Davd laughed. "Come around then and I'll show it to you. In the meantime..."

He busied himself at the human-style keyboard and a sea of stars appeared in the oval screen. After a lot of jiggling, a fuzzy dot centered itself, grew in size, and sharpened into the image of a feathery coil of light with a golden yolk at the center.

Bram caught his breath. Jun Davd had shown him more spectacular sights through the telescope, but there was none that caused the sudden gripping pain in his small chest that the sight of humankind's home always did. If he had been allowed to, he could have sat and looked at it for hours, making up stories in his head.

"Jun Davd," he said at last, "do you think Original Man could speak the Great Language?"

The old apprentice looked at him sharply. "No, I'm quite sure he couldn't. They were the same as us, those prototype humans who sent the Message—or we're the same as them, with a few bad genes edited out, of course. Why do you ask?"

"They—they rose so high. Higher than the Nar. Everybody says so, even Voth. How c-could they, if they were like us?"

All of sudden salt tears were rolling down his cheeks. He tried to stop them and smile at Jun Davd, but the smile only made things worse.

Jun Davd took him by the shoulders and turned him gently around to face him. "What happened today, Bram?" he asked softly.

Between sobs, Bram told him about Tha-tha's promotion to an adult touch reader while he, Bram, couldn't even understand a toccata on a child's reader. About the growing facility of his touch brothers in the Great Language while he himself had a growing sense of being left behind. About the feeling of increasingly being left out of things, even though Tha-tha and the others always tried to remember to speak aloud for his benefit.

"I see," Jun Davd said grimly. "And you wonder what kind of place the world holds for you, especially when you look around at older humans like me and see the limits on how far we can go. I know how you feel, Bram. I was a protégé of the old director—the one before Pfaf-tlk-pfaf—just as you're a protégé of Voth, and even though he was very close to the Change when I was growing up, he saw to it that I was firmly established before his final metaplasis, and Pfaf-tlk-pfaf has honored his wishes. On the whole, it's been a good life—the best, I think, that's reasonably possible."

Bram flung his arms around Jun Davd's neck. Hugging a human being was different than hugging a Nar. Human beings had bones that you could feel through the skin. "Why do I have to be different, Jun Davd?" he wailed. "I asked Voth once, and he said it was because I was made of human stuff instead of Nar stuff."

Jun Davd disengaged him gently and held him at arm's length so that he could look into his face. "Voth-shr-voth was right; you're different just because you're a human being. That doesn't mean you're better and it doesn't mean you're worse. Only a different *sort* of person. That's why Voth started to bring you here to the observatory when he first saw that you were interested in where humans come from—so that you could have some sense of

your own heritage and be proud of it, not think of yourself
as some kind of flawed Nar. I think it would break Voth's
heart to have you apprenticed here instead of with his
own touch group, but he was willing to take the chance
of losing you so that you could be happy and fulfilled."

"I'm sorry I cried, Jun Davd."

"That's all right, Bram. You cry whenever you feel like
it. That's part of being human, too."

"I thought that . . . maybe if Original Man could speak
the Great Language, I could learn how someday, too."

"They reached the heights their own way, Bram. The
human way, not the Nar way. And whatever heights the
second human race reaches here in *this* galaxy, we'll do
as humans, too."

Bram looked at the tiny glowing helix displayed in the
viewer. "I'm going to go there someday," he said with a
child's seriousness.

"You know that's not possible, Bram. We've discussed
it often enough. We can reach a few of the nearer stars
within a human lifetime—though we'd be very, *very* old
by the time we got much farther than Juxt or Next. And
the Nar can travel about ten times farther within *their*
lifetimes. But the limit will always be about a hundred
light-years—maybe a few thousand light-years within our
own galaxy if we ever learn to travel at relativistic speeds.
But that's a lot different from crossing the void between
galaxies—especially galaxies that aren't even in our own
cluster. No, child, it's a fine thing to be able to look
through a telescope at these distant objects, but they can
never be reached across an ocean of time, any more than
you or I could return to our own egghood. Voth wants
you to be happy in your life. And that means making your
way here, in the real world, as best you can."

It was one of those adult speeches that Bram had learned
to shut his ears to. His eyes had never left the golden
spiral in the screen.

"I didn't mean right *now*, Jun Davd," he said complacently. "I meant someday."

The someday never came. Bram became immersed in
life. As his touch brothers outdistanced him, he spent

more and more time with friends from the human enclave
and shared their purely human concerns. By adolescence,
few of the humans had much in common with their Nar
touch brothers anymore, and Bram was no exception.
Tha-tha made an effort to keep in touch with him—still
peeled down his waxy outer integument and unfolded his
inner surfaces while they jabbered away in their childhood
patois of Inglex-laced Small Language—but Tha-tha had
his own Nar life to live, a life that grew ever more in-
comprehensible to Bram.

It didn't matter. Bram, full of the juices of youth, had
the heady excitement of human society to sample. All
around him was a ferment of art, music, literature, fashion—people busily assimilating the sketchy outlines of
human culture as it had been transmitted in the Message,
and building on it. People *doing* things!

He left mama-mu Dlors' nest and moved into the bach-
elor lodge. He was on his way to an adult life with new
freedom to explore. He forgot childish dreams; the visits
to Jun Davd at the observatory became less frequent and
finally ceased entirely. Astronomy was a dead end for
humans anyway, as Jun Davd's example had shown. Bioengineering was where the honors lay—where there was
a hope of practical results that could have a recognizable
impact on the miniature human communities scattered
through the Father World. A human named Willum-frth-
willum had even been granted a Nar-style honorific for
his contributions to the development of viral monofilament, and then had gone on to achieve celebrity among
his fellow human beings for recreating additional terrestrial life forms, such as the tomato, by working backward
from existing genes of human foodstuffs included in the
Message. There was an old human saying to the effect
that the invention of a new sauce contributes more to
human welfare than the discovery of a new star; how
much more important, then, was it to bring more variety
to the limited human diet? When it came time for Bram
to make a career choice, Willum-frth-willum's shining example was already there before him.

So Bram made his adult compromise with life. Voth's
bioengineering touch group had always been waiting with

open tentacles to take him in as a sponsored human; he was under the mantle of the great Voth-shr-voth, after all. But Bram proved to have a natural talent for the work, and soon he was holding his own. He had a greater affinity for the Great Language than most humans—he could even manipulate a touch reader well enough to call forth basic menus, and could find his way around the files with a minimum of help. In no time at all he was given greater responsibility, formed genuine working relationships with the Nar juniors, and was allowed to run his own subprojects.

Bram threw himself into his work; it was solid and useful, gave form and purpose to his life, and gave him status in the human community.

He avoided Jun Davd; he could not have said why. Every once in a while he would find himself staring at the blank patch of night sky that contained the faraway galaxy of the first human race. But you couldn't see anything without a telescope. Bram would shake off an obscure, nagging sense of loss—a feeling he was not willing to examine—and allow the realites of daily life to absorb him.

There was a brief affair with Mim—but they lived in two different worlds now. He was part of the larger concerns of the Father World—minor though his role at the biocenter was. Mim had withdrawn more and more into the purely human ambience of the Compound, where a feverish minority of Resurgists tried to ignore the Nar civilization that supported them, and worked to recreate a semblance of an imagined human past. Eventually Bram lost Mim to an older man—Olan Byr, a musician like herself, who had made a name for himself as a tireless interpreter of the old music.

In due course, Bram formed a relationship with an exciting young woman named Kerthin, a sculptress with some radical ideas about human ascendancy in the sea of Nar that submerged them. Bram was entranced by her; he tried to show her that his thinking was as advanced as hers, but she laughed at him, told him that he was stuffy and conventional, but that she liked him anyhow.

Bram was ready to settle down by then; he formally

proposed a visit to the gene co-op with Kerthin. Preliminary gene mapping had given him every reason to hope that the two of them would be allowed to contribute a preponderant number of their genes to a composite genome and rear the child as their own. It would be the final step in the settled existence he had contrived for himself.

But Kerthin was evasive. She teased Bram about being too complacent. There were still great things to be done, she told him. She was not ready to settle down.

For the human race had reinvented politics.

The human population of the Father World, small as it still was, had grown to the point where it supported a remarkable number of factions, calling themselves by such names as Partnerites, Schismatists, Resurgists, Ascendists. Kerthin's friends were a fanatical splinter group of the staid, old Ascendist party.

Unwillingly, Bram was drawn into the conspiratorial schemes of Kerthin and her friends, at first only to keep an eye on Kerthin, and later to protect a startling secret he had uncovered through his work at the Nar biocenter.

Human beings were meant to be immortal!

Bram's unusual facility with touch readers had provided the key. While rummaging through the old files, he had discovered that the original human genome constructed by Nar bioengineers was incomplete. A codicil to the great Message of Original Man, received some fifty years into the second cycle of the transmission, had contained instructions for a synthetic virus able to infect human cells with the disease of eternal life. The tailored DNA had the ability to insinuate itself into human nucleotides and turn off a "death gene"—a genetic switch that expressed itself after a certain number of cell generations. The information had rested in the files for a thousand years—either unrecognized, or interdicted because of environmental dangers associated with it.

Bram shuddered to think what Kerthin's wild-eyed friends might do with such information. At best they would use it to inflame human passions, to put an end to the trust between human and Nar. Bram did not believe that the information had been hidden on purpose. He believed in the good will of the Nar, and he waited for the opportune moment to bring the matter up with Voth. But first he wanted to be sure.

While Bram was still trying to decide what to do, a starship arrived from Juxt One. Aboard it, having traveled for seven years, was the Ascendist messiah for whom Kerthin and her friends had been waiting.

His name was Penser, and what he preached was a mindless violence that he described as a "cleansing." The universe belonged to man by right, he told his disciples, and could not be shared with the Nar. He dismissed Nar largess. "To share is weakness," he said. "To accept is weakness." He advocated taking by force what the Nar were giving voluntarily. On Juxt One he had stirred his followers to acts of sabotage in which Nar had been killed. The abortive revolution had been hushed up by the horrified human settlers, and had not been recognized for what it was by the peaceable and unsuspecting Nar. Penser had fled under a false identity stolen from one of his disciples.

Now Penser proposed to hijack one of the great living starships and, with a few hundred followers, use it to take over a thinly inhabited moon of Jumb, the gas giant orbiting the Lesser Sun. The small Nar population there would be deported—killed if they resisted; the human colonists, Penser believed, would have no option but to go along with his plans once the deed was done.

The takeover would be accomplished before the Nar on nearby IIf, the Lesser Sun's principal inhabited planet, realized what was happening. After that, according to Penser, the Nar commonwealth would accept the situation to prevent useless further violence.

"They'll let the humans have their one little world," Kerthin assured Bram, mouthing Penser's words.

The seized moon was to be the focal point from which humans would crowd the Nar out of the cosmos. Penser intended to step up the human breeding rate without bothering about gene editing. Humans could easily outbreed the Nar. "Do you realize that the human population of the universe could be *doubled* every twenty years?" Kerthin had said, her eyes shining.

Other worldlets would be taken over, one at a time—

each as an accomplished fact to be presented to the Nar, with the dust allowed to settle between conquests and the Nar encouraged to believe that this time was the last. Penser had studied the ancient history of Original Man. Hitler, Napoleon, and Alexander had failed because they had bitten off more than they could chew. By the time the Nar woke up, Penser said, the human race would be ready to swallow Ilf—even scour the Father World itself!

But the starship hijacking went horribly wrong. The Nar, with a casual swipe of their great powers, put a stop to the mutiny and took all the humans aboard into custody—Penser's followers and innocent passengers alike, making no distinction between them. Bram was one of the innocent bystanders caught up in the net.

It was very bad. Penser was dead—a suicide. But there were dead Nar, as well. Among them was Bram's old tutor, Voth-shr-voth.

Voth's death was a particular atrocity to the Nar. He had died under torture when Penser's henchmen had attempted to force him—as the space tree's acting biologist—to override the tree's tropisms and make it spread the leaves of its light-sail on a course to the target moon.

Worse than that, Voth's death had interrupted the final flowering of his life—his terminal change from male to female. All of Voth's budding children had died with him when he had failed to reach a breeding pool in time.

The Nar had not understood until this time that their pets could bite. Their civilization ground briefly to a halt while they met in one of their grand touch conclaves to decide what to do about the human species.

Tentacle pressed to tentacle, radio sleeves linking the parallel meetings on all the nearby worlds, the entire Nar race became a single immense organism whose process of deliberation passed human understanding. The humans at the center of the vast tribunal—a sea of living Nar that stretched mile upon mile—waited and shuddered.

It was the Day of Wrath.

The humans were heard. When it was Bram's turn to speak, he told them about the immortality virus that had been withheld from all the generations of reconstituted man, condemning humans to short, unfulfilled lives in a long-lived Nar society. He told them of his childhood dream of returning home—home to the distant, unreachable galaxy where the first human race once had dwelt, and from which the tremendous Message of Original Man had been sent. His touch brother, Tha-tha, emerged from the packed throng to speak to him directly, and perhaps to intercede for him. "It is true, then, Bram-bram," he asked sadly, "that all your life you felt you had no place here?"

All around Bram, other humans were simultaneously unburdening themselves to the collective Nar consciousness: Partnerites telling of their struggles to be accepted in a society that saw them as ephemeral mutes; Resurgists admitting why they had given up and surrendered to a daydream of past human glory; even some Penserite radicals attempting to explain why they had been driven to violence in their effort to find a place for humans in a Nar universe.

Perhaps the Nar had never before realized the depths of human alienation and anguish. But they were getting an earful now. The sea of tentacles seethed. Bram could not read what was happening out there. No human could. But he could sense a great surge of sorrow and revulsion, distress and pity.

The human race might get off lightly, he dared to hope. The present generation might be allowed to live out their lives comfortably—under closer supervision, of course. It was even possible that the human species need not vanish from the universe a second time; limited breeding or *in vitro* gene assembly might keep a few dozen specimens around as curiosities for future generations of Nar to gawk at.

But the Nar, in a huge tide of nonmammalian empathy, were more compassionate than Bram could have imagined.

When the verdict was announced, the human race found that it had been sentenced to immortality.

The Nar had no use for immortality themselves; for them an eternity without aging and what lay at the end of it was an eternity without fulfillment. So perhaps they simply had not realized what such a gift would mean to humankind.

Bram was put in charge of a human-run project to reconstruct the virus; the Nar, with exquisite tact, had recognized that this must be a human achievement, not an act of charity. It would be the work of years or decades, even with Original Man's blueprint. For Bram would have to find an alternate route to the same result to avoid the biological dangers associated with the immortality nucleotides—dangers that, some thought, may have contributed to the demise of Original Man.

But immortality was only part of the Nar gift—a means to an end. With the complete gift, the Nar gave Bram back his dream.

The Nar species was on the verge of an enormous technological leap. Travel between stars, until now, had meant riding the worldlet-size space-dwelling trees that were part of Original Man's bioengineering bequest. They had replaced the first crude boron fusion-fission starships of the Nar's early space age, and could travel at up to one-seventh of the speed of light. With them, the Nar could spread slowly from star to star and hope to populate the galaxy in a million years or two.

But only recently a conceptual breakthrough had raised the possibility of a relativistic spacecraft that could reach the core of the galaxy in only fifty thousand years. With it, the Nar could do on a smaller scale what Original Man had done so grandly—use it as a robot beacon to broadcast their own genetic code to the billions of stars that would come within its range. If the probe hit the jackpot only once or twice, then the Nar race could spread from new foci, sending brothers among the stars who would be waiting to greet them.

To this lofty purpose, the Nar species had allocated a tremendous share of the wealth of their civilization. The robot spacecraft project had been given a timetable that might make it a reality in only a few centuries—a fraction of a Nar lifetime.

Now, in an act of stunning generosity, the Nar decided to speed up the timetable—and bequeath the relativistic engine to the human race.

With it, those humans who wished to—the restless ones, the unhappy ones, the adventurous ones—could return to their mythical home in another galaxy. The trip would take thirty-seven million years of real time, of course, but it had been calculated that by traveling within one hundred millionth of one percent of the speed of light, the time dilation factor predicted by the theory of relativity would have a value of approximately seventy thousand. So to the travelers, the journey would seem to last only about five hundred and forty years.

And when you had eternity to play with, that didn't seem like too high a price to pay.

To reach that tremendous terminal velocity—to become pregnant with enough kinetic energy to coast between the galaxies in a fuel-less void—the ramjet craft would first have to dive to the heart of the departure galaxy, gulping the rich H-II clouds as it went, then let the gravitational center of the galaxy sling it above the plane and out into emptiness.

So it all worked out to everybody's benefit. The humans would be able to do the Nar's little chore for them on the way home.

One problem remained. Robot ramjets were not very hospitable to life. They were *hot*! And even if a way were found around *that* problem, there was still the question of living space and a reliable supportive environment for a substantial fraction of the human race on a trip that would last for more than five hundred years.

How would it be managed?

It was simple. The spacecraft would tow a tree.

Mim appeared in a stunning green off-the-shoulder party dress with a five-pointed hem that, though it was a bit old-fashioned compared to some of the newer styles, suited her very well. Over it she wore a short pleated chlamys that left her right arm bare—an old cellist's habit.

She bent over the chairpuff and kissed Bram lightly above one eyebrow. "What are you sitting here brooding about?" she said.

"Oh, I was just thinking about the Father World," Bram said, getting up. "It seems very far away now."

"It *is* far away! Tens of thousands of light-years away!"

"Which means that tens of thousand of years have passed since we left. We're in their historical past, Mim. After only a couple of decades of travel. I wonder if they've forgotten us."

"Not a chance. The Nar never forget anything."

"All the Nar we knew are dead now. But there ought to be some fifty-thousand-year-old humans that we used to know walking around. I wonder what it's like to be fifty thousand years old. *We're* still under a hundred."

"And getting younger every day," she reminded him.

"Yes. I wonder if fifty thousand years is long enough for a human being to learn the Great Language. Jao swears that it's possible, with cortical transplants, electronic interfacing, and prosthetic touch sleeves."

"It must be a very different society from the one we grew up in," she commented.

"We'll never know," he said. "The people who stayed behind made *their* choice and we made ours. Speaking of which..."

He inclined an ear to the noise in the outside corridor. Some drunk was singing a Bobbing Day carol—off key—and his friends were making it worse by attempting harmony. Mim winced.

"Yes, we're developing our own traditions, aren't we? How would you like to try to explain All-Level Eve to the folk back home?"

"It's all very natural to the younger set. Mim, do you realize that there are children who've been born on Yggdrasil—who've never known anything else? Some day they'll outnumber us old-timers. By the time we get to the Milky Way—"

She took his arm. "Right now we'd better worry about getting to the Forum. It wouldn't do for the year-captain to be late."

He smiled at her and drew her a little closer. Together they stepped out into the corridor and let the crowd carry them along.

CHAPTER 3

The Bob dangled from five hundred feet overhead, its displacement showing just how badly askew the wooden chasm of the Forum was. Its carved onion shape, taller than two men, had been repainted in gaudy green and vermilion stripes by this year's Bobbing Day committee. Though it was only about twenty degrees out of plumb— Yggdrasil had prematurely swung the bough ten degrees toward the true before being checked—that was enough to hang it above the chalked line at a point that was nearly two hundred feet from the painted bull's-eye in the center of the floor.

"I don't like sitting this close to it," Mim said, taking a sip of her All-Level Eve cocktail. "I always think it's going to fall and roll right over us."

"It would roll in a circle," Orris said. "That's why it's that shape."

"It won't roll at all because it's not going to fall," Marg said firmly. "I won't allow anything to spoil Bobbing Day."

Everybody at the table laughed. Marg was still the commanding presence she had always been. She was large, formidable, and matronly at this stage of her youthening, and poor Orris seemed a collection of sticks beside her.

"You'd better have a word with the acrobats, then," Bram teased her. "If the one on top isn't careful, he's liable to get himself brained."

They all looked across to where the acrobats were forming a human pyramid, no more than thirty feet from their table. There were six of them: five brawny lads in

54

loincloths and a little lightweight fellow in rainbow skin-tights at the apex. They had managed to hoist the little fellow high enough to reach the Bob and set it spinning.

"Who are they?" Trist asked. "I think I recognize the one at the bottom right."

"They all work together in the glucose-extraction plant. Nice boys. They've been practicing for months."

Next to Trist, who had been holding her hand as if they were still in their early bonding years together, Nen said, "We all have to congratulate you, Marg. This is one of the best All-Level Eves ever. The decorations, the food, the entertainment—everything!"

Marg flushed with pleasure, and Orris beamed proudly. "Everybody on the committee worked very hard," Marg said.

Bram looked around the Forum at Marg's handiwork. The immense arena was lit by torches in wall brackets that cast a resinous red glow around the perimeter, where almost the entire population of the tree, with the exception of the few hundred who remained on duty tonight, were seated at tables, each defined by a circle of light cast by a sputtering resin stick. Garlands of silver leaves criss-crossed the walls, making a pattern of reflections.

There was no way to decorate so vast an area as the main floor of the ellipse, so Marg had very wisely left it in darkness, except for a central blaze of illumination where colored spotlights mounted high on the walls picked out the bull's-eye where the Bob would come to rest. A few reddish glints here and there, where leaf arrangements had been strategically placed, gave an abstract geometric shape to the pool of darkness. More spotlights were aimed at the Bob itself and followed the entertainers.

The final touch, lending a sense of awe and mystery to the annual rite of rotation, was the beam of sullen, red-shifted light from the starbow, filtering down from a len-ticel somewhere high above. On past All-Level Eves, the starlight had been jolly, multicolored, but now the sur-rounding vault of higher frequencies had contracted to a point forward of the direct line of vision from here, leaving only the bloody light that preceded darkness.

"Yes, here's to the committee," Bram said, raising his

glass. "What else are you going to have in the way of entertainment?"

"Oh, we'll have pattern dancing—three very talented couples from hydroponics—and some people who sing, and some very clever body puppets." Marg turned to scold Mim. "And I'm very disappointed in you, Mim. I thought you were going to play the cello for us tonight."

"Oh, nobody wants to hear concert music tonight," Mim said. "This is an evening to have *fun* in. Besides, some of these people have been waiting a whole year for a chance to be on stage."

The acrobats had given the little fellow a boost that allowed him to do a backflip past the onion bulge of the Bob, and now he hung by one knee from the suspending cord and swung the Bob in greater and greater arcs while the audience clapped and cheered.

Across the table from Bram, Ang dug her fingers into Jao's beefy arm. "He's going to swing right over us!" she squealed.

"Somebody pass the poor fellow a drink, then." Jao belched. He took a mighty gulp from his glass and set it down. He squinted critically at the surface of his drink. "Still an ellipse," he said. "You know, it's an awesome thought. At the very moment the Bob becomes plumb, five thousand ellipses in five thousand glasses are going to become five thousand circles."

"And we'll stop being all tipsy," Ang said.

"Ah, that's where you're wrong," Jao said with a sly wink at the company. "The geometry of alcohol is not the same as the geometry of space. The object of All-Level Eve is for the people to become progressively more tipsy while the environment becomes progressively less so."

"In that case, you're doing very well," Mim said with a laugh.

Out on the floor of the Forum, the rainbow-clad acrobat had dropped lightly to the shoulders of his fellows, to the applause of the surrounding ring of revelers. Noisemakers razzed and rattled. The human pyramid disassembled itself, acknowledged the applause with outflung arms and a curtsy, and tripped offstage. A singing duo took their place—a man and woman in clown costume: she with enormous quilted breasts, he with a braided rag phal- lus that trailed on the floor—and began singing bawdy songs to the rowdy encouragement of the onlookers.

"Who's the Momus?" Trist asked.

"Don't you recognize him?" Marg replied. "It's Wil- lum-frth-willum."

"He's lost considerable dignity."

"He doesn't need it anymore. He's got his youth to look forward to."

"I didn't know he had such a good singing voice," Mim said.

"He's kept it hidden all these years."

A lot of table hopping was going on as the time grew near for the swing of the Bob. People made their way across the tilting floor to drop off little Bobbing Day gifts, drink a toast with friends, embrace and kiss.

"It seems as if there's always been a Bobbing Day," Mim said, leaning against Bram's shoulder. "I can hardly remember how it got started. What are we going to do when we leave the galaxy and stop accelerating and there's no more annual tree turning?"

"We'll think of something," Bram said. "Human beings will always celebrate some sort of a year-festival."

"It's going to be a long, featureless ride between the galaxies," Jao said. "Nothing to mark the years."

"Sounds dull," Orris said. "But like Bram says, we'll think of something. We ought to appoint a revels com- mittee to look into it." He looked fondly at Marg. "We're putting you in charge of it."

"Almost time," Bram said, feeling his waistwatch with his fingertips. Some of the younger generation had taken to wearing timepieces on their wrists—clever little holo displays that showed the ten hours of the day visually, in human numerals—but for Bram, old habits died hard.

At this moment, in the heart of the tree, Jao's grand- daughter would be checking and rechecking her meters, adjusting the voltages and gas pressures that would tickle Yggdrasil into one-twelfth of a revolution—or, rather, the portion of those thirty degrees it had not already antici- pated. Once, early in the voyage, the humans had tried to accomplish the maneuver by brute force, using the

plentiful hydrogen trapped by the drive section. ButYgg-
drasil had fought back and returned to starting position
four times before the humans finally gave up. It was better
to trick Yggdrasil into following its own imperatives.

"Too bad your granddaughter can't be with us tonight,"
he said to Jao. "She missed the festivities last year, too;
seems to me she ought to be able to alternate with other
staffers in tree systems."

"Oh, Enyd? Don't waste your time feeling sorry for
her. She could be here if she wanted to. No sense of fun,
that girl. She's happier pushing her buttons. Sometimes
I wonder if she's really our granddaughter." He clapped
a hairy hand on Ang's haunch. "What do you think, pet?
Is she a case of mislabeled genes?"

"Oh, Jao!" Ang exclaimed. "She's just a little *serious*,
that's all."

"Here comes Smeth," Trist said. "Rounding up votes,
no doubt."

Bram looked across the torch-lit perimeter. Smeth's
gangling form could be discerned threading a route through
the tables, lurching awkwardly across the tilted floor. A
party of young constituents tried to detain him, but Smeth
seemed distracted; he exchanged a few words, made a
gesture declining an invitation to sit down, and kept coming.

"Something on his mind," Nen said. "And it isn't votes."

"Now, Jao," Ang said. "Remember you're not on duty
tonight. You said yourself that your deputy can handle
anything that comes up."

Jao patted her hand. "Wild forces couldn't drag me
away."

Smeth stumbled the last few yards and loomed over
the table.

"Sit down, Smeth," Orris said. "Have a drink."

"Uh, thanks, but I just wanted to have a word with
Jao," Smeth said.

"I knew it!" Ang said.

"Nothing wrong with the drive?" Jao said. "Everything
working all right?"

"The drive's fine...uh...at least it's coping with
everything the core's throwing at us."

"Oh?" Jao's tufted eyebrows went up. He rose from his seat and steered Smeth by the elbow to a little distance away. Bram could see them talking earnestly, heads close together.

Jao came back to the table while Smeth waited. "Look, I'm just going down to the remote bridge for a few minutes—we've got the one in this bough hooked up now. Never fear—I'll be back in plenty of time for the turning. Marg, mix me up a libation."

"Do you want me to come with you?" Bram offered.

"No . . . I'm just going to take some readings. Sit tight and enjoy the festivities. You too, Trist—no, don't get up."

He rejoined the fidgeting Smeth, and the two of them left.

Ang had begun a litany of complaint about Smeth. " . . . always dragging Jao off for some nonsense. Just because *he* lives for his work, he thinks everyone else does. I hope that when he gets young again, he'll find some woman who'll take him in hand." Marg listened sympathetically.

Mim asked Bram unobtrusively, "Why does Smeth look so worried? I know he's a fusspot, tending his engines and guarding the sacred fusion flame like some kind of keeper of the mysteries, but he's got Jao worried, too."

Bram told her about Jun Davd's concern over the gas infall that had made the center of the galaxy a denser place than it ought to be. "Galactic cores are active places, but this one may be more active than most. More collisions between stars. More stars exploding or being ripped apart by tides and feeding the black hole. Smashed stars forming a soup that circles the hole at tremendous speeds, creating more turbulence, more friction, stronger magnetic fields."

Mim gave a shudder. "And we're heading toward *that*?"

"We're bending ourselves around it at a safe distance. Smeth may want Jao to alter our trajectory somewhat, based on what he can deduce from the junk falling into our scoop."

"Is that what he meant by coping with what the core's throwing at us?"

"Probably. We've run into the fringes of gas jets so far, and a couple of minor storms of relativistic electrons."

"Storms?"

"Caused by shock waves in the plasma. They accelerate the stripped electrons. Gives the ramscoop quite a diet."

"Oh, dear, I don't like the sound of that!"

"Don't worry. The more energy that's thrown at us, the stronger our fields are. The chief effect is the spurts of extra acceleration it's caused, before feedback can compensate. You've probably noticed times during these past weeks when you've felt heavier."

"I thought it was old age delaying its farewells."

He smiled. "No. There've been some episodes of minor accidents and breakage that no one paid attention to. Fortunately, outside travel isn't allowed without a tether, for vehicles *or* people. Otherwise . . ."

"Otherwise, what?"

"Somebody could've gotten left behind. Traveling at almost the speed of light in some heavy weather. Not that they'd know anything. The instant they left the shadow of our intake area—"

"Please, I don't want to know about it!"

"Sorry. But as I was saying, the chief effect is extra acceleration. And that may have put us a few days ahead of schedule on our black hole flyby." He hesitated. "I've been thinking about sending everybody to the trunk when the time comes, to wait it out."

Mim looked alarmed. "Will that be necessary?"

"Oh, I doubt there's any real danger. If we ever ran into something we couldn't handle, the trunk wouldn't be any safer than an outer bough. But while I'm still year-captain, everybody's safety is my responsibility, and moving to the trunk would put us in toward the center of our umbrella, where the field is strongest, just while we're swinging around."

He caught Trist looking at him from across the table. Trist compressed his mouth as a signal for Bram to shut up.

"That wouldn't make you very popular," Mim said. "Everybody's getting settled into their new quarters, unpacking and sweeping out rooms they haven't seen for twelve years, and tomorrow morning the floors will finally be level."

Bram left it there. Across the table, Trist said loudly, "Who wants another drink? I think we've got time for one more before Leveltide."

"Look," Orris said. "Here come the clowns!"

Jao still hadn't returned when the Bob began to swing. "Twenty...nineteen and a half...nineteen..." the crowd chanted in unison, counting the degrees as the bulbous painted shape followed the chalk line toward the bull's-eye in the center of the Forum. Globular membrances lit from within by a coating of biolights drifted down, released from somewhere high above. Hitherto invisible sparklers were touched off, making a star pattern on the floor. To one side, the clowns were still gamely performing their skit, though nobody was watching: Two of them wearing twelve-foot body puppets were vying for possession of a papier-mâché imitation of the Bob, while three more, making a Nar with too many legs, danced around them, trying to make peace.

"Where *is* he?" Ang fretted. "He's going to miss it."

"Never mind," Trist said gallantly. "I've saved an extra kiss for you. Jao'll have to kiss Smeth. It'll serve him right."

"Five..." the crowd chanted. "Four..."

Bram could feel the faint trembling in the floor as Jao's granddaughter, a hundred and fifty miles overhead in the trunk, began to cancel inertia in order to bring the Bob precisely level. He had to admit that she was an artist at it. In some previous years, before she had become tree systems officer, the Bob had been as much as three or four degrees off. Everybody had had to make the best of it—the clowns would rush out with a big, round target-painted rug and wrestle it into place under the Bob while people egged them on, and Yggdrasil would gradually be corrected over the next few days. But Jao's granddaughter—he must remember that her name was Enyd—never missed.

"Here's to all you lovely people and another safe year," Marg said, raising her glass.

The Bob settled into place, swinging in a small diminishing arc that finally came to rest. More sparklers went off, and noisemakers raised a din. People were shaking hands, kissing, embracing.

Bram felt the shudder.

Others must have felt it, too. Around the arena there was a sudden dip in the noise level, then, as people decided they had been mistaken, things warmed up again.

Trist was staring at the Bob, his eyebrows knit together. Bram followed his lead. The Bob had started swinging again, making a small ellipse that finally settled precisely over the center of the bull's-eye once again and hovered there, trembling, only a few feet above the floor.

"Your granddaughter's losing her touch," Orris teased Ang. "She usually gets it on the first try."

Bram and Trist exchanged glances. Orris had missed the point, and so had most of the others at the table and in the festivities beyond. The babble of happy ringside voices continued undiminished.

It was not some small adjustment in the angle of radius that had set the Bob swaying again. If that had been the case, the Bob would not have returned to the same spot.

No, something had bumped Yggdrasil here in the interstellar night. Something violent enough to buffet a planetoid-size object stubborn with relativistic mass.

Bram rose to his feet. "I think I'd better—"

And then the thing struck again, knocking him off his feet.

Nobody could miss it this time. People went sprawling, tables overturned, and drinks went flying. Some reflex screaming was going on. The Bob swung in great pendulum arcs over the heads of the crowd. Some wall torches fell to the floor, and a few quick-witted people moved to stamp out the flames. The electric lights flickered, dimmed, then grew bright again.

And from above, where the red-shifted light had been filtering through the lenticule, there was a sudden hideous flare as great snakes of fire flashed by and dopplered through the spectrum.

Orris, white-faced, said, "What's happening?"

"Everybody better stay put," Bram said. "There's a lot of broken glass around." People were milling around, but the situation seemed to be coming under control again. "Orris, you look after things here. Trist, I'll need your help." Trist nodded and rose.

And then, suddenly, Jao was at Bram's elbow, his forehead bleeding from a gash where he must have fallen against something.

"Better come to the bridge," Jao said. "Jun Davd's trapped in the trunk, but I've got him on the fiber-optic link. And Smeth's in touch with his black gang in the engine section."

"What's wrong?" Bram asked.

"The galaxy is exploding."

Bram stared straight ahead into a representation of hell.

The viewscreen that showed the spectrum-corrected forward view was a smear of red-hot coals punctuated by glaring white intersections and eerie violet blobs that throbbed at the headachy limits of vision.

At the center of the screen, a multicolored vortex of fire swirled around a tiny central blaze of eye-hurting brightness. Time was speeded up enough so that Bram could see the crushed stars breaking up, lengthening, feeding their substance into the rushing swirl of light.

Another flattened whirlpool flamed at the edge of the screen, tilted just enough to reveal a similar blinding center. The second vortex seemed even bigger, more violent, than the first.

The whole screen pulsed. At regular intervals of a few seconds, brightness swelled, the field of coals seemed to ripple, and a dazzling shower of sparks danced in front of the view. Each time this happened, Bram felt the floor beneath him shudder, heard the vast creak and groan of the wooden worldlet around him.

"It's not a literal view, of course," Jun Davd's calm voice came over the communications link. "It's the entire electromagnetic spectrum done in visible light. But I've done it in a logarithmic progression, so you can more or less trust your eyes between blue-green and yellow-orange. Then it really starts to stretch out. In the blues, you're seeing by x-rays. In the far violet, between four thousand and forty-five hundred angstroms, you're seeing by gamma radiation. And those dull reds are very long radio waves. I had to do it that way so you could make some sense of the view. The dust obscures everything. But infrared gets passed from particle to particle, and some of the energetic gamma punches through."

"Thank you, Jun Davd," Bram said. "You must have stayed up all night to do that."

Jun Davd chuckled. "I don't imagine there was much sleep for anybody."

That was true enough. Bram rubbed at his grainy eyes with a fist. They were red, burning. All his joints were stiff.

The others in the long, sweeping loggia that served as this bough's bridge had suffered equally from lack of sleep. Smeth looked bedraggled, his salt-and-pepper hair sticking up in tufts. Jao and Trist moved as if they had weights attached to their feet, and Bram could see the weary, drawn faces of the people hunched over the monitors.

Mim gave him a wan smile. She was still in her party dress. She had stayed here through the long night, making herself useful. Marg was here, too. She had put Orris to work cleaning up the shambles of the festivities, then she had gotten busy organizing hot food and drink for those on duty.

The bridge itself was fully functional, with everything plugged in, though a lot of unopened cases were still shoved against the rear wall, and some of the equipment was dispersed helter-skelter wherever convenient.

A great gout of incandescence leaped out of the screen. Bram flinched. It reached toward him, a violet serpent with a beady red and orange gut showing through, and writhed offscreen. Bram turned his head to look out the observation wall and saw a cross section of fire flash by, flaring from yellow to red in seconds. Yggdrasil gave a lurch.

"What was that?" Bram said.

"Jet," Jun Davd said. "I'd estimate it at about twenty-five light-years long and still growing. It's moving at about three-fourths of the speed of light, but of course it's emitting a lot of relativistic electrons that are traveling faster."

Smeth looked around, strain showing on his face. "We swallowed some of the fringes. That was the bump you felt."

"What caused it?" Bram asked.

Jun Davd's composure was undisturbed despite the backhand swipe the cosmos had just taken at him. "It's that black hole we're heading toward. If you'll keep your eye on it, you can see the process as it gets ready to toss the next one at us. The hole must be spinning very fast. It must have a very strange geometry—sliced off flat at the poles, but with the curvature of its circumference undisturbed. The gas and dismantled stars flowing into it would have a very strong magnetic field. You can't anchor a magnetic field in a black hole, but some of the field lines would penetrate the accretion disk and attach themselves very close to the event horizon. Then it's crack the whip— a million stars at a time."

"Why are we heading directly toward it?" Bram asked Jao. "I thought we were on a course that gave it a wide berth."

"We were," Jao said, his face grim.

"We still are," Jun Davd's voice said. "That object you see is not the black hole at the center of the galaxy."

"What is it, then?" Bram said, but he was afraid he already knew.

"It's another black hole—in orbit around the galaxy's central hypermass. The black hole at the center of the galaxy has a second black hole as its satellite."

Except for those who were not able to leave their monitor boards, everyone on the bridge had gathered around the viewscreen showing Jun Davd's display. Nobody was doing much talking.

Bram stared, fascinated, at the flat, double-ended funnel of fire that was sucking in the stars. You couldn't see the black hole itself, of course. You couldn't even see the accretion disk. But you could see those whirlpools of superheated gas by the inferno of radiation they gave off as they fell down that cosmic drain. And that intense, tiny blaze at the center was where the condensed matter crossed the static limit and doomed itself to leave the universe forever.

Jun Davd's model of binary black holes explained a lot of things. It explained the rolling yawn of the satellite hole: that was caused by the precession of its spin axis. And it explained those fingers of fire across the bed of coals: the satellite hole was sweeping out the rotating gas cloud of its primary. The geometry of space-time must be very complicated in there. Eventually the orbit of the satellite hole would decay, and it would fall into its primary.

And *that* would make quite a splash! If anyone in the nearby universe was trying to prove the existence of gravity waves, it would make his day.

"How did it happen?" Bram said.

"The black hole may have been snatched from the Bonfire when the two galaxies met," Jun Davd said. "That might help to explain why the Bonfire lost its shape."

Jao spoke wonderingly. "That would have been quite a meal for our galaxy to digest. First it nibbles around the edges. Then it reaches in and pulls out a plum."

Jun Davd cackled appreciatively. "The stolen hole would have fallen to the center, sweeping up stars and gas," he went on. "By the time it took up residence as part of a binary pair, it would have been quite massive. We can assume, from the present remnants of the Bonfire, that its central black hole could not have been much more than a hundred million solar masses. However, the satellite hole appears to be three or four times that mass. In fact, I'd put it at a fourth to a third the size of its primary, which I now estimate at well over a billion solar masses— much bigger than I expected. Or..."

"Or?" Bram prompted.

"Alternatively, the orbiting black hole might have been born right here in the galactic nucleus—maybe with the help of turbulence caused by the passing of the Bonfire."

"You don't sound very convinced."

"The dust is certainly thick enough and stellar collisions frequent enough to aggregate a second black hole of a few thousand solar masses. A single collision would be enough to start the process if the stars were massive enough to begin with."

"But we're dealing with a hole of three or four hundred million solar masses."

Jao burst in: "Why stop at one orbiting black hole? Why not a whole planetary system of them?"

"Exactly," Jun Davd said. "Of course, a number of additional black holes may exist. In fact, I'd be surprised if they didn't. And two or more of them may have consolidated to form a larger hole. But nothing big enough to explain what we're facing here."

"What, then?"

"What we've got here is a binary system, not a planetary system. Both of them have a very rapid spin, they're very close—only a few diameters apart—and one is at least a fourth the size of the other. In fact, they fit almost perfectly the picture of contact binaries."

Bram struggled to remember his rusty astronomy. "Contact binaries. When the primordial cloud gains too much angular momentum as it condenses and relieves itself by forming a disk. And the disk condenses into a companion, not a planetary system, because it contains too much material and the lines of magnetic force aren't strong enough to cause spin-down and the spiraling outward of the disk." He frowned as if Jun Davd could see him. "But you're describing the formation of stars."

Jun Davd's disembodied voice said, "What, essentially, are black holes?"

Outside the observation wall, the flickering tongue of ionized gas continued to rattle through the spectrum, a slice at a time. How long had Jun Davd said it was? Twenty-five light-years. It had grown another light-year while they were talking.

The viewscreen gave him a better impression of what the tongue was doing. It appeared as a mottled serpent swinging laterally away from them on its whiplash path, swallowing stars as it went.

Bram saw something that must have been a supernova—a wink of brilliant light that was gone in an instant, on Yggdrasil's speeded-up time scale. Then another flash and another, each of them bathing space in a cosmic instant of inconceivable radiation, each blowing most of its substance off to add more fuel to whatever was happening here in the heart of the galaxy, leaving its core behind as a neutron star.

Chain reaction!

In the galaxy outside, perhaps forty or fifty days had gone by in the last few minutes. Supernovae weren't supposed to occur that close together. They were supposed to occur once every century or two.

Now he could see another cosmic jet forming at the hub of whirling gases that marked the central black hole. It whipped around, growing by the light-year, ready to slap Yggdrasil when it was long enough.

"Jun Davd," Bram said, feeling sick, "how long can these jets grow?"

Jun Davd's voice was grave. "Millions of light-years in the most extreme cases we know. More often, a few tens of thousands of light-years."

"And in this case? From what you've been able to observe?"

"Long enough to reach the edge of the galaxy. That's what you wanted to know, isn't it?"

"And they're growing at seventy-five percent of the speed of light?"

"They'll slow down a bit as they proceed outward. Some of them will fall back."

Bram grasped at a slender hope. "Then there would be time to warn the Father World, wouldn't there? We could stop broadcasting the Message and use our radio beacon to beam a warning. We know they're listening to the center of the galaxy. They'd have at least twelve thousand years to get ready. Maybe ... maybe build a fleet of ships to migrate. Or ... or set up ramjet screens for whole planets."

"The primary threat isn't the jets themselves," Jun Davd said gently. "It's the wave front of radiation coming from the events that have already begun here in the central region—and *that* travels at the speed of light." He went on as if he were giving one of his lectures. "The jets themselves contribute to that wave front—relativistic aberration makes them radiate most intensely in the direction of their motion. But they're only a part of the story. The supernovae are adding their increment of radiation. But, chiefly, it's coming from that whirligig of black holes and their accretion disks. The soup of matter that engine is feeding on is getting progressively thicker—it's now a self-sustaining process—and friction is causing the smaller, four-hundred-million-sun hole to spiral inward at an increasing rate."

How can he be so calm, Bram wondered.

Jun Davd's voice remained steady. "The radiation is pulsing outward in a series of shells that at this point are only light-days apart. You've noticed the flickering of the viewscreen and the rhythmic surges of acceleration as our engine harvests H-II pushed by that broom of photons. I've been taking measurements over the last shipboard hour, and those pulses are coming closer together."

Bram snatched at another straw. "The inverse-square law! By the time the shells of radiation reach the outskirts of the galaxy—"

"They'll still be fatal," Jun Davd said flatly. "In any case, no life anywhere in the galaxy will be able to survive the final event, when the two black holes merge."

A stunned silence pervaded the bridge. Everybody had been listening, of course—trying not to let it all sink in, taking refuge in Jun Davd's lucid exposition, clinging to some last atom of hope that out of his calm parade of revelations would come the one final fact that was a reprieve for the Father World and its two races.

Now people avoided looking at one another, as if in some obscure shame.

Out of the silence came a strange sound—one that became a shocking sound a moment later as people on the bridge realized that it was the sound of Jun Davd sobbing.

Bram shocked them further by putting the question that sooner or later would have to be asked.

"Will Yggdrasil survive?"

Jun Davd needed a moment to regain control of his voice. "We are now disposing of more energy than is available to the entire Nar civilization. The fields are still holding. We are protected for the time being. But I don't know if we can handle something on the scale of a climactic merger of the primary hole and its satellite."

There was a delayed moan of grief from someone on the bridge. Grief for the loss of the Nar and all their works. These were superb people, Bram's racing mind said. Personal fear would come later.

Jun Davd took refuge in more pedantry. "When two black holes become one, the resulting event horizon has a greater area than the sun of the areas of the event horizons of the original holes. It does not attain its final shape immediately. During the fraction of a second when the collapse takes place, there is a shifting and complicated topography. The geometry of space-time around it is ... irregular. The mathematics to describe it does not exist. And the ... distorted ... event horizon *vibrates*. The gravity waves generated by two vibrating masses equivalent to a billion and a half suns will be tremendous. What that will do to the surrounding plasma, you can well imagine. Next, angular momentum will increase abruptly at the same time that queer event horizon expands—and because the conjugate hole is spinning rapidly, the accretion disk will be embedded well *below* the static limit, transferring mechanical energy and magnetic force. A tremendous explosion of gamma radiation will travel outward at the speed of light, followed by a sphere of stripped matter traveling at relativistic speeds. We can hope to outrun the matter. But our ability to survive the shell of radiation may depend on our distance from the core when it overtakes us."

There was one last question for Bram to ask.

"How soon before the holes merge?"

"We'll be lucky to make it around the core."

"We're making a run for it, anyway," Jao said.

"That we are," Bram agreed. "All we can do is to pour on the gravities."

He lay propped on the floor pad, feeling the oppressive weight on his chest, his shoulders, his neck as he tried to hold his head up. All down the length of the observation loggia, dozens of people lay similarly sprawled on pads,

working prone, their instruments on the floor beside them.
Bram had ordered everybody to crawl, not walk, if they
absolutely had to move about. The bulk of the population
of the tree were in their quarters, lying down. It was still
half a day till periastron, and they would remain there
until then.

Jao said, "No, that's not all we can do. Bram, I've got
to ask you about something."

"Ask away."

"There's a decision to make about the core maneuver."

"Why ask *me*? I'm only year-captain. Discuss it with
Jun Davd."

"I've already discussed it with Jun Davd. But it's not
strictly a technical decision. It involves the lives of everyone aboard. Jun Davd says you're the only one who can
make the decision, and I agree."

With a sinking feeling, Bram said, "Go ahead."

"We've got to get in and out of the galactic core *fast*.
There's no way we can simply back up, the laws of physics
being what they are. We've got to use the mass at the
center to bend our path in a hyperbola and swing around
and out. Now our patron mass turns out to be *two* masses,
very close together—right?—but for the purposes of our
hyperbolic orbit, we're treating it as a single mass."

"Yes," Bram said, wondering what Jao was driving at.

"Even if there were some magical new law of physics
that would let us dump all our inertia at once and come
to a dead stop without rattling the glassware, it wouldn't
do us a bit of good. Because we'd have to back out from
a standing start and build up all our lovely gamma factor
all over again, and that would take us fifty thousand years
longer than whipping around the focus of the hyperbola.
So we're committed."

"Yes, certainly. Everyone understands that."

Jao tried to wave a leaden hand, gave up the effort.
"We also have to add a vector to angle the outward path
somewhat above the plane of the galaxy if we want to
aim at the Milky Way. That makes it even more tricky,
but I won't go into that now."

"Yes, yes," Bram said, wishing Jao would get to the
point.

"So, as you said, we decided to pile on all the acceleration that Yggdrasil will bear in the hope of beating the merger of the two black holes and the final explosion by the widest margin possible. But the extra speed means we need an even tighter hyperbola—we've got to brush that doomsday engine ever closer, and that has its own dangers."

"We all decided to take the risk."

"Otherwise," Jao said, ignoring the interruption, "we'd escape the galaxy, all right, and save our own skins. But we'd sail on out into intergalactic space and miss our target." He looked around and lowered his voice. "Of course, there may be some who are frightened enough of the core maneuver to want to do that on purpose."

"If you're asking—"

"Bram, there's a way we can pick up some extra velocity without adding more g's and taking the risk of cracking Yggdrasil's branches—to say nothing of our own sacroiliacs."

"Go on."

Jao hitched himself closer on his elbows. He took another look around the bridge to make sure that he would not be overheard.

"We use the satellite hole as a gravity machine."

"What?"

"We're *already* going to pick up the rotational energy of the primary hole. It's got a rotation parameter of point nine nine eight, and it's doing weird things to the space around it, and the field lines from the accretion disk are going to reach out with magnetic fingers and fling us along by our own magnetic field. Now, what I'm saying is that we can refine our orbit and loop around the satellite hole, and pick up its orbital energy. It's whizzing around its primary at a ferocious rate at this point. We could pick up fifty thousand g's of acceleration without it costing us a thing. We wouldn't even feel it!"

"We'd have to fly between the two holes to make that loop."

"Uh huh."

"Jun Davd says they're only a few diameters apart at

this stage. And they're spiraling closer. The final dive could happen at any moment."

"He thinks we have enough time to squeak through."

Bram's heart was pounding. "He said that at the present high rate of spin, the static limit is well above the edge of the accretion disk. The region between them must be very weird. We could get sucked into the hole with no warning. Into either one of the holes."

"Yah. That's why he says it's your decision."

Bram was going to ask for an estimate of their chances. But that would be begging the question—asking Jao and Jun Davd to make the decision.

"Do it," he said.

Jao nodded and crawled off on his elbows and knees to confer with Smeth.

The ghost of a star drifted by, a ball of red so dull as to be at the limits of visibility. The universe outside the long observation wall was no longer blind; it was filled with a meaningless red fog that showed a suggestion of vast billows, specks, twisting sheets. The phantom star cleared a tunnel ahead of it, but that was an illusion; actually, the star was going the other way, and the tunnel, of course, was its wake.

"Can you see it?" Jun Davd's voice said over the loudspeaker.

"Yes," Bram called to the directional pickup.

"Interesting," Jun Davd said. "I wasn't sure it would be visible. That shows you how chaotic the galaxy's final act has become. Imagine the odds against encountering a fellow traveler at anything like a fraction of *our* relativistic speed! I wish I had a window here."

"There isn't that much to see, Jun Davd. Just red mist."

"Yes, a pale reflection of events *behind* us. Supernova explosions proceeding outward, perhaps. Possibly local turbulence in those expanding jets, sending shock waves in the opposite direction. Puffs of stripped matter, relativistic electrons, moving inward to add to the mischief. The death throes of a galaxy."

Mim's hand sought Bram's. Her floor mat was pulled up close to his. He had tried to make her nap, but she

was unable to. The party dress was bedraggled. It had
been a long time since she or anyone else had eaten; Marg
and her helpers had had to give up when acceleration
increased.

"Easy," Bram said. "Remember, the Father World is
still alive at this moment. Nothing will happen to them
for almost fifty thousand years."

"Oh, Bram, it's so awful! Isn't there anything we can
do?"

He shrugged. "You heard Jun Davd. The first shells of
radiation are already on their way. The big one will be
right behind us. We can use the Message beacon to send
a warning as soon as we swing around the core, but our
warning would reach them only a few years before the
radiation front did. It would almost be cruel. Then what?
Suppose they managed to fit out a few space arks with
ramjet drives to save a few thousand Nar and humans.
They have no time to build up their gamma to the point
we have, and they can't outrun the expanding shell. They
can't reach another galaxy, anyway, not in a million years
of subjective time, because they can't use the H-II in the
inner galaxy to accelerate the way we did."

"It's all so ironic," she said bitterly. "We were supposed
to ensure the survival of the Nar species. We came all
this way. And now it's all gone for nothing. Instead of
broadcasting their Message, all we can do is to give them
their death sentence."

He squeezed her hand. There was absolutely nothing
he could say.

The people around him, fanned out on mats in front
of the forward viewscreen, didn't have much to say, either. Where two people lay together, they might murmur
at each other at intervals, but mostly they watched the
view painted by Jun Davd's computer.

Other screens around the bridge, and the screens in
the living quarters where the bulk of the people lay waiting
it out, had now been plugged into Jun Davd's program.
Some of the people watching with Bram and Mim had
access to their own screens, but there seemed to be a
compulsion to watch in groups.

"Hold on, everybody," Jao's voice said over the loud-speakers. "We just have to give it one more nudge."

The tree lurched. Tortured wood fibers groaned. Something somewhere gave with a snap. Interior lights flickered.

"How did Yggdrasil come through that?" Bram asked the tree systems center through the portable console on the floor next to his head.

The voice of Jao's granddaughter, Enyd, answered. "We're all right. We lost a few minor branches—all deadwood, anyway. Yggdrasil's reacting to the increased g-forces by acting to strengthen its compartments, but it won't last long enough to cause any serious imbalance."

"How are you people doing in there?" he asked.

Her voice softened, lost its formality. "We're all right, Captain," she said.

He switched off. The view in the forward screen was astonishing. A maelstrom of star-stuff churned around and around, fast enough to see. The private whirlpool of the satellite hole could be seen at this flattened angle of approach as an eddy in the main vortex—an eddy that itself circled around the main swirl of gases, dragging streamers with it. The tilt of its precession gave a peek into its heart of brightness every time it came around. Rags of plasma glittering with embedded stars enclosed the double whirlpool like a disintegrating bird's nest made of fire.

The background stars were squashed, stretched around the immediate vicinity of the holes, their light bent. A circle of splashed stars followed the smaller hole around, snapping back when it had passed.

Nowhere could Bram see a path through the torrent of radiance. The concentric swirls of gas seemed to make one bean-shaped disk whose irregular contour, twisting with the secondary hole, smoothed out almost to an oval with distance from the duel center.

The sky around that cosmic gullet—if you could call it a sky—was crowded with stars of every possible color, jammed so closely together that in places the blackness of space seemed to be nothing more than pavement showing through. Gigantic irregular blobs of glowing gas wandered among the stars, grazing on them. Every once in a while, the flash of a supernova explosion, speeded up twenty thousand times, could be seen through an engorged blob. The blobs had an average drift toward the black holes; the ones closest to the double maelstrom bulged yearningly toward it.

A cloud rushed toward them. "Hold on again," Jao's voice said. "We're going through."

The tree shook as the fields compensated. Weight fluctuated. Bram hoped nobody was moving about; otherwise, there might be broken bones that couldn't be attended to for some hours. Starfog enveloped them, dimming the fire ahead but not hiding it. Violet stars bobbed by, bloating themselves on the feast of gas; their violet color was the computer program's translation of the x-rays kindled by that rain of starmist.

Outside the clear elastic windows, the cloud manifested itself only as a dull red flicker—random flashes caused by encounters of gas molecules with relativistic electrons and orphaned protons that happened to be traveling in the same direction as Yggdrasil.

They broke through the cloud a minute later, into the awful radiance of the galaxy's inner heart. The whirlpool was just ahead, a roaring cataract of flame.

"Here we go!" Jao's voice said.

An enormous force seized the tree. Abruptly, weight was gone. Yggdrasil's acceleration was insignificant within that tremendous grip; it was like rowing upstream against a waterfall.

"Stay down!" Bram shouted.

His voice cut through the sudden babble, and people who had started to move clung to their mats. Bram thumbed the intercom switch and repeated his warning for those in their quarters.

Tidal forces changed their orientation as Yggdrasil, now in orbit around the outside hole, swung loose on its tether. The probe, uselessly spitting hadronic photons, must similarly have been trying to align its axis with its strange new parent body.

Bram fervently and irrationally hoped the probe's drive was pointed *down*, not *up*. Not that it would significantly matter in these few minutes and in view of the greater forces acting on the vehicle. In any case, he reminded himself, breaking free of orbit now would be every bit as deadly as diving into the black hole itself.

Equipment went sliding and crashing. People gasped as they felt the tidal pseudogravity change its direction. The hole didn't care which axis it struck through the wider diameter of the dumbbell-shaped body it had captured, but Yggdrasil, bless it, did, and the tree's struggle to "remember" its Bobbing Day vertical saved the humans from injury.

"Hold on to something if you can!" Bram shouted. "Try to stay in contact with the floor!"

Yggdrasil held together. Jun Davd had done his calculations well. The smaller black hole, with a solar-system-size circumference of over a billion and a half miles, was big enough, and their orbital distance from it great enough that tidal forces could not pull the tree apart. And the size of an individual human being was too insignificant to matter. Bram could feel the differential in the tug between his head and his feet, but it was no worse than the second-rate artificial gravity to be found in a spinning space vehicle that happened to have a diameter of only forty or fifty feet.

"Here comes the fun part," Jao said over the loudspeaker.

Yggdrasil swooped around the focus of its orbit. It was now attaining the inside loop of its curve. It was no longer speeding around the black hole in a direction contrary to the hole's own path around the parent hole, but was picking up fifty thousand g's worth of acceleration from the hole's orbital motion.

All for free, as Jao had pointed out. It was fifty thousand gravities that would have crushed them to paste if they had not been in free fall around the body that was providing it.

The only scary part of it was the fact that the inside loop was taking the treeful of humans between the two black holes.

"Oh, Bram," Mim whispered, squeezing his hand in a death grip. "Can such things be?"

The screen was blinding, even though it showed a bow-dlerized version of the radiance outside. They passed be-tween cascades of fire that sheeted to infinity. The eye followed those ravening walls along a path of bent light that made nonsense of perspective—on and on past the point where they should have recurved and eclipsed them-selves.

At the center of each infinity, the fires poured into an iris: nothingness surrounded by violet inferno.

"I wasn't sure we'd be able to see the holes them-selves," Jun Davd's awed voice said. "I thought the ac-cretion disks and the surrounding infall would block them from sight. But geometry doesn't mean anything here. We're within a few billion miles of each of them—less than a light-day away. If you're willing to accept an ar-bitrary definition of distance in the vicinity of gravitational fields like these, that is."

Bram's fear that there would be no path between the two accretion disks proved to be unfounded. What had appeared from a distance to be a merging of the twin vortices was a less substantial barrier up close. The ac-cretion disks traded material, it was true, but the gaseous zone between them was tenuous enough to pass through. And Yggdrasil wasn't going to be here long enough to worry about orbital decay. As they plunged between the fountaining sheets of flame, a curtain seemed to open up continually before them.

There was a moment when a giant eye looked in at them through the observation wall. People cried aloud in wonder. In the yawning eternity that the hole's gravity had made of time, light was downshifted even more than Yggdrasil's tremendous speeds had done thus far. The-oretically, there should have been nothing visible.

And nothing was what they were seeing.

Then the hole flung them away. The tree whipped around the loop, its path bent back on itself, and headed out of the galaxy. The transfer of orbital energy had been tremendous, and the hole's precession had given the tree the additional vector that would angle its path above the ecliptic.

The weight of acceleration returned. People picked

themselves up and started to move about. The g-forces were back to normal now. There was no need to force the pace. Whatever the danger from the front of radiation that would inevitably overtake them at some undetermined time in the years ahead, they had successfully navigated between those terrible whirlpools without being caught in the ultimate collapse.

Bram helped Mim to her feet. Together they went to the view wall. Other people were lined up along the safety rail, looking out.

There was something to see now, for the first time since the starbow had moved out of sight.

The universe was filled with light. Light of all colors, in wisps and ribbons and streamers.

An elongated blob of mottled blues and greens stretched, writhed, broke up into smaller blobs of violet and orange. A long pennant of pale blue flapped and disintegrated into a thousand filaments. Iridescent tendrils reached after the craft and fell behind. The striations of color played against a background of white radiance that cast long multiple shadows behind the people at the rail.

Yggdrasil was riding the shock waves out of the galactic center. In the nearby volume of space, collimated beams of accelerated matter were traveling in the same relativistic frame as Yggdrasil and shedding some of their radiation in the visible part of the spectrum.

The grateful tree dwellers drank in the spectacle, chattering happily after the tension of the past hours. Nobody was stopping to think about what it meant.

"It's beautiful," Mim said.

Bram said nothing. It was the beauty of death.

"It's hard to believe two hundred thousand years have gone by since we left the galaxy," Marg said. The tiny curved smile on her lips indicated an attempt at whimsy. "You don't look a day older, Mim. In fact, quite the reverse."

Mim, holding the new baby, beamed. "I'm going to name her Lydis," she said. "It comes from the tonality that Beethoven chose for a quartet movement he intended as a song of thanksgiving."

"Very appropriate," Orris said, "seeing that she was born on Safepassage Day."

"I was going to wait a few more years before getting pregnant," Mim said. "But then I decided I was young enough."

"You're not going to get much younger," Marg said. "None of us are."

Marg's own baby was two years old now. She and Orris had finally taken the plunge when Jun Davd had announced that they had officially left the exploding galaxy behind. There had been a rash of births that year.

"Oh, I don't know." Jun Davd laughed, trying to extricate a gnarled finger from the baby's grip. "Some of us elders still have quite a few years to go before we lose our wrinkles."

Bram, hovering proudly over Mim and the baby and trying not to look too smug, said, "I don't like to think of it as two hundred thousand years. Let the outside universe take care of itself. I prefer to count it in Safepassage Days—three more of them. We're all still alive, and we're even ahead of schedule."

The first Safepassage Day had been celebrated the year after the black hole maneuver. Nobody had thought it up—it had just seemed to happen by itself. It came the day after Bobbing Day, and the two holidays had naturally merged into one extended festivity. A new set of rituals had quickly sprung up around Safepassage Day, with gift giving, overeating, and much hilarity. Bobbing Day was still observed, though the reason for it was now gone, with Yggdrasil under spin. It was mostly for the children, who celebrated with miniature trees, candy, and little gaily painted plumb bobs.

"Yes," Trist said. "We picked up a tremendous boost not only from Jao's gravity machine, but from all that dense stuff the ramscoop swallowed on the way out." He grinned at Jao. "Jao, my hairy friend, what's your refined estimate of our terminal velocity, and how long before we reach the galaxy of Original Man?"

Jao fidgeted on a seating puff next to the maternal nest. Mim had passed the baby to a cooing, clucking Ang, and he was afraid that he was going to be asked to hold it.

"Well," he said, "there's still a lot of plus and minus in the observations, but Jun Davd's latest figures show us coasting at within a hundred millionth of one percent of the speed of light. That means we should cover thirty-seven million light-years in about five hundred and twenty-eight years, our time."

There was a harrumph from the fringe of the little group, where Smeth had parked himself at a safe distance from the baby.

"Not precisely," he said. "The ramscoop is still on standby. We're bound to pick up a stray hydrogen cloud or two, even between galaxies. We still may shave a few years from that estimate."

Smeth had finally been elected year-captain. He took it very seriously, even though there wouldn't be much to do during the next five hundred years. He was driving everyone crazy, poking his nose into the cellulose plant, the glucose-processing operation, housing expansion, and the kitchens.

"How about it, Jao?" Bram asked.

Jao scowled. "I hope not," he said. "We've got too much velocity to shed as it is. The Milky Way was supposed to be a pretty fair match for our galaxy in mass and configuration. Nobody figured on binary black holes and core explosions."

"How are you going to brake?"

Jao shrugged. "We'll spiral in, spiral out. We've got thirty-seven million years to figure out an approach. By that time the Milky Way's own hypermass may have grown some."

There was an uneasy shifting in the circle of people around Mim's nest. Jun Davd said quickly, "A larger black hole at the center of a galaxy should in itself present no dangers. In any case, with a normal accretion rate, no black hole could swallow its galaxy within the probable lifetime of the universe."

"Hey, hear that, little Lydis?" Trist said with theatrical heartiness. "Your new home is going to be around for what passes for forever!"

People made themselves laugh, but a small pall had

invaded the maternity chamber. Bram knew that everyone was thinking about the Nar and their vanished civilization.

His eyes strayed to the window wall. There was nothing to see out there anymore except Yggdrasil itself— mile after mile of great twisting subbranches and carpets of leaves, lit up by the banks of spotlights that were trained on them from the shaft of the probe: not only to give Yggdrasil a sense of its own rotation, but to provide the human passengers with a sense of place in a universe that otherwise had gone blank.

Somewhere beyond Yggdrasil's horizons was an exploding galaxy, its light blotted out by red shift. It didn't bear thinking about. But it was impossible to shut it out of the mind.

Nen cleared her throat. "What heights must they have reached in the fifty thousand years they had left to them?" she asked. "They spread so *fast* through their arm of the galaxy in that little time. Expanding their domain. As if they knew they were racing against the end of everything."

On the way out of the galaxy, Trist had used the antenna array to monitor the radio emissions of the spreading Nar civilization until they stopped—replaced by the random radio noise of frying suns. Bram had watched Trist change, become progressively haunted during those last years, and he knew that Trist must have brought some of his despair home to Nen in their quarters at the end of each day.

"In another million years they might have started up Skybridge, toward the Bonfire," Trist said softly.

"That wonderful web of life—it's all gone now!" Jao's granddaughter said with unexpected fervor. "The Nar, the humans and other organisms they brought into being, the forests of space poplars multiplying through the cometary halos from star to star!"

Bram wished the conversation hadn't taken this turn. All this was upsetting Mim on what should have been a happy day for her.

But it was Mim herself who wouldn't let it go. "Trist," she said. "Do you think they ever received our warning?"

"We can't ever know," he said. "It couldn't have made any difference anyway."

Mim had retrieved the baby from Ang. Bram thought that it made a pretty picture—Mim's dark hair spilled down around her shoulders, the baby nuzzling at her breast. Life, he thought. Life out of the ashes of universal death.

"They gave life to humankind twice, you know," Mim said almost in a whisper. "And there's no way we can pay the debt."

A slow dawning overtook Bram. He smiled at Mim. "Yes," he said. "Yes, there is."

Halfway across the night, Yggdrasil encountered a star. It was a fading red dwarf, so dim that they were almost upon it before the sensors reacted. In minutes of treeboard time, it was light-years behind them—too quick to call the passengers for a real-time look—but Jun Davd made a record for later replay by anyone who was interested.

"It must have broken free from its parent galaxy a very long time ago," Bram said to Mim as they watched the replay in their quarters. "Any star much higher on the main sequence would have burnt out long ago."

"Oh, Bram," Mim said, moved by the sight. "Could a star like that have planets? With living creatures on them?"

He touched her arm. "If so, they live in a very lonely universe. Under a sky with nothing in it except a fuzzy patch or two."

"Like us," Mim whispered.

"No," Bram said, "not like us. Someday we'll have stars in our sky again."

CHAPTER 4

"It'll take us about forty more years to stop," Jao said. "But we should end up in the approximate volume of space that Original Man used to inhabit."

People were starting to bunch around the optical boundary of the gigantic holo projection that dominated what, by convention, was the forward end of the observation lounge. More spectators were trickling into the fanshaped chamber. Yggdrasil had just burst out of one of the globular star clusters above the plane of the Milky Way, and word was going around that there was a magnificent view to be seen.

Bram stood a little aside with the rest of the astronomy and physics group, so as not to block the view. He'd been here about a half hour now, but he still couldn't take his eyes off the image.

The central bulge of the galaxy loomed head on out of darkness: a spectacular incandescent yolk with the flattened disk spread out around it. The fires of the nucleus glowed yellow, those of the disk shading to the paler blues of older stars. Nearer, a hail of intervening stars streamed by, Yggdrasil's tremendous speed putting them in visible motion.

The holo vista was startlingly realistic—much more so than the kind of flat computer display Jun Davd had made do with at the beginning of the voyage. But that was hardly surprising. He'd had centuries to improve on it and five generations of brilliant engineers to assist him.

This blazing vision was everything Bram had dreamed

of all his life. A knot of indescribable longing formed in his chest. It was easy to forget that this was illusion—that in deceleration mode, with the tethered tree straining forward and a torrent of hadronic photons aimed along the probe's axis through the focus of the sheltering ramscoop fields, the scene rushing toward him was actually beneath his feet.

Jao was taking some good-natured heckling from the crowd of onlookers. "Forty years is a long time to wait," someone said.

"We could do it faster," Jao said. "The limiting factor is the number of g's we want to take over an extended period of time."

"I don't understand how we'll be able to brake at all," somebody else said, "when we're not approaching edge-on through the spiral arms."

"We've already shed some velocity diving through the globular clusters," Jao said. "And there's plenty of mass in the central bulge, even though it's not as concentrated as the one that sent us on our way." His hands sketched the glowing egg in the holo behind him. "We dive straight down through the nice, nourishing H-II regions we're going to find in there, we make a tight demiorbit around the central three parsecs, a safe distance outside the core that contains the black hole, the central star cluster, and the rotating inner ring of ionized gas. The normal orbit at that radius—if we wanted to stay there—takes ten thousand years, so we apply vector to turn it into a powered orbit. Nevertheless, we start to spiral out in spite of ourselves, in flatter and flatter spirals that bring us into the plane of the galaxy. And the spirals are retrograde, of course, so we're using the magnetic brake of the nucleus itself. Nothing to it! It's as easy as tomato pie! Isn't that so, Bram?"

Bram, startled out of his reverie, said, "Uh, certainly. The Milky Way turns out to have a very strong magnetic field at the center from what certain of our observations seem to indicate, and we ought to be able to use its rotation to slow us down considerably—just the opposite of the magnetic assist we got at departure."

He glanced at the peculiar arc that could be seen growing out of the center of the galaxy's golden yolk like a spray caused by a pinprick. It wasn't a very large scale feature—only a few thousand light-years in extent—and its meaning was still being debated by the astronomy department; there was no need to go further into it at this moment.

"The galaxy's made a quarter rotation in the last seventy-four million years," Jun Davd interposed smoothly. "Or, rather, Original Man's neighborhood in one of the spiral arms has. We had to allow for that, too. I hope everyone appreciates the brilliant job of orbital plotting that Jao's department did."

Jun Davd was as imposing as a young man as he had been when he was old. He'd become even taller with the reversal of calcium loss in his spine and carried his slim, smooth-muscled body with an easy grace that his older incarnation had only hinted at. Bram could never quite get used to seeing him without white hair, though.

"Well, I suppose if we've come this far, we can wait another forty years," Jao's heckler conceded grudgingly. Bram recognized him as one of the younger passengers who had been born on the trip. He was probably under a century old, and forty years would seem like forever to him.

"Oho, hold on minute," Jao said with a malicious glint in his eye. "After we get to the volume of *space* we think Original Man's message came from seventy-four million years ago, we still have to find the suns he used. *That* could take us another century or two if we don't get lucky right away. We can do some preliminary sifting from a distance, but every time we want to stop and examine a G-type star firsthand, we've got to spend a year boosting down from relativistic speeds, a year boosting up to get to the next one, and at the low gamma we build up for these short hops, at least a couple of years in between. Unless you don't mind gaining a *lot* of weight, that is!"

"Why do we have to find one of Original Man's worlds at all?" grumbled the slender youth who had once been Doc Pol. Young he had become, but he hadn't lost his grumpiness. "We're here, we're safe in a galaxy that isn't exploding—why not settle down in the first G-type system we find? Put down roots. Let our descendants go gallivanting around looking for Original Man's world if they've a mind to."

There was a chorus of opposition to squelch that idea. Nobody wanted to give up on the search now that they were so close. Doc Pol hunched his faunlike head between his shoulders and looked stubborn.

"We've waited this long—we can wait a little while longer," said a woman wearing one of the leaf tabards that had been popular five hundred years back. The costume placed her as one of the old hands—now a minority.

"That's right," another person said authoritatively. "Man's worlds are our best bet, anyway. There's bound to be *some* sort of a surviving DNA-based ecology we can adapt to instead of having to start an ecology from scratch from our vats and gardens here. In the meantime, Yggdrasil is a fine world to live on."

"Too fine," someone else said. "We have folk aboard who've never known any other world. There may be some who'll prefer to stay in orbit with Yggdrasil. It makes a more benign environment than most planetary surfaces. I know I'd be tempted to stay myself."

"Until one day you found yourself sailing off to the cometary halo or heading for a nearby star that Yggdrasil thought had the right absorption lines," some wag said, and everybody laughed.

Jao's granddaughter, Enyd, claimed attention with a frown and a gesture. She was still chief tree systems officer after all these years, still smooth, cool, and unapproachable. She picked a lover briefly every twenty years or so, but most of the time she remained seemingly wedded to Yggdrasil. The unattached men who had wooed her to no avail called her "the dryad" behind her back.

"Whatever we do, we'll have to slow down enough to let Yggdrasil absorb a comet or two before too long," she said. "It's been showing the effects of drought these last few years."

The current year-captain, a colorless hydroponicist named Ploz who'd had the support of the sociometrics clique, said with quick concern, "How critical is it?"

"We're not losing leaves or anything like that. But the reproductive cycle is on hold. And the more recent xylem rings are getting extremely narrow—Yggdrasil's pretty much shut down its growth these last few years."

"How much longer before it *gets* critical?" Ploz persisted.

"I wouldn't want to wait more than another century or so," Enyd said severely.

There was a general sigh of relief. Jun Davd said, "Yggdrasil will have its comet long before then."

Bram hung around until the press of people got too thick for comfort. Then, with a last regretful look at the galaxy's swollen heart of fire, he elbowed his way out to make room for someone else.

"Don't forget the meeting tomorrow," Jao called after him. Bram waved acknowledgment.

When he emerged from the crowd, he found a delegation of four waiting to intercept him—three members of the glib younger set who seemed to be running things these days and one of the former oldsters who'd been around at the start of the journey.

Silv Jaks was the group's spokesperson, and that was Bram's clue that the sociometricians had taken a hand in whatever this would turn out to be. Bram wasn't quite sure what sociometrics was, other than the fact that it had something to do with people in groups—it was one of the jargon-packed new sciences that had sprung up during the trip's later generations—but its disciples had definite ideas about the running of the tree, and they wielded a lot of influence among the new people.

"Bram—we hoped we'd find you here," she said briskly. "Do you have a minute to talk?"

"Sure, Silv." Bram nodded to the group's senior member. "Hello, Torm."

"I'll come to the point," Silv said. "We represent a committee that wants you to run for year-captain this term."

"That's very flattering," Bram said warily, "but I haven't been year-captain for over two hundred years. I'm just a working biologist and part-time astronomy assistant these days. There are plenty of qualified people around."

She set her jaw and drew a breath. "We believe you're the candidate who's needed at this time."

"I thought you were going to throw your weight behind Ploz again. Everyone says he's doing a good job."

"He was the sort of year-captain we needed while we were still coasting. With deceleration, we've become a migratory society again. And there will be further upheavals as the populations of the outlying branches are assimilated into the annual branch once more. We're going to undergo a lot of societal stress in the coming years. More important, our *goal* is in sight now." She gestured past the crowds toward the overpowering panorama of the Milky Way's bright center. "We need a renewal of our sense of purpose as a society."

"What's it got to do with me? It seems to me that we've hung on to our sense of purpose all right—even though the Father World is only a legend to most of the folk who were born between the galaxies. As to adjusting to an annual migration again, I wouldn't worry. People manage." He smiled reassuringly. "It might even breathe some life into All-Level Eve and Bobbing Day again."

Silv was having none of his levity. "You're a symbol of the old days for a lot of the people who weren't around then. And for the original embarkees, you're the leader who started them on this voyage. You were the first year-captain—I looked that up! We've run profiles of all the old leaders through the computer, and we believe you're the one who's best suited to bring the two moieties together."

"The two what?"

It sounded like more of the jargon that Silv's colleagues in the Theoretical Anthropology group were always culling out of the primal Inglex dictionary. They were always creating computer models of imaginary human societies and drawing fanciful conclusions from them. They claimed to use rigorous statistical methods, too, but from what Bram had seen, some of the more overweening practitioners of the arcane speciality had a rather shaky grasp of real math.

Silv metered her words to him carefully. "One-third of the population of the tree had been born within the last hundred and fifty years. Approximately one-fourth consists of the original embarkees and the generation immediately following, who share their values to a large degree. In between is an amorphous group who tend to be polarized in one direction or the other. Thus there has been an evolution toward endogamous moieties which—"

Torm interrupted with a twinkle. "What she's trying to say is that the older and younger voyagers tend to divide into two groups as defined by their cross-mating practices." He winked. "Not that I've noticed it myself."

Bram laughed. "Tell that to my great-great-great-granddaughter Ame," he said. "She's been trying to fight off Smeth's attentions for years."

"Naturally, in an evolving culture the lines aren't yet rigidly drawn," Silv said with signs of annoyance, "but we've drawn up charts and applied statistical methods, and we believe there's a developing pattern of custom and taboo."

Torm allowed his eyes to glaze, though not enough to be impolite. The lively old fogy of the Bachelors' Lodge had again become the smallish, dapper young blade he must once have been. Bram would not have put it past him to have cast an eye on Silv herself for a little endogamous tumble.

"What it sublimates down to," Torm said, "is that Silv's crowd think I have enough influence with the old-timers to be worth cultivating and that if we can get together behind a candidate with across-the-moieties appeal, we'll have the votes to win."

"And that's me?"

"You're the only one we can agree on. If you say yes, the votes are guaranteed."

"Will you accept?" Silv asked.

Bram looked past them at the fiery egg in the holo projection. "I'll think it over," he promised.

"A symbol of the old days," Bram repeated with relish. "That's what they're calling me now. They want to dust me off and set me up as year-captain again."

Mim paused in her work. She was feeding the score of a new string quartet by one of her protégés into her computer and punching in the program that would separate it into players' parts for next Tenday's performance. "That might not be such a bad idea," she said.

"Oh, Mim, you know the job's nothing but a headache," he protested.

His daughter, Lydis, said, "What are you going to tell them?"

Lydis had hardly changed at all in the last five hundred years. She was still the same slender, dark-haired edition of her mother that she had been when she reached her final age, without an added ounce, worry line, or shift of body mass. Even her teeth seemed always to come in as identical replicas, not changing the shape of her mouth an iota. Lydis had not inherited Mim's talent for music, though; she was a gifted and relentlessly practical engineer who had designed the hardware for some of the tree's most important industrial biosynthesis plants. Currently she had taken an interest in piloting and was spending a lot of her time exploring the hangars where Yggdrasil's fleet of landers was stored and practicing in the simulators.

"I haven't decided," Bram said. He went to the coldall and helped himself to a gourd of sapbrew. "The next few years are going to be very exciting ones for astronomy. We have the chance to study the galaxy we're going to live in from the inside out, over a real-time frame of tens of thousands of years, so we can observe processes. There's that peculiar feature in the nucleus—the gas arc I mentioned. It suggests a powerful magnetic field, but at right angles to where one ought to be. We may find an answer in the inner parsec of the galaxy. We'll never have the chance for a close-up view again. Jun Davd's offered me the chance to be an important part of it. Being year-captain is time-consuming."

He took a sip from the gourd. "And then there's my own bioengineering project. Genesis Two. I'd have to shut that down entirely for a while."

Mim put the string quarter score aside. "The observations will get made whether you're there or not," she said. "It will take years—decades—to sort them out and draw conclusions from them. You have all the time in the world. There are still tons of data from the explosion of the old galaxy that are lying there waiting for someone to go through them. Jun Davd can wait. And as for your genetics project, I know it means a lot to you, but that can wait, too. Your assistants can keep it warm. In any case, you couldn't implement the project until we're re-settled."

"I don't know, Mim," he temporized.

"I'll tell you this," she said. "For the last two hundred years we've had year-captains who immersed themselves more and more in the housekeeping details of the job. When they weren't officious busybodies who tried to in-terfere with people's lives, that is. Because for at least that long, a majority of the population have been people who think that the human past is a sort of fairy tale. They've never lived on a planet, never had a Nar touch brother—never even seen a real Nar, for that matter. They think that babies have always been made by two people in a nest together—not constructed out of nu-cleotides. They don't have any real comprehension of the fact that the human species ceased to exist for thirty-seven million years, and that we're here now by the grace of a wonderful race that's ceased to exist itself, and that we escaped by the skin of our teeth, and that Yggdrasil is just a temporary habitat to get us back to the original seedbed of humanity." She paused for breath. "Bram, do you realize that most of the people on this tree have never in their lives seen a real star—only holo projections? Maybe Silv is right. Maybe we *do* need to remind our-selves of what this trip is all about!"

He grinned at her. "I think you just like the privileges that go with being married to a year-captain. Like always having a meal or your sleep interrupted by some problem, and never having any privacy, and sitting through long boring meetings where everybody pushes their point of view on you for the thousandth time, and you smile and nod for the thousandth time so that nobody thinks their views are being slighted."

She grinned back at him. "Shall I tell you why Lydis is here?"

"To check up on the old folks and make sure their synapses haven't gotten all stuck together?"

"Oh, Bram!" Lydis said.

Mim said, "So I could ask her how she'd feel about being older sister to a new sibling. A five-hundred-year-older sister."

"I think it's a wonderful idea," Lydis said. "It's about time. The new people hardly wait till one child is grown up before having another one. They breed like yeast. I certainly think the demographics of the tree entitle you to another baby. And I'd enjoy having a sibling."

Both of them looked Bram's way. He said with feeling, "Lyd is right, Mim. The end of our journey's in sight. Yggdrasil could handle five or ten times our current population without any strain—but I doubt that even the new people can breed fast enough to fill it up before we reach home territory. You're certainly as eligible as any centenarian to have a second child. But are you sure you don't want to wait until we find a planet?"

"No," she said. "Call it an act of faith."

Bram embraced her. "Careful, oldsters," Lydis said. "You might tempt *me* to have a second child, too, like my silly granddaughter."

Mim, her dark eyes shining, said, "Think of the exciting younghood the child's going to have. A plunge through the heart of the galaxy. The strange sights at the core. A trip to the spiral arm that was the cradle of humanity. And—and the *stars* coming back!" Her voice took on fervor. "A curtain of stars drawing back little by little as we slow down, stars spreading till they fill the sky again, shifting back to their true colors . . . until finally one day our destination star lies before us, big as a sun."

"Yes," Bram said, caught by the vision. It was what another child had dreamed thirty-seven million years ago in another galaxy.

Mim, warm in his arms, felt what he was thinking. "It's come true, hasn't it, Bram?" she said softly.

"I wonder what we'll find there," he said.

"You're seeing the husk of a quasar," Jun Davd said, "left over from the quasar epoch of the cosmos."

He gestured toward the dizzying scene behind the observatory's holo wall. The fabric of the universe seemed to writhe as stars were wrenched from their true positions and yanked into the illusory halo surrounding the black hole's event horizon. Then, as Yggdrasil continued its headlong dive past the hole, the stars smeared around the heart of darkness pulled free and popped back into place. The queer stellar mirage was visible because Yggdrasil, on its first pass, was in a polar orbit—dropping down from above the nuclear bulge, where the hole's accretion disk did not obscure the view.

You could see the inferno of light representing the disk if you stepped close to the transparent shield and looked down into the imaginary space behind the wall. But most people took a look and stepped right back again. You knew it wasn't real, but something about it made you feel as if you were falling.

Smeth, working hard to impress Ame, cleared his throat to get noticed. "It might be a husk, but if so, it's a husk of a hundred million solar masses. Not in the same league as the binary holes at the center of the Father World's galaxy, but massive enough to have caused periodic core explosions of its own. We've detected a sort of smoke ring ten thousand light-years out that seems to be a remnant of the last explosion." Then he made the mistake of condescending to her. "Of course," he said importantly, "you weren't born yet when we made the passage between Scylla and Charybdis—that's what we old hands call the binary hole maneuver, from an old legend of Original Man—but those were the great days! You had to have been there!"

"Yes, I've played back the sequence many times," Ame said offhandedly. "Jun Davd, is there any danger of the next core explosion wiping out life in this galaxy, as it did in the old one?"

Bram watched Ame with a pride of authorship he felt for all his descendants—though in Ame's case he could claim only one thirty-second of the credit. His great-great-great-granddaughter had turned out well, he thought. She was a pert, direct, lively girl with wide green eyes and corn-colored hair. Though she was scarcely forty years old, she was a complete person with good sense and integrated views.

Her interest was in something she called reconstructive paleontology, and with a small group of similar-minded young people who styled themselves such things as comparative geologists and theoretical terralogists, she was attempting to come up with a self-consistent picture of the bygone planet, Earth, that had spawned Original Man. The store of data they had to go on was skimpy—the highly condensed primers of various descriptive sciences that had been included in the Message plus whatever clues they could gather from literary works, dictionary line drawings, parallel processes on the Father World, and similar sources. But she and her friends had been ingenious and had gone surprisingly far with their small database.

To Smeth's chagrin, Ame had brought along two colleagues from the paleoearth department: a woman named Abiga, whose specialty was comparative geology, and a young man named Jorv, who was only in his twenties and who bubbled over with enthusiasm for something he called "deductive zoology."

Bram felt sorry for Smeth, watching him hover and fuss around Ame. Youth had not been kind to the gawky physicist; it had robbed him of a certain acquired gravity and left him awkward and abrasive again. When Smeth had invited Ame to watch the hole approach with the astronomy and physics group, he had expected to monopolize her—and now she could not be pried loose from her chums. Smeth still was trying to figure out if Jorv was attached somehow to Abriga or whether he represented sexual competition.

As if that weren't bad enough, Jun Davd was being courtly.

"No, we believe the Milky Way is reasonably tame now," Jun Davd said in answer to Ame's question. "The quasar epoch used up the tremendous quantity of material within the core that might fuel an event on *that* titanic a scale and stored it conveniently in the form of the black hole we're orbiting now. The subsequent explosions— like the one that caused the 'smoke ring' Smeth mentioned—obviously could not have been violent enough to wipe out life in the Milky Way... though they might have had some minor effect on species."

Ame and Jorv exchanged a peculiar glance.

"When did the last core explosion take place?" Ame asked. "Or is there any way of estimating it?"

"Yes, indeed, there is," Jun Davd said. "We've been observing the so-called smoke ring over a period of more than fifteen thousand objective years during our dive into the galactic bulge. It keeps expanding and contracting to strike a balance between its rotational velocity and the gravitational attraction of the center. From the rate of oscillation, we calculate that the last core explosion took place approximately one hundred and forty-one million years ago." He smiled. "And I gather that Original Man evolved after that event, since he broadcast his Message only seventy-four million years ago."

"Jun Davd," Ame said, hesitating, "when is the next core explosion due?"

Smeth opened his mouth, but Jun Davd beat him to it.

"Theoretically, there shouldn't be one. The last explosion should have depleted the galactic center of the necessary mass. The smoke ring's velocity and distance suggest an ejected mass of one hundred million solar masses—and an explosion powered by converting the equivalent of ten thousand suns completely into energy. Now a black hole of one hundred million solar masses sits in the center, and except for the observed stars around it, the center should pretty well have been swept clean." He frowned.

"But?"

"By generating artificial profiles of the twenty-one centimeter line, we've determined the amount of invisible matter that must be rotating around the galactic center." He paused, decided to add to his explanation. "You see, that gave us the Doppler shift of the neutral hydrogen present."

She seemed to know what he was talking about. "The faster the rotation, the greater the mass?"

He brightened. "Precisely. And the figure we get is two hundred million solar masses."

"Twice what ought to be there?"

He nodded. "And we don't know where it came from."

"Jao has a theory about that, though," Bram put in.

"I've heard about Jao's theories, Bram-*tsu*." Ame laughed. She was a dutiful descendant, always giving him an ancestral honorific in the abbreviated Chin-pin-yin form. He had told her over and over again to simply call him Bram, but like so many of the young people, she was a stickler for convention; it was as if the newest generation were trying to revive a structure of human tradition all by themselves.

Jao, hearing his name, twisted his shaggy red head around from the console he had been working. "Yah," he said, "there has to be some kind of mechanism for renewing matter in the core of the galaxy. It doesn't have to amount to much—about seven-tenths of a solar mass per year."

"The problem is," Jun Davd said indulgently, "that this hypothetical flow of matter isn't coming from the galactic plane, and it isn't coming from outside the galaxy, as when the Whirlpool cannibalized the Bonfire."

"So that leaves one place, right?" Jao continued. "The nucleus of the galaxy itself. Matter just appears there."

Smeth found his voice. "That's preposterous!" he said. "It's nothing more than a rehash of the old discredited theory of the continuous origin of matter!"

"No, listen, this is a new idea based on the heavy-neutrino model of the universe," Jao insisted. "If neutrinos have mass, then they could account for ninety percent of the mass of the universe, and ordinary matter is a film wrapped around great clumps of neutrinos. And where do the clumps come from? I'm glad you asked that. They're simply the walls of a great spongy cellular structure, one of whose bubbles is our own dear old universe. This all takes place in eleven-dimensional space-time, needless to say. The different domains are a necessary consequence of the first moments of creation—and you'll notice that the domains would be nonregular in shape, and that fits in well with the observed fibrous structure of the universe. So how do we create matter in the nuclei of galaxies without violating baryon conservation?"

He glared around at everybody.

"I have a feeling he's going to tell us," Bram said.

"We *don't*!" Jao proclaimed triumphantly. "We have an exchange of neutrinos and un-neutrinos through the walls of the domains. The walls leak. Why are the leaks located in the centers of galaxies? Easy. Because of the hypermasses there—the super black holes sinking deep into the plenum and stretching the warp and woof of space-time to its limits. You may well ask why no right-handed neutrinos have ever been observed, despite the predictions of theory! Because the scales are balanced in *other* domains, that's why! So symmetry is preserved in the larger sense. Baryons—like protons and neutrons—can't cross the domain walls without instantly decaying. But un-neutrinos exhibit antidecay and assemble themselves into elementary particles, in the reverse of beta decay."

Smeth was beside himself. His face was red as a tomato, and he seemed in danger of bursting.

"You can't *do* that!" he said, his voice cracking. "How can you change leptons into baryons?"

"With mesons as the mediators, naturally," Jao said. "And while we're at it, what do you think happened to those missing solar neutrinos you tried to detect in that chlorine tank experiment of yours back on the Father World? I'll tell you. They were falling in, not out. They were being funneled through the domain wall to another domain. There must have been a black hole on the other side."

Smeth opened his mouth indignantly to reply, but Ame cut in to get the subject back on track.

"So what it boils down to is that, by whatever mysterious process, there's enough material in the center of the galaxy for another explosion, even though it shouldn't be there?" she asked.

"Admirably put," Jun Davd said.

"And that presumably this process acted in the past to cause periodic explosions?"

"Yes."

Ame mulled it over. "Could core explosions be a by-product of some other process? Or vice versa?"

Jun Davd pursed his lips. "That's an interesting question. More interesting than you know. Why do you ask?"

"I'm trying to pin down periodicity. You said that the last core explosion in the Milky Way must have taken place one hundred and forty-one million years ago?"

"Thereabouts."

"It's a very interesting coincidence."

Her zoologist friend, Jorv, nodded energetically.

"Coincidence? How?" Jun Davd asked.

"Because one hundred and thirty-nine million years ago was when the dinosaurs became extinct."

Jorv burst out, "Practically on the heels of the explosion!"

"What is a dinosaur?" Jun Davd inquired.

"It was a very large animal that predated humans on Earth. Though they couldn't have been as large as the Message described them—there must be some error or misinterpretation of scale. We have line sketches of several of the main types. They were the dominant form of life on Earth for about one hundred and thirty million years, then they abruptly vanished."

"Like Original Man," Jun Davd murmured. "I take your point."

"How big were they?" Jao asked.

"They were built on the same general plan as human beings," Ame said. "Four limbs, bilateral symmetry, bony skeleton—so I suppose it's possible that they could have been as much as three or four times human size. We've done computer simulations of them, and with a thicker bone cross section as compared to a human, certain efficiencies in oxygenating tissues, a slower metabolism, and so forth, we think it's possible for them to have weighed as much as a ton."

Jao whistled. "That big?"

"The Message data has some of them attaining a length of ninety feet and weighing as much as fifty tons." She smiled. "But of course that's nonsense. No creature with an internal skeleton could attain that size. It would have to have some sort of exoskeleton supporting its weight like a scaffolding, or an external shell, like the orthocone creatures on the Father World—and of course, then they couldn't be very active."

Jorv's boyish face had been working, and now he said,

"Don't take away my big dinosaurs, Ame! I've been running a different set of assumptions through the computer, and I can get bipeds up to twenty feet tall and quadrupeds twice that scale."

"Bone is bone, and histology is histology," Ame said tolerantly, "but if you want to postulate more efficient absorptive surfaces than human beings have, and a food intake of a quarter ton a day, and radiators to get rid of body heat, you're welcome to your big dinosaurs."

It was the usual sort of professional banter, but Bram could all but see Smeth's suspicious mind working to make something more of it. Poor Smeth, he thought. The case was hopeless, but it wasn't up to him to tell Smeth that!

"So these . . . dinosaurs disappeared at the approximate time of the core explosion?" Jun Davd mused. "Hmmm . . . allowing time for some undefined process to spread to Earth's latitude in the galaxy at the quite reasonable rate of about one and one-half percent of the speed of light?"

"Not just the dinosaurs, Jun Davd," Jorv said. "They disappeared completely—every last one of them—but many other land animals and most marine species disappeared at the same time. If the record that we've been given is correct."

"And about one hundred fifty-five million years before *that* mass extinction," Ame put in, "there was another major extinction in which half of all animal families were wiped out. And one hundred and fifty-five million is almost an exact multiple of twenty-six million."

"What's the significance of twenty-six million?" Jun Davd asked.

Ame and Jorv fell over themselves to be the one to tell him. Ame won out. "The geological record we got from Original Man—and you must realize it's only a summary, without the detail we'd like—shows that there seem to be major species die-offs at intervals that work out to an average of about twenty-six million years."

Jorv amended: "In two cases, there seems to have been a follow-up extinction of species at an interval somewhere between thirteen and fifteen million years."

"That's what worries me," Ame said. "There were two

cycles of extinction that followed the dinosaur disappearances that don't appear to have affected the precursors of *Homo sapiens*, but add another thirteen million years to *that* and you get a value pretty close to the time when Original Man's Message was cut off."

"Jao," Jun Davd said, turning around. "What sort of correlation can we get on that major date of one hundred and fifty-five million years prior to the last core explosion?"

Jao's fingers flew over his board. "It's hard to say, Jun Davd. We got one scenario that could have put another core explosion about there. You know, the one where we factored in the expanding molecular ring at the center. But we don't know enough yet."

Jun Davd turned back to Ame. "There's not enough to go on," he said. "We have one striking correlation of a core explosion with one of your two major extinctions and one more possible correspondence. But there's been no more explosion since the dinosaurs disappeared and no periodic phenomenon that subdivides the major events into twenty-six-million-year cycles."

"How about this?" Jao said. "Imagine something that sweeps the galaxy like the spokes of a wheel. Imagine eight spokes. Four major spokes, like the arms of a cross. And in between, four minor spokes, also arranged roughly as a cross. As Man's sun orbits the galactic center, it encounters a spoke approximately every twenty-six million years."

"Why eight spokes?" Jun Davd inquired.

"You have to start somewhere. Eight has a nice symmetry. Besides, it works out in lots of ways. You'll see in a minute."

"What do you mean?" Ame asked, leaning forward.

"Look," Jao said. He did something to his console, and the tremendous scene behind the holo wall vanished, to be replaced by the rough scrawls Jao was tracing on his touch pad with one meaty forefinger.

"Hey, wait a minute!" Smeth protested.

"The universe won't go away," Jao said. "I'll bring it back in a minute. I want everyone to see this."

A bold vertical line in screaming orange grew in the

illusory void behind the wall. "We start with a two-spoke model," Jao said. "Two opposing arms, like a lot of cosmic phenomena. Like galactic gas jets, for example. Now we add another pair of arms at right angles."

He slashed another orange line across the first. It wasn't quite horizontal—apparently by design, because as everyone watched, the second pair of arms, responding to whatever crude instructions he had punched into his board, slowly turned until the adjustment was made.

"You see, there's some repulsive force holding them equidistant from the two previous arms," Jao said. "Like magnetism. Now we subdivide one more time."

Two more crude slashes turned the cross into an asterisk. This time the finger-painted lines weren't as thick, and they were a paler orange. They were also slightly out of position, but after a moment the second cross rotated with respect to the first until all the angles were equal.

"These are the baby arms," Jao said. "They're not full-grown yet. They're weaker. That's why I drew them skinny."

Jorv, with growing excitement, said, "What did you mean when you said it works out?"

"For starts, when you multiply these twenty-six-million-year events by yours by eight, you get a figure of two hundred and eight million years. Which is a pretty good match for the length of time it takes Man's sun to make one complete orbit around the galactic center."

"Very suggestive," Jun Davd said. "Eight events per solar orbit. Of course, you're assuming either that the spokes are stationary, or the sun is stationary, or the spokes are rotating at twice the sun's speed at the radius of the sun's orbit."

"Like I said, you have to start somewhere," Jao said. "I like figures that come out even. So you begin with a nice regular series—two, four, eight. And multiples of orbital speed—which incidentally would put the end of a full-grown spoke somewhere at the rim of the galaxy."

"Why not a ten-spoke model?" Smeth interrupted, with a sidelong glance at Ame. "You'd get a multiple of two hundred and sixty million years, which is closer to the two-hundred-and-fifty-million-year galactic year that *some* of us prefer!"

Jao shrugged. "Suit yourself. You could make that work, too, with a little fiddling with the relative velocities. You can work out the figures if you like. But an eight-spoke model's more elegant."

"I take it there's more," Jun Davd prompted.

Jao brightened. "Yah. Watch this."

His thick fingers busied themselves on the board, and a bright yellow dot appeared about halfway out on one of the orange spokes. It began tracing a slow circle around the center of the geometric figure. A moment later the eight-armed figure began to revolve, too, at a somewhat faster rate, with the arms continually overtaking the dot.

"Now, let's label the arms so we can keep track of them," Jao said.

Letters popped up, alphabetizing the arms. Jao did not stop the process quickly enough, and a second round of letters began to subtend the first.

"That's okay, leave it," Jao said. "If I were laying this out flat, I'd be going past eight into the next cycle, anyway."

Ame and Jorv were intent on the garish sketch hanging in the space before them. Bram could see Ame's lips moving as she counted to herself.

"Now we take those forty-five-degree angles and subdivide them again," Jao said.

Eight more lines grew within the spoked figure. These were dotted lines, even paler and more tentative than the lines of the second cross. Not all of them were full-length. Several of them still fell short of the yellow dot's circular orbit.

"These are your follow-up extinctions," Jao said to Jorv. "The ones you say sometimes follow the main events thirteen to fifteen million years later. They subdivide the twenty-six-million-year intervals, and they're growing outward at different rates, so we can't fit all of them into the picture. Yet."

"Very thin," Smeh said.

"So we start with what we *do* know. Here's the dinosaurs."

One of the arms of the original cross thickened and darkened to burnt orange. The tenuous dotted line following it began to blink for attention.

"Okay, anything there?" Jao asked.

Ame and Jorv looked at each other. "The Miocene crisis," Ame said immediately. "A mass wipeout of shellfish, plankton, some land animals. But it's only twelve million years later."

"Close enough," Jao said. "Now, let's skip back one hundred and fifty-five million years to the other really major crisis. The one that wiped out half of all animal families on Earth. Have we got a secondary extinction associated with it?"

"Yes," Ame said, catching her breath. "A bigger one this time. A very large extinction of marine organisms that *could* fall within a ten- to fifteen-million-year period. We couldn't fit it into our data before without stretching it."

"All in knowing how," Jao said with a grin, while Smeth smoldered.

Jao thickened the axis and shaded it over to include the following arm. "Very interesting," he said. "The two big ones are at right angles to each other. Forming two arms of the older cross. And it's the arms sprouting in their wake that turn out to be the real killers."

"As if whatever it is was getting stronger," Ame suggested.

"Yah."

"Jao—"

"Not yet. Let's fill in as many blanks as we can first."

Over the next several minutes they assigned eleven extinction episodes to the rotating spokes. Nine of them fit the pattern of the eight major spokes, and two fell within the secondary following position.

"How do you explain the missing pieces?" Smeth asked.

"How should I know?" Jao rumbled. "Insufficient data. Fluctuations in the strength of the spokes. Maybe factors that we haven't figured yet. The sun catches up with a spiral arm every hundred million years or so and stays inside for ten million years. It bobs up and down through the plane in a thirty-three-million-year cycle, if it behaves like the other stars at that radius. Maybe the dust intensifies the killer effect on some passes. Maybe it does the opposite and acts as a shield. Why don't you try to combine all the cycles and see what you can work out? The important thing is that everything we *do* have fits the pattern."

His belligerence died. Like everybody else in the observatory he was staring at the one big fact that hung before them in the rotating holo image.

"The ninth extinction and the first extinction are doubled up on the same spoke," Ame said in a half whisper.

"It came back again for a second swipe," Jao said.

"The second visitation was the last extinction before human beings evolved."

"The first swipe was the big double event," Jorv said. "First the trilobites and all that plankton—ninety percent of sea life. Then half of all animal life on Earth."

"And if there was a . . . a similar follow-up," Ame said, "it would have come at just about the same time that Original Man disappeared from the universe."

Smeth's harsh voice grated through the ensuing silence.

"It couldn't be. Man is an intelligent being, not a—a dinosaur! He would have found some way to protect himself. Or flee. After all, it isn't as if the entire Milky Way was sterilized the way the Father World's galaxy was. *Some* life survived each of these—extinctions and went on to evolve."

"When the dinosaurs disappeared," Jorv said, his young voice getting away from him, "no species of land animal weighing more than twenty pounds survived. Man's ancestors were very small and primitive. It was the highly evolved species that went. The second time around, that was man."

Jao stared thoughtfully at the rotating orange arms of his holo model. "Original Man had only spread a few hundred light-years. At most, a few thousand. You can't travel faster than the speed of light. You can't outrun something that extends to the galactic rim and sweeps the galaxy laterally. They could only have caught up with the *previous* killer arm."

He retreated into gloomy contemplation. Nobody else seemed very lively, either. Bram was just about to say something, when Jun Davd did it for him.

"Let's not jump to conclusions," Jun Davd said. "This is all highly speculative. Jao doesn't have a theory, just a hypothesis. We need more data. We'll set up a long-term computer model and keep feeding our observations into it."

"Yah, I'll get on that today," Jao said.

Jan Davd went on, "Original Man's sector of the galaxy is about thirty thousand light-years from the center, and on our outward spiral, we'll sweep great areas of the disk over a real-time period of tens of millennia. We'll be able to make observations that were not possible for Original Man, no matter how much further advanced than us he was."

Ame and Jorv looked puzzled, and Jun Davd added gently, "The *time* wasn't there for him, you see."

As it sank in, the tension began to go out of the room. A few tentative smiles made their appearance. Ame brought her chin up and said to Bram, "You've brought us this far, Bram*tsu*. Nothing can frighten us now. This galaxy is humankind's heritage, and we're here to claim it."

Smeth edged forward, trying to reestablish contact with Ame. "That's right," he said. "The whole thing may be nothing more than a statistical fluke, anyway."

"There's just one thing." Jao's voice brought their heads around again. "If the eight-arm model is correct, our sector of the galaxy is due for another brush soon."

His hand swept the board, and the rotating orange lines snapped out of existence. The universe came terrifyingly back into sight, a raw torrent of light that slammed them across the eyes and turned the human figures into stark silhouettes. Yggdrasil's plunge toward periastron had carried it past the black hole's equator, and the accretion disk had risen out of the floor.

CHAPTER 5

"There's a star in there somewhere," Jun Davd said through his suit radio. "Its light may be blocked, but it's shining its heart out in the ten-micron infrared range."

Bram clung to a cleat with one gloved hand to keep the trunk's slow rotation from shedding him into space and turned up the magnification of his helmet visor. "A body-temperature star," he said. "That fits the picture, all right."

He peered past the leafy horizon at a void that was frosty with stars again. After more than two decades of braking, the starbow had separated and strewn its baubles across the sky. The drive was off, and Yggdrasil was towing the probe now, not the other way around.

But despite the magnificence of the sprinkled stars, it was the sight in the center of his image compensator that occupied Bram's full attention.

There was a scratch across the sky—a perfectly straight line, as if a cosmic thumbnail had scraped away the black. Next to the long scratch was a collection of bright squiggles, like cursive writing in an unknown language.

"The straight line's about ninety million miles long," Jun Davd said. Within the crystal bowl of the new space suit, his dark profile was intent on the distant object. "That's about the same length as the radius of the infrared emission shell the instruments can detect. Does that suggest anything to you?"

"The only astronomical phenomenon I can think of that's that straight and that long is a Type I comet tail,"

Bram said. "Except that there's no coma at one end. In fact, the brightest part, if I read the instruments right, is in the middle."

"Yes," Jun Davd agreed. "And it doesn't extend outward from where the mass indicators say our shrouded star ought to be. It's tangent to it."

"So that suggests very strongly that it has something to do with the structure that's enclosing the star. And that those curved scratches—the arcs and hooks—are part of the same manifestation."

Jun Davd turned to face him. Somehow Jun Davd managed to be limber, even in the bulky envelope of the human-shaped space suit that had been developed during the last ten years of deceleration by a team under the direction of Lydis. He had the toe of one heavy boot hooked under the horn of a cleat to check his outward drift, and his long-limbed body swiveled halfway around at the hips with a natural grace. He was not one of those people you saw bobbing around at the end of their safety ropes and having to haul themselves in.

"I agree. I have a computer working on an analysis of the curvatures to see what kind of a three-dimensional shape we can make them fit into. But clearly, we're looking at an artifact."

Artifact. Bram tasted the word with disbelief. From the size of the infrared emission shell, the unseen sun ought to have been a red giant—a swallower of solar systems. An artifact of that radius at the center of the Father World's system would have engulfed the two inner planets and the Father World itself.

"A trap around a star," Bram said slowly. "A trap for energy. When we first began searching for an enclosed star radiating in the ten-micron part of the spectrum, I somehow visualized something like a sphere. I think we all did." He paused to stare again at the distant wonder. "It's hard to imagine how any rectilinear material body the size of *that* could maintain its shape without gravitationally collapsing."

"There's only one answer, then. It's not straight."

Bram looked again, but the line was just as straight as before. "It's not?" he said.

"We're looking at the illuminated limb of another geometric form," Jun Davd said. "One that *can* maintain its shape. I can think of at least two: a cylinder and—"

"Yes," Bram breathed. "A disk. A spinning disk. Seen edge-on. But it's still unbelievable."

"We don't know what was possible to Original Man at the height of his glory. Perhaps, given another forty or fifty thousand years, the Nar might have learned how to utilize the total energy of a sun."

"Do you really think that's Man's sun in there?"

Jun Davd wrinkled his brow. "One of the suns he used, perhaps. The sun that gave him birth, no. I can't see him dismantling his own father world to make a beacon. There's nothing in this system larger than an asteroid. Nothing but a swarm of comets orbiting an invisible mass. And we're lucky he left us the comets."

He broke off to stare across the miles at the cagework trumpet bell of the ramscoop, which was no longer bathed in the spilled energies that had made it bright. A couple of comets had already been stuffed down its throat as start-up fuel for the next intersystem hop—the hop that the absence of worlds here had made unavoidable.

A space tug floated nearby, waiting to field the next slushball to be sent onward. Two tugs, actually, with a five-mile-wide net strung between them. It was the net that was visible as a fleck of light from a reflected spotlight beam. Bram wondered if his daughter Lydis was one of the pilots.

Closer at hand, against the fibrous wall of the root system across the way, a work crew was prying another ensnared comet away from Yggdrasil—a small one, less than a mile in diameter. With his magnification up, Bram could just make out the tiny space suited figures. They were melting away the clinging ice with dozens of two-man torches. It would require exquisite nicety of timing on the part of the foreman to make sure that the frozen sphere broke loose at just the right moment to cast it toward the waiting tugs instead of outward into the dark.

Yggdrasil could spare a few comets. Scores of the captured iceballs beaded the thirsty surface of its root hemisphere. The tree was working bravely to redistribute mass, but the unassimilated treasure trove still caused a wobble in the crown that took some getting used to. There was a lot of dropped glassware in the living quarters these days, but nobody was complaining. Abundance had returned to the tree after the long drought. The pools were filled, there was boating in the lagoon again, and water sports in the spherical pond at the center of the trunk. More important was the increase in metabolic products as Yggdrasil went through a growth spurt—sugars, starches, complex resins, and new cellulose for the factories.

Bram remembered the excitement when they had entered this queer, gutted system. Four previous ten-micron emission sources had proved to be false alarms—supergiants with circumstellar emission shells that were probably heated dust grains, not worth slowing down for. But the fifth candidate had shown all the symptoms of what the search team had jokingly taken to calling "Jao's shell."

It was Jao who first had proposed the theory of an enwrapped star whose output—by whatever unknown means—had been translated into the cosmos-spanning radio waves of Original Man's beacon.

"Where's all that building material going to come from?" Smeth had scoffed.

"From the dismantled planets," Jao had replied. "And maybe they'd have to haul over the planets from a couple of nearby systems, too. They'd be turned into some kind of supermaterial made mostly of hydrogen, carbon, and oxygen—the atmospheres of a couple of gas giants mixed with the goodies at the core, and some cometary ice— you get the picture."

"How are you going to keep the shell from drifting off center?" Smeth had expostulated. "And if it rotates, how do you keep its substance from collecting at the equator?"

"Details," Jao had replied airily. "We'll worry about them later. The main thing is to look for infrared sources that fit the basic picture."

The search area had been narrowed down to a sphere a thousa light-years in diameter. The Nar, long ago, had pinpoin an approximate location for Original Man's sun by analyzing wave fronts on a line stretched between the Father World and the new outpost on Juxt, and they had arrived at a value for the galactic year at that radius. Jun Davd, during the thirty-seven-million-year head-on approach to the Milky Way, had refined the figure still further. When the M supergiants and the small hot objects shining through dust had been eliminated, the number of candidates was small. Even so, it was surprising to have found it, apparently, on the first try.

"I calculate a total energy output for our invisible sun of four times ten to the thirty-third power ergs per second," Jun Davd had announced shortly after Yggdrasil had settled into a cometary orbit. "That's based on the number of ergs per square inch falling on our collectors and applying the figure to an imaginary sphere at the radius of our own orbit. All in the deep infrared! It's consistent with the normal output at all wavelengths of a G-type dwarf similar to both Original Man's presumed sun and the Father World's primary. An attractive sun for our type of life, and the Nar's."

Jao had worked out approximate orbital periods for the first few comets Yggdrasil had chased. "Yah," he'd said. "The comets are moving at the right speed for the postulated mass at the center. Maybe just a little bit high— but, like I said, the beacon builders might've dragged in an extra gas giant or two from another system."

It was going to be hard to pry Yggdrasil away from the comets after its long thirst. Bram—year-captain again for the fiftieth time—was under a lot of pressure to let the tree graze peaceably for a while in the outer reaches of the cometary halo. The human population of the living spaceship was now up to twenty-five thousand. It was getting a big crowded along the axis of acceleration. The younger generation in particular had its eye on all the congenial real estate that would open up in the other branches if Yggdrasil went on permanent rotation mode.

But Bram did not dare give in. He had the feeling that if the populace spread out this time, he'd never get them back to the axis.

At Yggdrasil's leisurely rate of travel, it would take decades to drift from star to star—centuries or even millennia to search out the G-type dwarfs in this sector of the galaxy for the traces of Original Man. The new people did not have the same sense of urgency—the idea of a goal. For them, Yggdrasil was a way of life. It was more than possible than the citizenry could vote to settle in the first system that had rocky bodies to mine, a cometary shell to seed with a crop of more Yggdrasils.

Sometimes, on bad nights, Bram had a nightmare that he would never make planetfall again.

No, he thought. The only solution was to get his little convoy under fusion acceleration as quickly as possible, investigate the mystery at the heart of this system, then boost out again at one g.

Certain it was that Yggdrasil, left to its own devices, was not going to get much of an outward kick from the starlight to be found *here*!

Beside him, Jun Davd said, "I saw something just then."

Bram looked, but saw nothing except the faint scratch in the darkness and its attendant squiggles.

"Within the curve of the larger arc," Jun Davd said.

Large, at this distance, meant nothing much more than a fairy's hangnail, even under full magnification, but Bram stared till his eyes watered.

Then he could just make it out—the dimmest of patches, like a foggy speck in his faceplate.

"It's leaking light," Jun Davd said. "There are holes in it. That's diffuse reflection on a surface. Keep watching. And if I'm not mistaken..."

As if someone had punctured the fabric of space with a pin, a star peeped forth.

"It's not the whole star, of course," Jun Davd mused. "It's probably the light from no more than ten or twenty percent of its surface to judge by the apparent magnitude. But we wouldn't have seen a disk, anyway, at this distance, just a point of light."

Bram didn't need a spectroscope to tell him what he was looking at. "It's a G-type sun," he said.

"Yes, indeed," Jun Davd said. "Well, we'd better uproot poor Yggdrasil again and go in for a closer look."

"It's embarrassing," Ame said. "I have as many children as my great-great-great-grandmother."

She held up the twins for inspection, one in the crook of each arm. They were beginning to lose the wrinkled, recently boiled look, and it could be seen from their coloring and button features that they were going to take after Ame, not Smeth.

"Never mind, they're beautiful babies," Mim said, nudging Bram in the ribs to keep him quiet. "And dizygotic twins are nobody's fault."

Smeth puttered nearby, a fatuous grin on his face. Ame's firm stewardship had done wonders for him; the rough edges, if not gone, were ground down a bit, and his friends pronounced him almost civilized. He and Ame had been together for ten Bobbings now. She teased him by telling him that it had simply become too much trouble keeping him at arm's length and that she had decided that maybe he was salvagable after all, despite five hundred years of bachelordom; to which he responded by swelling with pride and pleasure.

"I've used up my quota on my first try," Ame said ruefully.

One child per century was the rule nowadays, enforced by society's unspoken displeasure. Those who had bred too thoughtlessly during the profligate days of middle-passage now sheepishly waited for the passing years to rehabilitate their reputations.

"You can have a share of mine or Lydis's," Mim said. "We're not a prolific family. It all averages out."

"Yah, you want to talk embarrassed, look at Marg and Orris," Jao said heartily. "Five children, like clockwork. Hey, I bet they have a cesium clock hanging over their sleeping nest so they can start working on number six the nanosecond it's licit."

"Jao, you're awful—stop that!" Ang exclaimed. "Excuse him, everybody."

"Why? What did I say?" Jao said innocently.

Bram, suppressing a smile, said to Ame, "Quotas may be a thing of the past sooner than you think. We ought to be ready to leave this system in a few years, and then it's just a question of time till we hit on a suitable planet."

He carefully refrained from specifying the father world of Original Man. He didn't want to appear to be too much of a visionary to these practical young people like Ame and her friends. It was generally accepted that there ought to be any number of suitable planets of G-type suns in Original Man's neck of the galaxy that once had been used by the vanished race and that therefore would possess breathable atmospheres and benign ecologies. Any sensible person aboard ought to be ready to settle for one of these. And any one of them would be a treasure trove for the paleontologists and the archeologists and the rest of the practitioners of the new theoretical sciences.

"Yah, as soon as your cohabitant here starts up the fusion engine, we'll be on our way," Jao said. "How's it going, Smeth?"

Smeth, startled out of his slack-jawed adoration of his firstborn, replied, "I've got a crew aboard the probe overhauling the systems now. The four-wave mirrors need realignment, and there's been some minor damage to the web of the scoop, but it held up pretty well, considering. I'd say we ought to finish in a two of Tendays, and then we'll be ready to travel again."

"We ought to be able to *land* on the outside of whatever's walling off the sun!" Jao said enthusiastically. "The temperature's a nice comfortable three hundred degrees Absolute. Then we hightail it out of the system and start looking at yellow dwarfs. There's only eight or nine possibles within a twenty-light-year radius, and I'm betting one of them is the birthplace of Original Man. The stars around him would've had different relative motions—the guidepost constellations in the Message are no good to us now—but they'd have the same general orbits around the galactic center, and I'm betting they didn't drift too far apart. This beacon would've been one of the two or three closest." He showed all this teeth to Ame in a gargantuan grin. "You'll be able to multiply with a clear conscience by the time the twins are grown."

Bram marveled that Jao was able to be so bluff and nonchalant on the subject in the fact of his own tragedy. His second child, by some fluke, had proved to be immune to the immorality virus. The boy had grown into a humorous, likable chap with Jao's talent for physics. He had made some notable contributions and had left offspring himself before dying at the age of a hundred and thirty. That had been two centuries ago. Jao and Ang had never had another child after that.

Bram thought about his own new son, Edard. He and Mim had been lucky. Edard was a fine young man, still in his twenties but already making a contribution to human culture. From the first it had been evident that he had inherited Mim's musical talent. He had picked out tunes on the keyboard at the age of three, and by five he was well on the way to teaching himself to play Mim's cello, when Mim had taken a hand and started giving him formal lessons. Now, Edard was devoting himself to composition. He was obsessed by the six old symphonies that had been transmitted in score in the Message of Original Man and had applied himself to the task of recreating a live symphonic texture. He was probably the first composer in the history of the tree who was in a position to do so. With the increase in population, there were now enough first-rate players for an orchestra of thirty-eight people. They gave a concert every Tenday evening. Tonight they were going to introduce Edard's twenty-second symphony, the first in which he had totally abjured all electronic fill-ins for missing instruments and had limited himself to what the live players could produce. It promised to start a new, revolutionary trend.

Thinking of it reminded Bram to check his waistwatch for the time; the newer people might think him an old fuddy-duddy for clinging to habits learned on the Father World, but any honest person would have to admit that it was more polite to unobtrusively feel for the time with your fingertips than to read it off a visual wrist meter.

"We'd better think about going, Mim," he said when he had a chance to get her attention. "It's only two hours till the concert."

Mim made the announcement general. "Sorry to rush off," she said, "but I'm not cellist emeritus *yet*. I have to do my share with the others. Edard insists on a *thick* cello sound—he says he needs at least four."

"I'd better go, too," Ang said. She was in the violin section. "No, you stay a while if you like," she said to Jao.

"I wish I could hear the concert, Mim-*tsu-mu*," Ame said, "but I don't think I'd be welcome with two yowling babies."

"I'll stay with you," Smeth said.

"No, you go," Ame told him. "Don't you dare miss Edard's premiere."

"I can hear it later on tape," he said.

"*Tape*?" Jao exploded. He put on an indignant expression for Mim's benefit. "Have you been paying the remotest attention to what Ang and Mim've been saying? The whole point is that it's living, breathing music. If you're going to hear it through a speaker, Edard might as well've done it all on a synthesizer!"

"Since when are you the great music lover?" Smeth snapped.

Ame stopped him with a look. "You go on," she said. "One of us ought to be there." She apologized to Mim. "Tell Edard-*tsu-hsiung* I'm sorry. I'll hear another performance of it." The punctilious honorific she added to Edard's name meant something like "ancestor-brother." Immortality was stretching the language out of shape.

The door rasp sounded. "I'll get it," Smeth said, glad to escape.

While Mim and Ame said their good-byes, Bram heard raised voices at the door. Someone was wroth with Smeth. When leave-taking was done and Bram accompanied the two musicians to the entry chamber, he saw that the agitated caller was Jao's granddaughter, Enyd, the tree systems officer.

"I didn't expect to find *you* here, Captain," Enyd said. "I came here to ask physics supervisor Smeth if it's true that he plans to put Yggdrasil under acceleration again, and if so to lodge a protest."

Smeth blustered, "The decision to reactive the drive is entirely the prerogative of—"

Bram cut him off. "Yes, it's true, Officer Enyd. I planned to discuss it with you first thing in the morning. I apologize for the fact that word apparently got to you in a roundabout way before I had that opportunity. You should have been the first to know."

"It was one of the technicians working on the overhaul," Smeth fumed. "That loudmouth Perc, I'll bet. He must have spread it all over the place. All I did was to flash the workcage to ask how soon they could promise start-up *if* we decided to go! But I told them to keep their mouths shut."

"We'll have to make an announcement," Bram said.

"Captain, Yggdrasil's barely had time to recover," Enyd said. "It wants to spin normally for a while. It can't go back so soon to the artificial rhythm of adjusting its lateral growth once every Bobbing."

Bram looked at Mim. "Go on ahead, Mim. I'll catch up." Mim and Ame left after a belated, perfunctory exchange of greetings with the distracted Enyd.

"How is Yggdrasil's ice reserve?" Bram asked, before Enyd could resume her complaints.

She hesitated, then said scrupulously, "Adequate, I suppose. But if we are to resume traveling, I would prefer to achieve satiety."

"I'll tell you what. When we get the fusion drive started, we'll chase down a few more comets for Yggdrasil before proceeding inward."

"Captain, water and trace elements aren't the only point. Yggdrasill needs a summer season, relief from stress, time for sustained photosynthesis. I wouldn't mind if you turned on the fusion fire for *that*; right now, Yggdrasil's trying to make do with starlight ... and the minor portion of infrared that it's able to convert into the six-hundred-sixty- and seven-hundred-thirty-millimicron range."

Her voice was almost tremulous, belying the cool, remote beauty that drove her suitors wild.

Bram spoke gravely. "I'm confident in your ability to monitor Yggdrasil's metabolism and do whatever is necessary, Chief Officer Enyd. I'm going to ask you to keep this tree happy for two more years. That's the time we'll need to penetrate to the center of this system under one gravity's acceleration. Then we can let Yggdrasil bask in the light of a real sun for a while, while we explore."

Edard sat in the cello section with Mim and the other two cellists, but sometimes in the finicky passages he would leave off playing and beat time for the other musicians. Bram watched the slender, dark-haired figure with pride. The music was first-rate; everybody said so, Mim had told him after the rehearsals. Even the old diehard, Kesper, had said with tears in his eyes, "If Mozart had written another symphony besides the *Jupiter*, it would have sounded like this!"

In the seat beside Bram, Smeth was trying to suppress a cough. Jao glared at him fiercely, and Smeth grumbled, "Where's the *tune*? Everybody's playing something different."

There were whispers of "*Quiet!*" from the surrounding seats, and Smeth subsided. Bram looked around the great, carved wooden chamber. Every one of the eight thousand seats was filled, and a repeat performance had been scheduled for those who were unable to get in. Edard had refused to allow a microphone pickup, saying that it would only encourage people to listen in their own chambers.

The live sound was glorious, Bram had to admit. The acoustics of the wooden cavity, refined over the centuries, helped.

Stringed instruments had come a long way in five hundred years. The new cello was like a truncated pyramid the height of a child, and the performers played it vertically instead of horizontally on a stand, as before. The bow weighed only a couple of pounds now and could be played without an elbow clamp; it was a lightweight plastic framework with its own power source to keep the continuous friction band running smoothly around its sprockets. Mim was a stickler for proper bow technique. She told her students that the bow should hardly be moved at all—just raised or lowered on the eight strings.

The music was coming to a climax. The cellos all buzzed in unison; the violins soared; the horn players raised their long, conical instruments and blared in thrilling harmony.

It was over. Bram stood with the rest and applauded. On the central platform, Edard looked flushed and pleased. Mim went over and kissed him.

"You've got a talented boy, all right," Jao said. "Too bad he has no head for science."

Bram laughed. "Are you trying to sound like Smeth?"

"I'd *never* say a thing like that," Smeth protested indignantly. "I thought it was . . . very good."

The applause rose, swelled. The other musicians were closing around Edard, clapping him on the back, grasping his hands. Edard looked no younger than the others, but Bram could not help reflecting on his age. What will he develop into, he thought, with all eternity ahead of him?

The audience had settled down again for the encore. Edard had wisely refrained from repeating his own music and was giving them the familiar slow movement of the *Jupiter* Symphony—deliberately inviting comparison, Bram thought, smiling at the arrogance of youth. He closed his eyes and listened as the long-drawn cello melody gravely climbed its steps while the violins scolded it. The audience held its breath. Even Smeth sat rapt and silent beside him.

There was a tap on his shoulder, and he turned toward the aisle to find Trist leaning apologetically toward him.

"I'm sorry," Trist whispered, "but something's come up. I think you'd better have a look at it. Jun Davd's waiting for us."

The violins had succeeded in wresting the theme back from the cellos. Bram looked longingly at the communing musicians on the platform. Mim and Edard would expect to see him backstage afterward. He gave a resigned shrug and eased his way out while people glared at him. He followed Trist up the aisle. The heavenly music floated after him. A backward glance had told him that Jao was trailing along behind, prodding a resisting Smeth.

"Now, what's this about?" Bram said when they were out of the hall.

"We're getting some very strange radio signals," Trist said.

Bram stopped in his tracks. Smeth and Jao piled into him. "Intelligent?" he said.

"Let's just say they're nonnatural," Trist said.

Jao's big hand grabbed Trist by the shoulder and spun him around. "Where are they coming from?" he said hoarsely.

"From everywhere," Trist said.

"What do you mean?" Bram said.

Trist bit his lip. "I mean from half the sky. From every star in a volume of space that—" He broke off. "Best come see for yourself."

"But what kind of—"

"Jun Davd's still sorting out the data the computer dumped," Trist said. "He'll probably have a simulation ready by the time we get there."

And that was all they could get out of him during the trip to the Message center. It was a ride of over twenty minutes, even on the high-speed mag-lev tubeway that had finally replaced the outside slingshot pods on eight of the twelve major branches. Bram had to watch Smeth fidget and listen to Jao grumble all the way. He found it hard to contain his own curiosity, but he knew there was no point in pressing Trist.

The Message center had been gathering dust during the five centuries of coasting between galaxies, and had been reopened only in recent years, as an adjunct of the observatory. It had been thought worthwhile to begin searching for possible evidence of artificial signals as they approached the volume of space that once had held the civilization of Original Man—if they were going to have intelligent neighbors, they had better know about it—and the radio installation still held a lot of specialized equipment and the old programs that Trist had used in monitoring the Nar wavelengths on the way out of the Whirlpool galaxy. But the search program still took a back seat to the long-range radioastronomy programs that Jun Davd had set up using the Message center's antenna ray, including the accreting computer model of Jao's magnetic eight-spoke theory to account for the periodic extinctions of Earth's life.

The tremendous cylindrical arcade was darkened and silent as they floated through it; with the fusion drive turned off, the tree was practicing a few small economies in its use of electric power. Far down an avenue of shadowy capacitors, Bram could see the bobbing lights of one of the skeleton maintenance crews that made periodic inspection tours here. Trist led the way in a series of shallow touchdowns. The gravity was almost nil this close to the tree's center of rotation; they had to wait once for Smeth, who incautiously bounced too high and got himself captured by what had been the ceiling when the tree had been under acceleration.

"Here we are," Trist said, letting them into his old office.

Jun Davd looked up at them from a jumble of printouts and scrawled summaries spread out around him on a variety of work surfaces. Screens and variously organized date windows were fine, but there was nothing like paper when you wanted to see everything at once.

"Ah, here you are," he said. "Did you tell them?"

"Yes," Trist said.

"*Tell* us?" Jao roared. "He told us nothing except that we'd better come have a look for ourselves."

Jun Davd said imperturbably, "You know that we have a number of ingenious computer programs written by Trist, designed to search likely wavelengths for patterns of various types, with all sorts of Doppler compensations—for our motion, the motion of stars, the motions of presumed planets orbiting in a variety of presumed planes, shifts in limb brightness along the edges of the presumed planets as the planets themselves rotate around an infinite number of presumed axes . . . it's all very complicated, particularly when we ourselves are moving."

"Yes, yes," Jao said impatiently.

"Some of the data goes back over a year—we'd already spotted the infrared emission of our invisible star and were decelerating toward it. But the computer never sounded the alarm. Neither did the technicians who conducted the occasional random sampling. But that's not surprising. The data picture didn't become really interesting till we came to rest."

Seeing Jao redden toward explosion, Bram said. "Take pity on the man, Jun Davd."

"Here it is translated into audio," Jun Davd said. "With a little guesswork, of course."

He flipped a switch, and the room was suddenly filled with clicks and snaps, as if a million demented children were all breaking twigs at once.

Bram felt ice down his spine. "What is it?" he said.

"It has no information-bearing content that we can see. On the other hand we can't make it correspond to any natural radio phenomenon that we can imagine."

Trist broke in. "So we decided it must be a by-product of some artificial process. Like back-lobe leakage from the space-based antennas of solar power satellites."

"Then an analysis of the wave forms suggested strongly that the clicks were acoustic in nature," Jun Davd said. "So we discarded the idea that they were some kind of static, either natural or artificial."

Bram listened to the hard, dry snapping sounds for a moment. Regarded as actual physical noises, they were even more puzzling. "They'd have to be produced in a medium: solid, liquid, or gas," he said.

"Ridiculous," Smeth said. "There *must* be a natural explanation. Remember how pulsars fooled the early radio astronomers? It's some property of the stars in this arm of the galaxy."

Bram frowned. "Trist said that the signals come from everywhere. From the invisible star we're orbiting too?"

"No. Everywhere *but*," Trist volunteered.

"Now we come to the interesting part," Jun Davd said. "Bear with me a moment. This is still very crude. But it will give you an idea."

He fiddled with a console, and a holographic window lit up in the display board. It was a three-dimensional star map, reasonably realistic, with points of colored light scattered through the velvet darkness. A dull red bead began winking in a lower corner.

"That's our position," Jun Davd said. "Or the position of our infrared star. We're somewhere in the cometary belt—we won't quibble about half a light-year or so. And now here's the route we took from the center of the galaxy."

A yellow dotted line grew from the blinking bead, angling inward in the holographic illusion, and disappeared behind the windowframe on the opposite side.

"Now, all of this space is filled with these odd radio emissions—they've all had different times of origin and the oldest of them are presumably spreading in spheres many hundreds of light-years in diameter. Far beyond the boundaries of my little map. But that's not what we're concerned with. We want to show the stars of origin."

He fiddled with the console again, and a whole swarm of stars in the center of the holo image began blinking. The swarm was in the shape of a lumpy sphere—as near to a perfect sphere as the actual distribution of stars in space could make it.

With one exception. There was a curiously flat, squashed area on the part of the sphere directly opposite the bead representing the infrared star, which hung just outside the boundary of winking stars.

"I don't think that part of the sphere is actually flattened," Jun Davd said. "That's about forty light-years away—at the furthest distance from us. I think any emissions originating there have started fairly recently and simply haven't reached us yet."

Trist nodded in agreement. "Yes, we intersected a small chord of this . . . spherical volume of space on our way here, and when we crank back the data we find that we've witnessed several discrete jumps in the size of the globe. It seems to be growing quite uniformly, at about one-tenth of the speed of light."

Jun Davd's fingers flicked buttons, and a star at the surface of the shell sent a spray of three dotted lines toward the line embedded within the sphere that represented Yggdrasil's route, making an equilateral triangle bisected at the vertex. He added three little green Yggdrasils where the dotted lines met the route.

"No reception," Jun Davd said, tapping the first Yggdrasil at the earliest position on the route. He went on to tap the second Yggdrasil, where the bisecting line showed the shortest distance to the star. "First reception," he said. Then he pointed to the third little tree symbol. "And we're still receiving at the same radial distance as the previous no-reception zone, so knowing our speed and the distance covered, and throwing in a little Doppler anaylsis of about a dozen similar cases, we get a pretty good value for the rate of growth of the shell."

"And virtually every single star within the shell is giving off radio clicks," Trist said.

The other three looked at one another. The thought was inescapable. "Original Man?" Bram said.

"No, impossible!" Jao said.

Smeth was getting excited. Too excited. "Why are we wasting time *here*?" he said. "Whatever this phenomenon is, it's growing from a center." He squinted at the pinch of stars in the middle of the representation—a couple of yellow dwarfs, one with a smaller orange star and a red dwarf for companions; a solitary red dwarf; a blue-white giant attended by a burnt-out cinder. "Let's investigate the *center* of the sphere and see if we can find out what's causing it!"

Jao bellowed in outrage. He could see his lovely enclosed star slipping away from him. "What? That's twenty light-years away! You're talking seven, eight years of ship time by the time we build up enough gamma at one g! We're here *now*! We can be at the center of *this* system in less than two years!"

Jun Davd was no help. He stood there smiling. Bram turned to Trist. "How fast did you say that sphere of clicking stars is growing? At about one-tenth the speed of light?"

"That's right," Trist said.

Bram exercised his prerogatives as year-captain. "In that case we can stay here and wait for it. This star is due to give off clicks any time now."

CHAPTER 6

The sky was full of disks.

The nearest one, only a hundred million miles away, turned half the sky blind. It stood almost edge-on—seen only as a paper-thin rim faintly traced by light, sketching the partial outline of a tall ellipse whose shape could be inferred from the stars it blotted out.

It was immense. Unbelievably so. A planet would have been imperceptible against it, a sun a mere pinprick. Its diameter was, in fact, that of a planetary orbit.

Another disk, equally huge, bracketed the other side of the sky, showing as a somewhat fuller ellipse. But this one presented its inner face and was visible as a pale wash of refracted light.

Between them hung a whole collection of similar shapes, like paper cutouts all dangling at the same level from invisible threads. Directly ahead was a great illuminated circle on what must have been the opposite side of the hidden sun. A smaller circle was a black silhouette trying unsuccessfully to eclipse it. On either side of the smaller circle were attendant disks, canted inward to make narrow ovals. Their inner faces, closer to the unseen sun than the gigantic disk opposite, made brighter daubs against its inferior illumination. A bite had been taken out of the edge of one of them by the eclipsing circle.

Through the spaces between them could be seen a whole swarm of still smaller disks—if objects that were millions of miles in diameter could be called small. The glimpsed shapes were in a different plane than the outer disks; the ellipses they presented were horizontal, not vertical.

The tiny dot of a sun in the center of that bewildering arrangement had never peeped forth again in all the two years they had been traveling toward it. In view of the complicated schedule of eclipses, its brief emergence must have been an exceedingly rare event.

Bram stared over the heads of the crowd at the flat, queer shapes floating in the darkness. He swallowed hard. Reason said they could not exist. But they did.

"There can be no stranger sight in the universe," Jun Davd said to no one in particular.

People jostled and crowded around him at the safety rail in front of the long, curving observation wall. This was a real view, not a holo. Naked space was on the other side of the transparent polycarbonate sheet, and people had been gravitating here even though Yggdrasil's slow rotation periodically turned the scenery on its head. The holo still ran at the opposite end of the lounge, but even though it showed close-ups, there was no added detail to make it worth watching.

"It works out to an ingeniously timed energy trap," Jao was burbling to anyone who would listen. His burly form was at the center of a knot of people, the nearer ones in danger of getting clipped by his waving hands.

"Listen to him," Smeth grumbled to Bram. "You'd think he was taking credit for it himself. It's nothing like the continuous bubble he theorized about."

"...though the timing's decayed somewhat after seventy-four million years," Jao went on. "Otherwise, we wouldn't be seeing the disks by so much leaked light, and we *never* would have seen the star itself."

A pretty admirer who must have stretched Jao's uxoriousness to the limit spoke up. "I know you explained it before, Jao, but it's awfully confusing. It gives me a headache just to think about it."

"It's beautiful, beautiful!" Jao boomed. "Look, there are four shells of disks—an outer and inner shell in equatorial orbit, and an outer and inner shell in polar orbit. The polar shells are the itsy ones on the inside, and their main job is simply to reflect all radiation into the equatorial plane."

"I understand that, but..."

"Each shell consists of three disks whose diameters are equal to the radii of their distance from the sun. Actually, it's their centers of gravity that're in that orbit. But they don't swivel. Each one of them has exactly enough spin to make its day equal to its year, so that the flat side always faces sunward." He frowned. "Except that one of the inner ones once got a nudge from something that messed up its synchronization—probably a solar flare. That's why the sun was able to pop out in the equatorial plane when we were in the cometary belt."

"But why don't they all just crash into one another?" his admirer wailed.

"Look—each set of three consists of disks whose centers of gravity are at the points of an equilateral triangle, thus occupying the same orbit in a state of equilibrium. It's a very stable arrangement. And the fact—now, get this—the fact that the diameter of each disk is equal to the radius of its orbit means that the zone of interception of the *inner* set is equal to the zone of interception of the *outer* set—so that when you project that cone, it's like having a solid fence of *six* disks, all tangent to each other." He smiled benignly. "Except that you *don't* have to worry about them crashing together. To say nothing of all the mass you save."

"By using littler disks?"

He nodded. "Almost all the mass of the energy trap is in the three *big* ninety-million-mile disks. The next shell inward—the one that orbits at thirty-six million miles—contains only about a sixth as much mass. Call it four twenty-fifths. And the ratio holds as you keep diminishing—so that *all* of the inner disks put together add up to less than the mass of one more big disk. Original Man was very clever. He made his fence out of geometry instead of mass."

"It's a fence with a lot of gaps, though, isn't it?" said a smart aleck who looked as if he were the boyfriend of the girl or aspired to be.

"Not as much as you think," Jao said indulgently. "Let's

figure it out. Hey, Smeth, what's the formula for a hy-pocycloid—never mind, I'll graph it."

He grabbed for the touch pad he had dangling from a chain around his neck and poked at it with thick fingers. An electric-blue circle grew on its photoplastic surface, followed by a horizontal line that bisected it, then two curves with the same radius as the original circle that sprouted from the ends of the line and met at the top. Little boxes began to subdivide the resulting figures, get-ting smaller and smaller until the eye could no longer separate them. The negatively curved triangle in the cen-ter differentiated itself with a change of color. Jao's fingers asked the touch pad a couple of questions, and he read off the answer.

"Yah," he said. "The equatorial fence intercepts about seventy percent of the solar energy that comes its way. So does the polar shell. Together they cover somewhat more than one-fifth of the surface of an imaginary sphere enclosing the sun at any radius. I guess that was good enough to do the job."

"What ever happened to Jao's Bubble?" his opponent asked maliciously.

Jao was totally bland. "Oh, yah, the idea of enclosing a star inside some kind of a continuous shell. It wouldn't work."

"I can't stand it!" Smeth groaned. "Now he's going to disown the whole idea."

"He has no shame." Bram laughed. "Jao throws off ideas, but he isn't attached to them."

Jao was lecturing the young man earnestly. "In the first place, there's no way to keep it from drifting off center," he said. "You might start with the star perfectly centered, but once the slightest drift started, it would keep getting worse, because the attraction from all other directions would keep decreasing..."

"That's exactly what I told him," Smeth complained to Bram.

"...and can you imagine the centrifugal force at the equator if the thing rotated at all? Your sphere would suffer from slump. Everything would tend to collect at

the equatorial plane. No, my friend, your sphere's a pic-
turesque idea, but you can't have it."

"How does he do it?" Smeth grumbled.

"And who needs it, anyway?" Jao said before his young
antagonist could open his mouth to protest. "Let's figure
out how much energy Original Man had at his disposal
for his intergalactic beacon."

He reached for his pendant touch pad again and began
tapping at it one-handed without looking.

"Look at him showing off," Smeth said in disgust. "He
hits wrong numbers all the time that way, but that doesn't
stop him."

"Each one of those big disks has a surface area of...
hmm... call it six point three six quadrillion square miles.
A six followed by fifteen digits. On each side. If you're
trying to make sense of a number like that, it means
that—" He punched numbers again. "—one side of a disk
has *thirty-two million* times the surface area of an ordinary
planetary body like the Father World."

"Why one side?" his admirer queried.

"We're only concerned with the side that's soaking up
energy."

"Oh."

Jao continued. "We've already got a value for the solar
constant at the distance of the cometary halo, a light-year
out. Now let's crank it back according to the inverse-
square law, and we've got—" His fingers busied themselves again. "At ninety million miles, it works out to...
hmm... one point four kilowatts per square meter... times
sixteen times ten to the nineteen square meters—"

"Oh, for pity's sake!" Smeth burst out. "All that ri-
gamarole! He wants to say that each of the three large
diskworlds receives twenty-three times ten to the twenty-
first kilowatts of energy!"

"Thank you, Smeth," Jao said equably. "Twenty-three
sextillion kilowatts. And we're not through yet. We multiply by six, and—"

"Multiply by three something, you mean," interrupted
his rival for the young woman's attention.

"No. Don't forget the three disks of the inner equatorial
shell may be a lot smaller, but they're closer to the star,

and they intercept exactly as much solar radiation as if they were big disks in the outer orbit."

"But—"

Jao sailed on serenely. "Which means that in the equatorial fence alone, Original Man had one hundred and thirty-eight sextillion kilowatts at his disposal to turn into radio waves." He paused for effect. "That is *ten trillion times* as much power as Nar civilization produced on the Father World."

Bram caught his breath. The figure was staggering. He had never bothered to work it out himself, though he had known it must be very high.

"They thought big, those people," he said to Smeth. "By now the human genetic code will have reached the Virgo cluster. I always assumed that was the target. But with that kind of power, I wonder if they were aiming beyond."

Smeth snorted. "Huh, don't let Jao's raving impress you too much. We don't know how efficient those... constructions were at converting energy into the longer radio wavelengths and modulating them."

"It hardly matters, does it?" Bram responded. "The waves will keep spreading through the universe. If they were meant to reach Virgo, the limit of their detectability must lie many times beyond it."

Over by the view wall, Jao was unleashing one of his terrifying smiles on the girl. Though he was utterly faithful to Ang, he didn't mind going through the motions.

Jao's young competitor glowered and made another try at impressing the girl. "If most of the mass of the system is in the big disks," he said belligerently, "how come the sun hasn't drifted toward one or another of them over a period of time—just as it would toward one side of a 'Jao's Bubble'? Excuse me— 'Jao's *shell*.' The same thing would apply—the attraction of the other two disks would decrease with distance, and it would keep getting worse!"

He must have been a physics apprentice. He stole a glance at the girl and went on in a classroom voice. "In a synthetic system like this one, which is essentially three big masses mutually revolving at the points of an equilaterial triangle, a mass occupying the center can't move *above* or *below* the equatorial plane because of the combined pull of the three major components." He stared a challenge. "But it *can* and *will* move *within* the plane!"

"I didn't say most of the mass of the *system* was in the big disks," Jao said kindly. "I said the big disks contain most of the *planetary* mass. Actually, the only mass about the same as a good-size gas giant—maybe a few tenths of one percent of the mass of the G-type star in the middle. So they're in orbit around it in the normal way."

"But that would mean—"

"Right. We *know* they're very thin—maybe as little as fifty miles across the rim. But even so, with a diameter measured in orbital distances, that would give them a volume of maybe four thousand times the volume of your run-of-the-mill gas giant. So they're lighter than they have any right to be."

The boy did some quick figuring in his head. "Four thou—but that would make them lighter than air!"

"Correct. About three and a third times lighter. In fact, they have a density of only about twice that of helium, on average."

"But that's impossible."

"I said on average."

Smeth bustled over. "One might posulate that they're hollow, or honeycombed, or a gas enclosed by a membrane. Or made of a rigid, infinite-length polymer with properties we can't imagine."

"What could be that light—and strong enough to maintain its shape over interplanetary distances?" the boy said.

Jao stared out the window at the strange floating circles that had taken the place of most of the sky. His face was flushed with excitement.

When he finally spoke, it was in Bram's direction. "We'll have to land on one of them to find out, won't we, Captain?"

Bram kissed Mim good-bye, feeling self-conscious in front of all the spectators. A crowd of about two thousand was jammed into the cavernous hangar, waiting to see the takeoff, and the rest of the population of the tree must have been watching on their holo sets. Bram could see the camera crew perched high on the spidery platform of an interbranch shuttle vehicle, where they had an overall view.

"Be careful," Mim said, pressing herself against the tough hide of his vacuum suit. "I wish you weren't going this trip."

He embraced her one-armed, his bubble helmet tucked under the other arm. "The year-captain's expected to lead the way," he said. "That's why they elect him. But don't worry. Lydis is the best landing craft pilot we have—and it's not going to be like landing, anyway. It'll be more like docking with a nonrotating branch. She's practiced it in the simulator a hundred times."

"But it's spinning."

"So slowly at the rim that it makes practically no difference. You're thinking in terms of a body like Yggdrasil, with a diameter only a few hundred miles across. In *this* case, the spin isn't there to *provide* gravity. It cancels it. So when we match for it, we'll touch down as lightly as a leaf."

"I'd still feel a whole lot better if I knew you were landing on the flat side."

A few feet away, under the skeletal arch of a landing leg, Jao left off nuzzling a clinging Ang looked across her golden head toward them.

"That'd be a lot trickier, Mim, even though it *looks* simpler," Jao boomed past Ang's ear, making her wince. "Your normal instincts don't apply on a body as bizarre as that. Neither do your first mathematical assumptions about up and down. Landing anywhere between the hub and the rim on a disk-shaped body would give Lydis some complicated gravitational gradients to cope with. The vertical component and the horizontal component don't behave the same way in relation to the center of gravity. And then there'd be the added factor of centrifugal force tending to make us slide outward, though we don't *think* it'd exceed the diagonal gravitational vector tending to pin us down. To say nothing of all sorts of unpredictable edge effects to get past before we could cross to those interesting structures on the rim. No, Mim, this is the simplest way. We've got it all worked out."

Bram had felt Mim stiffen at Jao's mention of "sliding outward" and "edge effects." He turned it into a joke. "What Jao's really worried about is having to hike across a ninety-million-mile plain to get to where we're going."

She smiled gamely. "I guess I don't understand physics."

"That's all right, Mim, I don't understand Bach," Jao said.

"Don't worry, we'll be very careful," Bram told her, "and we'll be locked in to Jun Davd and his computer the whole time."

The third member of the exploration team, a dour geologist named Enry, pushed his way through the well-wishers and said apologetically to Bram, "Lydis says she's about ready. Says it's time to get these people out of here and climb aboard."

Enry stood there, stolidly waiting. He was a blocky, square-jawed man who long ago had been a touch associate with a geology touch group on the Father World. Though the Father World no longer existed, Enry had never given up his speciality; he pored over the old Nar records in the library and published a monograph every quarter century or so. He was the nearest thing to an expert the tree possessed, and he handled himself well physically in the null-gravity sports at the trunk's center. Bram had thought of him immediately when choosing the exploration team.

"All right," Bram said. He gave Mim a final peck that turned into something more as their lips touched again, then went with Enry to pry Jao loose from Ang.

A warning blast came from a two-tone bass whistle. Exasperated monitors wearing headbadges rushed back and forth, trying to shoo lingering spectators out of the drop area.

"Behind the ropes, behind the ropes! Everybody behind the ropes! Other side of the air curtain track!" The crowd moved as sluggishly as sap. "Keep it moving, keep it moving, unless you want to breathe vacuum!"

Bram got Enry and Jao started up the landing leg ladder with their gear and was preparing to climb it himself when he became aware of a disturbance at the fringe of the retreating crowd. A small, agile figure was darting past the monitors, getting chased by them, and darting back into the forbidden area. The interloper evaded a pursuer and made a beeline for the base of the ladder.

Bram saw corn-yellow hair flying and green eyes on either side of an upturned nose and recognized his great-great-great-granddaughter. "Ame!" he exclaimed. "What are you doing here?"

"I'm going with you," she announced. "Here, take this."

She unslung a lumpy shoulder bag and thrust it at him. The clinking sound of some kind of equipment came from within.

"You can't," he said. "We don't know what we may run into. Anyway, it's only a scouting trip. You'll have plenty of opportunities to go along on the later landings, like everybody else."

"That's the point, Bram-*tsu*. You ought to have a palentogist along on your first survey, and I'm the only authentic specimen you've got." She grinned engagingly at him. "Besides, I've turned myself into a pretty fair geologist, so I'll carry my weight."

"We've got a geologist, a good one."

"Oh, Enry knows his subject, I'll give him that. But his subject's the Father World. Those disks out there are something nobody's an expert on. But my group's been doing theoretical studies for twenty years now—you'd be surprised at some of the computer simulations we've come up with!" She wrinkled her nose. "We really ought to have an archeologist with us, too."

"An archaeologist, is it? Spare me! A theoretical paleontologist's farfetched enough on a preliminary scouting expedition like this."

"Does that mean you'll—"

A monitor came puffing up, a man with a broad, law-abiding face and a long-suffering expression.

"Sorry, Captain. She slipped past us. I'll get her out of here."

Ame turned on him. "I'm *not* going with you. I'm going aboard, isn't that right, Bram-*tsu* Captain?"

The monitor looked doubtfully at the lightweight knee-lengths and slipover she was wearing. "If you want, I can get one of the other safety marshals and we can escort her forcibly."

"No, it's all right. I'll talk to her," Bram said. "Go on, Marshal, I'll take responsibility for sending her back."

The monitor raised a quizzical eyebrow and withdrew. Bram turned to Ame. "You haven't rehearsed with us. There's the question of equipment—"

"Oh, that! There are spare space suits in the ship, and one of them is bound to fit me—it isn't as if they had to be custom fitted. I've ridden with Lydis lots of times before—on trips to other branches and even to the probe. And when it comes to that, I've spent as much time in vacuum as anybody. If I can climb around the branches under spin, I ought to be able to manage on one of those nice flat things out there."

Bram refrained from bringing up Jao's speculations on the nature of disk gravity gradients. "Are you sure you want to leave the twins alone for that long?"

"Smeth will take care of them. They adore him. He spoils them like mad. They're two years old now—they don't need to have me around constantly."

Bram sighed. "Everybody and their gene sibling wanted to be included on this trip. I almost had a riot. I had to promise that if there are no problems, everyone who wants to will get a turn while we're parked in this orbit. And here I am, giving preference to a descendant. They'll have my hide for nepotism."

"I can go, then?"

He gave in. "Your great-great-grandmother is the pilot. It's her decision. If she says you can go, then you're on. Otherwise you promise to leave quietly, all right?"

"I promise."

Above, Jao stuck his head out of the hatch. "What's holding you up? Lydis's already lost a turn while you've been palavering."

Ame scrambled up the landing leg ladder, with Bram behind her carrying the sack of equipment. It was bulky; he felt the handle of a digging tool through the fabric as it swung against his hip.

At the top, Bram twisted around and caught sight of

Mim waving to him from the other side of the barrier. He waved back and squeezed through the hatch after Ame.

Jao filled the air lock, huge and grinning. "Stay here a minute with her," Bram said, "while I—"

"Lydis says it's okay," Jao said. "Let's get going."

A great rumbling sound filled the bay as the curtain rolled around its track and sealed off the cylindrical launch chamber. The crowd on the other side would be streaming toward holo monitors to watch the drop as relayed by the exterior pickups.

Bram turned sternly to Ame. "You had it all arranged with her in advance, didn't you?"

She wrinkled her nose at him. "She said you'd only be stuffy about it, and she was right."

Bram shrugged and sealed the outside hatch, then, after herding Jao and Ame through the air lock, screwed the inner lid into place.

He looked around the dome-shaped cabin. The landing vehicle was basically a squat hemisphere supported on five arched legs. It had started out as a Nar design with the pilot's seat in the middle, but like the rest of the considerable fleet the tree had been stocked with, its interior had been rearranged during the intergalactic crossing to give it something resembling front-back orientation, and the controls had been shifted to conform to human morphology. Lydis and her copilot sat facing one of the five bulging ports—the one that had been designated "forward." The rear of the cabin contained passenger couches—more than the current mission profile called for—storage, equipment, and minimum amenities.

"You have exactly ten minutes to tie yourselves down," Lydis said. "I don't intend to sit here for another go-round."

"Sorry," Bram said.

He nodded to his daughter's co-pilot, a wiry, nonchalant fellow named Zef, then helped Enry and Jao stow their gear. Ame went to a locker and helped herself to a spare vacuum suit. While she struggled to get into it, Bram hefted the clanking sack she had given him and, after a moment's reflection, shoved it into a padded locker. "I hope there's nothing breakable in there," he said.

"Nothing *very* breakable," she said.

They climbed onto their couches and fastened the arm-pits-to-hips webbing in place. Jao cranked his couch to a sitting position.

"I want all you treelubbers to lie prone for the drop," Lydis said. "And while you're at it, put your helmets on."

She herself was sitting upright, as was Zef. Jao pointed that out.

"You do everything by the list when you ride with me," Lydis said. "Otherwise, you can get out and walk."

Grumbling, Jao complied.

"It's surprising, the number of things that can go wrong," Zef said cheerfully. "Why, I saw a fellow explode once because he forgot to screw his helmet on all the way and nobody'd told him the cabin wasn't going to be pres-surized that trip."

"Oh, stow it," Jao said. "I'm not falling for any more of your stories."

Zef laughed. "It's not that we care about the safety of our passengers. We just don't want a lot of helmets float-ing around and bumping into things."

Jao started to reply, but his voice was cut off as Lydis watched the passengers off the Talk circuit. Abruptly Zef dropped his smile and became all business. Bram found himself gripping the armrests of his couch. Drop must be imminent.

He was still plugged into the Listen circuit, though. He could hear Lydis talking to Jun Davd back in the observatory.

"I have your readout," she said. "Please confirm."

"Three minutes more and you'll be in optimum drop position. As tangent as you can get. Do you want the computer to open the trapdoor for you?"

"No, I'd rather do it by feel. The computer doesn't have nerves in its bottom, and it has too much faith in the invariance of mechanical systems. I'm going to have to make a lot of small burn corrections, anyway, once we're out there. Just keep feeding me the figures."

It was a point of pride with Lydis to be in fingertip control. She believed piloting was an art, not a science.

"A computer with nerves in its bottom!" Jun Davd chuckled. "My goodness. We'll work on it."

By craning his neck, Bram could see one of the duplicate screens left over from the original Nar installation, next to the observation blister closest to him. In a simplified computer cartoon it showed a great dull-red disk, slightly angled to give a sense of perspective, and a jolly little green representation of Yggdrasil, much out of scale, floating above and to one side of it. Discreetly flashing and dotted lines showed the direction of rotation of both bodies and their intersecting orbits around the rice-grain sun shining through a cluster of red lobes at the center of the system.

It obviously hadn't been very practical to put Yggdrasil into orbit around the rim of a disk-shaped body with a circumference of two hundred seventy million miles. And parking Yggdrasil sixty degrees ahead of the disk—at the stable point which in this crazy system neatly coincided with the point of equilibrium with the disk ahead of it in orbit—would still have placed them an inconvenient forty-five million miles away from the forward edge of the disk and all of one hundred million miles away from the present "top" of the disk, which they had chosen as their likeliest base of operations.

So instead, with Jun Davd's help, Bram had put Yggdrasil into a solar orbit that intersected the disk's orbit at a tilted angle. It started above and behind the disk at a distance of only a few million miles, slanted down at a tangent that almost grazed their target point on the rim, and continued on past to a point ahead of the disk in orbit that would place Yggdrasil directly "above" the spot where the disk's own slow rotation would have brought the explorers' base of operations by that time.

Thus, for at least the first half year, travel time between Yggdrasil and the main landing site would be measured in days rather than months. At that point, Yggdrasil's solar orbit could be converted into a powered orbit around the rim, which would take it back to its starting point for another such orbital stern chase.

Bram kept his eye on the pulsing orange line that emanated from the tiny cartoon Yggdrasil on the screen and ended tangent to the disk. It represented a vector of the momentum that would be imparted by Yggdrasil's own orbital motion plus the added kick from Yggdrasil's rotation at the moment of release.

Lydis would add her own increment of momentum by firing the spacecraft's engines once she was in a position to judge how well lined up she was. Then she would have to cut it fine at the other end, killing all her pseudoorbital velocity and matching the speed of her target on the rotating edge of the disk—so that the net cancellation of both would come out even at the precise moment of touchdown.

No wonder she didn't trust the computer.

Once launched, the complex orbital mechanics boiled down to an eyeball-and-seat-of-the-pants job, and Bram himself trusted Lydis's instincts more than he trusted the unreeling chains of glowing figures superimposed on the computer cartoon that kept changing their final decimal places.

"Hold on to your valuables," Zef warned through the helmet circuit.

The trapdoor beneath the spacecraft sprang open, and they fell through. Sudden weightlessness was a faint thrill along Bram's spine till his body adjusted. He made an incautious movement and floated an inch off the couch, held down by the webbing pressing against his chest.

He lost interest immediately in the computer display and applied himself to the view outside the blister. Yggdrasil's great gnarled branches floated by, pierced by random points of light from people's living quarters.

The tree rose until it was a green cloud above them. It began to dwindle and in minutes was far enough away that its shape could be seen against a sprinkling of stars: a double-ended mushroom divided by darkness.

He turned his head to see how Enry was taking it and saw that the man was sweating inside his helmet. Of the four passengers, Enry was the only one who had never been away from the tree; Ame had gone on jaunts with Lydis, and Jao had gone with Bram on comet-chasing expeditions. Bram could understand how Enry felt. It was

a wrenching experience to part from the entity that nu-
tured you in blind universe.

From this angle, line of sight was out of the system,
and nothing could be seen except the stars. Now, with
Yggdrasil shrinking overhead, Lydis rotated the ship to
point toward their destination.

An uncanny collection of glowing circles rose to fill
the viewport. Here, above the equatorial plane of the
system, one could look down past their scalloped fence
into the inner heart where the polar disks orbited. Their
tininess was an illusion of distance; they still dwarfed the
enclosed sun. One of them was skewed; Jao had been
right about that. A collision with a leftover planetoid or
a solar flare some time in the past had altered its carefully
timed spin. The sun spilled its light through like a glowing
egg in a nest.

The turning of the craft continued, and now an enormous knife edge cleaved the sky: the disk that was their
destination.

Lydis applied a touch of her lateral jets once more,
and the turning stopped until the knife edge was suspended directly overhead. Bram studied it through the
bubble dome. At the tip where the line ended was an
illuminated dot, like a tiny flower on a stem.

"You can see the moon from here," Lydis's voice came
through the suit radio. "It looks as if it's resting on the
rim from here, but of course it's not. The structures we
sighted through the big telescope are beneath it. We should
begin to make *them* out at about a quarter million miles.
They're huge."

The diskworld had proved to have moons—eleven of
them, equally spaced, in synchronous orbit around the
rim. Where the twelfth should have been, the narrow
ribbon of landscape slumped suggestively across a span
of twenty million miles.

The orbits of the moons were impossible—too close
and too slow. "They have no right to hover like that,"
Jun Davd had said.

For once, Jao had had no theories, except for a
halfhearted, "Antigrav, maybe?"

"What I'm interested in is, what are they hovering

over?" Jun Davd had mused. He had kept his instruments trained on the moons during Yggdrasil's long inward sweep from the outer limits of the plundered system, and had done much juggling with computer enhancement and other techniques. Some two billion miles out, he had been rewarded. "It's some kind of support complex," he had announced, showing dubious pictures of a patchy grid, which might have been nothing more than the computer's desire to please. "Roadways, maybe. Ditches or canals or the remnants of a buried transport system. Street layouts with the rubble showing differently in the infrared ... casting low shadows ..."

He had set a course for the largest of the complexes on the disk whose orbit they could most conveniently intercept. It struck Bram as finicky and bizarre, and Jun Davd agreed with him. But it was a planetary body with interplanetary distances; the next largest complex was a third of the way around the rim—ninety million miles away. Too far to walk. It was definitely a problem in space navigation.

"Hold on," Lydis's voice said. "I'm going to give you some weight now."

There was a gentle shove on Bram's chest, pressing him into the couch. A rain of small objects came from above; someone had forgotten to secure some minor gear. Zef turned to glare at the culprit, and Jao grinned sheepishly within his helmet.

The burn was a leisurely one, lasting a half hour at what Bram estimated to be about a quarter of a gravity. There was plenty of hydrogen and oxygen to be profligate with since Yggdrasil had drunk its fill of comets.

Lydis saw her passengers fidgeting. "I know it's hard to lie still when there doesn't seem to be any reason for it," she said, "but I don't want any mass moving around while I'm doing this."

At last they went weightless again. "All right," Lydis said. "You can get up now. Take off your vacuum suits if you like. I'm not going to fire the jets again for about two days."

Everybody gratefully desuited. Jao scratched mightily.

"I don't think you were worried about leaks at all," he said. "I think you just wanted to keep us quiet."

"Where'd you ever get an idea like that?" Zef said.

They all crowded to an observation blister to have a look at their destination; Lydis had rolled the ship over after the main burn so that people wouldn't have to crane their necks to look through the overhead dome.

Enry, pale, said, "How wide is the rim? It still looks like a one-dimensional line from here."

"About fifty miles," Jao said. "Talk about *thin*! We wouldn't see it at all from this angle if it wasn't for scattered light from over the edge."

Ame said, with a trace of awe, "The former human race was efficient. "Just about all the working surface is on the flat sides."

Jao nodded. "But don't forget, even a fifty-mile width gives a surface area on the rim alone of thirteen and a half billion square miles. That's equivalent to the surface areas of *seventy* of your normal, terrestroid-style planets like the Father World. That's a *lot* of elbow room, even if it *is* all east and west."

"I'm glad we don't have to dig it *all* up," Ame said, with a glance at Enry to see how he was taking her presence.

Enry rose to the occasion. He was stuffy but nice. "I could use a little help," he said.

A perfunctory laugh went around. Bram asked Lydis for a magnified view through the ship's telescope and got nothing more than a fuzzier line topped by a blurred speck that might have been construed as a crescent.

"It's going to be a very strange place," he said.

Part II

TESTAMENT

CHAPTER 7

The diskworld was a very strange place indeed.

Bram, weighing no more than an ounce or two, stood at the front of the landing ladder and looked out across the red twilight at a thin slice of landscape that stretched away into darkness.

Its edges were sharply defined against the starry night. Strictly speaking, there was no horizon at the end of it; the bleak, uniform vista dwindled to a vanishing point long before the eye could reach that hypothetical sykline some millions of miles beyond.

It gave Bram the illusion of standing on a very high, infinitely long ridge. Ahead was a flat, narrow plain of rubble that turned into a needle point piercing the black sky. On either side of him, not many miles away, was a sheer cliff that dropped down ninety million miles to a chasm filled with stars.

His weightlessness contributed to the dreamlike feeling of the place. The next person down the ladder jostled him unintentionally, and they both drifted a foot into the air before settling to the ground again.

Bram glanced into the other's faceplate and saw by the blue glow of the helmet telltales that it was Jao. For once the red-bearded physicist was speechless. Both of them turned by common consent to look at the inner rim of their thin-sliced world.

The universe of stars gave way to a sky erased by stray luminescence, over what appeared to be a geometrically straight edge with no hint of curvature.

The brink of the world.

The great disks rose like goblin faces peering over the precipice, glowing a dull red of dying embers. As this queer world turned, they would rise in unison until they filled the sky. Even now, the big one ahead of them in orbit showed an angular diameter of fifty degrees, a hundred times wider than the sun would have been had it been visible.

From the present angle of view, almost forty million miles above the plane of the sun, one looked down on the inner disks. The three in the next orbit inward faced each other in a circle, like a conference of goblin children. Only one of these showed its glowing face; the other two were circular blots of darkness. Still farther inward hung more disks, getting smaller and smaller.

"I think I figured it out," Jao said.

"Figured what out?"

"How to manufacture a diskworld."

"How?"

Jao affected jauntiness, but his voice shook a little. "Oh, spin-up, foamed materials, superfilament, anchoring masses. I'll tell you more when the geologist's report is in."

Bram looked across to where a squarish space-suited figure on its hands and knees was chipping away at rock with a little hammer. Each blow tended to lift him into the air, and then there would be a wait until he was sufficiently anchored to strike again; it must have been a maddeningly frustrating way to work. Enry had wasted no time. He had started collecting his samples only a few yards from the ship.

"What do you say, Enry?" Bram said.

His radio crackled. "Looks like ordinary rock so far," Enry's voice said. "Under a layer of dust."

"Yar, from the spin-up," Jao countered. "Plus seventy million years' worth of micrometeorites. You're going to have to dig a lot deeper before you get to what this planet's made of."

"Which is?"

"Mostly nothing. Wrapped around gases—oxygen, mostly, I'd guess. Combined with aluminum and probably carbon. You'll have to get a chemist. But I'll tell you this, Enry-*peng-yu*, when you get to it, it's going to be a job taking the sample."

Enry grunted and continued his chipping. He was gradually working out a low-gravity technique—striking his little outcropping from one side, then quickly reaching around to strike it from the other, and staying more or less in orbit around it.

"The rest of the answer's there," Jao went on, pointing at the moon overhead.

Bram raised his eyes to the zenith and instinctively wanted to duck his head. Everybody did. The ellipsoidal moon was so close—only a few diameters away—that it seemed in danger of falling.

You didn't have to look up to be conscious of it. You could almost *feel* it hanging there with its pointed end aimed at your head. Feel it literally, perhaps. Its gravitational pull would not be insignificant compared with the diskworld's feeble tug at the rim. Perhaps the fluids of the cells sent a message to the brain.

The pockmarked body measured scarcely a hundred fifty miles through the long axis. It might once have been an asteroid towed here by Original Man, Jun Davd had suggested, or a smaller moon of one of the dismantled gas giants.

There were artificial structures on the underside of the moon, visible even to the naked eye—a distinctly geometric jumble at the lower tip, with four enigmatic hairlines converging on it from the satellite's waistline. The airless clarity brought it tantalizingly near.

"It makes you feel that you could almost jump up and touch it," Bram said.

Jao chewed a hairy lip. "You know...I bet a spacesuited man *could* reach the moon by jumping," he said in a serious tone. "Assuming he could jump with an initial velocity of, oh, sixteen feet per second. Escape velocity ought to be somewhere around there. The surface gravity here's about like a small asteroid. Like that comet head we visited." His eyes almost clicked as he started doing calculations in his head. "Suit jets would help," he conceded. "The trick would be landing safely on the moon, with only a pair of legs to come down on."

"It might be quite a crash," Bram said. "How far would he have to fall after capture—about a thousand miles?"

"Less than that."

"We'll visit the moon after we get organized here, I promise you. But I think we'll do it in workpods."

"There might be an alternative."

"Huh?"

"We might be able to get there in climbers. We'll know after we get to the ruins."

The ruins—or their apparent focus—lay directly underneath the lower tip of the ellipsoidal moon. Lydis had wanted to land closer to them, but Jao had insisted that she land at least fifty miles away. "It might be dangerous," he had said, but he had refused to say why. Bram had taken him seriously enough to order Lydis to comply. The distance would be inconvenient, but they had brought along a pair of walkers adapted to airlessness and low gravity.

"What are you talking about?" Bram asked.

"See anything over there? Use your top magnification."

Obediently, Bram searched the distant ruins with his helmet telescope. The liquid crystal display emerged from its clear plastic sandwich and formed a circular image in front of his right eye. He squinted and adjusted the focus.

"I don't see anything."

"Turn up the contrast."

"I think I see some kind of streak or scratch. It's hard to be sure. I think it's in my helmet . . . no, it stays put when I move. It may be a beam of light or a reflection. It's pointing straight up in the direction of the moon."

"That's it," Jao said.

"That's what?"

"Oh, no. I'm not saying. I'm not sticking my neck out till we get there."

"Watch out!" Bram's suit radio said.

He stepped to one side and saw Lydis and Zef wrestling one of the walkers out of the hatch. They let go, and it floated down to the ground, where it unfolded, shook itself off, and inflated its passenger bubble. The biodevice was a tried and true version of the basic model the Nar had used for airless planetoids and nonrotating space structures. Its fragile, elongated frame would not have stood up under any semblance of real gravity, but it was strong enough for places like this. It had a submetabolism that worked on hydrogen and oxygen, and besides supplying energy, the auxilliary system had water and oxygen to spare for passengers.

"Well, let's not waste time," Jao said, with a hop and a dive toward the vehicle. "Did anybody pack a lunch?"

Enry was engrossed in his work. Now he was putting dust samples into little vials. Ame came bounding over from a fissure she had been studying. "That's more like it," she said. "Wait till I get my kit."

Lydis drifted down the ladder and stationed herself in front of the spidery biovehicle. "Hold on," she said. "We go out two at a time, at least till we know more about this place, and we keep the voice and homing circuits on at all times."

"What d'ya mean?" Jao said. "The walker'll carry three."

"Sorry," Lydis said. "That's the way it's going to be."

Jao assumed an expression of great regret. "Sorry, Ame. You can take the next trip. Do you want me to bring back any rubble samples for you?"

Ame sputtered. "We're going to have a first look at the ruins, and it needs someone with some archaeological and paleontological training." She appealed to Lydis. "Isn't that so?"

"I'd say so," Lydis replied.

"Well," Jao said. "Your daughter has spoken. I guess it's Ame and me. Sorry, Bram. I'll give you a running report over the radio."

"Not a chance," Lydis said firmly. "Neither your nor Ame is qualified on a walker. Bram's the driver."

It was Jao's turn to sputter. "There's nothing to steering one of those things."

"There's too much trouble an inexperienced driver can get into in low gravity," Lydis said. "You could turn over.

Bounce it too high and come down the wrong way. Misjudge a ravine."

"Sorry, Jao," Bram said. "You can have the second ride. I'll find out what that thing is. And give you a report over the radio."

The walker loped across the jagged landscape, bouncing upward in great buoyant swoops that ate up the miles. Bram, with an occasional corrective jerk of the reins, kept a watchful eye through the inflated bubble on the route ahead. The tumbled lines of rubble they had to cross were not really dangerous to the walker, which was nimble enough to compensate for its stiff-legged gait when it came down wrong-footed on a boulder or crack. But of course it had no long-distance judgment.

"It's shivery," Ame said, glancing toward the great glowing hump of a disk that rose out of the ground to their left. As dull and rusty as the light was, it cast long gloomy striations of shadow across the stark plain.

"Shivery?" he teased her. "Is that some sort of technical term you paleontologists use?"

She nestled for comfort against him on the narrow bench. "It's been dead and broken for millions of years. But I feel that it's been waiting for us."

"It has."

"And that it's watching us right now."

"Nothing could live here."

"*We* do. And this thing we're riding in *sort* of lives."

"You're letting your imagination run away with you. But that's not surprising. This place is haunted. By the entire human race."

"Yes." She shuddered. "It's like our own graveyard. We're supposed to be immortal. But so were they."

"That's why it's important to find answers here, Ame. And that's your job."

She shook off the mood with an effort. "A job for more than me and Enry. We're going to have to develop a real science of archaeology very quickly. We've never had the subject matter before. We don't want to blunder about, destroying knowledge."

"How do we go about it?"

"We'll need a large labor force from the tree," she said briskly. "We'll have to establish a grid first, and a cataloging system. The librarians can help there, and everybody else will have to pitch in. Chemists, cultural scholars, everybody." She challenged him with a direct gaze. "I can hardly wait to get a real team here and start the dig. How soon do you think that will be, Bram-*tsu*?"

"Right away, if everything looks all right. We'll spend a few days here first—find a good place to set up a base camp, get an idea of the layout. Lydis ought to be able to move the ship a bit closer. That thing up ahead isn't a danger now that we know where it is."

The walker was at the top of a leap, and as it drifted slowly down, both passengers looked ahead through the bubble. The elusive streak at the center of the compound still could not be seen with the naked eye, even from a few miles away. But a couple of stops during the approach and a look through the helmet telescopes had confirmed that it was still there.

Bram had tried bouncing light off it from a hand laser, while Ame made photometer readings. Slashing back and forth with the beam, he had still obtained readings at what a rough triangulation told him was a height of over twenty miles.

Whatever it was, it was indubitably solid matter, and it reached straight up.

"Stop here," Ame said. "I want to look at something."

Bram reined the walker in. It reared up in the low gravity, then its front legs settled into the dust. Bram made it kneel, then followed Ame out through the lips of the bubble.

It made a primitive air lock, but it was the best that could be done within the limitations of the scrawny biomachine. Very little atmosphere was lost if you managed the egress properly. You learned the technique quickly—arms stretched out with your head tucked between them, as if you were diving, then squirm the rest of yourself through sidewise, while the fat inflated edges sealed themselves around you, and a quick pop as you drew your foot through. He and Ame had stayed in their suits with their helmets on even though the bubble was fully pres-

surized with a breathable atmosphere of fifty percent oxygen. Lydis had insisted on that for safety's sake.

Ame headed for one of the low ridges of rubble that
crisscrossed the area, as she had done on previous stops.
It looked no different from any of the other ridges of
rubble as far as Bram could see.

"What is it?" he asked.

"Another rooftop," she said. "Pretty intact under there,
I should think. A warehouse or distribution center, maybe,
from the size of it and from the way it's situated—you
can see how long that unbroken ridgeline goes on."

"But why—"

"Come on. This way." She had already planted a lo-
cater beacon in the debris for future reference, and now
she scrambled up a low slope, sending up clouds of dust
and chips that hung there in the inconsequential gravity.

"Careful of your suit," Bram cried, but she had already
disappeared over the edge. With a sigh he leaped after,
soared over the peak with his legs tucked up, and dragged
a toe to put himself down just on the other side. Unexpectedly, he found himself standing next to Ame on a
forty-five-degree slope that ended at the base of what was
ummistakably an uncovered wall of stone one hundred
feet away.

"I thought I saw it when we were at the top of that
last jump," she said complacently. "Collapsed roof. Quake,
maybe—we'll have to ask Enry how quakes would work
on a body with stresses like this one. Or maybe a meteo-
rite strike. Look, it took four levels with it—it must be
all tumbled down underneath there."

She pointed, and Bram saw the broken ledges on the
wall opposite, each with its cap of dust.

"And *that* will tell us how deep the regolith lies on a
body like this one after we measure the slump," she said.
"You know, there must have been a lot of leftover junk
in this system after Original Man got through with his
construction project. We've got seventy million years'
worth of impact debris and dustfall. Lot of digging to do.
Small bodies tend to lose mass because of high-energy
impacts. The gravity doesn't hold on to the stuff that
fountains up. But on a body like this, even though the

surface gravity is low because of rotation, there's still the attraction of all that mass. The impact debris has no place to go, really, and over the eons it settles down in a slow rain and stays."

"You've been studying your astronomy."

She gave a pleased laugh. "It's the same as geology in a place like this, isn't it?"

"What do you expect to find under all that rubble?" He gestured at the tipped slope they stood on.

Her eyes shone. "Fossils, if we're lucky. There'd be organic material if this was a food depot—or even if people lived or worked here, away from the operational center. People leave garbage. And garbage means mold, bacteria, microfossils. Maybe even the bones of vermin. Original Man must have had vermin."

Bram remembered a childhood tale: *The Dappled Piper of Shu-shih.*

"Yes, indeed," he said. "They called them rats."

"Member of the order *Rodentia*," she said with a frown. "They're in the mammal list, but Original Man doesn't have much to say about them."

"I'll settle for a few dessicated bacteria. Would there be any DNA left after seventy million years?"

"Maybe. This place isn't cold. But it's airless and dry. Original Man ressurected something called *Tyrannosaurus rex* from a bone fragment after a similar period. In his twenty-first century. They kept them in zoos."

He caught something of her excitement. "What a find a few bone fragments of Original Man would be! If we could do some DNA sequencing on a big enough sample, we could find out if he edited us before broadcasting our genetic code."

"We don't know his burial customs. But millions of people must have lived here over a period of time to operate the beacon. There would have been accidents . . . illnesses that got out of hand . . . the rare individual who was immune to the immortality virus—" She broke off, abruptly aware that Jao would be listening through the radio link.

"We'd better get going," Bram said. "You've left a marker; we can send an excavation team later."

But Ame was unclipping a folding shovel from her belt. She flexed the stub of a handle once to activate the memory plastic and an instant later had a proper shovel. "Let's see how deep the regolith is where it's slid down here," she said. "Help me clear some of this away."

Bram worked with his gloved hands while Ame shoveled, and within a tenth of an hour they had uncovered a smooth, hard gray surface.

"No miracle materials, those," Ame said. "They made the walls and roof of ordinary melted and poured stone. They could afford to mold it thick enough to cover expanses like this. There was plenty of stone, and power to spare before they switched on the transmitter."

"Twenty-three sextillion kilowatts, Jao figured," Bram said. "Trillions of times as much energy as the entire Nar civilization had at its disposal. It's a little disappointing to find that their building construction was so prosaic."

"Sophisticated megaliths," Ame said. "That's what they are. Great slabs meant to outlast eternity. Only this one didn't."

She rapped the end of her shovel sharply; hydrogen atoms spilled from the reservoir they had fled to, preempted bonds again, and once more the shovel handle shrank to fit into her belt. She occupied herself for a moment chipping a rock sample from the slab. "I'll take this back to Enry for analysis," she said.

She bobbed to her feet a little too quickly, and Bram pulled her out of the air. "Ready?" he asked. He was anxious to return to the walker and continue toward the apparent center of the complex.

"Just a minute," Ame said.

She looked down the rubble-strewn slope of where its edge abutted the vertical wall and studied the V-shaped trench it made. "There's broken rock in places along the edge," she said. "If any of them correspond to broken sections of the underside of the slab, we could get underground without digging."

"No," he said. "We're not going to crawl through caves without any backup. It's too dangerous. This place will still be here when we get back. Let's get going. We're wasting our air supply on the outskirts."

"As long as we're here, let's just take a *look*," she said.

"All right."

He gave in and followed her down the slope. He didn't like it. They were in a deep groove, cut off from sight of the walker and the never-ending landscape. Only the stars burned overhead.

Ame was unconcerned. She played the light of her torch along the join of the two surfaces. Color vision returned, showing Bram vitreous streaks of green, brown, and yellow mixed with the gray. Even to the naked eye it was apparent that the rubble had slid down the slope to cover any possible cracks to a depth of many feet. It would take a lot of work to clear it away.

But he was wrong. Ame's torch played on a gaping black aperture that ran down the rocky crease in a spot that seemed remarkably free of rubble. In fact, the rubble seemed to be piled higher on either side of it.

"It goes all the way down," she said. "About twenty feet to where the floor is. Big enough to squeeze through, and then there's a sort of triangular tunnel made by the edge of the roof slab and the angle of the floor and wall. The tunnel's clean—hardly any debris to clear away. I wouldn't have expected that. The roof must have collapsed with miraculous precision. Half our work's been done for us already. And when we explore the whole length of the cleft, we're *bound* to find places where we can get through into the main part of the ruin." Her voice rose with excitement. "Acres and acres of undisturbed ...*anything*! Bram-*tsu*, why don't we just—"

"No," he said firmly. "We're not going to go crawling in there now. For one thing, we'd be out of radio contact. Come on, Ame. We've seen everything there is to see for the moment.

"I suppose you're right," she sighed. She played the beam of her torch in widening spirals around the entrance. "But I don't understand where all the rubble went."

Then they saw the footprints.

The tracks converged on the hole from all directions. Heavy traffic. The reason they weren't obvious in the immediate vicinity of the hole was that they became too thick there, obliterating outlines and churning up the dust.

Besides, getting in and out of the hole meant belly crawling, further erasing any tracks.

But they were very plain farther away.

They were longer and narrower than an ordinary human footprint, but they covered about the same area and presumably would have supported a body of similar weight. The foot that had made the imprint had been encased in a tubelike boot with a ridged underside.

When he was able to catch his breath he said, "How long ago?"

Even his untrained eye could see that the outlines of the footprints were not as sharp as the prints he and Ame had left.

Ame produced a tiny measuring stick and compared the depth of the two sets of prints. Then she poked the rod into the dust in several places.

"They're recent," she said.

That startled him. "How recent?"

Her features worked within the helmet. "We'll have to assume that the dustfall on this world has been diminishing during the last seventy million years, as the disks swept out their orbit. Dimishing on a logarithmic scale, maybe. Most of the dustfall must have taken place in the first few million years. But the roof must have collapsed, too, within a few million years of the time when Original Man abandoned the place, because of the later buildup that replaced the dust that slid down into the crevice."

"Ame—*how recent*?"

"It could have been within the last thirty million years."

Bram swayed in the low gravity. "More than forty million years after we thought the human race died out," he whispered. He grasped her space-suited arm. "Could these prints have been made by a human foot?"

She shrugged. "Depends on what you want to consider human. It took the human foot only a few million years to evolve from a grasping organ that looked something like our hands. I suppose that in another forty million years, it could have evolved into something that looked like *that*."

She splashed her light around the prints. "It's hard to tell what might have been inside that boot," she said finally. "But the elongated proportions aside, that *could* be a foot with the normal configuration of heel, instep, and toes. They always bend in the same place, so they had bones. Not like a Nar footprint that varied from step to step."

"They brought animals with them."

The light revealed meandering chains of shallow little paw prints, hardly larger than a human thumb. Then it struck Bram.

"What kind of animal could live in vacuum?"

The paw prints divided into five slender toes. Whatever had made them had been bare to space.

Ame leaned for a closer look. "A terrestrial animal. We've got quite a few drawings to go on. All terrestrial vertebrates had limbs based on a plan of five digits—even those that evolved into hoofs or wings. Bram-*tsu*, I've *seen* pictures of paws that must have looked something like these, on little climbing creatures like tree shrews, and raccoons, and . . . and squirrels!"

"And rats?" he suggested.

"Yes, those, too."

"Could this world once have had air?"

"N-no. Not with the low gravity. Besides, these prints show no signs of weathering. They're perfectly preserved."

Bram stood up. His knees felt weak. "We've never seen another terrestrial animal," he said. "On all the Nar worlds, we were the only specimen. Now it appears that we're standing on a world that once held at least two more specimens. Let's get going, Ame. The sooner we finish our survey, the sooner you can start digging for fossils."

"Bram-*tsu*, have you noticed something?" She moved her beam of yellow light around the area, holding it low to cast shadows.

The little paw marks were always superimposed over the footprints. Never the other way around.

"The animals were later," he said.

"A *lot* later," she said. She rested the light on a nearby cluster of paw prints. "Look at these. They're very shallow because of the low gravity and because a creature that size wouldn't have massed very much. They can't be more than a millimeter deep. But even so, every detail is sharp. They're not at all blurred by dustfall. They couldn't *possibly* be more than a million years old." She traced the paw prints with the light to where they disappeared into the crevice. "They might have been made yesterday."

It was a ladder to the moon.

Bram and Ame left the walker at the edge of the massive circular housing and walked over to where the two thick ropes rose straight up into the sky, taut as bowstrings.

The ropes were semitranslucent and so thick around that it would have taken six or seven people joining hands in a circle to have embraced them. The bulge of the winding strands was sufficient to have served as a spiral staircase.

"The moon's tethered," Bram said. "Like a captive balloon."

They stared up to where the cables disappeared into the sky. They were visible, Bram guessed, to a height of a couple of miles.

One of the cars that once had plied the tremendous mooring line was stalled about a hundred yards up, like a bead on a string. It was a flattish ovoid with portholes around the rim, and the beam of torch reached high enough to show it to be painted a jolly shade of red. The cable passed through the car's center. Bram could only guess at the nature of the mechanism that climbed the braided cord—worm gears or ratchets or cogwheels. But there must have been an inner carousel that housed it, to keep the passengers from getting dizzy.

What a ride it must have been! Being whirled upward at thousands of miles an hour. How would they have managed turnover so that they could land on the moon right side up? Was there a way station at the point where the moon's gravitational influence took over? A transfer point linking the two cables? There would have to be one car coming down for every car going up, to maintain equilibrium: One didn't fool around with stresses like these!

His eyes moved across a mile of circular plaza to where a second set of sky ropes had been guyed. One of them had snapped. The end of the cable lay in ruins amid the buildings it had smashed. The dangling end of the rope was visible about a half mile up. The remains of an ovoid car that had slipped off the end of the rope lay strewn across the plaza.

Bram hoped no one had been in it. The disaster most likely had happened millions of years after the departure of man—maybe even millions of years after the time of the narrow-footed visitors. But the remaining set of cables had been strong enough to hold the moon down. The astonishing system had been engineered for redundancy.

Unable to resist, Bram reached out a cautious hand and touched the glasslike rope where it rose out of an encircling collar. He might have been touching a column carved out of solid steel. It was utterly hard, utterly immovable.

"Now we know what those hairline markings on the moon are," he said. "The moon's wearing a harness."

"Bram-*tsu*, Jao is going crazy," Ame reminded him delicately.

"Sorry, Jao," Bram said, switching on the receiver of his suit radio. "I guess you've been listening to me and Ame oohing and ahing. I forget that you can't see it."

A howl of the purest agony reached him. After a moment, Bram realized that words were embedded in the incoherent gargling sounds.

"Describe it. What are the dimensions? What does the surface look like? What colors do you get when you flash light on it? How's it anchored? Careful of loose threads, if there are any. You could lose a finger."

Bram gave him a brief description of the rope and the surrounding installation. "I can't imagine what it would be made of," he said. "And I can't see how it's anchored. It just disappears into the ground."

"Yar," Jao said, breathing hard. "Each thread is a single continuous molecule that reaches from here to the moon. My guess is that it'll turn out to be mostly oxygen bonded to silica, magnesium, and aluminum, with a carbon backbone to help out with all the connections. It'd be harder than diamond and with a higher tensile strength than amorphous boron to *start* with, and then there'd be some kind of submolecular weaving between adjacent chains ... And, oh yah, you won't find where it's anchored, because it reaches all the way down to the original core of this world, forty-five million miles under your feet. That's because it's only a guide thread—part of the warp and woof that held this world together while they were spinning it."

"Slow down," Bram said. "I can believe in your tied-down moon because I can see the evidence here with my own eyes—and by the way, you'd better radio Jun Davd right away and tell him that we've solved the mystery of why the moons are lower than they ought to be for synchronous orbit. I'll even accept your endless molecule till a better explanation comes along. But how could it support another forty-five million miles of its own weight?"

"It's the other way around," Jao said smugly. "The idea isn't to hold the moon down. The moon is what holds the world up."

Bram looked around at an apparently solid landscape. They were near one edge of the rim here. The avenues of rubble stretched to the opposite side, fifty miles away. The rectilinear mounds were higher at the lunar longitude than they had been on the outskirts of the enormous complex—the buildings had been taller and more important here. It had not occurred to Bram to wonder why the moonropes were peripheral and not centered, because, after all, the entire surface of the diskworld was the "equator."

"You're getting too farfetched," he said, and waited for the next dizzying supposition from Jao.

"Am I?" Jao retorted. "I'll bet you anything you care to name that when we cross that plain to the other side, we'll find *another* cable car station and *another* set of ropes. Making an equilateral triangle with a fifty-mile base and its apex on the moon. Wait a minute! Make that a *very* narrow tetragon! Why not? The angle of divergence is minuscule on that scale. You might as well have parallel tethers. No, wait again! How about spreading the moon terminal still *farther* apart? At an angle that converges at the disk's core? With a *little* truing of curves, you could have a ninety-million-mile section of parabola for your antenna. Bram, we've got to map the whole topography of this disk! I'll bet it has a *concave* cross section. Hard to detect, but it would make this razor's edge of a rim the *widest* part, except for the leftover bulge at the hub!"

"I'd have thought that even a few inches of overhang at a height of forty-five million miles would add up to insupportable stresses."

"Don't you *see*?" Jao's voice exploded in Bram's ear. "This world was built like a suspension roof! It *had* to be! Otherwise, with the spin needed to keep it from collapsing under its own weight, the synchronous orbital points would have been embedded somewhere below the *surface*! There wouldn't *be* a stable surface! All the people and the buildings and the topsoil would be thrown off into space!"

"What's a suspension roof?"

"It was an idea one of the Resurgist architects had for building our sports arena in the human compound. Arthe, his name was. You strung cables from supporting piers and laid roofing material over them. You kept the internal air pressure of the building higher, to bear some of the weight. It was a way to provide a larger interior space unobstructed by load-bearing pillars. Nothing ever came of it. The council was too conservative and decided to stick with a Nar-style shell."

"A whole *world* built that way?"

"Why not? It makes sense. And it fits the facts. We *know* this world is lighter than air. About twice the weight of helium on average. And when that average includes a rocky surface and two apparently rigid faces, then we're dealing with an artifact that for all its size is mostly a gossamer nothingness enclosing *more* mostly nothingness."

"Yes, I remember that Smeth proposed a honeycomb structure or a membrane enclosing a gas."

Jao snorted impatiently. "But how do you build *up* a honeycomb out of a gas giant's mass without it collapsing into a sphere after the first hundred thousand miles? Even if your honeycomb were as light as hydrogen? Especially when you're starting out that much closer to the center of gravity—not like out here on the rim, forty-five million miles away from it, where we're down to about six decimal places worth of zeros with a one hung on the end of them, and we're staying attached to the surface mainly by courtesy of the local gravity of the crust. As for a membrane, one meteor puncture and you'd have the deflated skin of a world."

"It would take more than one," Bram demurred.

"This world's *had* more than one," Ame said tartly.

"All right, gang up on me," Bram said. "Go on, Jao. Lydis, are you recording this for Jun Davd?"

"Yes," Lydis said. "I can always add it to the reserve air supply. After cooling it down."

"Who told you it'd be risky to make a cislunar landing approach?" Jao reminded her. "*That* didn't turn out to be hot air, did it?"

"Let him finish," Enry's voice broke in. "It fits in with my seismograph readings. The waves damp out a few miles down."

"Thank you, Enry. I'm glad there's *one* member of our expedition with a little vision." Jao continued smugly. "You start with an unremarkable rocky-type body—maybe the core of the gas giant they poured into their parts bin. Next you tow your twelve moons into place, positioning them so that they occupy the same synchronous orbit in a stable dodecagonal configuration. If you don't have twelve leftover moons handy, you fill in with a few hefty asteroids."

"Skip the details for now," Bram suggested, "or we'll never get there."

Jao made a pained sound. "Then you drop a line from each of your synchronous moons and anchor them at the planet's equator. While you're lowering the lines, of course, you have to keep judiciously raising the moons' orbits, to keep the center of gravity in the right place. Even with the lightweight filament you're using, the mass adds up as the line grows."

"So far you're describing the construction of an ordinary orbital elevator," Bram said.

"You recognized that?" Jao sounded pleased. "Not many people knew about that project."

"I worked on a part of the problem at the biocenter," Bram said. "Ordinary viral monofilament— the kind the Nar used for the bubble car cable network—tested well within the breaking strength limits, but there were still some problems with prolonged ultraviolet exposure that needed to be worked out."

"What's an orbital elevator?" Ame asked.

"You're looking at one," Bram said, pointing at the plaited crystal tower that rose into the sky with its impaled passenger vehicle still hanging from it like a spitted egg. "The Nar had a scheme for building a number of space docking stations on the same principle. Eventually they looked forward to a whole ring of them around the equator of the Father World, linked together for stability. It was well within the limits of theoretical possibility. But the Nar thought in terms of thousands of years, and there was no particular sense of urgency, oxygen and biologically produced alcohol for shuttle fuel being as cheap as they were."

"The big difference here," Jao rushed in, "is that Original Man's skyhook used *two* tethers, anchored fifty miles apart. That was important. Even if they came together at the apex of an isoceles triangle twenty-odd thousand miles up, the slight lean from the true vertical wouldn't have mattered that much. Not with the materials *they* had available."

"Okay, you've got your twelve moons, bobbing up there like captive balloons, and connected to make a dodecagon—"

"To make a *circle*, Bram. The line bellies outward."

"Okay, a circle. What next?"

"Next they started *spinning* the world. Faster and faster. At the same time, they began playing out more of their superfilament. They must have fed it out in a liquid form that instantly hardened—"

"There was a terrestrial animal called a spider that did that biologically," Ame put in.

"Yah, I wouldn't know about that. Anyway, they probably fed in the raw materials at the poles, from a couple of big gas clouds they had parked out in space. The oxygen and carbon could've come from carbon dioxide they siphoned off a hothouse-type planet—there's one of those in almost every G-star system, same as gas giants. *That* must've been a sight to see—the two big vortices whirling from the poles millions of miles into space, while the tethered moons spun out farther and farther weaving a gossamer web between them."

"You don't think small, I'll give you that." Bram laughed.

"*Now* you start extruding your foam—mountains of it, oceans of it, following the network of filaments into orbit, the trapped bubbles of gases blowing the material up to two or three thousand times its volume before the molecules cross-link and become rigid. It maintains the disk shape, reaching a predetermined orbit at the limit of the spin force, with an excess material falling back to the surface. Foam that squeezes laterally through the web shears off, making a nice smooth face. Depending on the altitude, the excess stuff either slides outward or falls back to the hub. It's *exactly* like the preliminary stages of the formation of a protostar...or...or a galaxy! The material settles more and more into a flat rotating disk! But now, with the growth of the disk, angular momentum is transferred and the spin slows down! So you get the stable situation we see here, with the moons traveling just a *little* faster—or lower—than they ought to be for synchronous orbit and maintaining the tension that helps hold the whole structure together."

He stopped, out of breath.

"What's happened to your rocky world at the center?" Bram asked.

"Oh, *that*? It's smeared all over the faces of the disk. *Some* of it's been flung out beyond the rim and fallen back, and we're standing on it. And the *rest* of it's a plug in the hole at the center of the disk, where the gravity is perpendicular to the disk surface. "It's *heavy* there, that close to the center of gravity, I promise you!"

"What about it, Enry?" Bram said.

"It could be." The geologist's voice was muffled; he must have turned his head away from the helmet mike to check data. "I've got samples that could have come from the rocky core of a gas giant that broke up. Silicates that show signs of once having been under tremendous pressure. Millions of atmospheres worth—the kind of pressure that turns molecular hydrogen into metallic hydrogen. The paleomagnetism's interesting. The orientation's every which way. As if the samples originated elsewhere and were scattered all over the place."

"What did I tell you?" Jao sounded smug.

"There's something else," Enry drawled.

"What?"

"The rocks show that there's a steady leakage of gases from the interior of this . . . world. Oxygen, and carbon dioxide, and lighter gases like nitrogen and helium. The rim can't hold on to an atmosphere, of course. But there could be a considerable amount of gas still trapped in the . . . cavities that Jao postulates." There was a moment of silence with an unmistakable frown in it. "More than there ought to be, from the rate of leakage, after seventy million years."

"The gases are subliming off the foamed surfaces," Jao said quickly. "And maybe off the superfilament as well. Nitrogen, did you say? I'm going to have to rethink the chemistry of it. Plenty of oxygen, that's for sure. Hey, we might be able to tap into it during our stay—take some of the load off Yggdrasil!"

"How far down would we have to drill to tap atmosphere?" Bram asked.

"I don't know. It would take some pretty fancy mathematics to figure out the thickness of the crust, based on too many variables—the size of the original core, rate of spin-up, disk gravity gradients, surface friction affecting the dispersion of material . . . I think we'll have to rely on Enry's empirical methods. Theory fails in a case like this. It can't be much, though."

"Those bare paw prints," Ame said. "Do you suppose . . ."

"Forget it, Ame. Any atmosphere belched out from the interior would instantly disperse. You'll have to find another explanation."

"There was life here within the last few million years—I'm certain of that," she said stubbornly. "It's . . ."

"What's the matter, Ame?" Bram said.

She flashed her light around the base of the moonrope. "Look," she said.

The tracks had been easy to miss in the permanent red twilight, especially when there was the awesome sight of that crystalline pillar drawing your eyes up instead of down. And the reflected light from directly above had tended to wash out the long, diffuse shadows cast by the horizon-filling sliver of the companion diskworld that rose above the brink.

But once you had noticed them, it was hard to see how the eye had skipped over them. Shallow as they were, they were perfectly plain, like inked thumbprints, a little smudged where the tiny paws had scrabbled in the dust. The myriad trails meandered a bit. But in the end pointed toward the soaring cable.

"They climbed it," Ame said. "That's where they went. They climbed to the moon."

They had six hours to explore the central complex, Lydis told them. After that, they would begin to tax the walker's ability to replenish their air supply. "I don't want you to use your reserve bottles at all," Lydis said. "That's cutting it too close. I want you to come in with your reserve bottles intact. Understood?"

"Understood," Bram told his daughter. He sighed. It had been five hundred years since she had been a little girl, but every once in a while it felt strange to be taking orders from her.

Ame was scrambling happily all over the mounds of rubble, leaving little electronic markers that would give off coded transponder signals when asked.

"Site number twenty," she dictated to one of them. "Probable auditorium or lecture hall." She followed with a series of dimensionless coordinates that would be fitted later into a triangulation grid by a computer.

"How can you tell it's an auditorium?" Bram asked. "It's just another dust pile, as far as I can see."

"It's fan-shaped," she said, tossing him a grin over her

shoulder. "We tend to think that public halls are supposed to be circular, with a stage in the center, because of the Nar influence. But this is a much more natural shape for human beings. And see, the focal point—abutting what might be classrooms or administrative offices   is at about the limit of distance from which a live lecturer or performer could be seen to any effect."

Bram followed her around as best he could, climbing in and out of the walker, helping with the measurements, and operating the little portable thumper that located cavities beneath the surface.

"Libraries," Ame exulted. "I'm sure of it. And museum warehouses and storehouses and depots and vaults for frozen samples. And all the support and recreational facilities you'd need for the population of millions that it would have taken to run this outpost—hydroponic farms, maybe even zoos! This will be a treasure trove for the archaeologists, Bram-*tsu*! And there'll be middens—we'll find seeds and organic refuse and bones . . ."

He didn't like leaving her alone while he went off on his own side forays, and at one point he coaxed her into the walker for an excursion to the rim's edge.

"Don't go out any farther," he warned. "I don't know how secure this thing is."

They were standing on the great skeleton arm of a gantry that extended out over the abyss—part of some sort of transport system that traveled an unknown distance down the face. Bram could see the stanchions that once might have supported an elevator or funicular dwindling with distance till they disappeared.

Hundreds—possibly thousands—of miles down the sheer face began a glittering fairy forest of tiny filaments that swept in a great arc until they could no longer be distinguished against the knife edge that cut the black night ninety million miles below.

"The feed array for the antenna system," Bram said. "There must be others, equally spaced around the disk, aimed at a reflector at the hub."

By this time they had worked themselves through to the opposite edge of the disk, facing the intergalactic night.

The antenna complex was lit from above by ruddy moonlight.

The buried city, limned by mounded avenues of detritus, stretched all the way across the diskworld from rim to rim. And Jao had been right: There was another set of cables climbing to the moon on this side, too.

"So this," Ame said, "was the voice of the human race?"

"Yes." Bram dug through the centuries for an old memory. "My teacher, Voth, once said that humankind had learned to tame a sun's power to shout across the gulf between the galaxies, but he couldn't imagine how."

He mused at the phased array, wondering at the scale that would allow its nearer ranks to be seen at such a distance. The elements must be miles high to be even remotely distinguishable—cantilevered or guyed against the topsy-turvy gravity. But that would have presented no problem to a race with moonrope at its disposal. And the gravity would be mild for the next few million miles, anyway. It would be a different story at the hub, where gravity would be crushing. Perhaps there were phase shifters installed at a safe radius. He would send an expedition down the face to see—in a space vehicle. And the physics would have to be carefully worked out so that the explorers would not find themselves slammed against a wall that had become a floor.

Bram shuddered at the thought of the mighty energies that once had been dispensed by that distant forest. In operation, it would have been a microwave inferno that would have sizzled a man to a crisp in milliseconds. No wonder a healthy stretch of no-man's-land had been left—and not just to get past the gravitational edge effects.

Bram inched farther out on the gantry for a better look. Jao was going to insist on a full description. Too energetic a toe push sent him doing a handstand, and he walked a few steps on his hands before his boots settled down, holding on for dear life and being careful not to let go with one hand before he had a firm grip with the other. The asterioid-strength gravity was deceptive, he knew. He still had all his mass, and it was a long way to fall. Already, though he was no more than fifty yards over the edge, he knew that the horizontal component of the disk-world's complex gravity was tugging every atom of his body toward itself in a complicated vector. He would have had to crawl out another million miles or so to feel anything, of course, but it was there nevertheless. But if he were to fall past reach of a handhold, he would be accelerated inexorably—at the dreamlike rate of about one thirty-millionth of a foot per second to start—until, at an unknown fraction of the distance to the center, the reaching forces of the disk would slam him into the tilted wall-scape at a velocity sufficient to abrade him into a long, wet smear.

It didn't help a whit to realize that he'd have been long dead of suffocation, thirst, or boredom before that happened.

Bram stopped his balloonlike four-limbed outward prowl and wrapped himself securely around a thick strut with an arm and a leg while he surveyed the cliff face from his improved vantage point.

There was movement beside him, and then Ame was pressed up next to him, peering past his shoulder into the abyss.

"I thought I told you to stay put," Bram said.

"Don't be silly, Bram-*tsu*. I'm perfectly able to take care of myself. What could possibly happen?" She leaned out alarmingly. "Do you think we have enough time to climb down there for a look at some of those caves?"

"*No!*" he said, hearing himself sputter. In a more reasonable tone of voice, he said, "We'll come back later with ropes and proper climbing equipment and a team of trained outside workers. Maybe we'll round up a few tame climbers from Yggdrasil's vascular system and ride *them*. And the *climbers* will wear safety lines, too!"

"It was just an idea," she said mildly.

She unclipped her torch from her belt and played it over the vertical surface below. Seen up close, Jao's "smooth face" was pocked with great pits and hollows. Looking at this cross section of a world, Bram could see where the crust began, a few miles below, like frosting on a slice of cake. The artificial material beneath was thinly covered with dust, and all sorts of domes, bulges, and the craters of burst bubbles poked above the rubbish of the sundered planet that had been used as a starter.

Closer at hand, vacuum welding over the eons had cemented a rocky cliffside in place. But here, too, even the languorous stresses that the diskworld was heir to had from time to time torn great chunks of material loose and left a pattern of cracks and cavities.

Ame's beam found one of the holes. "I wonder how deep—" she began, and stopped.

A pair of animal eyes shone in the beam of light for a startled second, then whisked out of sight.

"Oh!" Ame squeaked. She dropped the torch. It seemed to hang in space beside her, the light beam revolving in lazy circles. Ame recovered before the torch had drifted down more than an inch or two, caught it by the wrong end, and got it pointed at the cave again.

"Did you see it, too?" she whispered.

"Yes," Bram said.

There was life in this place. And it was shy.

They stayed clinging to their dizzy perch until Lydis's radioed warnings about their reserve air supply became too impatient to ignore. But the beady, luminous eyes never reappeared.

"It's hunkered at the back of the cave, waiting for us to go away," Ame said.

"Or there's a way out through the rear," Bram suggested. "There may be a whole system of burrows."

She had tried the light in every opening it would reach. Far below, at the limit of the beam, they thought they saw a pair of pinpoints of reflected light for the briefest flash, but it was impossible to be sure. Finally, when Lydis began making threats, they gave up and hauled themselves back along the gigantic crane arm to the security of the rim.

They had left the walker parked a short distance away in a square at the intersection of two avenues of raised gravel. As they approached it, there was an explosion of movement around it, and dozens of small furry forms streaked away into hiding.

Bram gave a start. The little beasts were gone in an instant, before he had time to react.

"We scared them off," he said.

"They must have been watching us the whole time, everywhere we went," Ame said. "The ones here got up the courage to investigate the walker when we were gone so long."

A wary little face peered out from around a block of stone, then jerked back as Ame's light beam found it. Bram had a quick impression of huge round eyes, button nose, tiny mouth, and the flash of a bushy tail.

He found himself laughing. "They're curious," he said.

"They're descended from terrestrial life," Ame said. "That's for certain. Like every picture I've ever seen. Everything in pairs—eyes, ears, limbs—just like us! And they're furred—they're not only vertebrates but mammals, too!"

"But how do they breathe vacuum?"

"I wonder . . . they've had millions of years to adapt to this place. Have you ever heard of whales?"

"I know the word. Stands for something big."

"It was a real animal once. It adapted to a new environment, too. It learned to go for long stretches without breathing."

They were at the walker now. The biovehicle was in the same kneeling position they had left it in. Bram gave Ame a boost, and she hoisted herself up to the passenger bubble. Then she froze.

"Bram-*tsu*! Look!"

He levitated to a position beside her, and she grabbed his arm. One of the little animals was trapped inside the bubble, scurrying about frantically, looking for a way out.

He stopped her as she as about to insert herself into the bubble. "Wait. Let's see if we can shoo that thing out of there first."

"Why? What harm could it do?"

"I don't like the look of those little teeth."

"It's more afraid of us than we are of it. Oh, *look* at it, Bram-*tsu*! It's so *small*! It's just a little *baby*! It must have gotten separated from its mother. It's terrified."

Without waiting for a response, she swan-dived through

the lips of the bubble. Bram followed, letting out at least a pound of air pressure in his haste.

"The poor thing," Ame said, reaching for the small creature. It cowered against the far side of the transparent bubble, chittering at them. It was a little roly-poly thing, a ball of soft brown fluff with enormous golden eyes that were mostly round pupil.

"Ame, don't touch it."

"Nonsense! It couldn't bite me through my vacuum suit even if it tried."

She picked the creature up. It squirmed in her grasp, then seemed to give up. A moment later it was in the crook of her arm, clinging to her with four tiny grasping paws.

"It wants its mother," Ame said. "Look, Bram-*tsu*, there's a third eyelid for when it's outside."

He bent closer and saw the transparent nictitating membrane flick across the golden eye when the creature blinked at him.

"And little flaps for the ears, too," he added, noticing the folds of pink flesh that creased reflexively to close off the entrance to the ear canal when he leaned too close, as if the little animal were trying to shut him out of its world.

"I think you're scaring it," Ame told him.

"No, it's getting used to me."

There were similar little flaps for the nostrils, but the creature's nose twitched as it sniffed at him, and the flaps stayed open.

"I've seen pictures of fur, but I never dreamed it could be so *soft*," Ame said dreamily. "Sort of like the twins' hair, only all over. It makes you want to stroke it."

"Ame, you keep those gloves on."

"All right," she said, patting the little beast with a gauntleted hand. It responded to the touch by snuggling up closer against her and wrapping its tail around her arm.

"We've got to start back," Bram said. "We'll come back and study them."

"Jorv will be pleased," Ame said. "All of a sudden, zoology isn't a theoretical science anymore."

"We'd better leave it here. We don't have the facilities

for keeping it alive during the trip back to the tree. It might not survive."

"Bram-*tsu*, I love you. You're a biologist, but it never even *occurred* to you to take it back as a specimen."

"Well, I . . ." He flushed. "There'll be plenty of time to study these animals at our leisure, find out what they eat, take tissue samples without hurting them."

It was the Nar influence, he supposed—growing up among beings whose respect for any sort of conscious life was innate. Bram hoped the human race wouldn't lose that trait with the passage of generations, but he had heard a few rather cold-blooded remarks from some of the younger tree dwellers.

"I hate to give it up," Ame said. "It's so cuddly and cute. You know, Bram-*tsu*, it's all fluff. Underneath, it's all scrawny."

Reluctantly, she pried the small clinging creature from her body and eased it through the lips of the bubble. Bram saw the little fleshy flaps wink into place over ears and nostrils, and the creature's fur seemed to puff up still further. Then it was floating to the ground with chubby grace, its tiny prehensile paws outstretched for contact.

It scampered off immediately. A larger beast darted from a cranny to intercept it, bowled it over, and nudged it with a button nose to a perch on her back.

"It's found its mother, anyway," Ame said with relief.

The mother beastie stood up on her haunches to bare her teeth at Ame and Bram, then scurried away with the baby fluffball clinging to her fur.

"I discovered them, and I'm going to name them," Ame said. "I'm going to call them Cuddlies."

CHAPTER 8

The airless streets were filled with space-suited tourists from the tree these days. They gawked at the massive excavated buildings, hunted for souvenirs in the rubble, and generally got in the archaeologists' way. About a quarter of the population could be found on the surface of the diskworld at any given time, and the proportion was increasing as quickly as pressurized accommodations could be provided and atmosphere plants cloned.

Bram strolled down the broad, roughed-out avenue with Mim at his side, trying to keep his feet on the ground and rubbernecking like anybody else. A lot had been accomplished since his last visit; duties aboard the tree had kept him busy there for several Tendays. The tops of more buildings had emerged from the gray dust, and the tallest of them now stood at a height of twenty feet or more.

"It's coming to life again," Mim said, reading his thoughts. "You can almost imagine what it must have been like."

"Hundreds of thousands of people going about their business—more than ever existed on the Father World, let alone gathered in one place," Bram agreed. "We've found shops, theaters, even a sports arena where they played a game in midair with a ball and stick, and you were out of bounds when your feet touched the ground. And we've only begun to dig."

Mim said wonderingly. "So *many*! As many as the Nar! And it looks crowded to me with only a few thousand here!"

"Most of the shirt-sleeve traffic between buildings would have been through the tunnel system. Still, it must have been pretty lively on the surface."

Two space-suited people walked by, bearing a huge slab of granite that seemed to be covered with bas-reliefs. They were walking almost normally, thanks to the tons of mass that kept their boots pressed to the ground. One of them freed an arm to wave at Bram and Mim as they passed. The slab dipped, but the person caught it before it floated too far down out of its inertial path.

Bram waved back, frowning within his helmet. "I wonder where they got that," he said. "They're supposed to leave things in place till an archaeologist can have a look at the site. There are too many helpful amateurs wandering around."

"Does it matter?"

"Very much, apparently. Ame says that the way finds are sited tells them as much as the finds themselves. And with bones especially, there's a question of missing pieces."

"Those long-footed skeletons?"

"She's got some fairly complete ones. There's a question about the dating. She sent word that there's something she wants to discuss with me."

"And lots of Cuddly bones?"

"Yes, and some they can't identify. She thinks that they may have been pets of Original Man."

Mim gave a subdued shudder and linked arms with Bram. "Ugh—bones! Still, it makes a good excuse for an excursion. The view gets more spectacular all the time."

They both looked toward the horizon at the half-risen disk. It was a swollen red orb that stretched across most of the sky, its oblique angle squashing it out of shape. A smaller disk, back-to, made a black shadow across the glowing field. With the overhead moon brightening up, the diskworld was a reasonably well lit place these days— about on a par with the Father World nights when the lesser sun had been in the sky.

They had been in the system long enough for the diskworld's rotation to bring this segment of the rim down almost to the plane of orbit. Yggdrasil, after some complicated maneuvering, was about a quarter diameter behind them again and catching up fast. At present, the trip from the tree took eleven days, the trip back even longer, but that didn't stop the excursionists. With Yggdrasil renewed and the crust of the diskworld itself to tap, there was fuel literally to burn.

They continued their shuffling stroll. A Cuddly popped up out of a hole in the ground in front of them, sat up on its haunches, and gave them a fearless, big-eyed stare. The little animals had quickly allowed their natural curiosity to overtake their initial caution of human beings, and now they were all over the place.

Mim gave a cry of delight. "Aren't they cute? Look at those clever little paws! They're almost human! Can we take one back with us?"

"Why not? Half the people on the tree seem to have adopted a Cuddly. Or vice versa. They're easy to tame, they eat anything, and they're nice to have around."

There had been some fear at first that the little burrowing beasts would spread uncontrolled through Yggdrasil's vessels and passageways and perhaps interfere with the tree's internal ecology. But that hadn't been the case. The Cuddlies seemed to prefer human company, and they hung around the living quarters, attaching themselves to a particular person or family. They were affectionate little things, rubbing against a person's leg until picked up and stroked, or even forcing matters by climbing up themselves to an arm or a shoulder. They were also shameless little beggars. Few people could resist them. They had quickly discovered all the outside exits, and during Yggdrasil's "night" they liked to prowl about in naked space, among the leaves and branches. They could go an hour or more without breathing, living off the compressed oxygen in their accessory lungs or trapped in their amazing fur with its overlapping erectile follicles.

"Oh, look, I think it's begging for food," Mim exclaimed. "Do you have anything with you?"

"Afraid not. I had half a cornwich in one of my sealpockets, left over from the shuttle snack bin, but I threw it away when we helmeted up."

The big-eyed little furball, its coat fluffed out for vacuum, was balancing itself on one foot and its tail, holding out its right paw and right foot in tandem, like a pair of tiny human hands. It held the pose for a long moment, decided that Bram and Mim weren't worth bothering with, and scooted off to find a better prospect.

"Oh!" Mim said, disappointed. "What are they, Bram? Were they brought here by Original Man?"

"Ame doesn't think so. They're too recent. She's found the bones of what seems to be a transitional form they may have evolved from—and *that* only goes back about twenty million years. Before that, there's a gap. All we know so far is that they have terrestrial DNA."

The avenue they were walking along was one of the spokes of the great circular plaza that centered on the moon ladder—the initial dig had started here, and so far about a square mile of the surrounding city had been dug up. Now, as Bram and Mim emerged into the open spaces of the plaza, they both looked up.

A climber was coming down from the moon, an angular leggy shape that was silhouetted against the eerie red glow of the rising disk. As they watched, the artificial creature detoured around the stalled moon car, stepping carefully over the smooth surface and finding a foothold on the rope below. The climber was wearing a transparent ten-legged space suit that had been designed by, of all people, Marg; it included an extra tuck of material that fit over the passenger cup and billowed out to provide a habitable bubble for the five-hour climb.

"They've found Cuddlies on the moon, too," Bram said. "Whole colonies of them. They've been established there for millions of years—and apparently they still travel back and forth. We've found fresh footprints around the rope. How they do it is a mystery. Even with a stop at the turnover station. Young Jorv thinks they have some way of taking extra air along, but that seems farfetched, clever little beasts though they are." He gave a wide grin. "Of course, now they're spoiled—they hitch rides with us in the climbers."

"Are they digging up there, too?"

"Yes. We've found the remains of some tremendous engineering structures—extrusion devices on a scale that can hardly be imagined. Evidently, the original engineers played out the supporting filament from both ends when they were manufacturing this world."

"So Ang told me. Jao can hardly contain himself now that his theory of suspension construction's been vindicated."

"We're trying to verify it at this end, too. We've sunk several shafts at a slant and found that the moonrope extends as far down as we're able to reach. We've gone past the crust now—it's easy with digging machines in this low gravity—and penetrated through to the foamed understructure. We have to proceed carefully, though, to avoid disturbing the Cuddly burrows. They're thick in the vicinity of the rope—it seems to be a main travel route downward. When the excavators started, they burst some of the bubbles and let the air out."

"Oh, Bram, did they—"

"Relax. You can't kill a Cuddly by taking away its air—they had plenty of time to squeeze through their little tunnels to the adjoining cavities. We messed up their gardens, though. No wonder the little rascals are such beggars."

"Gardens?"

"Yes, we've uncovered a whole ecology down there. Jorv thinks that the ancestors of the Cuddlies carried seeds back from their surface foraging expeditions to the old granaries and warehouses of Original Man. Buried the seeds in their dens or excreted them—and some were still viable enough to sprout. Millions of years of evolution would have done the rest. And they would have carried bacteria, fungus spores—even algae—too. There's insect life down there as well, marvelously adapted to the environment."

"How can things grow in the dark?"

"There's no visible light, true, except for bioluminescence. But the whole interior of the diskworld is suffused with infrared because of its energy-trapping structure, and the plant life's learned to use it. For that matter, the Cuddlies themselves see quite well in the far red. Jorv suspects that the Cuddlies may even take a hand in cultivating some of the edible plants. That's not unheard of in the animal kingdom. Something called an ant once did it—

grew a fungus crop in its nest. Planted it, fertilized it, even chewed leaves to mulch it."

"Could the Cuddlies be that smart?"

"It would be instinctual behavior. A survival characteristic developed through the ages. Mim, we're finding out so much about terrestrial life from the books and microrecords in the libraries we've unearthed and from studying the organisms in the Cuddly burrows. Earth must have been a wonderful place! There were flying things that wove nests, rodents that built dams! Animal societies that cared for their young cooperatively! And we're a part of that richness and diversity!"

She reached for his gloved hand and gave it a clumsy squeeze. "I know. Life will never be the same again." She darted a a mischievous glance at him. "The food, for one thing. Marg's been experimenting with some of those frozen seeds that were found in storage. She says we'll soon be eating something called an artichoke."

Bram laughed. "She'll have us eating King James's forbidden fruit next."

"We already are," Mim said quite seriously. "Wasn't that the fruit of the tree of knowledge?"

Bram sobered. "More knowledge than we can absorb during our stay here. We'll have to come back someday, Mim, after we find our world and get settled." He took her by the arm. "Come on, we'd better find Ame and find out what she has to tell us."

The archaeologists had chosen the big sports arena as their headquarters. It was the only place large enough to reassemble some of their finds. Most of it was still underground, a tall interior space that the diggers had gained access to after excavating only a couple of layers.

Bram and Mim followed the vehicle ramp downward to a domed receiving area where several of the monstrous Nar digging machines were parked awaiting service and a number of heavy-duty walkers were being carefully unloaded under supervision. A driver going off duty let them in through one of the small prefabricated personnel locks that had been ferried down from the tree and installed here.

The living quarters were a careless jumble of plastic cubicles around the perimeter of the dig. Bram and Mim gratefully accepted an offer of showers and fresh tunics before going on through to the huge cylindrical cavity proper; several hours in a space suit doesn't do much to make a person presentable.

Banks of powerful lamps had been mounted far overhead as work lights. In their harsh glare, the cavernous interior took on a stark pattern of bright surfaces outlined by black shadow. Small groups of people in smocks or tabards were scattered across the immense broken floor, working at some of the hundreds of long tables where fragments of artifacts were being sorted and cataloged. More treasures were on display along the tiers of former spectator balconies in arrangements that made sense to the various specialists.

The larger reconstructions, some of them fairly complete, rose at intervals from the floor. Bram saw an articulated eight-wheeled surface vehicle taking shape—a series of portholed balls connected by flexible access tubes—and a towering plinth with the legs of a colossal metal statue still attached to it. Elsewhere, a section of wall with an engraved gate was being put together from a pile of stone blocks.

Bram pointed upward. "You can see where we patched the roof to pressurize the place—and we only had to do that because we broke through it ourselves. Otherwise, we only had to put in a few minor seals to make the place airtight again. They built well, these former humans. The supporting walls were fused stone and carbon, yards thick."

"What kind of games did they play here?"

"We've found clues to that in some bas-reliefs we dug up. One game was played with a ball and paddles. You struck the ball with a paddle or kicked it with a foot while flapping the paddles to try to stay aloft as long as possible. There was a variation played only with a stick—the players dropped faster, and the plays were shorter. If you'll look way up toward the ceiling past the lights, you'll see the remnants of the drop grid. At the beginning of each play the teams were released simultaneously at a signal, in their starting positions."

They continued threading their way between the tables across the wide floor. Progress was tricky because the floor was not smooth enough for a low-gravity scuff, and there was a tendency to bounce too high when surmounting some block of rubble—but they couldn't sail over the obstacles, either, because they had to be careful of the tables.

"They drank out of strange cups," Mim said, pausing at a table spread with shards of plastic ware.

Bram examined one of the more complete cups, a two-handled affair whose top tapered into a sort of spout that one could put into one's mouth, almost like a nipple.

"Actually, that's not such a bad design for a low-gravity environment. Prevents sloshing. Better than our own lidded cups," Bram observed.

"That's not what I meant. It's the handles. They don't seem to fit the hand very well. I'd find it very awkward to drink from one."

Instead of being designed for one or two fingers and an opposing thumb, the handles were fat knobs with five vertical grooves. Bram could see what Mim meant. If one were going to hold a cup with two hands as if it were a bowl, the natural tendency would be to cradle it laterally, in the direction the wrists faced. If handles were needed at all, the grooves ought to have been horizontal—and there ought to have been only four of them, with a depression for the thumb on the opposite side.

"Maybe their wrists were more supple than ours," he said. He smiled at a sudden comic image. "Or maybe they had no elbow room at their tables."

"I'm serious."

"So am I. About the wrist joints, anyway. Mim, what if Original Man *didn't* become extinct seventy-odd million years ago, as we've always thought? What if he evolved past us—past the image of himself that he transmitted to the Virgo cluster?"

"Have you talked to Edard about the musical instruments?"

"What? No, Edard leads his own life these days. I haven't seen him for a ten of Tendays."

"They put him on one of the evaluation committees. Asked for his thoughts on fragments that seemed to belong to musical instruments. There's a sort of pottery . . . flute, I'd guess you'd call it, in the shape of a tapered ovoid. It has finger grooves like the cups. And Edard says that the finger holes are placed in a peculiar way. It would make it almost impossible to play."

"Well, perhaps Ame has an answer. Here we are. This is her bailiwick over here."

He steered Mim toward one of the open bays on the perimeter of the floor, under the overhang of the first balcony. The bay was perhaps a quarter acre in extent. The bones didn't take up as much room as the artifacts.

Ame came over to greet them. Her handful of assistants were working at tables with brushes and scrapers and buckets of plaster. One bushy-headed fellow was glued to a computer screen that showed animated images comparing the ways hip joints rotated.

"Bram-*tsu-fu*, Mim-*tsu-mu*!" she said, her face radiant with pleasure. "I'm so glad you could come!"

"How are the twins?" Mim asked, giving her a matriarchal kiss.

"Jabbering. And getting into things. Smeth's watching them now. We have rooms at the guest house across the moon plaza. But I think I'm going to ask him to take them back to the tree. The low gravity isn't good for their bones while they're growing." She laughed. "Besides, they're enough trouble in two dimensions without having them flying through the air as well."

Bram looked across at the row of skeletons wired upright to metal stands. "It looks as if you've put together some fairly complete specimens since I was here last."

"Yes," Ame said, looking pleased. "We were lucky enough to stumble across a burial ground. They seem to have interred their dead with much ceremony. That was a bonus. We're learning quite a lot about their technology from the grave-objects. Don't be deceived, though. The skeletons aren't *quite* as complete as they look. We've filled in a few missing parts with plaster and resin by mirror-imaging, inference, trading bones, and so forth."

Bram stopped the eager flow of words with a raised eyebrow. "Burial ground?" he repeated. "What did they die of?"

"Accidents, some of them. Degenerative diseases. Old age."

"Old age!" Mim exclaimed. "But human beings are immortal!"

"Not always, Mim," Bram reminded her. "The immortality virus was an *addition* to Original Man's message. It came somewhere between the cycles of the transmission." He turned expectantly to Ame. "The burial ground must have dated from the earlier epoch of the diskworld, then?"

"No," Ame said. "That's the problem. We haven't dug down that far yet. Though the levels are mixed in ways they ought not to be—they've been disturbed."

"How recent, then?"

"From everything we can surmise from the skeleton remains, the grave objects, the kitchen middens, and all the rest—the most recent habitation of this city was only about twenty-eight to thirty million years ago."

"Original Man's heyday was more than twice as long ago as that. Could you be mistaken?"

"Radiometric dating confirms that figure pretty much."

"Original Man's civilization fell," Mim offered. "They lost their immortality. Forgot everything. Struggled up from barbarism. Then a new civilization emerged. Went star traveling again. Found humanity's old beacon and began digging through the ruins—same as we're doing."

"That might fit," Bram said. "The mixed levels. And some of the artifacts. They're more primitive than the diskworld itself would suggest. That eight-wheeled jointed machine with the armored portholes and those crude metal-spring tires to absorb bounce in low gravity, for instance. Even we're beyond that, with our Nar technology. Doesn't it suggest a race with reborn self-confidence in the first flush of star travel?"

"Come over here," Ame said. "I want to show you something."

They followed her to the row of skeletons. A young assistant looked up from her work, smiled, and went back to wiring vertebrae together on a half-completed specimen.

"I've never seen a human skeleton, of course," Ame said. "Just Doc Pol's ultrasonic hologram of one. But you don't have to be an expert to see that these skeletons aren't right."

She switched on the hologram, which appeared in a tinted plastic booth at the end of the row of skeletons, like one more skeleton frozen in a block of ice. Bram glanced at it for comparison, then turned his attention to the others.

The long-footed skeletons were approximately human size and shape and looked remarkably similar to Doc Pol's study model if you discounted the long tail. But even without recourse to the hologram, Bram could spot the anomalies.

"They have the same general body plan as we do," Ame said, "and the same major bones in the same places. But the arms are too short. The upper and lower leg bones are in the wrong proportion. The thumb opposes, but it's the same length as the fingers. The cranial structures are wrong—the skull has about the same volume as ours, but it's long rather than domed. And the dentition is very different."

"And then there's the tail," Mim put in.

"Yes," Ame said. "Evolution might have made many changes in man over a forty-million-year period, but surely it would not have given him back his tail."

Bram chewed his lip. "It *is* possible, you know. There's such a thing as back mutation or reversion. The mechanism isn't well understood. But in this case you might envision it as the *loss* of a 'switch-off' **gene** that was an *earlier* mutation causing taillessness in some hominoid ancestor of man. The loss would leave the redundant tail genes that were still part of the DNA free to express themselves again."

"You mean we could all grow *tails* again?" Mim said, wide-eyed. "I don't think I'd like that!"

She cast a distinctly worried look at the short-armed,

long-footed skeletons with their long whiplashes of added vertebrae.

Bram laughed. "It must have complicated their space-suit design, I'll say that."

"Oh, we've found an almost intact space suit," Ame said. "The tail sheath was quite ingenious, with a whole series of little bleeder valves that allowed the tail to curl all the way around in a prehensile grip. Even in moderate gravity, they could have hung from their tails, leaving both hands free. We turned the suit over to one of the technology evaluation committees. You can see it on the upper balcony if you like."

"Ame, how large a population of them was there?"

"It's too early to answer that, but it must have been in the tens of thousands."

"Too few to have filled this city, too many to have been just a scientific expedition. Ame, what were they *doing* here?"

"I can't tell you that, either. We know that *one* of the things they were doing was exploring these ruins—just as we are. In fact, they've made our work a little easier. We've found at least one of their digs and its repository. They seem to have brought things up from a lower level—one where the artifacts definitely *were* made for hands like ours—and they've arranged and cataloged their finds most conveniently."

"Longfoot archaeologists."

"Yes. They seem to have been just as interested in Original Man as we are. But the level of archaeological activity wasn't high enough to explain their numbers. Otherwise, the whole place would have been dug up."

"And yet they lived and died here."

"For several generations, at least. We've found parts of children's skeletons, too, and fetal bones along with the skeleton of one pregnant female. Bram-*tsu*, they gave birth to a dozen young at a time."

"That doesn't sound like human beings," Mim said.

"No, not even after thirty million more years of evolution. But on the other hand, thirty million years before *our* line diverged from the hominids, our most probable direct ancestor was a small tree-dwelling animal called

Aegyptopithecus. It was about the size of a Cuddly and looked something like a cat." She halted. "Do you know what a cat was?"

"Yes. The little furry animals in the Goya painting."

Ame nodded. "So you see, a lot can happen in thirty million years, even in the human line. Tail aside, the longfoots don't seem that different from us."

Bram said, "Ame, what were they?"

"We're going to do some DNA studies and protein sequencing as soon as we can scrape together enough material. I'll let you know."

He got the answer to one of his questions a couple of Tendays later.

He was sitting in the cubbyhole he used as an office, going over Yggdrasil's accounts—one of the more onerous chores he had to do as year-captain. Enyd had sent him an enormous stack of tally sheets—glucose balance; starch reserves; projected production of fats, oils, alcohol, and glycine over the next kiloday; currently available hydrogen and oxygen—and he was expected to okay the allocations today, if not yesterday.

The rasp of the intercom made him wince.

"I'll get it!" Mim called. He heard her speak to someone, then she poked her head in and said, "That was Smeth from the trunk. The expedition's just docked. Trist is on his way down now."

"What's his hurry? You'd think he'd want a little time to collapse first and get reacquainted with Nen. Or at least allow himself to be lionized for a few hours."

Bram had been back on board Yggdrasil for only a few days himself; he'd left the disk city with the question of longfoot ancestry still unresolved. He'd had to plunge immediately into his accumulated paperwork and other duties, with no time to think about the matter further.

"Nen's in surgery with Doc Pol," Mim said. "Somebody managed to fall down a tracheid and smash an ankle. Trist prepared a preliminary report on the trip back. But he said he thought you'd want to know right away."

"Know what?"

"That," she said, "is what he's on his way down to tell you."

Trist arrived twenty minutes later; he must have been in free fall all the way. His yellow hair was disheveled, and he had a ripe space suit aroma—Lydis was still making her passengers suit up for drops and dockings—but he was full of unleashed energy, and his blue eyes, though rimmed with fatigue, sparkled.

He refused Mim's offer of tea—a new custom instituted by Marg after she had read about it in some of the library material that had been brought up from the disk-world, subsequently experimenting with infusions brewed from Yggdrasil's bark—and got right to the point.

"We did a thorough survey from space, of course," he said. "Went as close to the hub as Lydis dared. Spotted over a hundred of the sites over a nine-hundred-billion-square-mile area. Some of the structures were still inflated after all this time; others were flat as corncakes. It was pretty obvious what they'd been up to. But we couldn't be absolutely certain till we made a landing and deployed the climbers. We managed to visit four locations—brought back some goodies for the archaeologists, too."

"And," Bram said, knowing the answer, "what were they?"

"Camps," Trist said promptly. "Work camps. They must have lived there deciyears at a time, repairing antenna elements, installing their own equipment to fill in the breaks."

"They were trying to make the system operational again?"

"That's the only conclusion that can be drawn."

Bram leaned back and stared into space for a moment. "That would have been a tremendous undertaking, even with a work force of tens of thousands—or many times more than that, it may turn out. It would have meant committing themselves for generations."

"They were willing to do that, apparently. Bram, can you imagine the conditions they must have endured in those inflatable camps? The ones closer to the horizontal gravity sectors were built out on scaffolding—with no place even to *stand* for kilodays, except for the tents and stringers. Dangling over eternity all that time while they worked. It wasn't much better closer to the hub. Trying to adjust to the crazy angles, under heavy gravity with your weight tearing sideways at you. With the danger of falling with every step and an awareness of the penalties if you did. We didn't set foot within ten million miles of some of the farther camps, and I can tell you, I *still* didn't like it!"

Trist hadn't heard about the tails. Bram told him.

"Whew!" Trist whistled. "That explains it. You'd *need* a tail to work in a place like that."

"Ame thinks they may have been a species other than man. But the verdict isn't in yet."

"A new species to supersede man. I'm not sure I like that idea. It was one thing to deal with the idea that human beings were extinct. We've more or less accepted that from the beginning. But the idea of another species taking our place—that's something else again. Gives us competition in this neck of the galaxy, Bram. The planet Earth may be overrun by these long-footed characters. Where do we go, then?"

"They may be our cousins."

"Makes no difference. The fact that they were getting ready to patch up Original Man's beacon tells us all we need to know. Different species or different order entirely, they were preparing to spread their own image through the universe. It bears out that old idea we used to talk about long ago, before the Nar sped us on our way to this galaxy—that there comes a time in the life of every intelligent species when it begins to dawn on them that the means is at hand for species immortality."

"Yes, I remember."

"Now we've got three cases. Original Man, broadcasting his genetic code to the Virgo cluster and beyond. The Nar, sending us to the heart of their own galaxy to do the same job for them. And now these people with tails. Except that they're a little premature. They were able to take advantage of an installation that somebody else built. Bram, I just had another thought!"

"What is it?"

'You said that these tailed people weren't immortal.

Neither were the Nar. Neither was Original Man when he *started* broadcasting. What if this compulsion to spread around your genetic code is a stage that a species goes through *before* it attains personal immortality?"

"Hmmm. The night doesn't seem so dark, then. The universe isn't a bottomless hole. There's *time*. Time to travel to the ends of the universe yourself someday. At least that's what the little nagging voice inside you would be saying. Trist, you don't suppose..."

"That Original Man never became extinct? That he simply gave up, packed up and went home after he'd been infected with eternal life long enough for the idea to sink in?"

"Yes. And then, somewhere along the way, acquired an immunity to immortality. Forgot things. Evolved into a new species. And then one day set out on a path to the stars again. And found the old beacon."

"As I said before, it hardly matters. Whoever they were, they're not *us*."

"I'd like to send an expedition to one of the inner disks. And to the next disk ahead of us in orbit—see how close a duplicate it is to this one. We may have landed in the wrong place."

"I'd give my spare shirt to go. But Bram, there isn't time—"

"I'm going to call a tree meeting and call for a vote to stay here an extra year. We're digging up treasure troves of material—whole libraries of it, and we've only scratched the surface. I want to get as much material transferred to Yggdrasil as we can. We can't abandon a working party here, no matter how many eager volunteers there'd be. Not when the only habitable body in the known universe also happens to be our only starship. And there's no telling when we'll be back this way. It may be centuries before we grow another Yggdrasil and outfit it and can spare a population to crew it."

"A year." Trist furrowed his brow. "I'll have to work out some orbits. The distances are huge, of course, but it's not like ordinary interplanetary travel here...hmmm, we've got a body whose own orbital period is a year as our catapult, with no gravity to speak of to fight...add a modest boost . . . *de*boost to end up a hundred twenty degrees ahead . . . and for the return trip, a retro-orbit to *lose* orbital energy and rendezvous with your starting point in somewhat *less* than a year." He gave Bram an engaging smile. "But I get Nen to go along with me as a medical officer."

"Done," Bram said.

Mim appeared with a tray. "Don't worry, it isn't tea," she said. "Just old-fashioned cornbrew and some snacks."

"Mim watch out!" Bram shouted.

A little ball of fluff streaked between her ankles and almost tripped her. She recovered her balance and managed to keep the tray level without spilling anything.

"Loki!" she scolded.

The Cuddly scampered up Trist's leg, paused at his knee to be patted, then climbed to his shoulder and pulled at his yellow hair.

"Loki, get down and behave yourself," Bram said. He apologized to Trist. "He gets into everything."

"Oh, that's all right, we have one of our own," Trist said. He scratched the little creatures's neck. "Where'd you get the name?"

"Loki? It was an old human god who was always getting into mischief. It seemed to fit."

"Nen named ours Fluff. If she doesn't stop overfeeding it, we'll have to rename it Sphere."

"It's hard to resist one," Mim said. "They're the best thing we're taking with us from the diskworld."

Loki sat up and chittered at her as if he knew what she was saying. Trist broke off a corner of one of his cornsnacks and gave it to the little beast, which held the morsel in both paws and began nibbling at it.

"Yes," Bram said. "I think they mean more to us than we realize. They're the first terrestrial life form that humans have ever seen, after all."

"Other than vegetables," Trist said, popping a potato crisp into his mouth.

"Vegetables that we engineered ourselves or the Nar engineered for us. But Trist, just think of it, these little creatures carry an unbroken line of DNA that goes all the way back to the world that gave us birth."

"DNA calls out to DNA, is that it?"

"Something like that. We know without having to think about it that these little animals are a precious link with an earthly heritage."

Idly, Trist scratched the Cuddly behind one ear. It made a contented sound and snuggled against him. "There's something wrong there," he said lazily. "The first human being, as far as *we're* concerned, was mixed up in a test tube by a Nar bioengineer. From native materials."

"Ravel is Ravel," Mim said. "No matter what instruments play it."

"Hah! Good for you, Mim!" Trist conceded. "I'll desist." He took a sip of his drink. Loki tried to poke his muzzle into the cup, and Trist let him have a taste. The Cuddly sputtered and spat it out. Everybody laughed.

"Abstemious," Bram said. "Maybe we can learn something from them."

Trist fed the little pet another fragment of cornsnack to appease it. "It *would* be nice," he said, "to go home to an Earth that was inhabited by Cuddlies instead of those tailed people with the long skinny feet."

"Not likely," Bram said. "Ame says the Cuddlies evolved on the diskworld from more primitive forms. That isn't to say that some collateral branch with similar traits couldn't have evolved on Earth in the meantime." He frowned. "But we *know* what life form achieved dominance on Earth, don't we?"

"They were rats," Ame said.

She stepped back to let Bram have a better look at the exhibit that she and her section had prepared. Two of her colleagues—Jorv, the bouncy baby-faced zoologist whom Bram had met before, and a tall bony young woman named Shira, who was something called a "paleobiologist"—stood by with eager expressions on their faces.

Bram raised an eyebrow. "Rats? The pests of the 'Dappled Piper' legend?"

He scuffed cautiously closer. He hadn't had time to readjust to diskworld gravity yet, and he was still stiff and tired from the ferry trip to the surface, though it was down to five days now.

"*Rattus norvegicus* to be exact," Ame said. "The most successful member of the family and the one that would have been in the best position to succeed Original Man after man's activities had changed the environment. They were highly adaptable, they were omnivores as humankind's ancestors were, and in fact they resembled some of the primitive specimens on our own family tree."

The computer-generated hologram showed three skeletons in the same scale. The center one was a life-size projection of Ame's most complete longfoot skeleton—the one Bram had noticed when he first entered the workbay. He recognized the skeleton on the right, too. It was Doc Pol's familiar ultrasound figurine, the textbook example that Doc had learned his own trade from and that he now required his apprentices to memorize.

The third skeleton was something else entirely. Though the computer had made the bones stand in an upright position, the proportions were grotesque. The torso was absurdly long, with tiny little hands and feet and a head that was much too large for it. The bones would have been too spindly to support the creature in normal gravity. Bram saw immediately that the creature must have been a very small animal that the computer had brought up to the size of the other two skeletons for purposes of comparison.

Ame touched a button, and lines flashed from the center skeleton to the other two, showing correspondences. Though the longfoot skeleton and the human skeleton were superficially similar, it was immediately apparent that the disproportioned skeleton on the left had more in common with the longfoot specimen.

"You can see that what appears to be a backward-bending knee is actually what became a heel," Ame said. "The creature would have walked on its toes. The shaft of the leg bone became a long, narrow foot. And of course, the tail is there, bone for bone."

"Ame, this is marvelous," Bram said. "I'm enormously impressed. How did you do all this?"

She looked pleased. "We had a breakthrough. Literally. One of the digging machines broke through to a layer where the stratigraphy had been disturbed. The longfoots had been busy there. They had a—a sort of museum of their own there. And a library. And biosample vaults. They had brought up and catalogued a whole biological cornucopia preserved by Original Man. It must have come as a wonderful revelation to the longfoots. They were interested in their own ancestry, you see. Original Man's records predated their own fossil records."

Jorv's plump face beamed complacency. "Original Man did all the work for them," he said, "and they did all the work for *us*."

"We don't have enough archaeologists to go around," Ame said, "but all the amateurs are well trained by now. As soon as the digging machine operator saw what he was bringing up, he stopped, roped off the place, and notified the proper people."

"As soon as they saw they were bringing up biological specimens, they got *us*," Jorv bubbled. "You wouldn't believe it! There were mounted skeletons. Arranged in classifications. And metal plaques to explain them. And supplementary materials—actual books preserved in nitrogen. And tapes and holochips. In Inglex and Chin-pinyin. The longfoots probably couldn't read them, but we could—right away!"

The attenuated paleobiologist, Shira, ran nervous fingers through stringy brown hair. "And there were actual tissue samples, too, still in a remarkable state of preservation. The rat-people—longfoots—had broken some of the seals, but others were intact. We were able to extract enough DNA and protein for sequential analysis."

"There'll be more," Jorv interrupted. "We've only scratched the surface with this find. We're trenching now, looking for the rest of it. And they thought zoology was a theoretical science! Bram-companion, when we get to our world, we'll be able to recreate species! Stock our streams with trout, our forests with trees other than poplar! Did you know that Original Man had his own biovehicles—a sort of walker called a horse!"

"Well, that's certainly a program for the future," Bram said noncommittally.

Shira continued serenely, as if used to interruptions. "Until now, we've lacked the capacity to do molecular taxonomy in any meaningful way. Oh, we've been able to use cytochrome *c* sequencing to demonstrate that human beings are very far removed indeed from yeast—forty-five amino acid differences—not quite as far removed from cabbages, and closer still to heterochronic eggs. But now, of course, we have all those lovely tissue samples."

"Horses," Jorv said dreamily. "Zebras. Giraffes. Rhesus monkeys. Wolves. Original Man preserved them all."

"And of course we've brought up scads of mouse bones from our deeper excavations. Man inadvertently carried mice and other vermin to the diskworld with him—just as, I suppose, he carried them with him everywhere he went. The mice didn't manage to survive for long after humans departed the diskworld. They never adapted for airlessness, they weren't able to burrow deep enough, and they quickly exhausted the more easily available sources of food. We found no mouse bones more recent than seventy million years old. But they still contained traces of cytochrome *c*."

"And we had ourselves and Cuddlies available as a source of hemoglobin and serum albumin," Jorv said. "Oh, there was no doubt at all!"

Shira brushed her hair back. "The longfoots were at several removes from us and Cuddlies—well beyond the limits of family or genus, let alone species. Farther still from Jorv's giraffes, though we were able to do only DNA sequencing in that case. But the molecular differences between longfoots and mice—"

"*Mus musculus*," Jorv interjected. "Same family as rats. If you remember your childhood Chin-pin-yin, it's the same word. Big-mouse."

Shira spared a tolerant glance for Jorv and finished what she had been saying. "...but the molecular differences between longfoots and mice were practically nil."

Bram nodded at the longfoot skeleton. "That seems to settle it, then. Man did become extinct. And the next dominant species was that."

Ame said, "We found something else."
"What's that?"

"We know how the Cuddlies got here."

Bram picked his way down the tunnel, following Jorv's bobbing yellow light. Loose gravel under his feet started slow-motion cascades as he proceeded, coming to rest long after he had passed. The lanky paleobiologist was right behind him, shedding enough light of her own for him to see by, and Ame brought up the rear. Bram, as an escorted guest, went unburdened; the other three wore many-pocketed tabards over their space suits and lugged an assortment of picks, hammers, and other small tools.

After what seemed like an endless trek, the tunnel opened out into a wide, low-ceiling space shored up by timbers. Other tunnels branched off the space, glimmers of light from a couple of them showing the presence of other work parties.

The thick timbers were ordinary vacuum-poplar. Seeing them brought a lump of homesickness to Bram's throat till he remembered that vacuum-poplar had originated *here*, in the Milky Way, not in the Whirlpool galaxy.

Ame saw him looking. "The longfoots dug up a human lumberyard near here and took advantage of it. The wood must have been in vacuum and still good. Before that—" She indicated the branching tunnels where archaeological work was in progress. "—the longfoots used columns of native stone as well as steel griders that they brought with them. Evidently they didn't have much of a structural plastics industry. It bears out your theory that they were a young civilization, newly come to star travel, Bram-*tsu*."

"What was this place?"

"The longfoots had some of their own storehouses here. And living areas close by. We gleaned some insight into their social habits. There was some limited pair bonding in our sense, but mostly they lived in aggregates of fifty to a hundred members in which females were available to males on some kind of schedule of dominance. The living arrangements pointed to that, anyway. The females raised their young separately and cooperated in keeping males at bay for a period after parturition."

"They don't sound like a very pleasant people."

"Rats don't make very pleasant ancestors."

Bram shuddered, remembering the fragment of film Ame had been able to show him. It had been part of an exhibit associated with the mounted rat skeleton and had shown a bedraggled brown animal with beady eyes and a naked tail greedily eating its way thorugh a store of corn, excreting as it went. Bram had been ashamed of his instant and automatic revulsion, telling himself that the rat was a life form like any other, with a right to existence. But Ame had told him that his reaction wasn't unique— that rats seemed to raise the hackles of most humans.

"You're being narrow-minded, Ame," Jorv protested. "Seeing it from a human point of view. Different species, different biological imperatives. They might have been a perfectly decent folk. They acted cooperatively, after all."

"Come here, I want to show you something," Ame said.

She led Bram to a cache where specimens had been arranged with preliminary labels. There were bins of a dessicated, unfamiliar grain, shovel-size scoops, a broken ceramic jug.

But what caught Bram's attention was a small animal skeleton on a slab of wood. The skull was crushed, pinned to the slab by a copper bar that was attached to a large spring. But enough could be seen of the jaw to show that it was still clenched around something that looked like a fossil nut, which was attached by a wire to a sort of pivoting tray.

"A trap," Ame said. "The animal in it was a Cuddly."

Shira tossed her lank hair back within the bowl of her helmet. "They poisoned them, too," she said. "We've found piles of Cuddly bones around a feast of that same bait that one of them would have brought back to the burrow for the females and young ones."

Bram was appalled. "But what a terrible thing to do."

"No more terrible than what Original Man did to rats," Jorv said.

"The longfoots carried their own vermin into space with them, just as man once carried rats and mice," Ame said. "That's what the vermin were. Cuddlies."

"The Cuddlies' ancestral form, actually," Shira said. "They hadn't evolved for airlessness yet. You can see that the rib cage isn't enlarged for accessory lungs. And the toe of the rear foot is not fully opposable."

"But I think that if we were to see one of these creatures in its fur," Ame said, "we'd see it as a Cuddly."

Bram studied the trap with distaste. "Ingenious and cruel," he said. "The victim had to tug at the bait to pull it loose, and that released this strut that kept the spring armed. The animal's head would be in position for the copper bar. Even if its reflexes were good and it drew back, it would still get its neck broken."

"These little animals were *pests*," Jorv said. "They got into the longfoots' food supply. They were probably unsanitary. And they probably bit."

"The longfoots tried diligently to exterminate them back on Earth. We found a sort of children's picture book with a story about it. But the creatures must have been too clever, or too prolific, to be stamped out entirely. The longfoots must have been horrified to find that they'd transported them here."

"Well, the Cuddlies outlasted the longfoots here, at any rate," Bram said grimly. "Long after these . . . rat-people packed up and went back to Earth, The Cuddlies were able to survive on the diskworld long enough to adapt for vacuum. To adapt for space travel, when you stop to think about it—when you see the way they scamper around Yggdrasil's branches and seem to enjoy it."

"Their root stock must have adapted back on Earth, too," said Shira.

"Yes," Ame said. "If the human race was never able to exterminate rats, and the rats developed into an intelligent species after man was gone, the same might be true for the proto-Cuddlies. They might be the longfoots' successors back on earth by now. After all, they occupied a similar ecological niche."

"What a delicious thought, Ame!" Shira exclaimed. "A world ruled by cousins of the Cuddlies! But would a six-foot intelligent Cuddly be as *huggable*?"

Ame laughed. "I can hardly wait to get to Sol and see. But Bram-*tsu*, we mustn't leave till we finish our work here."

"That won't be for a while," Bram said. "We had an

all-tree meeting before I left. You've been voted an extra year."

The long plain was dotted with depots of crated material, each with a little band of partisans gathered around it vying for priority. Processions of cargo walkers, roped together in long caravans led by space-suited drovers, plodded across the starlit diskscape toward the staging areas where the rocket-assisted pallets were being loaded. All the wheeled vehicles had been pressed into service, too, and they could be seen bumping lazily across the flat vista, some of them achieving temporary flight.

Bram, helping Jun Davd to cinch a saddlebag full of astronomical data in place on a kneeling walker, paused in his work to watch a shower of sparks lift above the horizon and rise toward the blob of silver light that was Yggdrasil, hovering just to the right of the pendant moon.

"That's the third in an hour from the other side," he said. "The museum's launchpad, it looks like. They must be working overtime."

"They're overloading their pallets," Jun Davd said. "I'm surprised some of 'em got off the ground. I was over there yesterday helping the dispatcher to figure weights and balances, and we had to make them take off a big statue of three naked men wrestling a snake. Would have spoiled the trim—had the platform tumbling end over end. Had one of those art fellows almost in tears."

"I'm sure they got it off later."

"They've had a year and a half to loot that museum. I thought the idea was to take a small representative sample and leave the rest for the ages—or for whenever we can get back this way."

"You know how it is. All of a sudden we're about to leave, and they start having second thoughts. There's this last-minute rush. Everybody's suddenly discovered that there are things they just can't bear to leave behind—the historians, the archaeologists, the agronomists, everybody." He laid a hand on the saddlebags. "You, too, it looks like."

Jun Davd grunted. "It just occurred to me that it might be a good idea to abscond with part of the backlog of original plates—do you know, their astronomers were still recording images on light-sensitive paper for centuries after they had more advanced methods available? Oh, I've got all the electronically stored data I need, but it'll take years—decades—to go through it all, and I started worrying about accumulated signal errors."

"Have you made any more progress in locating Sol?"

"There are four candidates in the immediate stellar neighborhood. I've all but ruled out three of them—but I want to refine my mass estimates a bit further before I set a course out of this system."

"Waiting until the last minute, are you?"

Jun Davd hooked a thumb over his shoulder in the direction of the red-rimmed world-edge that overlooked the masked sun.

"I think I've identified our hidden friend, though. It must have been the star they called Delta Pavonis."

Bram tried not to show his disappointment. "Well, it's a possible reference point, I suppose. Though the relative positions of the stars in the neighborhood will have changed a lot in seventy-four million years."

"Delta Pavonis was almost Sol's twin," Jun Davd went on serenely. "It was a G-type star with ninety-eight percent of Sol's mass. It was about nineteen light-years distant. The other nearby G stars had masses of eighty or ninety percent of Sol, except for one called Beta Hydri— that was about one and a quarter solar masses—and one other exception. So the invisible star we're circling almost *has* to be either Sol or Delta Pavonis—and I think we've already agreed that Original Man would hardly have dismantled his own system for a radio station."

"Or it could be an interloper. A wanderer they used."

"In that case, the proper motion of *all* the nearby stars would be much greater than we've observed during our stay."

"Oh, right." Bram blushed like an apprentice. After more than five centuries of subjective time, Jun Davd could still make him feel like the little boy whom Voth had sent to the observatory to take astronomy lessons.

"The interesting thing is that the other exception is

also almost a twin of Sol—a G-4 of one point oh eight solar masses."

"So we still can't tell which—"

"Except for the fact that it was part of a triple star system that went by the name of Alpha Centauri. Which also happened to be Sol's closest neighbor—just a shade over four light-years away."

With mounting excitement, Bram began, "That means—"

Jun Davd nodded. "On the assumption that stars that close might have been gravitationally bound—however tenuously—I searched for matching G stars about that distance apart, one of which was part of a triple system." A grin spread slowly across his dark face. "They're still there, drifting hand in hand through the spiral arms, and they haven't changed position much with respect to Delta Pavonis, either."

"Jun Davd, you're incorrigible! I'll never forgive you for keeping me in suspense like that. How far?"

"Less than twenty light-years. Boosting at one gravity, we can be home in seven subjective years."

Home. The word had a strange ring to it. Bram slapped Jun Davd on the back. "Let's hurry and get started, then."

The walker, misinterpreting the slap, rose to its full height. The drover came over and said, "Are you ready to go?"

"In a minute," Jun Davd told him. He turned back to Bram. "There's one more datum."

"What's that?"

"The G star that seems to be Sol happens to be at the exact center of the sphere of radio clicks that's growing our way. As if it were the focal point."

"Original Man!" Bram whispered. "He *has* come back!"

Jum Davd shook his head. "That doesn't seem likely. We've had the longfoots in between. We may be about to meet the *next* contender on the evolutionary treadmill. Or Smeth may be right. It may be a natural phenomenon. In any case, we'd better go see."

He picked up the remaining pair of saddlebags and slung them over his own shoulder. The other walkers in the caravan, feeling the tug of the rope, struggled to their feet. In a few minutes, Bram and Jun Davd were following the swaying line of biotransports down the well-scuffed trail to the staging area.

There were plenty of willing hands at the other end to help the caravan unload. Ame was there, supervising the lashing of some bulky crates to an enormous wooden frame whose booster rockets, bolted to the corners and along the sides, must have added up to a hundred thousand pounds of thrust. Bram also spotted his son, Edard, clambering around at the top of a mountain of freight, unfurling a cargo net. Edard saw him and took a nicely calculated leap that brought him floating down to within a foot of where Bram and Jun Davd were standing.

"Hello, Father. Hello, Jun Davd. What have you got there? Documents mostly? If you have anything fragile, I've got room for it with my stuff. I'm riding with the supercargo this load, and I can keep an eye on it for you at the other end."

Edard was fair and slender, with a suggestion of epicanthic folds at the corners of his eyes that must have come from mama-mu Dlors after skipping a generation. Bram was sorry that Edard had never met his partial gene grandmother; Dlors had elected to remain on the Father World. As a dancer, she had been part of the musical world, and she would have been as proud of Edard as if she had been any latter-day grandmother contributing a full complement of grandmotherly genes.

"You're going to ride that thing?" Bram asked, casting a dubious eye at the rickety pile. "In nothing but a space suit?"

"It's only a few hours to Yggie now, and the super's got an extra bottle of air he's willing to share," Edard said cheerfully.

Ame sauntered over. "Everybody's hitching rides now," she said. "I'm going to ride up with my last load, too. I'm saving the delicate stuff for then."

Edard cast a glance upward to where the silver shape of the space tree hung overhead. "Got to take advantage of Yggie's favorable position while it lasts. Look at these mountains of souvenirs around us. It'll be half a Tenday before we load it all, and then we've got to get the walkers and heavy equipment up there, not to mention packing up our own personal odds and ends."

Bram conceded the point with a nod. Before coming down to the surface on this final trip, he had given the order for Yggdrasil's rotation to be stopped. The tree's inhabitants could put up with weightlessness for the few days it took to make the final transfer of goods. The swarms of cargo pallets were landing all over the branches. The limited docking facilities at the hub were being reserved for passenger vehicles.

"I'll accept your offer with thanks," Jun Davd said to Edard. "Here, give me a hand with these boxes of instruments. Be careful—there's a lot of glass."

Edard pitched in, and he and Jun Davd made a number of soaring trips in tandem to the top of the heap with boxes slung between them, while Bram unloaded the walker. Fifteen minutes later it was done. The cargo net was tied down securely over the mound of bales and crates, and the supercargo, after inspecting all the fastenings, walked all the way around the wooden platform, checking the weight distribution at intervals with a jack arrangement that lifted the whole thing off the ground.

While they waited, Bram said to Edard, "What have you got there?"

Edard's face lit up. "Musical instruments. Hundreds of them, all gathered into one place by the longfoot archaeologists. We would never have been able to collect them all ourselves in twenty years of digging! This is my fourth load. Bramfather, the violin—and the other stringed instruments—are entirely different from the way we've conceived them! They had only four strings, and they were played with an ordinary manual bow, not motorized disks or powered friction wands. And the instruments themselves are beautiful, curved, complex shapes sculpted of wood. We'll have to learn how to copy them! We'll hear music we never heard before! But learning to play such devices well will take a lot of practice!"

"Your mother will be pleased." Bram could not help thinking of Olan Byr, who had devoted his life to reinventing the old instruments.

"I've already given her one of the cellos," Edard said. "On my last trip a few days ago. She was practicing on it when I left."

"We're filling in all the blank places in human culture," Ame said. "Books of art reproductions—shelves of them. And thousands of actual paintings and pieces of sculpture from the later centuries. And holos of opera, dance, and dramatic performances. And in my field, a complete survey of terrestrial paleontology going back four and a half billion years."

"Biology, too," Bram said. "We have a complete DNA library of thousands and thousands of plant and animal species." Those had been among the first treasures to be moved; they now were in storage aboard Yggdrasil.

Edard hardly listened; he was carried away by his own enthusiasms. "And musical scores! More than nine hundred compositions by someone named Schubert—songs, symphonies, quartets! He must have lived after the discovery of immortality to have written so much! And thirty-two piano sonatas by Beethoven, all of them strikingly different. I never knew he'd written so many! And operas by Mozart! Oratorios by Handel! They all belong to us again!"

"We'll look forward to your next concerts," Jun Davd murmured.

The super made a few last notations on a tablet with a vacuum stylus, scribbled his initials, and tacked the sheet to the pallet frame. "All set," he said.

Edard climbed to a perch atop his possessions, got a firm grip on the cargo net, and waved. A Cuddly rode his shoulder. Bram, Ame, and Jun Davd stood well back with the caravan master and line of walkers. Flame bloomed behind the splash skirt, and the heavily laden platform lifted ponderously, seemed to hang poised for several seconds, then rose with increasing speed into the black sky.

Around Bram the tethered walkers pawed the ground in response to the vibrations. Their attendants calmed them by stroking the affected pseudoganglions. Bram followed the yellow square of flame with his eyes as it climbed toward the hovering tree.

Bram's eyes were still turned upward when Jun Davd grabbed his sleeve and said, "Look!"

Somewhere past Yggdrasil a new star bloomed. It was a bright blue spark, moving rapidly across the field of stars. It lost its proper motion and turned brighter.

"I believe it's a fusion flame," Jun Davd said calmly.

The caravan master and drovers, following their gaze, gaped skyward. On the surrounding plain, activity slowed and stopped as other people noticed.

The blue spark was the brightest star in the sky. It moved not at all against the constellations now.

"They made their course correction," Jun Davd said. "It appears that this is the disk they've chosen."

"Where..." began a stunned Ame.

Jun Davd squinted at the strange new constellations that had taken shape after seventy-four million years. By now he knew them by heart. "They seem to have come from the general direction of Sol," he said. "Of course, it was inevitable that they'd get around to Delta Pavonis sooner or later."

"All those clicking stars..." Bram said.

Jun Davd nodded. "They had to be some manifestation of their message traffic, whether *we* could extract a pattern out of it or not. And they spread like a tide—not by exercising choice. Inhospitable places like red giants and the burnt-out cinders of white dwarfs, whose planets have no future. You'd think they would have skipped to a few of the more congenial stars first. And now their wave front's arriving here, like clockwork."

Bram drew a sharp breath. "But why now?" he said. "Why *not* sooner? Or later? No one's visited the disk-worlds for over fifty million years. And just as *we* get here..."

Ame's face was flushed behind the sparkling curve of her helmet. "Because it's their *turn*, don't you see, Bram-*tsu*!"

"Your extinction timetable?"

She nodded vigorously. "The figures work out about right, don't they, Jun Davd?"

Jun Davd spoke without removing his eyes from the distant fusion flame. "*We* came back here in a multiple of thirty-seven million years—just as fast as we could after the Message reached the Father World, not counting the few insignificant millennia that fell through the cracks while the Nar remade us, and so forth. *They* got here in a rough multiple of twenty-six million years after the Message stopped." He pursed his lips. "They seem to have arrived about four million years early. That's within the limits of your timetable, isn't it, Ame?"

"Divided by three, yes," she said.

Around them on the booty-littered plain, people were gathering into groups, pointing excitedly at the sky. Bram knew that if he switched to the general frequency he would hear a babble of voices. A delegation of about a dozen people, spotting Jun Davd's tall space-suited figure and his own well-worn tabard, were bouncing across the flat ribbonscape toward them.

"Who?" Bram said. "Relatives of the Cuddlies? The collateral branch you postulated that might have evolved from the same root stock after the longfoots carried the Cuddlies here?"

"No," Ame said. "That would have been the last cycle—twenty-six million years ago. The proto-Cuddlies missed their chance. They never traveled to the stars."

Bram stared at the blue spark that was heading toward them. "Who then?" he said.

"We'll know very soon," Jun Davd said.

CHAPTER 9

The alien ship resembled a long jointed stick studded with budlike structures and a cluster of bubbles like white foam at one end. It was very large, as starships must be. It was not worldlike in Yggdrasil's sense, but the segmented shaft was many miles long, and each individual bubble was easily a half mile in diameter.

"It's a fusion vessel, all right, but not a ramjet," said Jun Davd's deep, composed voice from the screen. "They carried their fuel with them. They're using a deuterium-helium three reaction. But there are traces of tritium from previous burns."

Bram saw the implications immediately. "They started their trip with a deuterium-tritium reaction. And they've been at it long enough to have to switch fuels because of the decay of their tritium."

He turned his eyes from the sticklike image on the portable viewscreen long enough to exchange glances with Jao. Jun Davd had returned to the tree in order to have the full resources of the observatory at his disposal, but the burly physicist had left Trist to hold the fort and returned to the diskworld, where, he said, "the action's going to be."

The strangers' starship had been decelerating steadily for six days now at half a g. It had covered more than two hundred million miles since it had first been spotted approaching from the outer system. It would rendezvous with the diskworld in only a few hours—still with too much velocity, according to Trist.

Bram, waiting with Jao, had set up shop in the great sports arena, which was mostly cleared out now. A few people in casual dress moved through the empty spaces, picking over the remaining exhibits. Ame was among them, a distant figure working with a male associate to pack and label pods. Bram had sent all the junketing tourists—and everybody else who could be spared—back to the tree. He didn't want half the population milling around where they could not easily be rounded up. Not with this new development unfolding. But Ame had refused to go. "Not on your life," she'd said. "I wouldn't miss this for anything. Besides, you're going to need me, and Jorv, and all the other experts on terrestrial life." She was right, Bram knew. Only a few hundred people remained on the diskworld, but he had seen to it that a sprinkling of specialists in the once-abstract disciplines was included.

"Yes," Jun Davd's voice agreed. "If they came from Sol, they've been traveling at nonrelativistic speeds. Tritium's half-life is only twelve years and a bit. At the end of their first fifty or sixty years, most of it would have turned into helium three, their secondary fuel. And what does that suggest?"

Jao's eyes glinted. "Deuterium-tritium fusion is easy. But tritium's hard to come by. They would've made it back home as a by-product of their fusion reactors. Deuterium-helium three fusion's easy, too—but first you have to accumulate enough helium three. Deuterium's more plentiful. But I guess they're not capable of deuterium-deuterium fusion yet. Nor of the boron fusion-fission reaction the Nar used in *their* early starships."

He glanced at the bubble-and-stick image that was being transmitted from Yggdrasil's telescopes. "So this is a very early model starship. They're in the first stages of exploration."

"It isn't an exploration ship. It's a colony ship. They don't have enough reaction mass for a return trip."

"But the bubbles..."

"If they ever were fuel tanks, they're empty now. Our radar shows they're hollow. And they haven't collapsed, as a sensible membrane envelope would, nor have they been cast off. I suspect that they've been converted into environmental pods for a very rapidly expanding population."

"They could have planned to set up reactors here to manufacture tritium," Bram suggested. "Or mine a gas giant for helium three."

"Except that there *are* no gas giants in this system. Nor oceans to extract deuterium from. All they could have known about this system is that there was mass here. And energy."

Jao was agape, and Bram didn't blame him. "You mean they sent a shipload of colonists out—to travel for generations and breed aboard ship—without knowing for sure what they'd find here? They must hold their lives cheap!"

"And it must follow that they hold other lives cheap, as well," Jun Davd said hollowly.

"Jun David, what are you driving at?" Bram demanded.

"They're closing with the disk very rapidly, and they still haven't turned off their fusion drive. They *must* have seen Yggdrasil. And felt our radar probing them. They know there's life here."

Trist's voice cut in, sounding harsh. "They're going to overshoot, Bram. They'll have to cut right across the rim of the diskworld."

Bram was aghast. "They'd *have* to assume there must be intelligent life on the surface even if they didn't care about the artifacts they'd be destroying. And they have no way of knowing exactly where on the rim we might be."

"We're sending them radio messages," Trist said. "Just intelligent noises on every wavelength—number patterns and so forth. They don't respond. It's as if we don't exist for them."

"I can evacuate," Bram said, thinking frantically. "No, that would take too long, wouldn't it, with everybody spread out? It wouldn't matter, anyway. Yggdrasil's less than twenty thousand miles away, right in the path of destruction if the drive exhaust comes anywhere near here."

"Yggdrasil's safe, and so are you, we think," Jun Davd said. "These careless strangers will intersect the rim between moons—at least five or ten million miles from your position."

"You think," Jao growled.

A scattered crowd had gathered on the plain, facing the point where the long straight ribbon of land vanished into infinity. About three hundred people were left on the diskworld, and virtually all of them were here in their space suits. They stood in small, chatting groups or lounged against the landing legs of the waiting shuttles. A few enterprising souls had even climbed to perches atop the spaces vehicles for a better view.

Bram was still uneasy about everybody being out in the open. His first instinct had been to keep people as far underground as possible. But Jun Davd had assured him that the alien ship was holding its course. For all practical purposes, the enormous curvature of the rim was a straight line, and even if that dreadful inferno of fusing deuterium and hydrogen three passed only marginally below the theoretical horizon, millions of miles of diskworld would be interposed between Bram's people and death.

Not so for the Cuddlies inhabiting that distant latitude. Bram's mouth tightened into a grim line as he thought of the slaughter that would take place in a few minutes.

The Cuddlies here certainly had no premonition of what was about to happen to their faraway cousins. Attracted by the festive atmosphere, they hung around the people, popping in and out of crevices and sometimes pulling at space-suit legs to be picked up.

"You could see it now if you were hanging in a bosun's chair over the outside rim," Jun Davd's voice sounded in his ear. "It's cutting upward from below a chord drawn between you and its point of intersection. It will rise above your sunward horizon after transit."

"How soon?" Bram asked.

"Four minutes. If you sight along the outer edge, you ought to be able to see some lightening of the limb."

Bram strained his eyes. Beside him, Jao, fussing with the tripod of a theodolite, straightened for a look.

Yes, the precipice edge that faced the interstellar night had gained a silvery hairline illumination. It projected a short distance as a faint straight scratch against the darkness. Where the scratch ended would be the theoretical horizon.

"Got it?" he asked Jao.

Jao struggled with the theodolite. "Just a second. Yah. Here we go."

"One minute."

All across the pebbled plain, space-suited figures showed that they were listening in on the circuit by ceasing their activities and becoming still. The Cuddlies, sensing the humans' absorption, froze.

"Now," Jun Davd said.

Where the threadlike horizon narrowed to invisibility, there was a great flare. Garish light spilled over the plain, casting long black shadows. Human figures, their reflexes slower than their helmet filters, raised arms in a delayed reaction to ward off the light.

Bram saw streaks of movement through the awful glare: startled Cuddlies popping back into their holes. When his eyes adjusted, not a Cuddly was to be seen anywhere.

The light dwindled to a point and disappeared. Moments later, a bright star rose against the inward horizon.

Except that it couldn't be a star, because it was in front of one of the great, dully visible faces of a disk.

Jun Davd's voice in Bram's ear was tinged with sorrow. "The exhaust swept across one of the regions we never had a chance to send a survey team to. The one with the great elliptical bowl and the pyramidal objects rising tens of miles high on stilts. Radar echoes appeared to show a small city in the vicinity to service it, whatever it was. We thought it might be a research center of some sort."

"I remember," Bram said.

"There's nothing there now but thousands of square miles of melted slag."

Bram thought of all the Cuddly warrens that must have lain under the complex and about all the Cuddlies outside the zone of direct destruction that would be dying of radiation sickness in the days and Tendays ahead.

Beside him, Jao swore. "I was going to come back. Maybe in a couple of hundred years when we got ourselves established and could afford to lay off a little. The pyramid installation was the first place I wanted to look at."

In the disk-filled inner sky, the artificial star seemed to slow as if it were on a rubber band. Slowly, slowly, the rim of the diskworld pulled it back.

"They're not going to bother to go into an orbit," Jun Davd's voice said. "They're just going to hang there."

"Disposable ship," Jao said. "Or disposable colonists."

"A life form that just sets blindly out and goes anywhere," Jun Davd mused, "and takes root if it can. And now, I'm afraid, they're making their second pass to bring them to a halt over the rim. They don't bother to think things out in advance. They're empirical."

The star hung over the point of the horizon and winked out. Across the narrow plain, space-suited people eddied about, and groups began to break up. A few cautious Cuddlies popped up out of their holes.

"Show's over," Bram said.

Back inside a sports arena that buzzed and echoed with excited conversation, Bram and Jao conferred with Jun Davd and watched on their portable screen the images from Yggdrasil's remote sensors.

"We were lucky," Jun Davd's distant voice said. "One of our orbiting cameras happened to be no more than a quarter million miles from where our visitor decided to park. We've moved it closer in the last hour, and we're still closing."

People kept poking their heads into the alcove where Bram and Jao had installed themselves. It would have been hard to jam more people into the area where people were crowding around for a look at the screen. Outside, on the rocky floor of the arena, a number of people had been foresighted enough to fetch their own personal viewscreens from their quarters and slave them to Bram's circuit, and each of these had growing knots of watchers around it.

"They're continuing to ignore us," Jun Davd said. "Not a peep on any wavelength."

Bram studied the fuzzy image. The lack of definition took away the regularities that would have labeled the ship an artificial shape and made it look like a life form. A life form with a long lumpy stem whose segments swelled where they fit into each other and a living jelly of bubbles to cap it. The nodules along the shaft fostered the notion.

For a moment Bram toyed with the idea. Yggdrasil was a living spaceship, after all. Why not this? What kind of life form would look like a budding stick, and what function would be served by the gob of bubbles at one end?

Then he dismissed the thought. The thing *was* a machine, after all—a relatively primitive machine that generated a howling storm of hydrogen-helium fusion and probably poisoned its inhabitants.

"We make it at approximately twenty miles long," Jun Davd said. "It could alight in Yggdrasil's branches and never be noticed, but it's still an impressive achievement for a manufactured article."

"What are they *doing*?" Bram said.

"Nothing, as far as we can tell. No extravehicle activity, no electromagnetic emissions. No attempt to reorient the axis of the ship as a preliminary to achieving some sort of rational orbit. They just appear to be waiting."

"Waiting for what?" Jao rumbled. "They sit there like that, and eventually they're going to drift off the rim and get sucked down the side. Then they're going to have to turn on that torch of theirs and burn some more landscape."

"Perhaps they don't care," Jun Davd said.

Bram was staring at the glob of bubbles. Overmagnification had blended them into an undifferentiated mass, but despite the bleared focus there was enough mottled shadowing for the eye to appreciate them as a clump of hundreds of separate spherules.

They were hollow, according to Jun Davd's radar echoes. Empty fuel tanks, each a couple of thousand feet in diameter—big enough to hold millions of tons of frozen hydrogen in its different isotopic forms. And there would be a complex maze of piping to skim off the helium three as it became available and store that separately, too.

Tritium was biologically hazardous. It was hard to believe that the empty bubbles had been converted into environmental pods. Jun Davd's imagination must have run away with him. Surely no people would be that reckless with their generations.

The vague mottling seemed to shift, showing one of the globules more distinctly.

"Do I see movement?" Bram said. "Or is that just image shimmer?"

Jao grabbed Bram's arm. "No, it's movement."

As they watched, one of the bubbles detached itself from the foamlike cluster and drifted free. A fine mist spouted from it.

"Chemical jets," Jun Davd said. "They're matching velocity with the rim."

A hum of voices rose in the surrounding bay. "Hold it down," Jao thundered.

"You were right," Bram told Jun Davd. "They moved into their empty fuel tanks. If that one held tritium, there must still be residual radiation. They'd have to be desperate for expansion room."

"The original life-support system must have been confined to the budlike structures on the stem," Jun Davd said. "But with the fuel tanks, they'd have a hundredfold the living space in reserve, becoming available as they spilled over."

"What kind of intelligent race," Bram said in dismay, "would breed that unrestrainedly, with no sureties at their destination?"

Ame pushed through the surrounding press of bodies. "The longfoots," she said. "The females had a dozen young to a litter, remember? They've come back."

"Or their successors have," Bram said. "Whatever else the longfoots were, they were a thoughtful people. That ship doesn't look like their technology."

"Rise and fall, Bram-*tsu*," Ame said defensively. "Devolution and reradiation of species."

On the screen, the separated globule fell with alarming speed toward the narrow rimscape. "That's awfully big to be using as a lander, even on a low-gravity world," Jun Davd said. "But that's what they're doing with it."

"One mistake and they'll be scattered all over the landscape," Jao grunted.

Bram calculated spherical volume in his head. "There could be a population of thousands in that bubble. If *all* of the bubbles are inhabited..."

"These strangers must like to travel in large crowds and take their environment with them," Jun Davd said. "That detachable habitat of theirs is big enough to qualify as a self-contained colony. The ship could drop more of them off here and there around the rim and leave them to fend for themselves. Then flit around the system and seed the other disks."

"You talk as if that ship were a living organism."

Jun Davd laughed. "If the surviving colonies grow up to build more ships like it, then it fits the definition."

Trist's voice cut in. "We're getting message traffic now between the ship and the lander."

"Radio? Laser?" Jao's voice was impatient.

"Neither. They communicate by modulating polarized light—switching rapidly back and forth to different planes of polarization. We can't read the signal, but it's a signal, all right."

"What kind of pattern? Binary, or what?"

"No, it's positional. It codes for some kind of grid. And now that you know that, you know as little as I do."

"Why would they modulate polarized light?" Bram asked. "If you're going to communicate by light, there are easier ways to modulate it for a signal."

It was Ame, unexpectedly, who answered. "Perhaps because it corresponds to their natural sensory input."

"Now, Ame, *we* use radio mostly," Jao said condescendingly. "But we don't see by radio waves."

"No," she said, "but we use it the way we use visible light—by modulating its frequency. Or we use it by mimicking sound—by modulating the amplitude."

Bram pondered Ame's startling supposition. "But where does a positional grid come into it?"

"I don't know, Bram-*tsu. We* use radio waves to build up pictures or sound. And when we use laser, we use it more or less as if it were just an improved kind of radio. It has something to do with the way they think or perceive things."

"Trist, can you rig up something that'll modulate polarized light?" Bram asked.

"Sure, nothing to it," came Trist's cheerful voice.

"Can you beam some of their own patterns back at them—just as a recognition signal? Just to get them to *notice* us."

"I'll get on it right away."

"And get somebody working on that grid."

"The chess club's already taken it on as a project. So have the linguists."

"Get them together."

On the screen, the stick ship had moved out of the frame as Jun Davd's remote camera followed the life-support module. It showed as a pale blob against a rimscape that whizzed by at blurring speed.

"Looking for a spot to light," Jun Davd said. "They had a choice of two directions. They chose yours."

"How long before they get here?"

"At their present velocity? About two days."

Two days later, the thing passed overhead, looking very large. Everybody was outside again for the passage. As it sailed by, everybody waved. A few energetic jumping jacks leaped straight up fifty feet or more, wigwagging with both hands. But the bubble took no notice. It receded into the distance, blank as an egg.

"They almost nicked one of the moonropes," Jao said. "They're flying much too close to the rim's edge. And too low. The pilot's a bit impetuous, isn't he?"

Bram, sweating inside his helmet, hand-cranked the flywheel-mounted telescope to follow the enormous spheroid. The others crowded close to look at the photoplastic image in the visored plate at the end of the barrel.

"They're losing speed and altitude fast," Bram said. "They're going to come down about two hundred miles farther on, it looks like. We'll have them for neighbors."

"The pilot's braking *too* fast," Jao said, squinting at the shaded image. "As if he made up his mind on the spur of the moment. Whoops! He changed his mind. He's lifting up over that escarpment! Almost grazed it. He must be shaking up his passengers."

Jao's commentary may have been unjust. The huge globular object went into a long graceful glide, riding the plume of its jet, and set down with abrupt gentleness in the exact center of a flat circular feature where the plain was smooth.

"A seat-of-the-pants natural," Bram said. "Like Lydis."

"If he wears pants," Jao said. "Or has a seat."

Ame was looking thoughtful. "What do we do now, great-great-great-grandfather?"

Bram sighed. "I suppose we'd better pay them a visit."

Everybody wanted to go. Bram fended them off as diplomatically as possible when they came barging into the bay where he was trying to work out a plan with Ame and Jao.

"The first meeting is going to be very important," he told them over and over. "We'll have just a few specialists, each with a job to do. We can't take a crowd along."

And then, of course, everybody tried to convince Bram that he or she was a specialist.

"As a sociometrician," Silv Jaks said, getting strident, "my insight into the interrelationships of individuals will be invaluable."

"We don't even know if they're human, Silv," Bram said. "What we're really after is a paleobiologist."

After she stalked out, Jao said, "That was nothing. One of the archaeologists insisted on being included because, he said, he could tell us a lot about them by studying their pottery."

Ame wrinkled her nose. "It might not be a bad idea to take along *someone* from the Theoretical Anthropology group, though. It would give us *some* kind of benchmark for behaviors."

"Who do you suggest?" Bram said.

"Heln Dunl-mak," Ame said promptly. "She's a sociobiologist. She worked with us to try to analyze longfoot society from physical clues. She's even been studying the behavior of social insects from the old books and holos."

"All right," Bram said.

"And we'd better have Jorv."

Bram hesitated. "He's an awfully impulsive fellow. Establishing contact could be a delicate business."

"He knows more about terrestrial life forms and their development than anybody we've got," Ame said. "There's his assistant, Harld, but..."

"I'll keep an eye on him," Jao said, twisting around from his console. He winked. "With a steady hand like me to keep him in line, there won't be any trouble."

Bram said, "I thought you'd stay here and—"

"What?" Jao gave a roar of outrage. "Who's going to operate the equipment? I've rigged up a computer signboard. I've programmed it with an image library and everything."

"All right, all right," Bram said hastily. "I wish we had a linguist."

"They've all gone back to the tree with their tons of books and micromedia in their own pet languages. What do we need a linguist for, anyway? Languages all either have a grammar more or less like Inglex, or they don't, like Chin-pin-yin. And I remember my childhood Chin-pin-yin as well as anybody. And when it comes to non-human speech, *all* us old-timers have a smattering of the Small Language." He squinted at Bram. "And one of us, if memory serves, even has a smattering of the Great Language."

"There won't be anything like that from any kind of terrestrial stock," Bram said.

Jao turned back to his console. "Trist's getting more radio traffic between the stick ship and that camp out yonder. Want to hear it?"

He turned up the volume, and a series of rapid, hard clicks came out of the speaker, like twenty people snapping their fingers as fast as they could.

"When did they switch from modulated polarized light to radio?" Ame asked.

"At about half a million miles. But Trist's analyzed the signals. He thinks they simply reproduce the patterns of the polarized light version—same positional code on a grid. He still hasn't figured out how the grid is organized, though. One thing's for sure—it isn't any simple up-and-down-and-across raster. Trist thinks it's irregular." Jao looked troubled. "But that's crazy."

Bram listened to the snapping sounds for a while. "Maybe their receiving equipment is better than my ear," he said, "but it sounds as if those noises are coming on top of each other—overlapping. How can they extract an information-bearing signal out of that?"

"Trist's taken the signals apart. He says he thinks they're organically produced."

Ame scrunched up her features. "It's a language, then. A language where sounds have visual coordinates."

"I don't understand," Bram said.

"Bram-*tsu*, our group's done a lot of work on sensory impressions and perception," Ame said. "Back during the years when we were trying to build up the new sciences. Doc Pol helped us with the medical aspects."

"That old curmudgeon!" Jao exclaimed. "I thought he didn't believe in anything he couldn't tap, prod, or take a urine sample from."

"He says polysenses are very common among human beings—much commoner than is believed. People who hear sounds as smells, for example, or who taste colors."

"Crossed wires," Bram said.

"No, it isn't just that. It's normal in all of us to some extent."

Bram thought it over. "Like Edard reading an orchestral score and hearing the music."

"Something like that."

"Or Mim swearing that different keys have different textures—G-major being hard and brittle, D-flat soft and velvety. She had an argument with Ang about it. Ang said the only difference between keys is that they're higher or lower."

"Colors!" Jao said suddenly. "Numbers have different colors. That's how I remember them. Equations transform the colors. I thought *everybody* saw numbers that way."

"Drugs will induce that kind of cross talk sometimes," Ame said. "Your nervous system just happens to work that way naturally."

Jao grinned. "Hey, Ame, what if you see flashing lights when you bump your elbow?"

"What about it?"

"Me, I get a pain in my elbow when I see flashing lights."

Bram cut through the clowning. "So our new neighbors have a neural hookup between the sounds of their language and some sort of visual grid?"

"And they see the different planes of polarized light, don't forget that."

"What kind of eyes must they have?" he wondered.

"Nothing like ours. Or the longfoots. Or the Cuddlies. Or any other kind of mammalian life we know about." She hesitated. "They may not have a continuous field of vision. They may see things as a mosaic."

It was a very strange thought. "What would the world look like to them?" Bram wondered aloud.

"We'll have to ask them, won't we?"

Bram turned his attention to Jao's screen. Jao was fiddling with images. He had made a sort of netlike structure out of green lines. The net kept stretching itself out of shape and changing the relationships between its warp and woof. It also kept trying to bend itself around various abstract three-dimensional shapes.

The snaps and clicks kept pouring from the loudspeaker. Bram could see that each one generated an orange dot within the distorted squares of the net. The showers of dots kept trying to arrange themselves into patterns within the ever-changing net.

"Are we still trying to get their attention on the frequency they use?" Bram asked.

"Yar, I've got a loop going on the transmitter. Trist is trying to raise their ship with the same program. Imitating their grid without knowing the coordinates is gobbledygook, but they still should extract a pattern."

Bram shook his head. "I thought they might have tried to contact *us* by now. The way they set down so abruptly after their flyover of our camp."

"We're keeping watch from a little way up the moonrope," Jao said. "Some volunteers set up a telescope station on top of the stalled moon car. They'll let us know right away if anything starts moving in our direction." He adjusted a dial. "But I don't think they're coming. It's going to be up to us."

Jorv showed up a few minutes later, impatient to start. He wore a vacuum suit with the helmet tucked under his arm. "I've been suited up for an hour," he said. "When do we go?"

"Not for a couple of hours," Bram said. "They're getting the walkers wound up and rounding up supplies and equipment. And some of our people need time to get ready."

That was Heln. She was putting together her material on ants, bees, beavers, wolves, rats, apes, elephants, antelopes—all the vanished animals of Earth that had lived in groups. If intelligence had evolved from any of them, their descendants would resemble them as little as man resembled the tree shrew. Heln wanted to be prepared to spot basic characteristics and extrapolate from them.

"Why delay?" Jorv said pugnaciously. "Pick up a few extra air bottles and get going."

"Don't you want time to get organized?" Bram countered. Jorv had nothing with him, not even a camera or a pad to take notes on.

"What for? Get a look at them, I say. Plow through the data afterward."

Ame came around and put a hand on Jorv's arm. "It's not just a case of observing them, Jorv," she said. "We'll work from your opinions—but we have to try to communicate with them, too."

"Why don't you meet us at the vehicle air lock in, say, two hours," Bram said.

Jorv walked out, shaking his head and muttering.

Bram helped Jao pack up his computer signboard and image library, while Ame went to give Heln a hand and to collect Shira, her paleobiologist colleague. Heln turned out to be a small, pert redhead, loaded down with a portable reader, cartridges, pad and easel, recorder, and other equipment.

When they arrived at the walker stables, Bram saw

that only two walkers were equipped and ready for him, not the three he had arranged for.

"Where's the other vehicle?" he asked the ostler, a squat, muscular man who was strapping a spare air tank on one of his charges.

"He took it," the ostler said. "Your friend. Said he was getting a head start, that you'd catch up with him."

"Jorv?"

"Short chubby fellow, sort of a restless way with him? I told him that I wasn't finished packing it up, but he said as long as it had enough air and power on the meter to get him there, it was good enough. He almost wouldn't wait long enough for me to put in a reserve air tank. I said to him, you don't want to go out there without one—never mind that you're only one person in a life-support system that's supposed to handle three."

"How long ago?"

"About two hours."

Bram turned to the others. "I don't know what he's up to, but we'd better run him down before he gets there."

"We'll have to triple up," Jao said. He looked at the mound of gear they had brought with them, then his eye lit on the red-haired sociobiologist. "Why don't you and Ame and Shira ride together, and Heln and I can squeeze in with all this equipment."

The walkers loped side by side across the dim plain, stretching their legs of plastic and synthetic protein. Their yellow headlamps bored into the endless ribbon of rubblescape ahead of them. They had traveled far enough so that the tethered moon was at their backs, showing its shape like a child's top. To their right was the bloated face of a disk, casting a rusty light. To their left were the deeps of space with a hoarfrost of stars.

"Not a sign of him," Bram said.

"Don't forget, he's running lighter," Ame pointed out. She was squeezed against him on the narrow bench. On her other side, Shira's bony hip dug into her. The lanky paleobiologist said, "He's had a two-hour head start. But Jorv's not a good driver. He'll try to hurry his walker too much, and that'll mean that its legs will just be churning around in midair a good deal of the time."

"Could we have passed him somehow?"

"We can see clear to the edge on either side. We'd have noticed his lights."

"*If* he remembered to turn them on," Shira said, and fell silent.

"We've been running for three hours," Bram said. "We'll be there soon. If we were going to catch up to him, we'd have done it by now."

"Don't worry, Bram-*tsu*." Ame said. "Jorv is a very intelligent man. He won't do anything *too* rash. All he wants to do is study them."

"They may be studying *him* by now," Bram said, and urged the walker on.

An hour later, the great pearly dome of the alien bubble grew out of the dimness ahead. There was no question of it appearing over the horizon—not on the diskworld. It simply became visible as a dot and grew larger.

Bram slowed the walker and approached at a trot. Jao, driving the other walker, fell in beside him.

The aliens were deploying around their bubble, queer sticklike creatures who hurried back and forth, carrying huge cone-shaped containers that they peeled open to reveal equipment and housing materials. Wheeled vehicles, whose barrel-shaped tires seemed to be clustered at one end, leaving a tubular chassis projecting with an upward cant, were being readied. All the activity was taking place under the glare of work lamps set up on tall stands around the perimeter of the camp.

"They like things bright," Ame said, looking at the pool of light around the tremendous ball.

"Look, there's Jorv's walker," Bram said.

The spindly vehicle, its bubble deflated, stood a short distance from the equipment-littered area of activity. There was no sign of Jorv himself.

"Collapsed bubble," Bram said. "It should have reinflated itself by now. I hope Jorv's not—"

Shira tossed her head. "If I know Jorv, he was careless about getting out, that's all. Walked away and left it unsealed."

"Bram-*tsu*," Ame said. "Do you notice something strange?"

It struck Bram after a moment. "Yes, why aren't there swarms of those creatures around the walker for a closer look at it? It's just sitting there. Don't they have any curiosity?"

"Maybe Jorv's getting all the attention."

"No, he isn't." Jao's voice came through the suit radio. "There he is, wandering around in the middle of their camp, and they're ignoring him."

Bram spotted the human figure after a moment. Jorv was dawdling about in bemused fashion, pausing here and there to look at things that interested him. He might have been out for a Tenday stroll. The stick creatures hurried past him on their errands without stopping.

It wasn't quite true that they were ignoring Jorv, though. Jorv got too close to some piece of equipment that a group of them were setting up, and one of them detached itself from the work party long enough to make a number of short, aggressive rushes at the space-suited human. Jorv scrambled back out of the way. Bram couldn't blame him; even from a distance the rushes looked scary. Jorv kept his distance, and the alien went back to its work, paying no further attention to him.

As the walkers cantered closer, Bram was able to make out more details of the creatures. They were long, tubular beings with pipestem limbs that seemed to grow out in a cluster from just below an oversize head. They walked upright on all fours, like animated plant stands—keeping the trailing portion of their bodies from scraping the ground by curling it upward in balance.

"Our ancestors ran on all fours, too," Shira said, mostly for Bram's benefit. "They learned to knuckle-walk, so that they could carry things at the same time. That's why evolution let us keep forelimbs we could manipulate with."

"It made for the development of intelligence," Ame agreed. "But these creatures never adapted for a two-legged gait. I wonder if . . ."

Bram studied the distant figures. The beanstalk creatures seemed not at all handicapped by their quadruped stance. The forward pair of legs did double duty as arms, and when the creatures carried things—tottering in the low gravity and intermittently dropping a front limb for temporary balance—Bram was amazed to see the tubelike abdomen curve flexibly around to assist with the grip. There seemed to be a clasping member at its tip.

The creatures wore enormous boxlike helmets that were far too large even for the oversize heads that could be seen shadowily within. A human child could have curled up inside.

"They want lots of room in those helmets," Bram said aloud. "I wonder why."

He reined the walker to a halt next to Jorv's abandoned vehicle. Jao and Heln pulled up behind him.

"We'd better walk from here," he said.

The five of them climbed to the ground. The pipestem figures in their unwieldy many-faceted helmets made no move in their direction. They went on with their restless scurrying to and fro, never pausing in their chores.

"Do you see what they're doing?" Jao said, putting a hand on Bram's sleeve.

Bram looked over to where the floodlights lit the underside of the tremendous cloudy ball that had been first a fuel tank, then an environmental module, then a landing craft.

It was growing all sorts of attachments. An undergrowth of prefabricated polyhedrons. Huge glistening balloons that were blown up and sprayed with hardening foam to become permanent structures. A network of tubeways and covered platforms that connected with the beginnings of some kind of large excavation.

"That lander will never go anywhere again," Jao said.

Bram nodded. "They're here to stay. First spot they touched down on. I get the feeling it could have been anywhere on the rim. They didn't waste any time unpacking, either."

Heln came over, festooned with cameras and recorders. "This is all I'll need," she said. "I'm leaving the rest of it in the walker. I was able to go through most of the material on the way."

"Any ideas?" Bram asked.

"I may have. First I want to see if Jorv and the others

can pin down a working phylogeny for those creatures. I can tell you one thing, though." She hesitated.

"Go on."

"They're not a contact species. But they observe a hierarchy of space." She saw his puzzled look and added, "You see, it would affect their social organization—and the way they communicate."

"You can tell all that by looking at them from a distance?"

"On average, they maintain a uniform separation between themselves of about one point five limb lengths in close working situations." She gave a troubled frown. "The limits of fang and claw, you see. In humans, it's about three feet. But the real clue came from Jorv."

"You mean when he got too close to that equipment and was warned off? I suppose it shows that these beings are touchy."

"No, not necessarily. They may inhabit a different universe of perception. Communication with them may not be a matter of language, or symbols, or images."

She cast a glance at the folded easel of the computer signboard that Jao was removing from the walker.

"I don't understand," Bram said.

Heln hesitated again. "I don't believe they're aware of Jorv."

"But they *saw* him. They rushed him till he backed off."

"That's not what I mean. I mean they're not aware of him as an entity. They're aware of the alteration of hierarchical space that his presence caused."

Jao paused in his labors. "Just like physics," he said. "The shape of space is defined by the presence of matter."

Heln pursed her lips. "I know it might not seem to make much sense..."

"No, no," Bram said hastily. "In the physical sciences we reason from a single datum sometimes and reach the most astonishing conclusions. You've got a new science here. We'll take your word for it."

Ame was anxiously surveying the scene within the floodlit area. "Jorv just got himself chased again," she said. "We'd better get over there before he gets himself into trouble."

"Yes," Bram said. First he checked the air bubble of Jorv's walker. It had deflated because the thickened edges of the gasket were misaligned. Shira had been right about Jorv's carelessness. He must have shouldered his way out of the vehicle frontally, probably spreading the bubble's lips apart with his hands, then letting them snap back into place. Bram realigned the closure and saw some of the collapsed folds begin to stir and rise; they might need that air on the way back—Jorv hadn't bothered to set out with a full complement of reserve air bottles, and if he'd had to get back home on his own, he might have made a close thing of it.

Jao slung his computer over his shoulder, and Bram shouldered the folded easel. Ame, he saw, had a big pad under her arm; she and Shira relieved Heln of some of her excess equipment. Together, they danced lightly across the landscape toward the stick-people's camp.

As they approached the lit area, two of the spindly creatures trotted by at close hand, bearing a large, light-weight construction panel between them. Their gait was three-legged, and the long tubular abdomens, with gauntleted pincers on the ends, were curled around for extra support. They were backlighted by the brilliant lamps, and through the cloudy sheaths that covered their bodies, Bram got an impression of stiff, slender, many-jointed legs. The huge boxy helmets, concealing their secrets in the reflected glare, made them look like walking packing crates.

Jao stepped forward, holding up an outspread hand, but the creatures veered off to join a work crew at the perimeter of illumination.

"You'd think they'd have stopped," he said, affronted.

"Different body language," Shira suggested. "Holding up a hand doesn't mean the same thing to them."

It sounded reasonable to Bram, but he saw Heln's pursed lips and frown of concentration.

They moved into the light. Bram saw Jorv's space-suited figure ahead, stalking one of the stick-creatures. Jorv approached at a crouch, the lines of his body an exaggerated study in caution. The stick-creature was half turned away, flexing its reedy legs, its sheathed abdomen twitching slightly. It let Jorv get within eight or nine feet, then, abruptly, its legs bunched like springs and it soared over his head and lit down next to a pile of construction materials, where, without preamble, it joined its fellows in putting up one of the polyhedral structures.

Jorv straightened up, every line of his body showing disappointment, and began stalking another one of the creatures.

"We're not even going to get that close to one," Jao grumbled.

Every time Bram and his party seemed about to intersect the path of one of the creatures, it veered off and ignored them.

"Just hold on," Bram said, "and we'll be in the thick of them."

"I'm insulted," Jao said. "Am I invisible, or what?"

Heln said, "They see you . . . but they don't see you."

"Maybe they're some kind of hive creatures," Shira put in. "No real intelligence. The intelligence is in that bubble they landed in."

"They've got intelligence," Bram said. "If intelligence means handling tools and machinery."

Then, without warning, they were upon one of the creatures. It reared up in their path, the light shining full on it, and for the first time Bram got a good look at what was inside those cagelike helmets.

Its face was the stuff of nightmares—two bulging domes of jelly on either side of a masklike bulb that was split by a vertical cleft. Each of those jellied eyes—if that's what they were—was the size of a man's head.

The cleft parted in a hideous vertical smile that hinted at something spiny and complicated within. There was a flicker of movement in front of the ghastly face—and in a moment of startled disbelief, Bram saw why the creatures needed so much room in their helmets.

There was a separate pair of limbs within the helmet!

They grew out of the creature's face, or the sides of what passed for a neck. They were smaller manipulating limbs—shorter than a man's arm—and these peculiar beings kept them folded up on the floor of the helmet, like a person resting his elbows on a table.

The creature swiveled its complicated head as if looking for a way of escape, and the facial limbs lifted and swung with it.

A flash of crazy thought went through Bram's head: It must cramp their style to be deprived of the use of their grasping members whenever they wear space suits! But the creatures' anatomy gave them no alternative. Limbs projecting through sleeves in a smaller helmet would have immobilized their heads.

Or maybe they simply needed to have their forelimbs available for grooming or self-care. Maybe they would have felt uncomfortable having the limbs enclosed apart from their faces. Bram could sympathize with that—hadn't he suffered the agony of being unable to scratch an itchy nose while wearing a space suit?

Everything had happened in an instant. Through his radio Bram heard a couple of people gasp—he felt like gasping himself—and then the jelly-eyed horror spun around and galloped away.

"It saw us," Jao said. "I swear it saw us that time."

"No," Heln said. "It saw the effect we were having on its visual field."

"What's the difference?"

"Have you ever heard of an animal called a frog?"

"Huh?"

"*Wa*, in Chin-pin-yin. The children's story about the mandarin who turned into one."

"Oh, yar."

"It saw motion, not objects. It ate an animal called a fly, but it didn't see the fly until it moved. If you tried to feed a captive frog on dead flies, it would starve to death."

"Are you saying that these tomato-eyed beasts are frogs?"

"No," Heln said patiently. "I'm saying that they have a queer sort of brain wiring that enables them to cooperate as a species but that makes other life forms irrelevant to them—as irrelevant as a fly is to a frog...until the fly moves. We're no part of their experience—or their instincts—so we don't exist for them."

Bram looked around at the teeming campsite. "Aren't you overstating the case? These aren't primitive animals. They've got space travel. They *must* process information somehow in those heads of theirs. Can you have intelligence without curiosity?"

Something was bothering him. It was Jao's description of the creatures as "tomato-eyed." It was true. The eyes were reminiscent of gigantic green tomatoes. A memory nagged at Bram somewhere below the level of consciousness.

"Maybe." Heln stood her ground. "And maybe you can have intelligence without empathy. Maybe we're going to find that these new neighbors of ours lack basic empathy—that it's literally impossible for them to relate to any life form but their own."

"That would certainly make it hard to communicate with them," Ame said with a strained smile.

"To say the least," Bram said.

"I hope not," Heln said, shifting some of her technical accoutrements on their carrying straps. "There *has* to be a way for us to plug ourselves into their sensory wiring. We'll just have to find it. Let's hear what Jorv has to say. Maybe he has some ideas about their phylum by now."

Jorv saw them coming and ambled over to greet them. He seemed preoccupied. "They may be descended from terrestrial insects," he said without preamble. "Did you notice those wraparound eyes? They probably carry the efficiency of the compound type of eye as far as it can go—their visual acuity may surpass our own. And the muscle attachment—I wish I could make out more through those space suits. They don't *move* as if the muscles were operating proper skeletons!"

Bram tried a mild reprimand. "Jorv, you shouldn't have come out here on your own. We may be running up against a very queer situation."

"Queer? I'll say it's queer. They won't stand still long enough for me to get a good look at them. Did anybody bring cameras? Ah, Heln—you'd better start taking some pictures."

"Did you try to talk to them?" Bram asked.

"Talk? They won't talk. Ame, I think you may have

hit on something when you deduced a hookup between sensory input and a visual grid from their radio signals."

Ame looked excited. "The compound eye means there's no overall image—just a very large number of separately perceived patches. The visual information jumps from facet to facet, whether the object is moving or the creature's head is moving, and the sum of the signals is processed somewhere in the brain—"

She broke off. Everybody looked at Heln. "Your frogs," Jao said.

"What have frogs got to do with it?" Jorv said irritably. "These are *insects*!"

"Very big ones if that's true," Shira murmured. "Insects shouldn't be able to grow to that size, with exoskeletons as a limiting factor. And they were lungless, weren't they? They transported oxygen through tracheae. That would limit their size, too."

"We won't know till we examine one!" Jorv's eyes were gleaming. "Do you think you could help me get one back to our camp?"

"Sit on him if you have to," Bram told the three women. "Jao, let's get your computer signboard set up."

They worked at it for fifteen hours, taking turns going back to the parked walkers to replenish their air supplies and to fetch various items that Heln or Jao had brought along in hopes that they would help.

Nobody ate a lot during that time—just a few hasty handfuls of travelfood that had been included with their rations—and nobody slept at all, despite the fact that all of them had been awake for more than twenty-four hours.

They got nowhere.

Every once in a while one of the stick-beings would dart over and pause for a look at the computer display or at an earnestly semaphoring human being. At least they seemed to be looking. But they always trotted on past without showing any reaction.

Once an exasperated Jao had stepped squarely into the path of an ambulating beastie and attempted to herd it with blocking movements of his wide torso toward the little communications arena. An observer could not have said that the intercepted individual exactly tried to *evade* Jao. Simply, it was somehow past him without appearing to have noticed his presence.

It was a pity, because Jao had knocked himself out to prepare his visual displays. There was a beautiful sequence in simplified diagrams and actual images that showed the human itinerary from the Whirlpool Galaxy to the Milky Way to the vicinity of the enclosed star that was presumed to be Delta Pavonis. Another sequence ingeniously arranged as a query showed the presumed progress of the tomato-eyed strangers from a presumed Sol.

Jao never got anywhere near to unveiling his masterpieces—a sophisticated scenario that showed the ancient origin of humankind on a planet of Sol, showed bright schematic images of DNA, and showed the diskworld itself with stylized radio waves spreading from it toward the Virgo cluster of galaxies. It went on to show the Whirlpool in the Canis Venatici cloud, halfway to Virgo, being bathed in the radio waves, the reemergence of the colorful DNA schema, then the recreation of human beings and their return to the planet that had given birth to their genes.

"They don't take visual information!" Jao said in disgust. "And them with eyes as big as my head!"

"It's not visual information, it's abstractions," Bram said. "Let's show them something closer to home."

They displayed images relating human figures to Yggdrasil, with much pointing at the green blob that could be seen over the horizon. They showed the fuzzy images of the stick-ship and finally life-size holos of the jelly-eyed creatures themselves, played back from Heln's camera.

But when Jao projected one of the fearsome holos in the path of one of the trotting creatures, it passed through it without pausing. "It didn't see the image as real," Ame said. "Not polarized for their eyes."

"But sometimes they *do* seem to pause for a second and show body reactions, particularly with the moving images," Shira said, sounding frustrated. "And certainly when we get too close to their precious equipment."

"The same way your feet find stepping-stones when

you cross a stream," Heln said. "Doesn't mean *you're* really aware of the stones."

Heln, tree-born, had never seen a stream and certainly never had crossed one on stepping-stones, but Bram appreciated the aptness of the simile.

"Going to try just one more thing," Jao grunted.

He generated an animated image of a Cuddly, and the next time a stick-creature intersected their little communications arena, he sent it scampering toward the being.

The alien being stopped dead in its tracks and stood stock still for all of two or three seconds. For a moment Bram thought it was going to rear up and change direction, as it did when a human got in its way. The nightmare face seemed to expand as the central cleft widened, and Bram thought he saw a flicker of movement within the cavity.

Then, apparently, the creature dismissed the holographic Cuddly and darted off on its interrupted errand.

"We almost had it that time!" Jao exclaimed. "Did you see that?"

"But why?" Shira asked. "It couldn't have seen the holo as real."

"Something in its neural circuitry reacted," Heln said. "Something about the image *almost* tripped a switch."

"But what?" Bram wondered. "The Cuddly's size? Its movement? Its resemblance to something it *is* primed to react to?"

"Maybe all of that," Heln said. "But it shows that the switch is there, ready to be tripped. And maybe after we get back and have time to study our film and data, we'll be able to figure out how to get them to notice *us*."

They kept at it until their margin of reserve air was almost gone. And then they had trouble prying Jorv away. "They're insects, all right," he babbled happily. "Or at least in the insect line of descent. It's all there in the jointing of the legs—the two short basal joints, femur and tibia meeting at the knees, then the three short joints and former claws of the tarsus. I'd give my eyeteeth to see them out of their space suits."

Bram had Jao drive Jorv back; he didn't trust the pudgy zoologist not to return to the alien campsite. Before they entered their separate vehicles, Bram exchanged a few words with Jao.

"Did you notice there were no Cuddlies hanging around? That's odd . . . there must be a few burrows in the area, and they're such curious little beasts."

"Huh? They're probably just being cautious till they figure these insect-people out."

"Heln says that maybe we'll be able to figure out how to trip that switch in their brains after we learn why they reacted to a Cuddly image."

"What are you getting at?"

"Maybe we won't want to."

It was hard for Bram to keep the curious from sneaking out to the insect-people's base camp. "Not until we know more," he insisted. "The specialists are working on it. We don't want to take the chance of stirring them up till we have some chance of communicating with them."

In the meantime, Yggdrasil was drifting inexorably farther away. Smeth called several times a day to display fits of ill temper.

"We were supposed to leave this system within two Tendays from now. Jun Davd's got our course worked out for that window, and my black gang's warming up the fusion drive. We're halfway through our checklist. We've already got a starter ball of deuterium slush in the throat of the scoop, and it's evaporating with every second that goes by." His words became a wail. "And where's Ame? She was supposed to be back here *days* ago! The twins are acting up, and I don't have time to handle them by myself."

"I'm sorry," Bram said. "I couldn't get Ame to leave now if I tried."

"Well, it's not every day you run into a new intelligent life form," Smeth said grudgingly.

"I can't get anyone else to leave, either," Bram told him. "We may have to change our plans. We can't leave this system without knowing more about what's waiting for us at Sol. We may not own it anymore—not if these are the new inheritors."

"If we don't pack up and go soon, Yggdrasil will have

to make another circuit. It would use up our whole starter ball. We could be delayed another year."

Bram broke it to him gently. "I think that's what it may take. We're going to have to put it to a vote."

"Don't *say* that! Jun Davd spends all his time looking at the pictures and data you sent up. I've been trying to get some revised escape orbits out of him, but his computer's all tied up with an analysis of the radio traffic that—that colony sent."

"Sent?"

"Yes, it's stopped. They don't seem to have anything more to say to one another. Jun Davd says the colony's on its own."

"Is he getting anywhere with his analysis?"

"No."

Jun Davd was interested in Heln's theories. "A life form that lacks basic empathy on a neurological level. It's a chilling thought for us humans. Very frustrating. Our only other relationship with intelligent beings was with the Nar—probably the most empathetic life form in the universe."

"I've forbidden our people here to go visit. But I know they sneak over there anyway, make a party of it. Walkers are checked out and are gone for twelve or fifteen hours. I can only hope they're watching from a distance. The insect-folk themselves are sending out pickets. Those wheeled vehicles of theirs are spreading outward in reconnaissance patterns. They're probably looking for expansion sites. I hope there are no encounters."

"And if there are?"

"According to Heln, they'll see the human beings as a detail of their environment. An unimportant detail. Irrelevant."

It was an audio-only circuit, but Bram could almost see Jun Davd shake his head in bemusement. "What if some impatient idiot grabbed hold of one of these creatures?"

"Then he'd be a relevant fact of the environment. That's the kind of encounter I don't want."

"I hope your terrestrial life specialists come up with some answers soon. People here in the tree are agog at your pictures. We can't keep them penned up much longer. You're liable to have tourists."

Bram groaned. "That's all we need."

"Heln believes that there may be a switch in the neurological makeup of these insect folk—a switch that would make us a part of their perceptions—and that this switch can be tripped if we find the key?"

"Correct."

"And that once tripped, it will stay tripped for them as a species?"

"Yes."

"Extraordinary!"

"Heln's delved into volumes of biological lore from the buried libraries and says there are all sorts of examples of these neurological switches—they're called 'releaser' mechanisms—in terrestroid life. If the animal's nervous system is complex enough and there's a degree of social organization, the perception of the triggered individual becomes the perception of the species."

"What if the perception is something we won't like?"

"All we want to do is get them to notice us."

"Be careful."

"I'm on my way to see Jorv now, to see if he's made any progress in tracing their species."

"The claspers at the tip of the abdomen were characteristic of many insects," Jorv said happily. "Like paired forceps. Insects developed an opposing grip before our own ancestors did. Only they had it in a different place."

He looked up at Bram, pleased with his little joke. Jorv had gotten an artist to prepare diagrams from Heln's pictures, and these were spread out on easels around him.

"Odd place for a hand," Bram said.

"Not when you consider the purpose."

"Which was?"

"To assist in copulation." Jorv licked his lips. "A useful accessory, particularly for species that mated in flight."

"These creatures don't have wings."

"No, but I'll wager an autopsy would show vestigial wing muscles, just as human beings have vestigial tails.

They lost the wings somewhere along the way, as ants did."

Jorv pointed at a picture tacked on the wall, showing a spiny, many-legged creature with fearsome jaws—a blowup from one of the old texts he and Heln had been delving into.

"Are they ants?"

"No. I haven't been able to find a form they correspond to—not yet. There's something puzzling about them."

Bram looked again at the diagram of the abdominal claspers. They were heavily gauntleted, but their form was plain enough, as a gloved hand is.

Jorv continued happily babbling. "The female claspers for gripping the male would have been in a different abdominal segment, but that doesn't mean anything. The structures would have been there embryonically, and if evolution decided they would make a useful hand, a similar appendage could have developed from the ovipositor."

"Ovipositor?"

"For laying eggs. It was generally equipped to puncture holes in mud, vegetation, or some other hatching medium. Living flesh, I'm afraid, in the case of some of the nastier species."

"Insects seem to have been a remarkably single-minded life form."

"In the sense of a will to survive? So were our own ancestors, no doubt. But those creatures building their city out there have developed intelligence. They've learned how to survive and propagate through technology. Don't worry. Once we get a key to their developmental patterns, we'll find a way to communicate with them."

"I hope so."

Jorv frowned. "I still haven't decided whether their ancestors were plant eaters or meat eaters. The mouth parts are hidden inside that odd facial structure. There were over a hundred million species of insects, and so far I haven't been able to find anything like it."

Ame came over with a new sheaf of blowups. "Hunters or browsers?" she mused. "It would be nice to know before we meet them again."

* * *

As it happened, it was the insect-folk who made the first move. Bram was having a meal with Ame when he got a call from one of the watchers he had posted on the plain.

"Bram-captain, one of those tube machines is rolling in your direction. It zigzags a lot, but there's no doubt about where it's headed. It should reach the digs in about an hour."

"Thanks. Stay where you are. Keep an eye out for any more of them."

He stood up. Ame said, "I'll get the others."

"Tell them to keep their distance till we see what they're up to. Let's see what *they* have in mind, for a change."

He deputized a dozen people for crowd control. "Tell everybody to stay out of their way. Don't interfere with them. If any approach is made, it will be done by one of the specialists."

An hour later, the excavated streets were full of waiting people. Word had gotten around fast. They sat on ledges, hung over the low rooftops that had thrust themselves out of the rubble, and loitered in the stone arches. Bram had a vantage point from the top of one of the buildings facing the moon plaza. If the insect surveying party kept to the avenues of rubble leading into town, this would be the major route.

"There it comes," Jao said beside him.

A tiny shape appeared in the distance and soon resolved itself into one of the tube vehicles, bumping along on its fat tires at about twenty-five miles an hour. The four barrel-shaped rollers were all grouped close together under a cab that seemed to carry most of the weight; the long, slender cylindrical body tilted upward at a thirty-degree angle behind it, doing a lot of vibrating. Bram supposed it made as much sense as any other design for rough country; if the cab had to crawl over an obstacle, the projecting section had plenty of leeway to tilt downward without dragging.

The bizarre vehicle rolled by the crystalline shafts of the moonropes without slowing down and came to a quivering stop at the edge of the wide plaza. Bram could see human figures peeking at it from around corners.

He waited for a door to open, but none did. After a few minutes a boxy helmet emerged from the end of the tube, about twelve feet above the ground. The rest of the insect-person extruded itself, hung rigidly horizontal from the lip of the tube by the claspers at the tip of its elongated abdomen, and let itself drop lightly on all fours to the ground. Seven more of the creatures followed.

They stood around, conferring with twitching movements of their long sterns. Bram saw little, discreet flashes of lights from their helmets and assumed it was the polarized light version of radio communication. After getting everything settled to their apparent satisfaction, they slung equipment over their humped shoulders—or hips, if that's what they were—and began skittering down the long boulevard with lots of nervous, darting side trips, staying in a loose group.

People began to drift down from rooftops and emerge from side streets to trail after the insect-people at a respectful distance.

"We'd better get down there," Bram said.

He vaulted over the rooftop and floated to the ground, with Jao close behind him. He strode in thirty-foot bounds across the plaza and caught up with the little parade going down the avenue.

Trouble started almost immediately. A skylarking fool who had been leaping up and down in great swoops shot fifty feet into the air and came down squarely in front of one of the insect-people. Apparently he got a good look at the jelly-eyed face within the helmet, because he backed away with a jerk and stumbled.

The insect-being showed no signs of stopping, and the skylarker showed no signs of getting out of its way. Jao reached the spot in one long soaring arc and snatched the offending person out of the way with a hand hooked into the webbing of the life-support backpack.

He bore his kicking prize to Bram. He did not set the fellow down on ground, but held him out to Bram at arm's length.

The face within the helmet was that of a junior archivist

named—Bram rummaged in his memory—Alb something-or-other. Alb was less than thirty years old, having been born in the heart of the Milky Way, and hadn't lived long enough to develop good sense.

"Put him down," Bram said.

Instead of letting go, Jao rammed the errant archivist into the ground with some emphasis. Alb stood there with a silly grin on his face.

"Alb, I thought I told everybody—" Bram began.

"He can't hear you," Jao said. "He isn't tuned in to your frequency." He made twisting motions to get the idea across to Alb, but the young man just stood there stupidly, no doubt listening to the gibes of his own circle of friends.

"Oh, chaos take it!" Jao exclaimed. He dialed through his own frequencies till he hit Alb's. He must have turned the power full up, to judge by the way Alb flinched. Somewhere out there a number of other people must have acquired an earache too. Jao proceeded to give the unfortunate fellow a dressing down. Bram tuned in for the tail end of it: "...brains of a three-legged baggage walker!"

Alb gave Bram a sheepish apology and promised to behave. Bram heard group laughter on the frequency, and Alb turned pink.

They caught up with the insect patrol some distance down the avenue of rubble. Jao's lecture seemed to have had good effect; the trailing crowd of people was hanging back farther. One of those who wasn't lagging behind was Heln Dunl-mak. She skipped ahead of the alien party, just beyond what she had described to Bram as the insect-people's "avoidance zone."

Heln's slight figure was top-heavy with improvised equipment—a bulky pack that Jao had put together for her. It was flashing modulated polarized light, some of it drawn from frequently appearing patterns in the stick-ship's early radio transmissions, some of it repeating and stringing together "phrases" that the darting aliens were blinking at each other.

"Best program I could cobble together at short notice," Jao said apologetically as he waved at Heln's dancing form. "Heln doesn't really know what she's *saying* to them, but she can punch in a few crude menus based on their physical behavior, and the computer can try to correlate it with what they're flashing to each other at the time. Then it runs through all the combinations. With luck, we'll get a 'turn right,' or 'follow me,' or 'look at this.' It's up to Heln to recognize a response."

But there was no sign of recognition from the insect-folk that Bram could see. By stretching his imagination to the limit, he might at best have concluded that they showed a sort of irritation or brief annoyance—analogous to what a human might display if a light were flashing in his eyes or if he were trying to talk with a radio on in the background. But such distractions, really, were below the level of awareness.

"The computer's learning all the time," Jao said defensively. "Sooner or later it might hit on something."

"What you've done is amazing," Bram assured him.

Jao brightened. "Want to know what the hardest part was? It wasn't the program. It was inventing the gizmo to recognize the polarization through different planes of orientation, then to transmit the same way. That's what takes up so much room in the backpack. I had to scavenge the faceplates of a whole bunch of helmets to build it."

Heln, arms spread low, purposely penetrated the avoidance zone and dropped to one knee, then danced back as the creatures showed restlessness. Her equipment blazed a signal that looked sustained to human eyes but that to the aliens, of course, would have flickered. Bram saw the shadowy facial limbs lift as if to ward off something, but the creatures never stopped their prowling movements.

"They still don't see it as speech," Jao said. "Something missing."

"Very frustrating," Bram said.

One of the insect-people was using an odd camera—a sizable box with one curved face studded with thousands of pinhole lenses. It took its pictures by sweeping areas of the ruins in short arcs.

"Multiple fixed-focus lenses," Jao said. "Motion shifts

the pattern. They must have some way of reading the result. Like Heln said, it's the way they see."

"They're not much interested in the people," Bram said. "Or individual objects. They seem to want fields of view."

"Looking for another place to light," Jao said. "The digs here are ready-made of them—honeycombed with chambers connected by a tunnel system."

"No," Bram said. "We can't allow that. We'll be coming back here someday. We've got to talk them out of it."

"First we've got to find a way to talk to them."

The insect-people spent the next few hours exploring, completely ignoring the holiday crowd that tagged along. After a while, Bram became aware that their seemingly random forays added up to an extremely efficient search grid.

Besides the camera, whose purpose was obvious, they used a number of other instruments. One was a long stinger that came out of a cylinder on legs and penetrated the ground to a depth of—Bram estimated by counting the telescoping sections—thirty feet, at least. The tripod gave a little jump when it hit bottom. "Their version of a thumper," Jao said. "They're searching for cavities." Other instruments, with a little thought, were soon recognized as a surveyor's transit and a range finder, adapted to the peculiar insect vision.

The creatures seemed to get restive after a while, and after they had darted at one another in a series of little mock attacks, they all filed back to their vehicle, launched themselves up into the end of the angled tubular chassis, and disappeared inside. Bram waited, but the barrel-wheeled vehicle showed no signs of starting up.

Heln sauntered over. "Lunch break for them," she observed. "Or some kind of break. Whatever it is, they've got to take off those helmets to do it."

After twenty minutes passed, the creatures popped out of the end of the tube again and resumed their mysterious activities. Several of them could be observed preening their nightmare faces. Jorv appeared with an assistant, who took more pictures.

At the end of another couple of hours, the creatures

found the ramp to the parking garage under the sports arena. This seemed to excite them. There was another head-to-head conference, with eight long tail sections sticking out and wobbling, the gauntleted claspers working convulsively.

They knew about air locks. Afraid that they might damage the locks leading to the stadium interior, Bram had been about to order that the creatures be let through while someone held the door, but one of them figured out the human machinery at a jelly-eyed glance, and they swarmed inside. They even closed it behind them.

They seemed to be awfully good with machinery.

"They can notice inanimate objects," Bram puzzled, "but not a crowd of people."

"You don't understand," Heln said. "We *are* inanimate objects."

"Yar," Jao said, as if he were an expert. "We haven't impinged on them."

A thought struck Bram. "They must have seen the shuttles parked in the field on their way through. If not man, then man's works! Why didn't they take an interest in *those*?"

"Held no meaning for them," Heln supplied. "Wasn't important. Not like the air lock here. They *wanted* to get inside."

Bram spoke to his traffic control deputies. "Keep the mob outside. I won't evict anyone who's already in there, but I think we'd better keep the numbers down."

Without their space suits, the creatures from Sol were an unnerving sight—spiny legs, globular green eyes, and hard shiny integument bristling with stiff hairs. The four-fingered claspers at their projecting rears were pincers of horn, and the forward manipulating limbs, now revealed, were all tweezers and hooks.

They prowled the floor and balconies of the chamber, taking no more notice of the gawking humans than humans would have taken of moss on a rock. With the boxy helmets off, the clicking noises they made to each other could be heard like a high-speed rattle of broken sticks.

Their insect ancestry was fully apparent. "You see,"

Jorv said ecstatically, "how evolution modified the exo-skeleton in a way that permitted them to grow to size. It became a partially embedded, hinged, mostly external skeleton that operates as a system of levers. The extensor and flexor muscles operate separately, bridging the hinges on opposite sides."

The skeletal apparitions gave everybody cause to remember their childhood ghost stories in Chin-pin-yin; the word for a foreigner was, literally, a "bones-outside," and now Bram heard people around him starting to call the Earthlings that.

Jorv could hardly contain himself. "You see the pulsating of the abdomen? I think they breathe through their anus. I wonder what evolution gave them in place of lungs."

"What *are* they?" Ame asked.

"I don't know," Jorv said. "They may have been aquatic. In that case—"

He was interrupted by a chattering Cuddly that skidded to a stop in front of the group and climbed up the nearest person to reach the shelter of human arms. The person happened to be Ame, who petted the fluffy little beast and cooed, "There, there, nothing's going to hurt you." The Cuddly had ventured too close to a prowling insect-thing and had had second thoughts about approaching it.

The insect-beings, in fact, had quite an audience of Cuddlies by this time. When the strange creatures had arrived and shucked their space suits, the couple of dozen Cuddlies that normally mooched around the chamber looking for handouts had immediately disappeared. After a while, when nothing much happened and the human beings seemed unconcerned, a few cautious little furry heads had popped up.

Now the Cuddlies were getting bolder. One fat little creature sat up on its haunches and scolded an insect-being that had paused for a moment to survey the arena floor.

"Isn't that cute?" Ame said. "It wants the bones-outside to pay some attention to it."

"If *we* can't get their attention with computer displays and polarized light, there's not much hope for a Cuddly," Shira said.

The little beast hopped closer and chittered more loudly.

"It's getting awfully close to the avoidance zone." Heln frowned. "I wonder..."

"I think the thing's showing some reaction," Jao said.

The face-legs, liberated from their box, swung idly to and fro. There was something about the stick-creature's stance. It seemed to lower itself a few inches and become utterly still.

Encouraged, the Cuddly made another little hop forward.

There was a blur of motion so fast that Bram saw it only as an afterimage. The masklike face of the alien split vertically, and a long scooplike lip tipped with teeth flicked out and captured the little furry beast.

The hinged lip, longer than a man's arm, snapped back, bearing the ensnared Cuddly to a barbed mouth. There was a single high-pitched squeal, and then with two crunches, the Cuddly was gone. The lobes of the toothed structure folded over to become a mask again.

The hum of human conversation in the chamber stopped abruptly. People stood frozen. Every Cuddly in sight streaked for a hiding place and disappeared. The insect-being stood preening itself with its hooked facial limbs. Its fellows paused in their rambles and turned their jelly-domed heads in its direction.

In the stunned silence, Jorv stood with dropped jaw, breathing hard. Suddenly he exclaimed, "Odonata!" and before Bram could stop him, he stepped up to the immobilized creature for a close look at its face.

There was another blurred movement as the creature seized Jorv with its facial limbs and bit his head off.

A woman screamed. People came out of their trances. The creature calmly continued crunching its way through Jorv's neck and shoulder. Jao grabbed one of the picks that the archaeologists had left lying around. Bram found a steel pry bar. Several others joined them, and they ran to recover what was left of Jorv's body from the leggy horror that was chomping its way through it.

It wouldn't let go. A couple of men had Jorv's body by the feet and were trying to pull it away. Bram grabbed the creature by one of its facial palps and tried to lever

its jaws open with the pry bar. A hooked leg came up and
raked him across the ribs. There was a sound of ripped
cloth and a searing pain, but he held on. Jao swung his
pick handle and smashed one of the bulging green eyes.

Even then it wouldn't let go. It rotated in injured circles, still munching, lashing out at the struggling men with
its barbed legs. The long abdomen whipped around and
a man screamed as its horned pincers tore at his flesh.

Bram went berserk. He beat at the armored hide with
his steel bar while Jao, grunting, labored with his pickax
at the ruined jelly of the head. The thing refused to die.
The limbs slashed blindly at the air. But it dropped its
grisly meal, and the long toothed lip struck out again and
again, looking for prey . Finally someone got a sharpened
pole—one the diggers used for soundings—and ran the
creature through, repeatedly, till it stopped moving.

Bram stood wearily, drenched in blood and gore, holding the slippery pry bar. He couldn't tell how much of the
blood was his own and how much had spilled from Jorv.

Shouts and screams echoed through the huge arena.
The other insect-creatures, as if by a common signal, had
gone on the attack. On a high balcony, the tragedy of Jorv
was repeated as a stick-being pursued a fleeing woman
and caught her with its facial snare. People came running,
too late, to her aid. They beat and stabbed at the creature
with whatever came to hand. One of the rescuers was
flung away, disemboweled by a stroke of a hind claw. The
tattered body tumbled slowly through the air toward the
distant floor below.

Elsewhere, one of the spindly horrors ran at a group
of people and emerged with a screaming victim in its
mouth. It ran off with its prize, munching as it went,
dropping a trail of arms and legs behind it.

Two more of the insect-beings bore down on the group
of shaken people gathered around Jorv's headless body.
They were a terrifying sight, but no one ran. An extensible
lip shot out and clasped someone's leg in its prehensile
hooks, but two quick-witted people threw themselves on
the victim and prevented him from being dragged back.
Men and women with poles, shovels, axes—anything that
could be used as a weapon—converged on the monster

from both sides. It loosed its grip, leaving a mangled leg that would have to be regenerated if the victim lived, and swung its three-lobed head at its tormentors. The lip raked across one victim, tearing flesh, and another man went down under the onslaught of the barbed head-legs. But other people harried it from behind, and when it swiveled its killing apparatus around to deal with them, a brave woman with a pole leaped high into the air and jabbed at a globular eye from above.

Meanwhile Bram saw the other creature rushing straight at him. The facial limbs were already extended for grasping. He knew he would be no match for the lightning thrust of the feeding apparatus—it surpassed his reach, even with the iron bar in his hand.

He dropped the bar and wrenched one of the heavy display tables from the ground. He put his whole back into it, swiveling from the hips. It was a massive piece of rough carpentry, twelve feet long, laden with rock and metal fragments that the archaeologists had not bothered to pack up. In the infinitesimal gravity, he could have lifted a weight ten times as heavy, but speed was the problem, and he needed all his muscular strength to overcome the inertia.

The table became his shield as the creature's lip struck. There was a sound of splintering wood, and Bram felt himself being driven back by the thrust. A rain of jagged stone and metal pelted his adversary. Bram shoved back, hard, and the weight of the table helped him; his feet were braced against the ground, while his opponent, losing contact, clung to the table as Bram ran it at full speed into the wall.

Three or four people ran to help him keep the creature pinned against the wall while somebody finished it off with an ax.

They stood around panting. "We're monkeys, monkeys," Ame sobbed beside him, and he became aware that she was one of the people who had helped him keep the creature pinned. "I thought we were human, but we knew in our bones how to gang up on them."

"All the rocks and junk confused it for a minute," Jao said. "Just long enough."

That gave Bram an idea. "Throw things at them!" he shouted.

The carnage on the floor was terrible. The insects had better reach with their legs and facial snares than the humans did with their shovels and axes, and they were very quick.

Jao was the first to react. He scooped up an armful of archaeological detritus from one of the big tables and sent a hail of missiles at another of the spindly creatures that was heading in their direction. It veered off. A sharp fragment caught it in one eye. Its lip shot out reflexively to find an enemy.

People were quick to get the idea. There were plenty of sharp objects to throw: shards from the long tables, cast-off equipment, and rubble from the floor itself. A barrage of missiles peppered the creatures from ground level and pelted them from the balconies. They came from all directions, thunking into the stiff hides, finding pulpy spots. There was no way for the creatures to avoid them, as marvelous as their eyesight was and as quick as their reflexes were. Every time they made a dash at a group of people, they were met by a volley of hurled objects.

Not that they were always turned aside. Sometimes they barged into a group, knocking people over and lacerating them, and carried someone off. They seemed to have no concept that they were outnumbered.

And then some brainy person reinvented the spear.

It was only a kitchen knife lashed hastily to a pole, but its owner—maybe losing his nerve about running it into an enemy personally—flung it at an insect-thing as it passed him. The blade hit a soft spot, and the creature ran by with the pole sticking out of it. Another person threw another improvised pike, then everybody who had a sharp stick seemed to join in. The wounded creature began to run in circles, snapping at the skewers in its hide, then grew weaker and less purposeful, sinking to its four skeleton knees. When the surrounding people saw that it was safe to approach it, they hacked it to pieces.

Something new had entered human affairs—a thing that could kill at a distance.

It was over in another fifteen minutes—not without

more human casualties. The last insect survivor, seeing
that it was alone, fled.

"Don't let it get to its space suit!" Heln cried.

A bunch of people took off in pursuit, but it evaded
them. Later, Bram reconstructed what had happened. The
insect-thing had killed two people it found in the tunnel
on the inner side of the air lock, retrieved its space suit,
and charged into the crowd outside. With its coffer of a
helmet on—its facial limbs caged up, and, perhaps, its
senses muffled—it was no longer aggressive. Nobody
outside knew what had been going on. The crowd parted
to make way for it, and the deputies were pleased to see
that nobody interfered with it. It hightailed it back to its
barrel-wheeled vehicle and drove out of town.

The killing spree had left seven dead aliens and more
than thirty dead and dismembered human beings. It was
going to be hard to tell the exact number until the body
parts that were strewn over the chamber were matched
up. Bram moved among the weeping people, viewing the
butchery. One of the dead was Alb, the junior archivist
whom Bram had reprimanded. Somehow he had slipped
past the deputies and gotten inside; poor Alb, he had
thought it all a lark.

"I suppose it was the space suits," Heln said, white as
flour. "We didn't look appetizing to them inside ours, and
their own feeding impulses were stifled with a sheet of
plastic cutting off their sensory world." She shuddered.
"They like their food live and moving. I wonder what kind
of livestock they carry with them in that tube vehicle of
theirs."

Nobody had thought about *that* part of it. Ame looked
ill. Bram remembered the creatures' behavior just before
they had taken time out to return to their vehicle for a
rest break.

"Maybe animals about the size and shape of a Cuddly,"
Bram said. "Possibly even mammals."

"Yah, the Cuddly popping up in front of that thing was
what tripped the switch," Jao said.

Heln gave the others a bleak look. "Yes, that and poor
Jorv, sticking his face inside their unobstructed striking

range. Their brains are rewired now. They've been programmed to see human beings. As food."

They spent the next day burying the dead—what could
be found of them. Bram found some words in King James
that seemed to express what everybody was feeling and
read them aloud over his suit radio while the surviving
human population stood around the grave site, heads
bowed inside their helmets. The terrestrial biology group
under Jorv's assistant took charge of the insect carcasses
and began to do autopsies.

When Bram called Yggdrasil, Jun Davd urged him to
close down the digs and return at once. "It's an unlucky
place now, I fear. If Heln is correct, the danger's just
beginning."

"I'm sending the first shuttle loads out today. We should
all be evacuated by the day after tomorrow. In the meantime, I've posted a guard. The main thing is not to let
them get inside the pressurized buildings with us."

"You ought to know that radio traffic between the colony and the father ship has resumed."

"They've renewed their connection?"

"For the time being. They had something to say to
each other. You can imagine what it is."

"I take your meaning, Jun Davd. I'll try to speed up
the evacuation."

"It's hard to abandon what we've found of our heritage,
I know. But we were going to leave soon, anyway."

Bitterness clogged Bram's voice. "Yes, but we always
meant to come back one day. Now..."

"Yes," Jun Davd said somberly. "They'll have spread
to the other disks by then. But Bram, we've done wonders
in the year we've been here—thanks in large part to the
spadework the rat archaeologists did for us. We've got
the great libraries of mankind and a whole biological repository of extinct life forms..."

"I know, Jun Davd. We never thought we'd regain so
much of our heritage. Still..." He felt suddenly weary.
For the first time, the centuries of wandering seemed to
have caught up with him—more than six of them by now,

while the clock of the universe had ticked off its tens of millions of years.

"What did Jorv mean, 'Odonata'?" Bram said.

Jorv's assistant, Harld, faced him, a scalpel in his hand, still looking pale and shaken. He had a thick white bandage on his head, covering the scalp wound he'd received trying to save a woman from the jaws of an insect-creature, and there were deep scratches down one long bony cheek.

Harld put the scalpel down, looking thoughtful. He paused to look around behind himself where the other two surviving members of the zoology department continued their dissection of one of the insect corpses. The body cavity was laid open, with internal organs spread out fanwise, and Bram did not care for too close a look.

"Odonata? Is that what he said?"

"Yes. Just before he died. He said it after he saw the way the creature grabbed the Cuddly, as if that had made him remember something."

"It comes from a root in a pre-Inglex language called Greek. It means 'tooth.' Original Man used Greek prefixes a lot in scientific classification. Ever since Jorv got back from his trip to the insect camp, he'd been poring over the old archives for insect references, especially from an institution known as the Smithsonian. But there was just so much material to absorb..."

"What does 'tooth' have to do with it?"

"It sounds as if it may be the name of the insect order."

"Can you..."

"There's nothing to it, now. It's all alphabetical. Come back in an hour."

Bram spent the hour arguing with one of the curators from the art team, who wanted to pack an entire shuttle with a collection of paintings and photoplastic art that had been discovered at the last minute.

"It's irreplaceable," the man pleaded. "Originals that were on loan from Earth museums. Art that was produced here on the diskworld over a period of several centuries — some of it of the very highest order. We can make a selection—let me assure you that we're prepared to be very *stringent* with ourselves—and have it vacuum crated within a Tenday."

Bram tried to explain that there was neither the space nor the time. "There are still crates of last-minute finds out next to the shuttle pad that are going to have to be abandoned," he said. "Can't you make microreproductions of it?"

"You don't *understand*!" the curator wailed. "These are *originals*!"

In the end, it was decided that the curator and his staff would be allowed to take a selection of some of the smaller objects with them as their personal baggage. "The Rembrandt engravings," the curator decided. "The little votive figurines from the Falwellite thearchy. The photoplastic diskscapes from the neo-literalist period. And some of the small table sculpture. Oh, dear, how will I ever winnow it down?"

Bram suggested that the museum staff load all the excess artwork that they could manage during the next twenty hours on one of the unused rocket-assisted pallets. Some tens of the pallets were slated to be left behind along with a lot of cargo walkers and heavy machinery. "See Jao," Bram said. "He'll compute a rough trajectory for you. We'll have to shoot it off unmanned, but with luck, one of the interbranch vehicles from Yggdrasil will snare it and bring it in."

"B-but it could be lost forever," the curator said. "Better to leave it here."

"No," Bram said, looking him in the eye. "It wouldn't."

That got through. The curator nodded grimly. "I'll get moving on it right away."

When Bram returned to Harld, the thin-featured zoologist was waiting for him next to a table spread with photoplastic readouts. He handed one to Bram without comment.

Bram took the stiff sheet from him. It showed a slender, jewellike creature with bulging metallic eyes and four fragile, veined wings.

"*Odonata*," Harld said. "Suborder *Anisoptera*. Also

known as the dragonfly, or sometimes by such names as the devil's darning needle, the mosquito hawk, or the bee butcher.

Bram studied the photograph. He could see several features that suggested a possible provenance for the insect-folk: the domelike eyes, the long segmented body with the claspers at the end, the six wiry legs all grouped together just behind the head.

"Our neighbors across the plain don't have wings," he pointed out.

"Neither did their ancestors," Harld said. "You're looking at the adult form of the dragonfly. That creature on the dissecting table is descended from an immature form called a nymph."

Bram looked across at the grisly specimen, the liplike structure with its hooked clasping lobes was spread out to more than a fourth of the creature's body length. He shuddered.

"Dragonflies spent most of their lives as nymphs," Harld went on. "Years, sometimes. They lived underwater, breathing through gills, eating voraciously till they grew to size. They'd attack anything that moved—creatures bigger than they were. When it came time for them to change, they'd climb up a reed, split their skin, and emerge as that glorious winged creature you see there. The adult form—the imago—was the one that reproduced. It lived only a few Tendays and died after laying its eggs."

He handed Bram another photoplastic readout. This one showed a dragonfly climbing out of a pale, cast-off ghost of itself and spreading its gossamer wings.

"What confused the issue," Harld said, warming to his subject, "was that *Odonata*'s like no other insect order. There was a separate evolution of the nymphal and imagal forms—probably dating back to before Earth's Carboniferous period. The dragonfly larva lacked the specialized regeneration centers—'imaginal disks,' they're called—that in other insects formed the adult tissues from latent embryonic cells, while the larval tissues melted away. They never went through an intervening pupal stage. They changed by direct growth."

He was shoving more readouts at Bram. "The nymph

adapted for an aquatic life, while the adult dragonfly remained virtually the same," he said. "The nymph evolved independently. It developed gills. Then, at some point, apparently—like other aquatic creatures—it left the water *in its immature form* and developed the ability to breathe air."

Something ugly stirred in Bram's memory, the shadow of an ancient image.

Harld was trying to show him something on the autopsy table. "Jorv was perfectly right about the way they developed the equivalent of lungs. A portion of the alimentary canal just anterior to the rectum became enlarged into a sort of bellows."

One of the other zoologists, a freckle-faced fellow, grinned crudely. "What a way to inhale," he said.

Harld looked annoyed. "It was an obvious evolutionary step—that's where the gills were, with their ready-made oxygenating apparatus. In human beings, the embryonic gill structures are derived from the *upper* alimentary canal—and that's why breathing and swallowing are interrelated in us."

The shadowy memory nagged at Bram. There had been something, a long, long time ago . . .

Harld was saying, "So it was through these aquatic forms that evolution got around the problem of the breathing spiracles that had formerly placed limits on the size and intelligence of land insects. Plus the modification of the exoskeleton into a partially internalized support. It gave the *Odonata* access to the evolutionary niche previously occupied by the large mammals."

"And now they're the inheritors of the earth," Bram murmured.

Harld frowned. "But first they had to learn how to reproduce in the nymphal stage. Without having to metamorphose into the adult winged form. Because otherwise the need to fly would have placed a limiting factor on their size."

And then Bram suddenly remembered.

"It was an unstable allele. Original Man spliced a set of synthetic chimeras into dragonfly DNA. They were trying to modify the nymph to create an organism that would keep insect pests under control in their arctic regions. They thought it would remain an aquatic form and do man's work for him. But it got out of hand."

"What?" The three zoologists gave their full attention. "Do you know something of this, Bram?"

It all came flooding back. It had been buried for almost seven hundred years in a mind that had become overlaid by other experiences. Slowly at first, then with increasing fluency, Bram told them about the synthetic heterochronic gene that had made the self-reproducing hen's egg possible—about the way a DNA chimera had been contrived out of genetic material derived from the dragonfly and the axolotl. How, generations later, Original Man had discovered the dangers lurking in the construct and had radioed a warning in a codicil to his first great Message. And how the Nar, accordingly, had suppressed the file—though it contained the seeds of man's immortality. How he, Bram, a rare human apprentice in a Nar touch group, had stumbled upon the reference and confronted his mentor, Voth, with it. How the entire Nar nation had carried their burden of guilt and finally, stunningly, made amends.

"You're saying, then, that it was the nymphal dragonflies that exterminated Original Man?" Harld asked.

His eyes were filled with horror. He was wondering, Bram knew, if it was all about to happen again.

"No, no," Bram said. "Original Man solved the problem. Or thought he had. At great cost. The near destruction of his arctic ecology. But the mutation must just have been biding its time. It waited, buried in dragonfly nucleotides, for forty million years . . . fifty million years. Long enough for the human race to go the way of the dinosaurs and to be replaced by a dominant species evolved from rats. Long enough for the rat-people to go the way of humankind—according to that timetable of periodic extinctions that your department drew up when we first arrived at the Milky Way. And when the rat-folk were gone, there was an ecological niche vacant, waiting for a new intelligent, cooperating species about the size of a man. No mammal, no vertebrate, could have competed with such as the nymphs had become."

All of them, the three zoologists and Bram, involuntarily looked over to the dissection table where the latest inheritor of the Earth lay. Harld swallowed hard.

"Man did this?" he asked.

"No, we must not be so arrogant," Bram said. "Perhaps it would have happened without us."

Harld opened his mouth as if he were about to say something further. But at that moment Jao came bursting into the improvised morgue.

"Better come quick!" Jao panted. "They're on their way!"

"Here?"

"Yar. About a hundred of those ground vehicles of theirs. We've got to round everybody up and get out to the shuttles before we're cut off."

Bram whirled around to the three zoologists. "Get going. Put on your vacuum suits and tell everybody you see to do the same. We're going to let the air out of this place."

He turned to Jao again. "All right, let's start deputizing people. How many of those shuttles are ready to be flown?"

"Enough—if we jam them full of people and dump everything else. In a couple of hours we can strap pallet rockets to some of them. It won't take much of a boost to at least get them off the ground out of harm's way. The pilots can finish their countdowns in space if they have to."

"Good. Let's get going."

Jao was sweating. "There's more," he said.

"What do you mean?"

"Jun Davd's been watching the ship through his telescopes. He radioed at almost the exact time our own lookouts saw the ground vehicles starting our way."

A chill ran down Bram's spine. "Go on," he said.

"More of the environmental bubbles are detaching themselves from the stick-ship. They're just boiling off it. Drifting down to the rim of the diskworld. And some of them are heading toward Yggdrasil."

Part III

SECOND EXODUS

CHAPTER 10

"He went back for the Rembrandts," a terrified assistant babbled. "He said he couldn't bear to leave them behind."

Bram shook the man into coherence. "How long ago?"

"About two hours ago. He took a walker."

Bram released him. "The fool," he said. "The idiotic fool." He pushed his way across the crowded shuttle deck to the raised platform of the control section, where Jao stood conferring in low tones with the pilot.

The pilot turned a worried face toward him. She was a big-boned woman with brown curly hair, a member of Lydis's comet-chasing squadron and, therefore, a crack flyer. "We're ready to go," she said. "We ought to lift off within the half hour or . . ."

She trailed off and glanced meaningfully out the arbitrary forward port across the pale ribbon of landscape.

"Is everyone else accounted for?" Bram asked Jao.

"Yar. The curator was accounted for, too, on our preliminary name check. He must have slipped away right afterward."

"He ought to have been back by now. Unless something happened to him."

Jao, without apology, reached past the pilot and punched a telescopic view of the plain into one of the screens. He adjusted the angle of incidence until he got what he was looking for, then refined the focus. Bram saw a thin haze of dust, its forward edge advancing, its rearward margin slowly settling.

"Less than fifty miles away," he said. "They could be here in an hour."

Bram checked the latches of his helmet before putting it on. "I'd better go look for him."

"Are you crazy?" Jao exploded. "There isn't time. If he doesn't get back in time for lift-off, we'll have to leave without him."

Bram turned to the pilot. "Don't wait for me," he said. "I'll keep in radio contact, but if I go off the air or if I'm late, lift off without me. Is that understood?"

"I'll wait till the last possible moment, Year-Captain," the pilot said.

"Don't cut it too fine," Bram said. He lifted the helmet to his shoulders.

Jao retrieved his own helmet. "I'm going with you. No argument."

They squeezed into the air lock together. "Leave the outside door open." The pilot's voice rang in his radio. Jao nodded and deployed a rope ladder, but they didn't waste time using the ladder to climb down; they let themselves drop, with a little shove to speed them on their way.

"This way," Jao said.

He led the way across the field to where a helter-skelter collection of walkers and wheeled machinery had been abandoned. Boxes, bundles, and personal possessions were strewn at random where they had been dropped. Some of the walkers stirred nervously, giving the illusion of life. They had no consciousness, of course—they were just protein machines—but still Bram hated the thought of leaving them here on a dragonfly world. Though, he reflected, if a dragonfly tried to eat one, the walker would poison it.

"This one," Jao said. "It's Old Speedy, the one that won all the races last summer." He checked the reselin tendons to make sure they were hard and taut, eyed the diameter of the central ball of muscle to see that it still retained sufficient running time, and climbed inside. Bram followed him through the flap, and Jao put the biomachine in motion with a slap of the reins.

The walker ran flat out toward the digs, Jao urging it on at a gallop. Bram twisted around for a look at the launching pad. The first shuttle was mounting the sky on a tail of fire. There were six more to go, with the approximately one hundred eighty remaining evacuees crowded into them. The life-support facilities would be strained, but they'd survive until they reached Yggdrasil.

A half hour later, the moon ladder came into view, with the stalled car dangling from it. The low, regular rubble mounds of the outskirts of the city lay only a few miles ahead of them.

"We're running late," Bram said. "Do you see any sign of him?"

"No."

Behind them, another shuttle rose into the sky. It was the fourth. There were only three left to go.

"There's his walker," Jao said, slowing down.

The derelict walker stood spraddle-legged in a patch of loose gravel, its blunt prow facing the digs, not the landing field. There was no sign of the curator in the vicinity. Bram got out and examined the interior of the driver's bubble.

"Ran out of power," he announced to Jao. "He must have taken a walker that was already run down. I saw a few footprints. I guess he decided to walk the rest of the way in."

"What was it that he was after, anyway?" Jao said.

"A collection of Rembrandt engravings."

"You'd think they were germ plasm samples. Couldn't he have holoed them or something?"

"He said they were originals from Earth."

Jao looked nervously behind him. "There goes another shuttle."

Their pilot heard him. "I think you'd better start back now," she said. "Your time's running out."

"How close are they?"

"About thirty miles. They can probably see our shuttles by now. But they're still sticking pretty closely to the inner rim route that their scouts took. So far they've shown no sign of veering inland for a look at us."

"That's because as far as they know, all of the goodies are still waiting for them at the digs," Jao said gruffly. He turned to Bram. "Where would your Rembrandt lover have been headed?"

"Back to the sports arena, I suppose. That's where he left the things he wasn't able to carry."

"Serve him right if he got left behind himself," Jao growled. He made no move to start up the walker again.

"Bee butchers," Bram said softly. "That was one of the names for dragonflies. Bees were another kind of insect. They lived in communal hives. Original Man raised them for a substance called honey that they produced. Some dragonflies learned to hang around bee yards and wait for the workers to return with their loads. They'd dismember the bees on the wing, Harld told me, until the ground was littered with bee fragments."

"Like the way they massacred us in the arena," Jao said harshly.

"Yes."

Jao reached to the tiller. "You're right, of course, chaos take it. We can't leave the little fellow there."

The walker unlimbered its long legs and in a moment was flying at top speed toward the oval of reflected moonlight that marked the central city.

They came upon the curator a couple of miles farther on. He staggered toward them out of the rubble, carrying a huge portfolio that he seemed unable to lift high enough to keep from dragging, even in the microgravity. Jao came jolting to a halt, and he and Bram climbed down. The curator stared dully at them through his helmet, his face gray. They hustled him into the walker and cracked his helmet, while Bram checked his tanks.

"His air's almost gone," Bram said. "He never would have made it back on foot."

Jao tossed the portfolio into the back of the inflated compartment. "I hope these were worth it," he snarled at the curator. "You risked a shuttleful of lives for them."

Through blue lips, the curator said defiantly, "They're irreplaceable."

"So are we," Jao snapped.

The walker's long strides ate up the miles. Through the radio, the pilot's strained voice kept them informed. "Year-Captain, the main body of the dragonfly force just passed our position. But several vehicles have separated from it and are crossing the plain toward us. The other remaining shuttle is going to take off now."

Ahead, flame boiled from the landscape and climbed the black sky. Bram looked across at the rim road and saw a line of tiny specks heading toward the city.

"I can see the vehicles," Bram said. "We should reach your position in about ten minutes."

"I'm warming the engines. Please hurry."

"Oh, oh," Jao said. "Take a look at that."

The walker's movement had attracted attention. On the rim road, four of the specks left the dragonfly cavalcade and headed inland.

"Trying to cut us off," Jao said. "But a walker can outrun one of those rolling travel tubes without half trying."

"Don't be too sure," Bram said. The tilted cylinders were picking up speed, streaking across the surface like gigantic writing pens guided by an invisible hand. Now their speed was too much for the low gravity. They began to jounce into the air, higher and higher, between the brief scrabbling of the wheels at the ground. One of them bounced a good thirty feet and came down upright, still moving. The passengers within must be shifting their weight around to keep it stable. Wingless the nymphs might be, but they still had the instincts of fliers.

Bram could see the shuttle now, a minuscule dome on stilts. A haze of escaping gas covered its skirts. Beyond, a wave of the angled tube vehicles rolled toward it.

"It's going to be close," Jao said.

"Too close," Bram said. "We're drawing them toward you," he told the pilot. "It's no good. You'd better lift off *now!*"

"No," the pilot said. "I can see you now. The outside air lock door is open, and everybody's in a suit and helmet just in case. I'll hold for you until the last minute. Jump for the door, hold on to the ladder or a strut—anything—

if you have to. I'll use the docking jets to get us space-borne, so you don't have to worry about being cooked."

In the rear of the walker, the curator hugged his portfolio to himself and moaned. Bram wondered about jumping for the air lock one-handed. Perhaps he could throw the curator at the door. No, Jao could jump first, catch the curator and fling him inside, then catch the portfolio. It would be a shame to leave the etchings behind after they had risked their lives for them.

"We're not going to make it," Jao said.

Bram gave up the idea. The tube vehicles were fanning out to engulf the base of the lander—fanning out to engulf the walker when it arrived.

"Do as I say," Bram ordered. "You've got thirty people there to think of."

The pilot's voice was filled with anguish. "We'll wait. We've talked it over together."

Bram's eyes stung. Beside him on the narrow bench, Jao cursed and brought the walker to a rearing halt.

Off to the side, the four dragonfly vehicles that had moved to cut the walker off instantly made a slight course correction to adapt to the new vector.

"Listen," Jao said roughly, "there's still a pallet out there ready to go. I strapped the rockets to it myself. We're going for it. So forget about waiting for us."

In the rear, the curator sat goggle-eyed. He clutched the portfolio with a death grip.

"When you get back to the tree," Bram told the pilot, "tell Jun Davd to watch for us. If we miss, Lydis can try for a catch."

"Yar," Jao said. "It's line of sight all the way. It's not as if I have to *compute* it to the last decimal place."

With a sob, the pilot said, "Good-bye, Year-Captain," and cut off.

Jao started the walker up again. Bram peered through the transparent bubble at the lander. At its base, tube vehicles were jolting to a stop. Nymphs popped out of the ends of tubes and swarmed around it. Bram could see the sticklike figures clinging to the landing legs. Two of them were at the air lock door. One of them disappeared inside. It must have blown the inner door and been caught by the gust, because seconds later it came tumbling out. The big, box-shaped helmet made it top-heavy; by the time it hit the ground, it was falling head first. The transparent cage shattered.

"Glass," Bram said. "Their helmets are made of glass."

"So?" Jao, wrestling with the walker's controls. "They must have a very strange industrial base."

A brilliant puff of flame bloomed underneath the shuttle. She was using the main propulsion unit, after all— using it as a weapon. The flame spilled over the nearer dragonfly machines, swallowed the square-helmeted figures clamoring around the landing legs. Slowly the shuttle lifted, shedding dragonfly forms that twisted in the air and fell helmet-down. A few of them still clung to the air lock ladder and upper structures, to be carried like an infection to the tree. The humans would have to keep them outside somehow. Surely they couldn't carry enough air in their suits to last the whole trip.

That raised another specter. "Jao, are there any spare air bottles loaded on the pallet?"

"No. It wasn't intended to be manned. We'll have to take the walker with us for our life support."

Their four pursuers were closing in fast, along a broad front. Jao wrenched at the controls and spun the walker around. What made it scary was the fact that he was heading toward them at a slant, trying to beat them to the pallet. The other dragonfly vehicles—those which hadn't been seared by the lander's flame—abandoned the site where they had been deprived of their prey and decided to come after the walker.

"They're coming at us from all sides," Bram grimaced.

"Just hold on," Jao said. He pulled up at the pallet and scrambled out of the walker. "Help me unload some of this junk!" Bram tumbled out after him, leaving the helmetless curator huddled within, clutching his precious portfolio.

The pallet was dangerously unbalanced. The last-minute effort to load it had been abandoned halfway through. Piles of crates surrounded it, and more crates and sacks were heaped indiscriminately on its edges, waiting to have their weight distributed evenly and to be tied down.

Bram started heaving cargo overboard. He did not care to imagine what priceless human artifacts were being jettisoned. Jao worked beside him with frantic haste.

"That's good enough," Jao panted. "Just pray that it doesn't tip over when we get off the ground."

Together they lashed a cargo net over the remaining load. The top surface was fairly level; Bram could only hope that the different weights averaged out, too.

He stayed outside while Jao squeezed back into the walker and jumped it to the top of the load. Bram tied down the walker's legs while Jao crawled over obstacles to find the detonator.

Then a dragonfly vehicle skittered up, hitting the edge of the wooden platform with a jolt. The impact swerved it around. Bram looked up and saw the overhanging end of the tubular chassis above him. A hatch popped open, and box-helmeted forms came pouring out. The first of them floated downward—not so high as to make it fall on its head, but just high enough to give it a lazy half turn in midair and enable it to land on all fours.

More of the vehicles were crowding around, more hatches popping open, and then Jao set off the rockets.

He must have given it almost everything he had, because the platform lifted with an abrupt acceleration that batted the overhanging dragonfly transport aside and slammed Bram down.

The edge of the platform caught the helmet of one of the descending nymphs and shattered it. The mass of green jelly inside exploded sickeningly. Another nymph flailed for a clawhold, missed, and fell away under the rocket exhaust.

But two of the nymphs were on the platform, scuttling toward him. Bram had just time enough to note that one of the nymphs was carrying a flanged, open-sided box as big as its helmet, and then they were on him.

A pronged sleeve lashed out at him. He ducked and took it on his helmet. If it had ripped open his suit, he would have been done for.

The flexible abdomen, tipped with claspers, whipped around at him. He caught the pincers and then, with his toes hooked into the cargo net, swung the insect like a sling while the upper body twisted around trying to get at him. The glass helmet smashed against the corner of a crate, and the claspers relaxed just on the point of crushing his gloved hand between them.

But then the other nymph had him by two legs and its claspers and was trying to stuff him into the box. He struggled, but it was lifting him from behind, and he couldn't reach it.

Then he was in the box, staring through its open end into the cleft face of a tomato-eyed monster that was lifting him upward with blurring speed.

He tried to get his legs under him, but crammed into the box as he was, he couldn't untangle himself fast enough. The rockets had stopped firing. The pallet was coasting now, and free-fall turned him into the creature's plaything.

It held him at arm's length for inspection. The blank green eyes loomed through the glass, and the facial legs within the helmet stirred restlessly on their shelf. There was a latch at the bottom of the faceplate, a simple catch meant to be operated from inside, and one of the facial limbs was reaching for it. . . .

And then all of a sudden Jao was there with a wooden stake in his hand.

Jao swung, driving the stake through the glass of the square helmet. The glass showered in fragments. The lobed face burst, and the hinged eating apparatus—unfolding limply from the smooth mask—lolled amid the jellied ruin.

Jao helped him out of the box. "What are those flanges for? It looks like it's made to fit on to something . . . it's built sort of like a little air lock, isn't it?"

Bram looked over at the shattered helmet. He could see now that the front plate was made to slide up and down on grooves. His knees were suddenly weak from delayed reaction.

"It's an eating box," he said.

The tethered moon was far behind them, showing itself as pear-shaped with the wide end up. Even without Jao's crude thumb-and-nose sightings, it was obvious by now that they were way off course. The cargo platform had gone sailing hundreds of miles past the edge of the disk's rim, and they were looking down a ninety-million-mile cliff side.

"Too wide and too high," Jao said gloomily. "I had to fire all the rockets at once for a quick getaway. That jolt the nymphmobile gave us didn't help any, either."

The three of them had been cooped up together inside the walker's inflated bubble for an hour now, breathing by courtesy of the walker's hydrogen-oxygen submetabolism. The curator had recovered somewhat and was getting snappish.

"Does that mean it's going to take longer?" he complained. "I'm getting hungry. And my eyes and throat are burning from the atmosphere in here."

"Be thankful you're breathing at all," Jao said. "We're all going to be a little hungry after a while, but at least we won't die of thirst."

"See here," the little man said. "I insist—"

Bram interrupted. "If we keep on this way much longer, by the time we overtake Yggdrasil, we'll be thousands of miles off the rim. They won't know where to look for us. And our suit radios don't have that kind of range."

"Yah, I guess we better have a little course correction about now," Jao said.

"With what? I thought you said you shot off all our rockets."

"Oh, there were a couple of spares left over from when I rigged the pallet," Jao said casually. "They were still in the corner where I stowed them, fortunately. Under a tarpaulin. The stevedores must've thought they were part of the cargo. I lugged them over here while that walking appetite was trying to package you for its dinner."

He gestured negligently at the thousand square feet of lumpy cargo net on which the walker rested. Bram saw the two solid-propellant canisters lying several feet away.

"What good will those do?" he asked. "Two little booster rockets aren't enough to nudge a mass like this after the kick it got."

"Oh, we don't have to push the whole mass," Jao said.

"Even if we dumped everything—at least as much as we could manage in the next hour, working at top speed—the platform itself has too much mass. We'd never be able to kill enough momentum to come out with the right vector." He gestured at the receding rimscape and shrugged. "And after another hour of this..."

"We'll ride the *walker* in!" Jao said impatiently. "Use it as our lifeboat. It weighs practically nothing, and there's just the combined mass of the three of us. There's enough thrust in just *one* of those boosters to change *our* vector while conserving the useful momentum toward Yggdrasil!"

"Yes, but—"

"It's all in the angles. I'll retrofire the second rocket to slow us down at the other end enough to compensate for the extra momentum. Or most of it, anyway. We'll hang in Yggdrasil's space for hours—more than enough to zero in on our suit radios. And if we're still out of range, I can rig up a hydrogen flare or something."

They set to work with a will. There was more than enough cordage to lash the two canisters in position on the walker's spindly frame. "Best to secure the retrorocket now, while we have some footing underneath us," Jao said. "I can align it precisely with the median axis. When it's time to fire, we'll aim the whole walker by squirting oxygen or something."

"You going to clear the pallet the same way?"

"No...too many variables. I'm using the pallet as our launch platform. I *know* how it's tumbling."

Jao had done wonders with a few simple tools—the timer of his neck computer, a couple of wooden stakes marked off with measuring lines, a loop sight made of bent wire. "We can't miss," he said. "It's a three-hundred-mile-wide target."

Overcoming their distaste, they scavenged the dragonfly air tanks, then discovered that they were unusable. The air was thick with contaminants. One whiff set the curator coughing and wheezing.

"What's the air of their world like if they can breathe *that*?" Bram wondered aloud.

"Never mind," Jao said. "Take 'em along. We'll use 'em for attitude jets."

They were about to leave when they saw movement

amid the jumbled cargo. "We've got a stowaway," Jao said.

Bram tensed, but it was only a Cuddly. They coaxed the little fellow closer, then grabbed him. His fur was beginning to lose the trapped air that made it fluffy.

"We'd better take him with us," Bram said. "He can't last much longer here."

The small creature went willingly with them into the walker's inflated bubble, eagerly sniffing the air. He immediately made a nuisance of himself by attempting to curl up in the lap of the one person there who didn't care for animals—the curator.

"Get him off me," the curator yelled. "I don't want him messing up these etchings."

"Oh, for Fatherbeing's sake, he's not going to hurt any.hing," Jao said. "You've got them in nitrogen envelopes, anyway."

Bram lifted the little beast away. "He's an old one," he said. "Look at that grizzled fur."

"Yar, he's lived a long time, all right. His string almost ran out here, though. He would have gone spinning through vacuum for eternity. Lucky we saw him in time."

"Smart of him to come out and show himself, you mean."

Jao cocked his head. "Going to bring him home to Mim?"

The Cuddly settled contentedly in Bram's lap. "I guess I've got myself another Cuddly," he sighed. "I hope he gets along with Loki."

The furry animal responded to Bram's voice by lifting its gray muzzle and blinking at him with big trusting brown eyes.

"What are you going to name him?" Jao asked.

"Who was that character in King James who lived so long? Methuselah. I'll call him Methuselah."

"Hear that, Methuselah? I guess you've got yourself a new home." Jao spoke absently, his eye on the changing chronograph display of his pendant computer. "Five more seconds, then we'll be pointed just right. Hold on, here we go."

He set off the solid fuel booster with the yank of a

wire, and the walker flew like a cork into space. The square bulk of the pallet tumbled away from them and grew smaller against the disk-filled night.

"Hold tight," the voice of Lydis crackled through the static. "I'm coming to pick you up."

"Did everybody make it?" Bram asked.

"Yes, the last shuttle got here hours ago. Smeth's into his countdown. We blast off within the fivehour."

That explained why Yggdrasil had stopped spinning. The tree's green hemispheres filled the sky ahead of them, a sandwich with the void of space for a filling. The trunk was a stubby bar in the middle, eclipsing stars, seemingly pierced by the long skewer of the probe behind it. They were still too far above the surface to make out any detail of branches or leaf-clothed roots, but scattered here and there across the greener dome were the pinpoint lights of human habitation.

Bram looked for the yellow wink of Lydis's drive and found it to one side. There was a more ominous sight beyond it—the pearly motes of dragonfly bubbles floating among the stars.

"How far from Yggdrasil do you make them?" Bram asked.

"We'll beat them," she said shortly, and switched off.

The burn was a long one, lasting almost an hour. Bram watched the flame until it winked out. Ten minutes later it flared up again, many times brighter now that it was facing them.

"That daughter of yours doesn't fool around," Jao said admiringly. "Burn till turnover, and no corrections." He glanced at the chronograph window of his display. "She'll be here in less than nine decaminutes."

Actually it took a full hour; Jao had forgotten to allow for the fact that Lydis would have to shut off her engine a little early to avoid cooking them and coast the last few miles. Even so, she was still killing momentum with her hydrazine maneuvering jets when she arrived.

They watched through the clear bubble as the rhombohedral bulk bore down on them. Lydis was flying a heavy-duty space tug—a comet chaser—instead of one of the lightweight interbranch shuttles.

"Come on, let's go," Jao said.

He picked up one of the scavenged dragonfly air tanks—a ribbed ovoid with a stopcock in the form of two levers meant to be squeezed together—and slipped one arm through its webbing. Bram screwed the curator's helmet back on while the man fussed at him. After a moment's thought, he replaced the curator's depleted air bottle with his own half-full one; actually, any of them could breathe for about nine minutes on the cubic foot or so of oxygen-rich walker air trapped in their suits, but the curator wouldn't know that, and Bram didn't want the little man getting panicky and thrashing around.

Together, he and Jao grabbed the curator by the arms and hauled him bodily through the air flap. The Cuddly came tumbling out on the blast of released air and, making an agile recovery, landed on Bram's shoulder.

The tug hovered a few hundred feet away, its nets spread like wings. Bram could see the mists of the hydrazine jets as Lydis nudged the behemoth toward them.

While the curator squirmed in their grasp, Jao aimed the nozzle of the dragonfly tank at a spot ahead of the tug and squirted polluted air into space. Lydis saw what he was doing and compensated her vector for lateral motion.

They sailed across the gap, with Methuselah riding happily on Bram's shoulder, and slammed into a net with rather more force than was elegant. The curator's mouth popped open as the breath was driven out of him. Methuselah went head over heels, caught a strand in his tiny paws, and scrambled back to Bram's shoulder.

They hauled themselves and the curator's wriggling form toward the open air lock door while Lydis positioned the tug for the return journey. She hardly looked up as they came squeezing through into the cabin.

"Strap yourselves down," she said. "We're going back in a hurry."

The tug skimmed bare miles above Yggdrasil's branches as Lydis followed the curve of the crown. Close—too close to the tree's edges—was the vanguard of the dragonfly force. Bram saw the lead bubble, a whitish orb a half mile in diameter, floating to a landing in the treetop.

"Lydis," came Jun Davd's strained voice through the radio. "We're about to start fusion. Smeth's evacuated the probe, and all his technicians are aboard Yggdrasil. What are you doing?"

"Go ahead and start up," she said through clenched jaws. "Don't worry about us."

"Get in to the trunk," he said. "A docking crew's waiting for you."

"I can set down anywhere, even if we lose the tug. With no spin on the branches, I don't need to rendezvous with the trunk. That's the problem. Neither do those dragonfly hatcheries out there. How close is the first of them?"

Jun Davd hesitated. "We'll be under way before it makes contact," he admitted reluctantly, "but not by much of a fraction of a g."

Lydis gave Bram an inquiring glance. He nodded.

"That's not good enough," she said. "If any of those ... things ... get inside Yggdrasil and start to breed..."

She shuddered, and Bram shuddered with her. The thought of a bubble alighting in the branches and disgorging thousands of voracious nymphs was too horrible to contemplate.

"Yes, the same thought had occurred to me," Jun Davd admitted. "We have a number of armed groups waiting outside around the likeliest points of contact. But we're no match for them."

Bram leaned over Lydis's shoulder and told Jun Davd about the glass helmets.

"Thank you, Bram," Jun Davd said. "That ought to help. We can throw missiles. Humans are good at playing ball, at least. But we're spread too thinly through the branches. We'll be vastly outnumbered at any given attack site, until we can rush reinforcements—and that's going to take too long under acceleration, using the internal transport system."

"That's why I'm doing this," Lydis said.

"Good luck," Jun Davd said simply.

"What's going on?" the frightened curator asked. "Why aren't we landing?"

Bram tried to calm him down. The little man drew himself up. "You don't *understand*," he said with mustered dignity. "I'm not concerned for myself. But nothing must be allowed to happen to these Rembrandts."

"If the dragonflies get into the tree, they'll use them for napkins," Jao said. "So shut up."

The curator assumed an aggrieved expression. "If I can help..."

"I'll let you know," Bram said. "In the meantime, hang on to that portfolio."

The tug rounded the curve of the treetop with a virtuoso application of lateral jets by Lydis. Ahead, the dragonfly bubble rose into view. Its pilot was applying the brakes with a skill that matched Lydis's. It hovered a bare quarter mile above the crown of leaves, its chemical jets scorching the branches. The other bubbles were some tens of miles away, not yet a threat.

The opalescent sphere crowded the viewport. With sickening clarity, Bram saw hundreds of space-suited nymphs crawling over its surface, ready to swarm over the branches at the instant of touchdown.

The tug hit it broadside with its cushioned nets. The work vehicle was a mere speck next to the sphere, but its powerful engines had moved comets larger than this.

Bram saw a shower of nymphs wriggling against the void, shaken loose by the impact. The pilot of the bubble frantically tried to bring his own maneuvering jets into play—either to try to burn the tug or to slip out of its clutches. He and Lydis dueled, two masters of the pilot's art. But Lydis anticipated every parry. Slowly she drove the hovering bubble off its landing pattern, moving it farther and farther along a tangent away from Yggdrasil.

The bubble's main thruster was pointed down toward the tree, still spouting fire and helping Lydis. There was only one way the pilot could hope to break away from the mite that was pushing so hard at his ship. He turned the breaking blast on full force, driving himself away from the tree so that he could start over again—and incidentally char the tug to a cinder.

Lydis was ready for him. The instant she felt herself losing contact, she spun the tug one hundred eighty degrees on its steering jets. By the time a half mile of globe had slipped past her, she was zooming away at full acceleration. It was the dragonfly bubble that was licked by *her* flame.

Bram could see the cloudy orb fighting for control. They were still alive in there, but they were in trouble. The nymph pilot was trying to spin the globe around so that he could kill his outward momentum and dive toward the tree again, but his key maneuvering jets must have been damaged because he could achieve only an erratic wobble.

Again, he did the only thing he could. He cut the main jet to stop his headlong outward flight and began, slowly and painfully, to spin the sphere around by some internal means.

"Either they've got a whopping big flywheel in there," Jao said, "or there're thousands of nymphs running around an inside track."

The globe receded into the distance. But the rest of them were drifting toward the giant tree like a clot of foam.

But by this time, Yggdrasil itself was moving beneath them. Bram saw the bright ball of the fusion sun in its cage, shining through the polarized disk that had appeared on the viewpoint to eclipse it. A brilliant pathway of hadronic photons reached thousands of miles into space, like a sword with the probe as its haft.

"Now to get down there before they build up to a g," Lydis said through clenched jaws.

Her fingers flew over the console, and the tug began its downward descent.

An incoherent choking sound came from the curator. "L-look, they're all over us!"

Bram whipped his head around. All of the viewpoints were filled with dragonfly faces, boxed in glass. Armored claspers hammered at the hull.

"We're covered with them," Lydis said. "They must have swarmed over us when we jolted them loose."

"How many?"

"I don't know. Tens of them, maybe."

Jao assumed a noble pose. "We can't take them back with us. We'll have to—"

"Too late," Bram said. "Some of them are already breaking free. They can drift down to Yggdrasil on their own."

"There's only one thing to do, then," Lydis said. "Deliver them to one spot."

She conferred by radio with Jun Davd. The outside defenders were alerted. They were all keeping their eye on the approaching tug. A flare went up to indicate where Lydis should try to land.

It was tricky. Fortunately, they were headed toward the leading edge of the tree crown, so there was no danger of sliding down the effective side of an accelerating object and falling into the photon stream. But Lydis had to contend with a rough landing field whose surface was rising toward her at an increasing but unknown rate and whose counterfeit gravity was mounting by the second.

Jao tried to help her with the variables and derivatives until she told him to shut up and let her concentrate.

Below, where the flare had been, Bram could see a ring of bobbing lights—men and women with torches. The ring expanded, dispersed, as the defenders scrambled outward, away from the touchdown point.

From all directions, other lights converged on the target ring as other defenders abandoned their positions and came to help.

Bram waited out the descent, sweating. A nymph scrabbled at the viewport opposite him and seemed to be making progress in creating a loose place for prying away the frame.

Then the nymphs were hurling themselves away from the hull, abandoning the tug before it touched down and spreading outward to get away from the rocket blast.

"Hold on!" Lydis cried.

She cut the drive twenty feet up, motionless in respect to Yggdrasil. But Yggdrasil continued to accelerate, and when it met the undercarriage of the tug, there was a respectable jolt. The tug settled into a nest of charred leaves, broke through smaller twigs, and came to rest at a crazy angle.

Bram hoped the landing had been as hard for the nymphs that had jumped ship before the impact. He saw one snatch at a twig, miss it, and smash its glass helmet against a projecting branch. But other nymphs were managing to land right side up or to grab branchlets with their four legs and abdominal claspers and swing themselves around.

"Let's go!" Jao roared, and he headed for the air lock with a grappling hook in his hand.

"Stay inside!" Bram said sharply.

Jao turned slowly around, an incredulous expression on his face.

"We'd only get in their way," Bram said. "We're inside the circle with the nymphs."

The curator sat with his teeth chattering, hugging his portfolio to his knees. It would have been an injustice to say he looked relieved.

Bram went with Lydis and Jao to look out the main port. Methuselah leaped off his shoulder and scampered ahead of him, taking a lively interest in the proceedings. "That's right, old fellow," Bram said, patting his head. "We've got lots of friends out there."

The circle of torches converged inward, making a pool of light as big as a teamball field. Bram saw the flickering nymph figures darting back and forth amidst the shadows of leaves.

One of them made a run at the perimeter of the circle. It was met by a hail of small thrown objects. It scuttled back and forth, trying to escape, but several missiles found their target. The glass helmet flew apart in fragments. There was a brief greenish snowstorm within the square frame, and the long tubular body curled up in the agony of death.

The circle of lights moved inward. Bram could see more lights rising above the sharp curve of the branch's horizon and approaching in ragged lines from the longitudinal directions.

Another dragonfly made a rush and was driven back by brickbats. The circle of lights contracted again.

"Throwing things," Bram said. "That's what Ame says

our treetop ancestors were good at. It gives us a longer reach than creatures like these. They don't understand throwing."

"They're learning," Jao said. "Any minute now it's going to occur to them to rush in a group, and then some of them will break through."

Bram glanced at the approaching lights. Reinforcements. He wished they would hurry up.

"We'd better get out of this system fast," Jao went on. "Because the next time we meet these things in space, they're going to be wearing wire mesh over their helmets."

Two dragonflies charged the line of defenders, one behind the other. The first one went down, but the second reached the perimeter. Bram saw a man go down, then there was a flurry of activity as a dozen humans swung at the insect with bats and pikes until it stopped moving.

By now the contracting circumference of men and women had closed up the gaps in the line, and more people were arriving every moment. A hard rain of missiles filled the circle. Bram heard metal ring off the hull of the tug, and something sharp and fast made a small star in the plastic of the viewport.

"What a pitch," Jao said. "There must be a lot of teamball players out there."

"The gravity keeps changing," Lydis said. "It must be hard to judge."

"The human brain's a marvelous computer, Lydis," Bram said. "You ought to know that."

The pelting shower of hard objects grew thicker as more people joined in. The nymphs, with their wraparound eyes and their superb ability to detect motion, were good at dodging. But it did them no good when they were bracketed on all sides.

The flat trajectories of the missiles became shallow arcs as gravity increased. But by the same token, the rain of brickbats from above grew harder and harder.

The pitchers were learning to act in unison—picking out one or two targets at a time and concentrating fire on them. By the time the nymphs made the concerted rush that Jao had predicted, there were too few of them left.

These, too, went down under the concentrated stoning.

The fact that they were bunched together even helped the humans. Bram tuned into the common wavelength and heard a cheer go up. The defenders swarmed all over the battlefield, making a muddle of light. When Lydis opened the air lock door, quite a crowd was waiting outside.

The elongated figure in the old-fashioned accordion-jointed space suit was Jun Davd. A transparent sack that still held a few unused lumps of metal and ceramic dangled from his hand. He grinned at Bram.

"Did you get them all?" Bram said.

"Yes."

"There were some that jumped free early. And there are clouds of nymphs out there that the bubble ship shed when we bumped it. They had a net vector toward the tree at the time. I doubt that any of them could survive impact at what the relative velocity was at the time, but . . ."

"We'll search the tree. We'll hunt them down. We won't rest until we know for sure."

The curator came swiftly out, clutching the big floppy portfolio he had risked his life for. He refused to let any-one take it from him. Friendly hands led him away toward the nearest entrance to the branch.

"Another iota of the human heritage." Jun Davd sighed. "We've got more of it than we ever bargained for. But we're leaving so much more behind. After coming all this way, through black holes and exploding galaxies, it doesn't seem fair to have to run away like thieves."

Lydis came over and joined them. She had plenty of willing helpers pitching in to secure the tug to the big branch. It would not be sacrificed, after all; somewhere between stars, before Yggdrasil spun again, it could be flown or towed under no-g conditions to an airdock in the trunk.

She pointed at the clot of bubbles that was sinking below Yggdrasil's horizon. "We ought to be safe from them now," she said. "There's no way they can match velocities with us anymore."

"Let's be sure," Jun Davd said.

Five minutes later he had a patch in to Smeth in probe control central, in the trunk. An assistant had hurried over

with portable equipment. Bram hadn't realized the extent
of the communication coordination effort that had gone
into repelling the dragonfly invaders. There was even a
small videoscreen in color—though it was flat, not holo.

They sat outside on the branch to watch; there would
not have been time to go inside. Smeth's voice came in,
clear as a bell, from one hundred fifty miles away.

"The bubbles are rising over the horizon now," Smeth
said. "They're very low—not more than a hundred miles
from the treetop. Can you see them?"

In the little portable screen, flecks of spume emerged
from behind the curve of the aft horizon. Some remote
camera on the other side of Yggdrasil was taking the pictures—probably one of Smeth's probe monitors. Bram
was horrified to see the fiery sprays of exhausts coming
from the bubbles, pointing outward; the dragonflies were
still trying to land on the tree.

"They don't realize..." someone murmured. Bram
recognized Ame's voice; she must have gone to probe
central to be with Smeth when he returned from the ramjet
with his black gang.

"I don't think they use instruments," Smeth said in a
strained voice. "I think they do everything by vision and
instinct."

"Are you running a parallax on them?" Jun Davd asked.

"Of course," Smeth snapped. "I'm doing a continuous
prediction."

Bram put the question that was on everyone's lips.
"Are they going to make it?"

"I don't think so. *They* think they are. But it's going
to be very close."

The remote camera tracked the bubbles across Yggdrasil's sky, gave it up, and another camera—evidently on
the trailing branches—picked them up.

"There—they've seen their error," Smeth said.

The bubbles must have rotated all at once; the exhaust
plumes now faced Yggdrasil, trying to push the colony
vehicles away. But they'd been picking up momentum too
long; they continued to fall inward toward a tree that was
slipping inexorably past them. They fell past the edge and
into the blinding stream of the hadronic photon drive.

They simply vanished. The energy that had instantly vaporized them was such an infinitesimal fraction of the energy flowing around them that they didn't even make a brief flare.

Bram heard all the sighs of relief through his suit radio. He did a little sighing himself.

A million miles out, they allowed themselves to feel safe. Yggdrasil was hitting almost its full one-gravity acceleration by then—far beyond anything dragonfly technology was able to approach. In a few Tendays, they would be out of the system.

Bram had time enough to clean up, eat something, and grab a few hours' sleep before he and Mim had to attend the impromptu celebration that was being held in the observation lounge. Marg had decided to cater it at short notice. Word was out that it would feature wines fermented with the help of terrestrial yeasts that had been retrieved from storage on the diskworld.

When he and Mim entered the great curved gallery arm in arm, a couple of thousand people were already milling around. The atmosphere seemed a little subdued for a party. People's eyes kept stealing to the sweeping expanse of clear plastic that showed the rearward view.

There was no sky behind them—just a solid wall against the firmament. It was blank-faced, featureless, lit only by the receding inferno of Yggdrasil's artificial sun. Even at a million miles, the top of the wall showed almost no curvature.

Bram got drinks for himself and Mim at one of the bars, then steered her over to the big holo display at the end of the lounge. That had its share of spectators, too. Jun Davd was keeping his telescopes trained on the hairbreath of rim where what was left of the human race had spent a year digging up its past, and was piping the images to the public displays throughout the tree. Though the images used the holo apparatus, they were flat, showing only what the telescope saw.

Somehow, that made the sight more immediate.

At extreme magnification, the tethered moon was a child's top poised just above the knife edge of the rim.

Its waistline harness and the grid of its engineering structures could be seen fuzzily.

Directly beneath the moon's small end was the excavated city they had quit. There was no individual building large enough to be seen, except for a tiny bump that might have been the sports arena—if that wasn't merely an irregularity in the telescope's charge-coupled retina. But the crosshatched pattern of the streets could be made out, and the two moon plazas—one on either side of the rim— were a pair of tiny eyelets.

But what really drew the fascinated attention of the people standing around the display was the dragonfly settlement a couple of hundred miles farther along the plain.

It had grown large enough to be seen from space.

At its center, the original dragonfly bubble was a small white bead. A grayish honeycomb was spread around it, like dirty froth. The froth seemed to have crept a little farther toward the buried city than it had in other directions.

Trist drifted over with a drink in his hand. "I hate to think of that wonderful storehouse being overrun by those monsters," he said, nodding at the telescopic image.

Bram agreed. "All the buildings and underground tunnels need only a little patching to make them habitable— they'll just be breeding spaces for the creatures. Still, there are other human sites—on that disk and the others, and on all the tethered moons."

"They'll get around to them," Trist said, taking a sip of a pink concoction. "It won't take long for them to spread through this entire system, the way they spawn."

Mim, lovely in a gown that left her arms and shoulders bare, shivered. "I'm just glad we're away from there. And we've managed to take away so much in spite of everything—from the life work of thousands of tale tellers and composers to the genome of the giraffe."

She looked at the gray patch of the dragonfly colony and shuddered again. She had been practically in hysterics, Bram knew, when the last shuttle had returned to the tree without him. The tapes of the dragonfly nymphs were something no one could forget.

"And the science, too," Trist said, brightening. "The

latter-day physics of Original Man, when we're finally able to understand it. The vistas it opens up!"

"Let's not forget the human diet," Bram said. "It's going to be considerably more interesting from now on. What's that you're drinking?"

"Marg calls it elderberry wine. Made mostly from tree glucose, of course, but with an infusion of cloned cells added to the fermentation vats. She's bullied the gardening section into growing the actual plants, though, from cuttings that Oris developed."

"May I try it?" Mim asked.

Trist held out his glass, and she took a sip. She wrinkled her nose. "Sweet," she said.

"Yes, isn't it?" Marg said, appearing at Mim's elbow with Orris in tow. She eyed Mim's gown, then relaxed as she decided that hers was more attention-getting. Marg's opulent figure spilled out of a wisp of a frock that she would not have dared to wear the first time she had been young, but the centuries had taken away a lot of inhibitions. Orris was still the same lanky, self-effacing consort he had always been. She had made him dress for the party in one of the Old-Earth costumes that the archaeological excavations had made briefly popular: great, puffy, striped thigh breeches and skintight leg coverings that showed his knobby knees.

"*Too* sweet, I think," Marg went blithely on. "Cloying, actually. I'm going to make wine from grapes, next. That's what Original Man did, mostly. The secret is to allow most of the glucose to ferment out, evidently. Orris is cloning cells now from the samples we brought back. But it will take two years to grow the rootstocks."

Orris's shaggy head bobbed up and down in agreement.

The telescopic display caught Marg's eye. Even she was sobered by it. She bit her lip. "I wonder what we missed," she said. "I know it will take tens and *tens* of years to sort through what we've already got, but I can't help thinking about what we might have *missed*. Do we have parsley, for example?" She fluttered her long eyelashes at Bram. "Don't you think it would be a good idea if we went back? The disks are identical, aren't they? There must be *other* biological museums we could dig up before those horrid creatures get to them." She pouted. "I can't *stand* the thought of them swarming over it all!"

"We were just talking about that." Bram floundered uncomfortably.

Mim came to his rescue. "You know what I can't stand? The idea of the Cuddlies being hunted by those awful things."

Orris nodded vigorously. "Yes, they may be the last survivors of the mammalian age on earth. They were safe here for eons. And now they're just fodder for probably the most voracious life form that evolution ever produced."

"I don't know," Trist protested. "They're tenacious little animals. The rat-people couldn't exterminate them. They've prospered for millions of years in an inimical environment. They'll learn to keep out of the nymphs' way. Life may get tougher for them. But I have a hunch they'll be around for millions of years more."

"In any case, they won't become extinct now," Bram said. "All the pets taken aboard Yggdrasil will see to that."

That led to a rash of Cuddly stories. Cuddly owners could be terrible bores.

"Our little Mittens is *such* a scamp!" Marg gushed. "She's into everything, but I haven't the heart to scold her."

"Our Loki, too," Mim said. "He was determined that he was going to come to the party. We had to lock him up to keep him from following us."

"I hear from Jao that you've adopted another one," Trist said politely.

"Yes . . . Methuselah," Bram said. "He's pretty spry for an old fellow. Walked right in and took possession of the place. No nonsense about him. Right now, I think he's in the process of showing Loki who's the boss."

"Loki's an unusual color," Orris said. "Almost the same shade as Jao's beard. Say, you wouldn't consider letting us mate him with Mittens, would you? We've always wanted a red—"

He was interrupted by the arrival of Edard. Edard was tired and dusty, still wearing coveralls with a treeguard armband; he hadn't gone to his quarters first to change for the party.

"Creation, but I could use a drink!" he said. Bram handed him his glass, and he drained it. Marg signaled one of her assistants for refills.

"What happened?" Bram asked.

"We found one," Edard said. "One of the patrols flushed it out of a tunnel in the sapwood. We lost two men, but we got it." He looked around for another drink. "It was full of eggs."

"Do you think there are any more?" Trist asked.

"I don't know. I hope not. We'll have to build up the treeguard with more volunteers, step up the patrols. I'm going on duty again tomorrow. We may have to keep this up for years if we want to be sure."

"How horrible," Mim said.

"Inside the tree, of course, they're not at the disadvantage they are in space suits. Spears aren't the whole answer. We need something smaller that can kill at a distance."

"A dart of some kind, maybe?" Trist suggested.

"Could be. With something like a spring to hurl it."

"Interesting idea. Maybe the physics department could come up with something."

"I've thought of one thing," Edard said. "A sort of bow, like a violin bow. With the string under lots of tension. It could throw a short shaft with a pointed end. Of course, it would take a lot of practice to learn how to aim a thing like that so you could hit something with it."

"Oh, Edard, you sound so bloodthirsty," Mim said.

"Sorry, Mother. But if you'd seen two men killed by one of those filthy creatures..."

"It's only for self-defense, Mim," Bram said. "When we're sure this crisis is over... why, we'll just disinvent this bow thing."

Everybody's eyes were drawn to the telescopic image hanging in the holo backplate. "We should have burned them with the photon drive instead of being so finicky about where we aimed it," Trist said.

"Now who's being bloodthirsty?" Bram said. "It wouldn't have made any difference. Their father ship's dropped bubbles all around the rim, and even if we'd spent a year in orbit around the disk, there'd be other ships, now that they've found the way."

"That's not what I mean," Trist said. "The dragonflies are now in possession of the diskworld transmission apparatus. What if some day it occurs to them to use it?"

It was a horrifying thought. "It would take thousands of years to get the disks into operating condition," Bram said.

"The universe has *got* thousands of years," Trist said.

"Before the dragonflies could seed the universe with their kind," Mim said, "their transmissions would have to reach a race advanced enough to synthesize their DNA. And what race would be that naive?"

"The Nar created *us*, Mim," Trist said. "And we gave them Penser."

"You may be overlooking one thing, Trist," Bram said. "Before you can induce another species to unriddle your genetic code, you've got to be able to *communicate* with them. And the dragonflies aren't very good at that. In fact, they may be inherently incapable of it."

"They won't need to broadcast their genetic code," Trist said grimly. "They'll just spread from star to star. And when their ships are good enough they'll reach other galaxies the way *we* did."

"Don't be so gloomy, Trist," Marg said. "You'll spoil the party."

"Sorry, Marg." He swallowed the last of his elderberry wine. "I think I'll get myself another drink. Who'll join me?"

Before he could carry out his intention, Jun Davd came hurrying into the lounge, followed by an assistant. He spoke briefly to the assistant, who nodded and went to the holo to make some kind of adjustment; then Jun Davd came through the crowd to Bram and his group.

"You'll want to see this," he said. "We've been tracking the dragonfly father ship for the past few hours. They've finished seeding the rim with their spawning bubbles, evidently, and they're ready to go on to the next diskworld. They've been following the rim around, using their fusion engine to build up velocity."

"Oh, no!" Mim exclaimed.

"They've sterilized a swath over ten million miles long so far."

"Why . . . they'll burn their own colonies," Orris said.

"No, they shut down when they drop one," Jun Davd said. "They're not mindless, you know."

"Not when it involves their own species," Trist said tightly.

"They're flying low," Jun Davd went on, as if he were discussing an abstract problem in ballistics. "The interesting thing is that they haven't passed under a moon yet. It's over twenty-two million miles between moons. Ah, here we are. We're picking them up now."

The telescopic display at the end of the lounge jiggled and blurred, then centered on a brilliant spark skimming the top of the fantastic wall that stretched across the stars. People stopped their conversation to look.

"They're awfully close to the rim edge, aren't they?" Trist observed, his face suddenly alight with interest.

"Yes, aren't they?" Jun Davd said.

The spark died without warning. Bram could see the ship itself, a tiny splinter that he knew was twenty miles long from end to end. The cluster of bubbles at one end didn't seem appreciably smaller. It was hard to tell. The few dozen that might have been expended on this world still left hundreds with which to seed the rest of the system.

"They're not cutting it too fine," Jun Davd drawled. "They're about a half million miles from their first colony next to our digs. They're closing at a hundred miles per second. It won't be many minutes longer now."

The ellipsoidal moon hovered, waiting. The dragonfly ship was going to pass under its pointed end. Even at the scale of distance involved, the progress of the bubble-ended splinter seemed swift.

"They're going to—" Mim said, and bit her lip.

The splinter hurtled onward, its axis aimed obliquely in preparation for the escape orbit that would take it to the next big disk of the outer trio. The angle gave it a wider cross section along its line of flight. That would make matters worse, Bram thought.

At the last moment, a dragonfly eye must have seen a hairline flicker of movement and a dragonfly brain must have made an instantaneous connection. The fusion flame flared in a desperate attempt to push the ship out of the plane of the disk.

"That was a mistake," Jun Davd said.

The splinter sheared in half, peeling back along its entire length. Hundreds of tiny glistening beads spilled into space. Bram thought that a collision at a hundred miles per second would have smeared the occupants to paste, but—incredibly—he could see chemical jets starting up in some of them as the pilots tried uselessly to save themselves.

Then the primitive deuterium-helium three reactor—smashed, flooded, and compressed all at once—blew.

A ball of terrible fire appeared in an instant, engulfing the spilled bubbles, spreading outward in growing circles across the diskscape, lighting up the underside of the pointed moon.

The moon gave a jerk.

It joggled for a moment, like a balloon being yanked by a child, and then the second set of moonropes on the other side of the rim, weakened by heat and impossibly stressed, parted.

Like a stone released from a sling, the moon flew into space.

Mim gasped. She clutched at Bram's arm, her fingers digging into his biceps.

"It can't hit us, Mim," Bram said softly, watching the moon sail upward, blunt end first. "It left the disk's orbit on a different tangent than we did."

Jun Davd heard him. "No, there's nothing left in the outer system that it *can* hit. It will probably take up a tilted orbit somewhere between here and the cometary halo."

Slowly, like ocean billows, the surface of the diskworld collapsed under the place where the moon had hung. A great scalloped depression spread out on either side. Eventually, when that wave of collapse ceased, there would be a forty-five-million-mile bite taken out of the disk between moons.

Throughout the lounge, sobs were heard as stunned people realized that the city of man had tumbled into that abyss.

"It's all gone, isn't it?" Mim asked. "Everything we found. Buried, crushed under an earthquake that could have swallowed worlds."

Bram found her hand. "*They're* gone too, Mim. The dragonflies."

"They'll be back, though," Trist said, staring out the curving view wall as the universe outside came tumbling down. "There are billions of them, less than twenty light-years away."

Bram's holo, fifty feet tall, stood on the rostrum and looked out across a sea of faces. It always made him feel self-conscious to be magnified this way—you didn't even dare to scratch your nose—but it was the only way for a crowd this size to have any connection with the speakers. He thanked his stars that the year-captain election was only a few Tendays away. He had resolved not to let his name be entered this time. It was someone else's turn.

The hall of the tree had been enlarged over the years with the increase in population, until now it could seat more than twenty thousand people. But that still wasn't enough to handle the crowd that had shown up tonight; the overflow had been consigned to the small adjacent amphitheater, watching the same holos, but without the reinforcing sight of the distant minikin figures whose shadows they were.

Over two hundred ushers with ballot boxes on poles were stationed at the ends of the aisles, each responsible for ten rows. This was a vote that nobody was going to miss.

"All right, I guess we've heard from everyone who said they wanted to speak—and a few who said they didn't," he said, while the simulacrum of himself that towered over him boomed out the words through the sound system. "And I guess the experts have answered all our questions. So I'm going to call on Jun Davd to sum it up, and then we can get on with the vote."

He left the podium to sit with Mim and the others,

mopping his brow a little too soon, so that a departing slice of the holo image made a swipe with a bedsheet-size handkerchief before he was completely offstage.

Jun Davd nodded as he squeezed past, then got up and took his place on the podium. His holo image, lithe with the common youth of the human race, leaned toward the crowd and said mildly, "We're still on the previously set course that will take us to the star we believe to be Sol. If we want to change that course, we should do so now. We've reached approximately one-fortieth of the speed of light, and within a few more day's we'll be beyond the effective limits of this system."

A vast troubled murmuring went through the audience, and voices were raised in different parts of the hall.

Jun Davd's holo raised a billboard palm. "Please, we've been through it all before. We believe that all the nearby stars, to a distance of about twenty light-years from Sol, are—or soon will be—inhabited by our dragonfly successors on earth. If that's the case, we have no home here. There is a sizable faction among us who want to flee this sector of space without further ado and search for a home elsewhere in the galaxy. And I can't say I blame them, after what we've seen here."

There were shouts of agreement from the crowd. A man near the front rose, shaking his fist, and was shushed by his neighbors.

"But there is another faction," Jun Davd went on, "who believe we should have a look at Sol anyway. We've heard from some of them tonight. They argue that we can't know for *sure* that our recent adversaries come from Earth, though all the biological studies indicate that they do. What if we're mistaken? What if Earth is *not* denied to us? What if the dragonfly ship came from elsewhere or was a lone survivor fleeing some planetary disaster? In that case, it would be a shame to have journeyed so far without even getting a glimpse of our goal."

There were more angry shouts from the audience. Jun Davd's looming holo waited them out, hands on its hips.

"There's one more thing to consider," he said when the noise subsided. "Even if the worst is true, oughtn't we to know more about these terrifying creatures? How far have they advanced since they launched their colony ship? How fast are they likely to spread? How far ought we to flee before we're safe? A thousand light-years? Ten thousand? To the opposite side of the galaxy? And when we get there, will we find them waiting for us—having arrived in ships that set out centuries after we did but were a few decimal places faster?"

That got to everybody. A subdued silence fell over the massed rows as Jun Davd went on.

"We believe that we can fly through the Sol system without danger and make a survey from space. With our engine off, we're unlikely to be spotted. And even if we were, we ought to be safe from being boarded unless we went into the close planetary orbit, as we did here. I doubt that they would be able to match velocities with us on a hyperbolic orbit through the system." He paused. "And if they tried—why, we'd see them coming from a long way off, and we'd turn on our engine and outrun them."

A flurry of voices went through the audience as people turned to their neighbors to comment. Jun Davd let the commotion run on for a bit, then raised a flat palm again.

"Of course, after the terrible events that we're all familiar with, it would be perfectly understandable if we voted not to take that chance. On that subject, perhaps we ought to hear from a member of the patrol, who I believe has something to tell us."

Edard got up. He evidently had just come off duty and still had his treeguard armband on. His voice was tense as he spoke.

"We just found two more and killed them. No casualties this time. We have a new weapon that doesn't let them get close to us—provided we outnumber them by a fair margin, of course. We believe that was the last of them. Except . . ."

He looked troubled. He pushed back a mop of dark hair and continued. "Except that one of them evidently bored holes in the cambium of a passage and laid eggs—several tens of them. We came upon one of the hatchlings. They're about as long as your thumb and they look exactly like the adults, except that perhaps they're stubbier. And they bite."

His holo held up a bandaged hand.

"We destroyed all the eggs we could find—and we had some help. When our Cuddlies saw what we were doing, they took a hand, too. They're good at getting into small places . . . and they're wild about eggs! We saw them chase down hatchlings, as well. Let me tell you that Cuddlies can bite, too."

A subdued sound of nervous laughter went through the chamber.

Edard smiled in response. "At the moment, there are several hundred Cuddlies prowling through the passageways, looking for eggs and hatchlings. They're very imitative beasts, as we all know. Pickings were slim after the first few hours—but we've all seen how persistent a Cuddly can be. I don't think that after a few Tendays we'll have to worry about nymphs being aboard the tree." He sobered. "But of course, we intend to keep the treeguard patrols going indefinitely." His holo gave a grin. "And on *that* subject, we'd be pleased to have more volunteers."

He sat down next to Bram and Mim. Jao leaned across and said, "Nice going."

Jun Davd was smiling to himself. Bram said, "Why are you so pleased with yourself, you old reprobate?" Bram asked. You undermined your own case when you let Edard remind everybody how dangerous the nymphs are."

"We'll see," Jun Davd said.

The ushers moved swiftly down the aisles. A ballot box was shoved at Bram on its long pole, and he pushed the yes button. The box slid past him to pause at Mim and Edard. Jao tried to vote twice and looked unabashed when the usher caught him at it and said, "None of that, brother."

The voting was over in twenty minutes. Yes and no votes went much faster than multiple-choice votes, as when there was a slate of candidates. The ushers brought their boxes to the clerk, who plugged them one at a time into a tabulator.

The tally figures floated in holographic projection, huge, glowing, and changing so rapidly that the final digits were a blur. But the trend was clear.

"It's going to be almost unanimous," Jao said. "I don't believe it."

The last few figures clicked into place. The crowd waited a moment to take it in, then a great cheer went up.

"That's it," Jun Dayd said. "We're going to Sol."

CHAPTER 11

Earth hung before them, a soiled brown ball swirled around with dingy clouds. Its moon had an atmosphere, too, if that yellowish soup could be called air.

"What have they done to it?" someone whispered.

Brown oceans, brown air—it was a planet drowned in swill. But incredibly, there was life there. The planet was thick with life, in fact, to judge by all the microwave radiation, the chemical pollutants revealed by infrared spectra, the hydrocarbons that choked the clouds, the orbital junk.

"There are simply too many of them," Jun Davd said sadly. "A population of half a trillion if we've estimated their demographics correctly from that ... city."

Radar imaging had exposed a spongelike warren of habitation that stretched from end to end of the single sprawling continent—an irregular heap of stacked cubes that staggered miles high in places, reaching to where the filthy air thinned to the merely fetid.

The radar imaging had sparked a lot of controversy. There was a strong feeling that the close-up look at Earth should be limited to passive observation—radio eavesdropping, infrared, and the like. But Yggdrasil was a naked-eye object by now, and further caution seemed pointless.

At any rate, the radar didn't seem to have alerted the inhabitants of the Earth-Moon system. Perhaps their own microwave background was simply too noisy. When there had been no sign that the dragonfly civilization was paying attention to them, the treeload of humans had voted to risk putting Yggdrasil into a remote orbit a hundred thousand miles out, with the fusion engine kept warmed up.

"I thought somehow it would be ... lovely," Mim said, turning a disappointed face to Bram. "Like the Father World seen from space."

Alis Tonia Atli, now a historian, was among the people who had come crowding into the observatory. "Is it possible that they inherited this? Evolved for it?" the thin woman suggested. "Perhaps it was Original Man who poisoned Terra, millions of years ago. We know he had a population in the billions."

"No, it wasn't Original Man that did this," said a thick-featured man with blue-black ringlets. It was Dal, the dramatist, inspired by the diskworld finds to return to the writing of his verse plays. "Earth didn't look like this when he was still around. I remember the words of one of the lunar poets of the twenty-eighth century ... Taine, I think."

He struck a professional pose and declaimed:

> Oh, fair blue world, marbled in glory,
> Teach us beauty as you rise
> Above our bleak horizon ...

He was interrupted by Hogard, the librarian. "I don't think that's Earth at all. I know it has a large moon, but that one big land mass with its three lobes doesn't fit any of the maps I've seen."

"Continental drift," Enry said stolidly. "Seventy-four million years of it. They came together in one supercontinent."

"The rest of the system doesn't fit, either," Hogard said stubbornly. "Where are the gas giants? The solar system was supposed to have four of them, including one with spectacular rings. Instead, those orbits are occupied with a whole collection of terrestroid planets, all of them crawling with dragonflies."

Jun Davd stepped in. "We *know* that the moon was terraformed with carbon dioxide from Venus and hydrogen from Jupiter. Carbon dioxide broken down to liberate oxygen, hydrogen reacting with some of the oxygen to make water. We can assume that the process went on. Carbon dioxide and hydrogen are very useful commodities for an industrial society expanding into space. Jupiter and Venus were gradually stripped. Both became habitable. Venus, with the crushing load of its hothouse atmosphere removed and a modest helping of hydrogen brought in to react with liberated oxygen to make oceans—and perhaps even an infusion of cometary ice. And Jupiter—"

"Jupiter stripped down to its rocky core," Bram said in a flash of insight. "But more important, with that terrible pressure released, the shell of metallic hydrogen surrounding the core could've changed state and boiled off. Which would have removed Jupiter's magnetic field. And with it, the deadly radiation belt that Jovians have."

Jun Davd nodded approvingly at his former pupil. "Which would have made the moons of Jupiter habitable."

"Five new worlds," the stocky playwright, Dal, said. "The four large moons plus Jupiter itself. All the real estate Original Man could have used. Seven, counting Mars and Venus. That bears me out. Original Man was not responsible for that stinking stew down there!"

He gestured vehemently at the observation window, where the blotched brown world floated against the cleanliness of space.

"No, they have abused their legacy most grievously," murmured Jun Davd. "Original Man once had a ring city and linked synchronous satellites draped around the waist of his lovely world, did you know that?"

There were oohs and ahs from the visitors. While Jun Davd explained, Bram turned his attention to the most interesting of the holographic displays that had been set up around the observatory—the one produced by gravitational imaging. It showed a tangled belt of overgrown wreckage around the equator of the slowly revolving planet. The buried debris must have been millions of years old. It made ridges in the sea floor, a single straight line of low hills across the land. The devastation when it crashed must have been inconceivable. Perhaps it had been the planetary disaster that had cleared an evolutionary path for the ascent of the rat-people.

Hogard was still insistent. "Okay, there are five rocky worlds doing a complicated dance around one another where Jupiter ought to be. But what about the other three gas giants this system is supposed to have? Did Original Man strip them, too?"

"No!" Mim cried with sudden heat. "I've seen the pictures of Saturn's rings! Human beings never would have done that to her!"

Bram followed her gaze to the long gallery wall of planetary images that Jun Davd had put on display. It was a selection made from the hundreds that had been taken while Yggdrasil plunged through the Sol system. The one that upset Mim showed a grim, yellow-stained ball of rock where a scummy ocean lapped at a tarnished shore. Yggdrasil had passed within a million miles of it. Even at that distance one could distinguish the scab of habitation that covered much of the land surface.

"I agree, Mim," Jun Davd said. "Perhaps the rat-people did that. Saturn was the next world out. They may not have had our sense of aesthetics."

"Atmospheric mining is simple in principle," Bram said. "A satellite in low orbit with a couple of hundred miles of siphon suspended beneath it. The vacuum of space operates the siphon. The orbit has to be readjusted every once in a while to compensate for atmospheric drag on the hose, but there's plenty of reaction mass available to do it with. The rat-people could have mined *their* hydrogen that way and had another planet available after Saturn was sucked dry."

"Eight planets," Jun Davd said. "Of Saturn's satellites, seven are more than three hundred miles in diameter—including one moon as big as Mercury—and the dragonflies are using them all."

"That wasn't enough for them," Bram said grimly. "We've detected dragonfly broadcasts from the leftover cores of what must have been Uranus and Neptune—and all of *their* moons that we were able to get any separation on."

"They're breeders!" Dal blazed. "Any piece of rock big enough for them to light on!"

"Yes, indeed," Jun Davd agreed. "Our resident sociobiologist, Heln Dunl-mak, tells me that she estimates the total dragonfly population of Sol system to be more than ten trillion."

The figure was mind-boggling—too big to grasp. Bram heard the gasps around him.

"And they're pushing outward," Jun Davd went on. "If the diskworld system of Delta Pavonis represents their present limit of expansion, then they now occupy a volume of space forty light-years in diameter."

He was about to go on, when an alarm went off. He picked up an interphone and listened briefly. He reached out and switched on a display. "Yes, yes, I see them now," he said.

He put down the interphone set and faced the circle of suddenly quiet people. "That was Smeth," he said. "Our sensors have detected the firing of launch vehicles. It appears that the dragonflies have decided that Yggdrasil is a likely-looking piece of real estate."

Bram watched through the scope as a pattern of orange sparks rose above the brown curve of the atmosphere and died out one at a time.

"End of boost phase," Jun Davd said from his console a few feet away. "I make that eighty-four vehicles, launched from twelve separate locations."

"Eighty-four!" Bram exclaimed, remembering the colony-size environmental bubbles that had tried to settle in Yggdrasil's branches in the diskworld system. "So many for a target our size?"

"These are relatively small multistage vehicles," Jun Davd said. He put a computer-enhanced image on the big screen so that everybody could see it. Bram saw a flecked bottle shape with a pinched waist jiggling at the approximate center of the field. Glowing green lines showed where the computer had used its imagination to fill in the outline.

"Designed to come up through atmosphere, with a final stage carrying no more than fifty or a hundred passengers, from its size. Probably their regular Earth-Moon bus. Their numbers, I assume, reflect those they happened to have standing by in a state of near-launch readiness. Yggdrasil is a target of opportunity. A new world that appeared suddenly out of the miraculous plenum."

Somebody said, "Don't they have shuttles?"

"No, these are throwaway vehicles," Jun Davd said. "Typical of them."

On the screen, the bottle shape divided in two at its pinched waist. Bram looked through his scope again and saw a fresh shower of sparks.

"Their parking orbit didn't last very long," Jun Davd said. "Not long enough, really, to qualify as a parking orbit at all. They hardly bother to calculate, do they— just eyeball it."

The minutes crawled by as the blanket of sparks moved perceptibly against the murky face of the planet, then slowed, then stopped moving and seemed to hover there. Jun Davd had removed the isolated ship from the big screen and replaced it with the wide view for the benefit of his visitors. What they were seeing was not strictly an honest telescopic image but one enriched by infrared, gravitational sensors, and synthetic aperture radar.

Then the sparks went out.

"Final velocity of somewhat over a hundred thousand miles an hour," Jun Davd said. "They've done very well on their hydrocarbons and oxygen. They don't appear to have injected themselves into Yggdrasil orbit. They're going to try for a direct landing."

The visitors waited in silence, trying to make sense out of the dancing dots on the screen. But there was really nothing to see except the background planet.

A voice on the edge of hysteria finally said, "Aren't we going to *do* something?"

"We're going to have weight very soon," Jun Davd said soothingly. "I suggest that everyone orient themselves toward the floor."

The floaters drifted to upright positions. People used walls and handholds to nudge themselves into foot contact as best as possible.

Bram felt returning weight: a few ounces at first, then a steadily increasing poundage. Smeth had gotten the fusion engine going in record time.

Yggdrasil groaned and creaked with the stresses of

acceleration. The tree didn't like this at all. It had come into this system under its own power—the ramjet having been shut down at about one hundred astronomical units—and finished the last seven percent of braking with its lightsails. It had broken out of its hyperbola and taken up its present orbit under the hormonal and mechanical inveigling of its human passengers, and it was just settling down to enjoy the sunlight only to be subjected to the rude yank of the tether again.

Slowly, the tree began to outdistance the gnats that were pursuing it. The one-hundred-thousand-mile orbit straightened out into a larger curve. The pursuing craft were in no danger from the photon exhaust yet, but they would be when their interception trajectory intersected the line where Yggdrasil had been.

After an hour, when the tree had built up a velocity of twenty miles a second and it became obvious that the gap would continue to widen, radar showed that the dragonfly landing stages had simultaneously flip-flopped.

"Now, why would they do that?" Bram asked.

"I'm afraid I know," Jun Davd said.

The answer came a moment later. Once again, a cloud of orange sparks twinkled into life. The burn lasted for several minutes, then extinguished.

"They used their retrorockets to give themselves an extra boost!" Bram said unbelievingly. "There's no way they can come to a soft landing on the Moon, now! All they can hope to do is—"

"Crash into Yggdrasil," Jun Davd finished for him. "Project our delta-vee and gamble that by the time they intersect our path, the angle will be acute enough and the relative velocity close enough to zero to enable them to survive the crash." His face was somber. "They don't care about being able to get back, of course."

Bram scrambled for a console and punched out figures, while Mim watched him, biting her lip in apprehension. After a bad couple of minutes, he gave her a reassuring smile and turned to Jun Davd.

"They can't catch up to us," he said.

A general sigh of relief went through the observatory, though anxiety still showed on many faces.

Jun Davd said, "No, an eye—even a wondrous thing like a dragonfly eye—isn't a computer. Orbital interceptions can be misleading. But they had to try. It seems to be an imperative with them. Spread their wings, figuratively speaking—the wings they haven't got—and set out for new worlds. Nature can be profligate. It doesn't matter if most don't survive."

Something like pity appeared on Mim's face. "Can they be rescued, Jun Davd?"

"I doubt that the lunar dragonflies would care to make the effort," Jun Davd said. "Their territory's overcrowded as it is. In any case, the question is immaterial."

It took another hour to demonstrate that. Jun Davd slid back the cover of the observation well in the floor. It gave a good view backward along their line of flight, between the twin puffs of foliage and foliated root. The people in the observatory crowded around the safety rail and stared downward.

Jun Davd fiddled with dials, and the tough, transparent membrane became a magnifying lens. The expanse of tree crown fled past in a blur as the focus came to rest somewhere beyond. Filters masked the glare of the caged sun, spitted on the slender shaft of the probe; the darkened circle of eclipse also made bearable the beam of virtual photons, briefly swollen with abnormal energy by a factor of ten billion before it satisfied quantum theory by decaying into pions.

The swarm of dragonfly vehicles peppered the view. They were harshly lit on the side facing the hadronic beam, and their shape could be clearly seen as squat bells, with the spent cone of the descent engine for a clapper.

"No way they can stop," Jun Davd said. "Nor can we."

The beam was very tight, but there was a certain amount of scattering. To the watching humans, it seemed that each bell instantly evaporated while still some distance away. One by one, they flicked out of existence, soaked up by the terrible light.

In minutes, space was swept clean of the glittering cloud.

"We're safe," Dal said. "Let's get out of this cursed system."

He spoke too soon. Yggdrasil's straightening course was taking it past the Moon. It lay before them, huge and yellow through the grand observation blister that formed one wall. Through sulfurous wisps of clouds could be seen a landscape of round lakes, patches of sparse unhealthy vegetation, pocked scars softened by weather, oily seas dotted with ring islands that had once been craters.

And popping up through the murky atmosphere was a shower of orange sparks.

An alarm went off. Jun Davd picked up the interphone, said "I see them," and hung up.

Bram was already busy at the computer touch board. Jun Davd leaned over his shoulder to see what he was entering, nodded approval, and started feeding in supplementary data from the tree's sensors.

"What can they hope to accomplish?" Bram whispered when the answer appeared on the screen. "At best they've matched roughly for our *present* velocity. Those vehicles *could* be waiting for us in our projected flight path if we *stopped accelerating* in the next decihour. But we're still boosting. They'll only end up behind us, like the others, and get themselves vaporized in our drive exhaust."

"Then they must expect us to stop accelerating," Jun Davd said.

"Missiles," exclaimed Alis Tonia Atli, then had to explain the specialized meaning of the word from her knowledge of twentieth-century earth history.

"No," Jun Davd said. "We'd have seen them by now. At any rate, they wouldn't do much better at catching us than those piloted craft. It has to be something faster."

"A fusion exhaust," said Dal. "Remember how reckless they were with it around the diskworld? They might not quail at using it this close to home. And they might not realize Yggdrasil's combustible. If all they want to do is kill the probe and stop us, they wouldn't mind turning us into a ball of slag. We'd be another moon to settle on—bigger than most of those they use."

"There's nothing the size of their interstellar ship in orbit," Jun Davd said. "I'm sure they launch them as soon

as they make them. The largest objects I see in orbit are
those bulky cylindrical structures attached to mirrors—"
He stopped.

"Light," Bram said. "Light would be fast enough."

Jun Davd looked shaken. "I thought they had something to do with solar power. I can see that even now we
don't fully understand these creatures. They've mounted
laser defenses against unwanted colonization by their
brethren on Earth."

Even as he spoke, the laser beams struck Yggdrasil.
There was a flickering of images on the big screen as some
of the antennae elements dispersed across Yggdrasil's
crown burned out, then the computer redistributed data
to compensate. Bram saw the beams, hundreds of them,
sending their threads of light through space in a complex
skein that focused on Yggdrasil. The computer had assigned different colors to the threads to distinguish the
types of lasers—violet, red, blue, green, magenta, and a
deadly gray to represent x-rays.

One of the visitors went into hysterics, a little round
man who was calmed by two women and given a glass of
water.

Bram reached for the interphone before he remembered that he was no longer year-captain. He turned to
Jun Davd. "Somebody should get Enyd to rotate the tree—
distribute the heat absorption. Even though we're boosting, another few percent of g wouldn't—"

"We needn't bother," Jun Davd said. "We couldn't get
rotation started fast enough. Besides..."

He trailed off, looking thoughtful.

The tree continued to accelerate. One of the women
with the hysterical man said soothingly, "See, we're still
going."

"The sensitive part of the ramjet shaft's in the umbrage
of the leaves at this angle," Jun Davd said. "And as for
the leaves themselves, our sensors haven't yet detected
any fires."

He was trying to suppress a smile. He gave up the
effort and let his long face split in a big grin.

Bram took the call from Smeth when it came. He listened briefly, then hung up and addressed the expectant throng.

"Smeth wanted to warn us that we're all a few pounds heavier—but I'm sure you've all noticed that already. The laser beams are giving us a small additional boost—enough to take a little of the load off the ramjet and turn more of its work into acceleration."

A few of the people looked puzzled. Bram drew a breath and said, "Yggdrasil thrives on light. Up to and including x-rays—the Nar found space trees happily in orbit around x-ray stars."

He added his own grin to Jun Davd's. "When Yggdrasil felt things getting a little too hot, it turned its leaves reflective side out, in the lightsail mode. The dragonflies will take a while to realize it, but they're helping to speed us out of their system."

An hour later, they watched the second fleet of dragonfly ships fall into the consuming flame of the drive beam. Long before then, the lasers had been switched off.

As Yggdrasil sped past the orbit of the planet that had been called Pluto, Jun Davd sought Bram out during an intermission at one of Edard's concerts. It was a Tenday later, and life in the tree was returning to normal. "The next time we meet them," Jun Davd said, "they may be more advanced."

"Then we'll have to go far enough to be sure we *won't* meet them," Bram said.

Jun Davd did not reply directly. "Trist is looking for volunteers to help repair the antenna system," he said.

"What's the hurry? We don't have a Message to broadcast anymore."

"No. But we'd better start listening."

Seven years of listening had taken their toll on Trist. He had the same ready smile, the same willingness to banter. But his ice-blue eyes had acquired something of the haunted look that Bram remembered from the years when Trist had monitored the spread of Nar civilization through the Whirlpool galaxy—until the wave of radiation from the exploding core had put a stop to the radio emissions forever.

Trist had monitored the Nar emissions for fifty thousand years. He had listened to the spread of dragonfly civilization for only fifty odd years—about seven years in terms of tree time. But his eyes had aged at the same rate as the outside universe, Bram thought.

Trist looked up from his console as Bram entered the control booth. The Message Center had been stripped of its library over the centuries, as the archivists had gradually integrated its contents with the growing central databank. But its equipment—the leaning stacks of power and control elements that made long avenues down the cylindrical cavity—had been left intact and placed at the service of the astronomy department.

"They've reached Aldebaran now," he said before Bram could speak.

"Red giant," Bram said, searching his memory. "With a companion."

"It's a white dwarf now," Trist said. "The dragonflies have settled both components. They're not very fussy. Outer planets of the dwarf would be pretty cold...but that wouldn't bother the kind of creatures who settled Pluto. Any inner planets, if they survived the red giant phase and resolidified, wouldn't be much more habitable. Airless slagballs."

"How far?" Bram asked.

"About sixty light-years from Sol. It was one of the stars that stayed in the same neighborhood."

A crawling sensation went down Bram's spine. "Their technology's improving. They're spreading outward at about half the speed of light."

Trist nodded. "Since we first met them at Delta Pavonis, the sphere of space they occupy has grown to a diameter of nearly one hundred twenty light-years. At this rate, it will take them only two hundred thousand years to overrun the entire galaxy."

"Jun Davd said that we could flee to the opposite ends of the Milky Way and find them waiting for us."

"If they learn how to attain relativistic speeds any time in the next few centuries, yes." Trist was gloomy. "And if they don't, they could come calling fairly soon, anyway."

"The nearest large galaxy is two million light years away. Andromeda, former man called it." Bram swallowed hard as he remembered the first breathtaking sight he'd had of the Milky Way's sister galaxy, centuries ago, as a child at the observatory with Voth. "At one g, we could be there in thirty years, our time."

"Two million years, dragonfly time," Trist said. "Plenty of time for them to invent relativistic ramjets. And improve on them."

"Yes," Bram said. "And intergalactic beacons that broadcast their genetic code. They're already in possession of the prototype."

"We're using frozen Nar technology for the most part," Trist said. "We won't have a better intergalactic machine till we've settled down somewhere, expanded our population, developed an industrial-based society—"

"While the dragonflies have had two million years to develop theirs."

Trist spoke with a sort of controlled terror. "Long before then, they'll have swallowed the entire Milky Way. Trillions of them around every G-type and K-type star. Billions, maybe, around less hospitable stars ... And ... two hundred billion stars! Two hundred billion separate dragonfly civilizations, all of them competing to be the first for the next leap outward."

"Jun Davd was right," Bram said. "All they have to do is to learn to crowd the speed of light by one decimal place better than we can."

He turned to listen for a moment to the speakers, which were pouring out a torrent of dragonfly clicks and snaps from whatever lumps of rock were in orbit around Aldebaran and its companion. When he spoke again, it was half to himself.

"There's no place we can go in the entire universe where we'd be safe from them. No place at all."

Both of them listened to the clicks for a while. Then Trist spoke. "You'd better call a ship's meeting."

"I'm not year-captain."

Trist showed rare exasperation. "Oh, for Fatherbeing's

sake, by the time we get Smeth to do it and wait for him to sort out all the ifs, buts, and maybes, the dragonfly sphere will be another fifty light-years across!"

"I'll post a notice in the datanet," Bram said.

"I say we go back!" the man on the holo stage bleated. "Go back and sterilize all their worlds with our engine exhaust! All of them, down to the smallest asteroid! That's the only way we'll ever be safe!"

He was a narrow-faced man with an incongruously thick and muscular neck sticking up out of protective coveralls, and his voice was shrill with fear.

"Who is he?" Bram whispered to Trist in the seat next to him.

"Name's Perc. He's one of Smeth's technicians. Fusion specialist, I think. Big talker—always trying to organize the black gang, whatever that means. He's always at loggerheads with Smeth."

"The way to do it," Perc blathered on, "is to start back far enough to build up a tremendous gamma factor. Build up enough relativistic mass so that we devastate them by gravitational effects, too, just to make sure. But the main thing about going in at relativistic speeds is that we can flash by in fractions of a second, before they have time to react. They might not even realize we were there, in fact. To them it would just seem as if the surface of their planets just sizzled and went up in flame."

"Ferocious, isn't he?" Bram said.

"He's just frightened," Mim said. "We all are."

"He's one of the post-Milky Way generation," Nen said, leaning across Trist. "Have you noticed how all of the really bloodcurdling comments tonight came from the new people?"

Mim nodded agreement. "It's hard for those of us who were raised among the Nar to think of a life form—*any* life form—as being a threat."

"We're learning," Bram said grimly.

"Oh, my dear, yes," Mim said, reaching blindly for Bram's hand. She seemed on the verge of bursting into tears; she might have been remembering the long vigil when Bram had failed to return to the tree with the evacuees. But it took her only a moment to recover her usual spunk. "That was another time, another universe."

Perc's outside holo image was waving its mammoth arms around. "Just one quick pass over each planet," Perc said earnestly and reasonably. "We needn't go into a polar orbit that would cover the entire surface—and we couldn't, anyway, with the kinetic energy of relativistic speeds. Our exhaust would boil away the crust—melt a channel of slag from pole to pole. Split the planet like a rotten fruit. Turn the oceans to steam and strip away the atmosphere. Nothing could survive—not anywhere. And think of Yggdrasil's mass at seventy—or seven hundred—gamma. We'd rip them apart! I move that we start back at once. Burn them out. Descend on them like an avenging angel. Bring them their time of fire."

The holo lurched off the stage, and the little man who had cast it seated himself again. Smeth thanked Perc for his views as if it hurt his teeth, then gaveled down the uproar that started.

"Jun Davd, I think you wanted to make a comment," he said.

Jun Davd's holo rose, courteous and grave, and looked down at the audience. "There's no doubt that we could wipe out planets if we had a mind to do so," he said. "But I'm afraid that for us to exterminate the entire dragonfly race is a mathematical impossibility. You can't make U-turns in space, and by the time we backed up far enough for a second run—decelerated and built up gamma again—years would have passed. We'd have to do that for every single planetary body ... divided, perhaps, by a factor of three or four for those we *could* align, of course. In Sol system, there are thirty-five inhabited bodies of fair size, plus an unknown number of asteroids, cometary nuclei, and possibly space habitats. We could not be sure of ... sterilizing ... them all. And if we could, there still would be numbers of dragonfly vehicles in transit within the system, ready to settle on some of the cooling cinders after we passed."

A babble of voices broke out. Smeth pounded his gavel, and Jun Davd went on.

"And, of course, we're not talking about only one system. There are approximately one thousand five hundred stars and multiple star systems within a sixty-five-light-year radius of Sol. Most of them, by the evidence of Trist's radio survey, are inhabited. Even if we spent only five or ten objective years dealing with each, it would be millennia before we finished the task."

He paused. The hall of the tree had gone silent.

"And by then, the dragonfly sphere of habitation would have grown to a diameter of at least fifteen thousand light-years."

"Then you're saying that we can't keep up with their expansion?" shouted a man in the front row.

Smeth tried to gavel him out of order, but Jun Davd bent forward to reply. His holo loomed like a cloud over the first ten rows, but it was the man in front whom he addressed.

"We'd have to disinfect every star in the galaxy. And then we'd have to start all over again."

There was a clamor of competing voices, and Smeth granted the stage to a woman who wanted to be assured that flight was not entirely hopeless. "Can't we find just one little star they won't want—where they'll leave us alone? Somewhere between the galaxies where they wouldn't find us?"

"Where's Jao?" Bram whispered to Trist. "I don't see him up there. I thought he had something he wanted to contribute to this."

"The last I heard, he was still working on some calculations. He has a computer model he wants to stir some more figures into."

"What good will that do?" Nen said angrily. "Words, numbers—what difference will any of it make?"

"It's something he's been cooking up with Jun Davd," Trist said. "All I know is that they think it has some bearing on the present situation."

On the platform, Smeth was trying to stem further discussion and bring the proceedings to some kind of conclusion. The company had been at this for hours now, everything had been said at least twice, and people were getting cranky and tired.

"The time's come for us to make a decision," Smeth

said harshly. "We have a problem that can't be solved. But we've got to choose a course of action, nonetheless. Put quite simply, do we fight, run, or hide? Or pretend it isn't so? I don't believe I've heard any other suggestions tonight. So if anybody wants to start making motions, I'll put them on the board and we can—"

The ushers were already starting to move down the aisles to get into position with their long-handled ballot boxes, when a burly figure dragging a bulky piece of electronic equipment shouldered his way past them.

"Hold it, Smeth!"

Smeth's face showed annoyance. "The discussion just closed, Jao. There's nothing more left to say. Take a seat with the others."

Jun Davd leaned over to whisper something in Smeth's ear. A slice of his face appeared in the holo projection, but the words weren't audible.

"All right," Smeth said. "Have your say. But try not to hold things up."

Jao climbed to the stage with his gear and started plugging light fibers into the exposed holo panel while the projectionist hovered nearby. He said something to the projectionist, who nodded and took over the task while Jao strode to the lectern. A gigantic red-bearded face, disembodied, hovered over the auditorium; he hadn't bothered with the niceties when he made his rough-and ready connections.

"When we dropped into the nucleus of the Milky Way from above the galactic plane about fifty of our years ago," Jao began without preamble, "we saw a peculiar sight. It was a sort of arc of hot gas rising up out of the core at right angles to where you'd expect it to be for a galactic magnetic field."

The audience stirred restively at what seemed to be an astronomy lecture coming when everybody was wound up with tension and ready to release it in the form of group action.

Jao appeared not to notice. The suspended face cocked a gigantic red eyebrow and went blithely on. "We postulated that something at the center of the galaxy was acting like a stupendous dynamo. The obvious candidate was a rotating black hole—the one we later used as a brake when we dived through the core."

The blank part of the holo was suddenly filled with the Milky Way, making the disembodied head appear to be cloaked in the magnificence of stars. Jao had improved on the crude animated holo of finger-painted orange lines that he had first sketched so many years ago to illustrate his theory. Now a realistic image was there, drawn from the observatory's photographic files and turned on its side to show an edge-on representation of the galaxy, with the central bulge glowing yellow.

The lines of force were still orange, though now they were an elegant computer sketch that made them flow in magnetic loops. The Milky Way tilted slightly, and now one could see the loops spinning faster around their common axis and flattening out to lie more within the galactic plane. Not all the lines of force were trapped, however. A small arclike spray still rose at the pole.

"The magnetic field was much more powerful than it ought to have been," Jao said, "and it was growing. There was twice as much mass rotating around the galactic center as there should have been—the equivalent of two hundred million solar masses. It should have been gobbled up by the black hole, swept out by core explosions during the quasar epoch of the universe. But *some* process is replenishing it—maybe from a universe on the other side of the plenum."

The Milky Way spun all the way up like a coin and presented its face. Now it could be seen as a great swirl of stars with an incandescent center. Jao's holographic head presided over it like some raffish deity.

He had their attention now. The crowd had stopped fidgeting, and the background buzz of conversation had died down.

"We set up a long-term computer model at that time and started feeding data into it. The program was authorized to change its suppositions if data didn't fit. We left the model running and plunged into the galactic core. All the senses of the tree were plugged into it. It saw, it listened, it sensed radiation and magnetism and gravitation, and it drew maps covering whole slices of the galaxy as we passed through."

Shaded areas appeared briefly in the hologram to show the path swept by Yggdrasil's spiraling orbit.

"Since our brush with the black hole, the computer has been processing sixty thousand years' worth of real-time observational data. It's a large enough sample of the history of the galaxy to show us how the charged arms grow. And to project into the past and future with the help of data from other sources. I've been awake for the last twenty hours polishing the results. And there's no possible doubt . . ."

Now Jao's theoretical plan of eight revolving spokes could be seen, superimposed in coruscating orange on a galaxy that was rotating at half their speed. They swept the spiral arms of stars like great flexible pinions, their ends trailing. They were growing outward all the time, becoming more vivid as they gained in power. It was very graphic.

The sun appeared as a yellow dot in the spiral arms of the galaxy, between spokes. And now one of the orange spokes brushed it.

"That happened three hundred million years ago," Jao said. "Half of all animal families on earth were wiped out. In the oceans, ninety percent of species disappeared."

Pictures floated in the holo, superimposed on the spinning wheel. They showed queer, scaly, flipper-limbed creatures with flat heads and big jaws, armored swimmers, many-legged bottom crawlers. They had come, Bram supposed, from Ame's files.

Another orange pinion swept past Sol, then another, and another. Some of them were thick and bright, some were feeble. Some of them had not yet grown long enough to reach the yellow dot. Images of strange life forms flashed, disappeared.

"Those were the dinosaurs," Jao went on. "They were *big*—bigger than our paleobiologists could believe at first, but we found bones in the diskworld museums. We'll remake those animals some day for our game preserves."

People gasped at the images: enormous armored quadrupeds with horned heads, finned backs, and spiked tails;

great, plodding, thick-legged creatures with long necks, tiny heads, and massive tails; a fearsome monster with stalactite teeth and tiny front limbs rearing high and trying to smash through the eighty-foot steel fence that held it so as to get at a human zookeeper who was only as tall as its knee.

"Gone," Jao said. "That was a major extinction. No land animal weighing more than twenty pounds survived. The little furry creatures who were humankind's ancestors were among them."

The great spoked mill continued to revolve. It had begun to subdivide again so that tenuous threads were trapped between some of the major arms, beginning their own growth.

"The extinctions come regularly now—about every twenty-six million years," Jao's floating head said somberly. "Some large, some small. And now we have some minor extinctions caused by these trailing arms, at intervals of from twelve to fifteen million years. The new arms haven't quite settled into place yet."

A thin orange wire passed across Sol like a wand.

"Twelve million years before the heyday of Original Man," Jao said. "Followed by the return of that first, powerful arm that wiped out half of all animal families on earth. Only this time, Original Man was the dominant species."

The audience sat stunned. In the silence, someone shouted, "I don't believe it. A technical civilization could have found some way to protect itself!"

Jao waited it out. "The rats survived in their burrows," he finally said. "They were small, prolific. They took mankind's place. And twenty-six million years later, it was their turn."

A thick orange arm, grown in intensity since its last circuit, came around and swatted the sun.

"There was no place for them to run, even if they'd known what was coming," Jao said. "The arms sweep the edge of the galaxy, now. They're thousands of light-years thick. An individual ship, shielded against radiation and traveling very close to the speed of light, might have been able to choose an orbit that would keep it between the advancing arm and the retreating arm till it got out of the galaxy entirely. But the rat-people weren't that advanced technologically."

The man who had previously interrupted Jao stood up and tried to speak again. Smeth nodded, and a monitor got to him with a portable pickup. His image sprang up on the holo stage in a double exposure that made the galaxy shine through him.

"But Original Man must have been advanced enough," he said. "Couldn't he have moved his whole population out and fled to another galaxy, leaving his beacon behind? Maybe *that's* the reason why the Message stopped—not man's extinction." His eyes, magnified against the swirling stars, pleaded at them.

"I don't know," Jao said. "With a population in the billions—maybe tens of billions . . . And anyway, he might not have known what was coming. *We* know, because we came to Sol straight out of the galactic core. Even if they had a ramjet like ours and sent a scout to the center of the galaxy, the round trip would have been better than sixty thousand years in objective time, and by that time it might have been too late—just as it was for the Nar."

Jun Davd stepped quickly into the holo frame and said, "Perhaps it *is* possible. The universe hasn't heard from Original Man since the Message was cut off, but perhaps that's because he hasn't reached refuge yet. He might have targeted a galaxy more than seventy-four million light-years away—in the Virgo cluster, for instance."

The man thanked him with grateful eyes and sat down.

Jun Davd said, with mild rebuke, "You'd better get on with it, Jao. "These people can't stand much more suspense."

Jao's holographic lips widened in a grin that was bigger than the entire central bulge of the galaxy.

"It's been twenty-six million years since the rat-people became extinct."

It took a moment for the impact of that to sink in, and then the entire hall erupted into a vast rumbling chaos. People leaped to their feet, shouting unintelligible questions at the rostrum.

Jao held up a hand that appeared in giant size beside the holo of his face and got partial silence.

"I wanted to be sure of my data before I came to this meeting. With twenty-six million years to play with, a five percent margin of leeway could have the dragonflies spilling out of this galaxy and halfway to Andromeda before the charged arm took its swipe. But that's not the case."

He grinned more broadly. "The leading edge of the next spoke is already brushing the dragonfly sector of space. We're getting radio noise from it now. It will meet the expanding dragonfly shell in less than ten thousand years. At this radius of the galaxy, it's only about eleven thousand light-years between charged arms. The dragonflies will have expanded to their limit by then, trapped between two arms."

The holo display showed the event graphically. A sphere of twinkling dots was growing outward from Sol, toward the orange barriers that fenced it in on either side. The arm swept inexorably onward, slicing the ball of lights thinner and thinner until nothing was left.

"Scrubbed clean," Jao said. "The universe is safe from dragonflies."

The assembly went wild. Jao could not have made himself heard even if he had wanted to go on. People were weeping, laughing, embracing—showing every form of emotion. Jao stood watching for long minutes, hands on hips, then left the platform. Jun Davd took his place and waited.

People crowded around Jao as he walked down the aisle, clapping him on the back, grabbing his arm, jabbering at him. He nodded pleasantly at everyone, mouthed words against the din.

He stopped at Bram's row and crowded in to loom over everybody. "This arm that's coming," he said. "It's grown since the last time around. It's going to make the Cretaceous extinction look like—what does Marg call them?—a tea party."

"No chance of the dragonflies surviving as a species?" Bram asked.

Jao shook his head. "Not a chance in a googol. If it doesn't get the dragonflies, it'll get what they eat. Evolution will have to start at the bottom again. There'll be breathing space of twenty-six million years. Time enough for another species to find its destiny."

Ame was there, leaning over the back of Mim's chair. She gave Mim a great-great-great-granddaughterly peck. "Maybe that species will be the Cuddlies," she said. "They're well established on the diskworlds, and they'll have a better chance than most of surviving in their shielded burrows. They can wait out the radiation for a few millennia. They're bright little creatures, well on their way to intelligence, and their weight lies below the twenty-pound danger zone."

"Oh, Ame," Mim said. "I hope you're right."

On the stage, Jun Davd had succeeded in getting a measure of attention. "It appears that spiral galaxies are not very healthy places to live," he said. "They tend to have hypermasses ticking away at their centers. Binary black holes splashing into one another and causing core explosions. Leftover black holes from the quasar epoch powering galactic dynamos. Perhaps it might he better to find a smaller, more congenial neighborhood."

He must have come to the meeting prepared for this, because Jao's holo of the Milky Way suddenly started to recede into the distance. As it dwindled, the field enlarged to show the fuzzy patches of globular clusters and some small, irregular satellite galaxies. The holo zeroed in on a pair of them.

"The Clouds of Magellan are not too far from home, I think," Jun Davd said. "The Large Magellanic Cloud is only one hundred fifty light-years away. The Milky Way would fill the sky..."

Loki and Methuselah came scampering over when Bram and Mim entered their quarters. It was past suppertime, and the two Cuddlies had firm ideas about when it was time to be fed.

Loki tried to lead Bram toward the cupboard, but Methuselah pawed at Mim's legs until she bent over and picked him up. Holding him in her arms, she frowned and said to Bram, "He's been acting a little funny the last few days. Do you think he's all right?"

"What do you mean, funny?"

"His appetite's been off. And I think his nose feels too warm."

Bram inspected the little beast. Methuselah's big brown eyes seemed as button-bright as usual. Were they a bit *too* bright? Bram ruffled the soft fur—brown, salted with gray. Methuselah's face seemed somehow different.

"Mim," Bram said. "Do you think his muzzle's getting darker?"

"Let me see." She pursed her lips. "Yes, there's less gray in it. It was almost pure white before. Some of the brown's coming back. What could make it do that?"

"I don't know. Original Man had animal doctors..."

"Well, we don't." She gave the little creature a hug. "We're taking him to Doc Pol."

"Fourth Cuddly I've seen this Tenday," Doc Pol said. "Marg and Orris were in with that spoiled pet of theirs just before you got here. Pesky critter nips a little too hard! Marg was carrying on. Thought her precious Mittens was at death's door."

"What was wrong with it?" Mim asked in alarm.

He looked up in annoyance. His irascibility was at odds with his boyish face and slender form. "Wrong with it? Nothing was wrong with it! It was pregnant, that's all!"

"Oh."

"Don't know what the fool woman expected, letting her pet run free like that. All the half-tame Cuddlies living in the branches. She said she thought her precious was too old—past the age of fertility."

"But that's right!" Mim said. "She wanted to mate her Mittens with our Loki...oh, about six ship-years ago, and Mittens was past the breeding age even then."

"That so?" Doc Pol said. He raised a faunlike eyebrow. "Well, let's have a look at your little feller."

For the next ten minutes, Doc Pol poked, prodded, tapped the tiny chest, shone lights into eyes and ears, managed to insert a thermometer abaft the twitching tail, and peered down the pink throat while Methuselah tried earnestly to bite him.

At last he released the Cuddly, who immediately settled in Mim's arms, clinging with all his might.

"Well?" Bram said.

"He's picked up a virus," Doc Pol said.

"Virus? How? What kind of virus? What could he have possibly caught?"

Doc Pol fiddled with his instruments and took his time about replying.

"Immortality," he said. "There's a lot of it going around."

Ame set it up. "Molecular taxonomy," she said. "The whole department's pitching in. We've got a team working on amino acid sequencing, another working on protein sequencing, and Doc Pol and his apprentices are helping us to measure the antigenic distances between humans, Cuddlies, and a number of primates whose serum albumin we've been able to clone from our diskworld biological samples. And, of course, we're doing extensive comparative anatomy studies."

"All of a sudden we're getting a rash of similar cases reported by Cuddly owners," Bram said. "Some of the children may have spread it after getting their booster shots. Or it may have been going on a long time. People today aren't really very familiar with the concept of aging. Oh, they understand it intellectually. But it wouldn't occur to a lot of them to wonder why their pets aren't getting old."

Ame bit her lip. "We really should have gotten around to a study of the Cuddlies sooner. But there was just so *much* for us to wade through in all those records and the frozen molecular zoo we took away with us from the diskworld . . ."

"How soon?" Bram asked.

"I'll have an answer for you in a few days."

"The Cuddlies are *Homo post-sapiens*," Ame announced.

A wave of shock went through the chamber. A reporter for the datanet said, "You mean these little animals are Original Man?"

"We believe they're a divergent species growing out of the extinct *Homo sapiens* branch, yes," Ame said.

An uproar started in the chamber. Ame looked helplessly around at her colleagues for support. She hadn't expected a mob this size when she had told datanet that she had a modest announcement to make. The announcement had had to be moved from the department's conference room to a small adjacent auditorium.

"What does that mean?" somebody demanded.

Ame faced them squarely. "It means that during the time of extinction, whatever *Homo sapiens* stock briefly survived on earth underwent adaptive radiation. Man himself would not have survived long, but a number of subbranches might have evolved to fit different ecological niches. The Earth would have become a very different place. Size and brainpower might not have been survival characteristics. Size certainly wasn't. There might have been back-mutations for such characteristics as tails and fur, night vision. The ancestors of the Cuddlies were among those divergent species. They were small, quick, burrowing omnivores. We know the rat-people considered them pests and tried to exterminate them. But they spread to the diskworlds as stowaways on spaceships, got into the granaries, learned to survive in pockets of trapped air. And they had millions of years after that to evolve into their present form—able to live in vacuum, to do without breathing for long periods of time, like Earth's extinct sea mammals." She shook her head ruefully. "It was obvious that the Cuddlies were terrestroid mammals, but we failed to take the step further that would have identified them as primates."

The datanet reporter waved for attention. "Couldn't the Cuddlies be descended from some *other* primate? Weren't there things like monkeys and apes? Lemurs?"

Ame shook her head. "We know the Cuddlies are hominids from the comparative anatomy studies—the teeth, for instance. But more important is the amino acid and protein sequencing. Molecular analysis shows that Cuddlies are as far removed from apes and monkeys as humans are. The cytochrome c sequence in man and Cuddly is almost identical." She paused, got some encouragement from Doc Pol, who was sitting behind her, and continued. "And there is no immunological distance at all."

"Is that why Cuddlies were able to catch the immortality virus?" asked someone else, probably a Cuddly owner.

"Yes," Ame said. "They're our very close cousins. They're what *we* could become."

At the back of the auditorium, Jun Davd turned to Bram with an amused smile. "How does it feel, Bram? You brought us across thirty-seven million light-years, hoping to find Original Man, and when we found him, we made him our house pet."

"We're Original Man, though, aren't we, in a sense?" Bram said. "And if you want to look at it the way Ame just did, *he's* descended from *us*."

The datanet reporter persisted in his questions. "Are you saying that we're going to evolve into little furry animals like Cuddlies, then?"

"No," Ame said. "Evolution doesn't repeat itself. We still have a long way to go. And so have they."

The Large Magellanic Cloud lay before them, a ruddy tiara spread across the night. From only a few tens of thousands of light-years away, it was brilliant, the teeming stars laced with torches of red fire.

"It's lovely," Mim said, holding Bram's hand. "What a breathtaking sky we're going to live under."

"Yes, the skies will be spectacular," Jun Davd said. "That red nebula at the end—the Tarantula, Original Man called it—will be brighter than Earth's full moon. And of course the Milky Way will be huge, and we'll see it almost head on. It will fill half the night sky—almost as large as we're seeing it now."

He switched on the rearward view for a moment to show them what he meant. The heartbreaking swirl of humankind's birthplace blazed against the darkness, a splendid pinwheel that revealed nothing of the deadly mill that was churning within her.

Bram felt the ache of its loss. "We'll be able to keep watch over it," he said with a smile he hoped was on straight.

"Don't look so glum," Jao boomed. "Not a dragonfly click coming from it, and it's been a hundred thousand years."

They had been fleeing for twenty-two years, ship time, and three years previously the dragonfly radio emissions had ceased—almost abruptly because of the extreme temporal condensation of the gamma factor they had built up by then. It meant that the dragonfly civilization had ceased to exist some ten to twenty thousand years after they had departed the galaxy and that, after a hundred thousand years, there was still no sign of it. For the first year of those three, Bram had lived in terror that one day Trist's listening post would pick up the clicking sounds that would mean that somewhere a dragonfly planet had survived and struggled back to the technological level again.

"You're right," he said with returning cheer. "It's the Cuddlies' turn now, on their diskworlds. They've got twenty-six million years to make the most of their opportunity. And who knows—before their time is up, we may even learn how to shut off galactic dynamos. In that case, we could go back and save them."

"Oh, Bram," Mim said. "What a wonderful thought!"

"But crazy," Jao said. "A crazy dream."

"Yes," Bram said. "I've been told that before."

Jun Davd switched on the forward view again. The torches of the Large Cloud shone forth once more. "We'll be safe in there," he said. "You can see there's no hypermass giving it shape. There are fifteen billion stars in there—old, young, and in-between. We ought to be able to find one small yellow star that the human race can call home."

"Amen to that," Bram said.

He smiled at Mim and squeezed the hand clasping his. Methuselah pressed against his leg. Humans and posthumans drew closer together to share an ancient tribal comfort. They stood in sacramental silence as the living tree that bore them hurtled out of the dark toward the cloud of fire.

Epilogue

SECOND GENESIS

Epilogue

SECOND GENESIS

"Why am I different?" the little decapod said.

He was about rib-high to Bram, hardly out of baby-hood, his saucer eyes disproportionately large around his waist, the undersides of his stubby tentacles still an immature mauve. Theth-theth, Bram had named him when the time had come to fish him out of the nursery pool. In the Small Language, it was a derivative of Voth. Mim had suggested the name: Little Theth.

Bram laughed and ruffled the velvety inner surface of a tentacle. He could feel the words that were trying to take shape there, gaining in form and lucidity with every passing day.

"Because I'm made of human stuff and you're made of Nar stuff," he said tolerantly. "We've been through it before."

"Just one more time," the small being begged.

"You want me to tell you the Story," Bram said.

"Yes," Theth-theth said contentedly, and snuggled up against Bram. Methuselah, trying to insert himself into the group, nestled against the little decapod's other side, making a sandwich of him, and Theth-theth stroked him with a lazy tentacle.

Bram sighed and settled back against the thick bole of the oak tree. There were oak trees now—whole forests of them—and this one was over a hundred years old. It had been planted, he remembered, the very day the bio-project to resurrect the Nar had begun.

He looked out across the wide valley, green with the grass and trees of Earth that had taken root here and flourished. A stream ran down the slopes, sparkling silver, and he could see a herd of zebra pausing to drink at one of the wide pools. The air was alive with the songs of birds.

Haven was a fair world, its contours softened by weather but barren of life until the coming of humanity. Now, after more than a century, the green cloak of vegetation was beginning to spread across the blue oceans to the other continents, and the oceans themselves were exploding with life—plankton and small fish, so far. Someday there would be whales, Bram thought.

The sky was a rich blue, piled high with fleecy white clouds. Bram could see Yggdrasil near the zenith, a bright star visible in daytime. People still lived there. Yggdrasil had scattered its seeds in the cometary belt, and other space poplars were growing there. In a couple of centuries, it would be time to harvest them; humankind would need more starships by then. The shuttles brought from the Father World were still in good repair, but a move was already afoot to start handcrafting orbital spacecraft here on Haven.

The sun overhead was warm and yellow—a perfect match for lost Sol. Jun Davd had searched long and hard before he was satisfied, and he had chosen well.

The twittering voices of children, both human and Nar, came floating on the summer breeze from somewhere close at hand. Bram turned his head and saw a group of them playing a children's game. In hide-and-seek, the Nar children were never "it"; their 360-degree vision and eyes that never closed gave them an unfair advantage. They were better at footraces, too. But the human children were better at playing catch and at such games as jacks, so it all evened out.

Some of the older human children, he saw, were wearing touch sleeves and the lightweight induction helmets that Jao's project had designed. It was a first crude step that filtered some of the touch language into the speech center of the human brain through mediation circuits. It would do for a start—human and decapod children could begin to learn the Great Language together. At this point, no Nar child in this first bioengineered crop was much older than Theth-theth.

Theth-theth tugged at Bram's arm with an encircling tentacle; Bram could feel the impatient rippling of the cilia.

"The Story!" the little decapod piped. "You promised, Bramfather!"

"Eh? I'm sorry. I must have been daydreaming. Too much lunch."

He was comfortably full and heavy from the Safepassage Day picnic; Mim had gone off to pick wild flowers with Ang and Lydis, and some of the men were playing a game of quoits in the grass, but he had not had the ambition to join them.

"The *Message*," the small flowerlike creature prompted. "How the race of Nar entrusted their faithful humans with it, but there was no one to receive it after the worlds ended. And—and how the humans sailed between Scylla and Charybdis, and how Yggdrasil saved the human race when the whole universe caught fire and burned up, and how the humans used the Message themselves to bring a new race of Nar into the world, just as the Nar had done for them—"

"Slow down a minute!" Bram laughed. "It seems to me that you're on the way to telling the whole Story yourself!"

"Go ahead, Bramfather," Theth-theth said. "You tell it *really*!"

Bram took a deep breath and began. "Once upon a time there was a beautiful planet called the Father World..."

He was winding the tale down, with Theth-theth's tentacles waving in a pleasurable trance, when Jao came hiking up the slope.

"There you are!" Jao blared at them. He bent to scratch Methuselah's head and offer a palm and bared forearm to Theth-theth. "Here you go, youngster, a little something for Safepassage Day."

He produced a miniature plumb bob molded of gaily painted polysugar. Theth-theth accepted it and said, "Thank you, Jao-uncle. May I save it till later? Mamamu Mim says I've had enough candy for now."

"Sure you can," Jao said.

Bram took charge of the candy bob, while Theth-theth ran off to play with the other children. Methuselah scampered off after him. The two were inseparable.

"Have to do something about the way Safepassage Day runs through the year—adjust it to Haven's seasons," Jao said. "Doesn't seem right celebrating it in the summertime, anyway. It ought to stay put."

"The children don't care," Bram said. "They don't *stay* children long enough to be confused by it. For Theth-theth, it's always *been* a summer holiday."

Both of them looked over to where the children were playing. Methuselah was getting underfoot, but they were tolerating him. Theth-theth had a tentacle twined around the forearm of a boy wearing a touch sleeve; they seemed to be choosing up sides.

"We'll have to keep improving the hardware," Jao said absently. "That induction cap's too bulky. Maybe something like a permanent implant . . . a second-generation mediation program . . . neural cloning. We can't let them grow away from each other, you know."

"No," Bram agreed. "But the real problem is life span."

They watched the frolicking youngsters, both of them reflecting on the tragedy of Nar mortality. "We could work on it," Jao said after a while, "but how do you keep them young without suppressing the Change? It would be like preserving a flower to keep it from going to seed. And that's what you'd have—a preserved flower."

"Well, the second generation of Nar is still a thousand years off. Maybe we'll think of something by then. In the meantime, we'll do our best for Theth-theth and the others."

"We've got to make sure that they grow up to be equal partners in whatever kind of society we develop, at the very least."

"Yes," Bram said.

Jao brightened. "We'll work something out. At least

we have this little corner of the universe to ourselves, for this hour of cosmic time, to do with what we want. Still no intelligent signals from the Milky Way, and when we hear any, it'll probably be the Cuddlies. But there's one thing I can't help thinking of..."

The summer heat and the digesting lunch made Bram too relaxed and comfortable to get *really* alarmed, but he knew that tone in Jao's voice. He sat up straighter against the bole of the resurrected oak tree and said, "What?"

"It's been almost seventy-five million years since Original Man began broadcasting his genes to the universe. That shell of signals is still expanding. It's reached its target, the Virgo Cluster, by now and enveloped hundreds—thousands—of galaxies..."

"Go on."

"Does the human race exist elsewhere in the universe?"

"We couldn't possibly know," Bram said. "Not for another seventy-five million years, at best."

"There's one other thing."

Bram sighed. "I think I know what it is."

"We've been edited. Oh, just for health, intelligence—things like that. And for all we know, the Nar did a little editing of their own. *We* did with them, so they could eat what we eat." He paused. "If these other human races out there were edited by *their* makers—what are they going to be like?"

They grinned at each other. "We'll just have to wait and see," Bram said.

ABOUT THE AUTHOR

Donald Moffitt was born in Boston and now lives in rural Maine with his wife, Ann, a native of Connecticut. A former public relations executive, industrial filmmaker, and ghostwriter, he has been writing fiction on and off for more than twenty years under an assortment of pen names, including his own, chiefly espionage novels and adventure stories in international settings. His first full-length science-fiction novel and the first book of any genre to be published under his own name was *The Jupiter Theft* (Del Rey, 1977). "One of the rewards of being a public relations man specializing in the technical end of large corporate accounts," he says, "was being allowed to hang around on the fringes of research being done in such widely disparate fields as computer technology, high-energy physics, the manned space program, polymer chemistry, parasitology, and virology—even, on a number of happy occasions, being pressed into service as an unpaid lab assistant." He became an enthusiastic addict of science fiction during the Golden Era, when Martians were red, Venusians green, Mercurians yellow, and "Jovian Dawn Men" always blue. He survived to see the medium become respectable and is cheered by recent signs that the fun is coming back to sf.